Po[illegible]

Edited by
Jay Faulkner

First Edition

ISBN: 978-1-61706-071-7

Printed in the United States & United Kingdom by
Static Movement
First Printing: December 2010

Powers

Edited by
Jay Faulkner

STATIC MOVEMENT

Table of Contents

Introduction by Jay Faulkner....1
Foreword by Cy Dethan....2
Crappy Birthday by Gary McKenzie....3
The Tripwire Trio by T. L. Barrett....8
The Last Day and Night Of Bill Stevens, Superhero by Jude-Marie Green....20
Dreaming of Nick Savage by Simon Forster....28
The Night Ghost Returns by Christopher McKittrick....37
Seven Years after Midnight (A novella) by John X. Grey....47
Family Secrets by Rob Rosen....69
Secret Origin of the Sack Man by Martin Zeigler....73
Dinner Guest by Frank Byrns....79
Space Scouts by David Perlmutter....85
Super Cleaners by Michelle Ruckoldt....93
Spandex by Alexander Bentley....97
Maxed by Bradley Descartes....105
Fanaticism by Gary Buettner....114
The Dragoon by Lane Kareska....119
The Stuntman by Matt Adams....123
The Last Laugh by Luke Johnson....137

Introduction - The Power to Believe

Jay Faulkner

My father was in the Royal Air Force and, as such, my family traveled all over the world, every few years, getting settled into a new place, new home, new school just as it was time to move on once again. The changes in physical location were always pretty easy to get used to but the changes in people – leaving friends behind only to have to make new ones, all over again – was a lot harder. I found that I could compensate for this by losing myself in fiction: fantasy worlds such as those given to me by Tolkien, Susan Cooper, and C.S. Lewis were my first love but then I discovered the four-color heroes of comics. American counterparts from Marvel and DC quickly joined British staples such as the Eagle and 2000AD and, no matter how often we moved, which country we ended up in, or how many friends I had to make I always had the X-Men, Spiderman, Animal-Man, the Justice League and numerous other heroes to keep me company and, as cliché as it sounds, to inspire me. My love of comics was often a great icebreaker amongst the new and strange faces at my new schools, a way in to the groups of people who would become groups of friends.

Many years later I don't read comics as much as I use to though (as my wife will vehemently complain to you, should you ever meet her) I do still have somewhere between fifteen and twenty thousand of them stored around the house, garage, cellar and even at my family's houses. It may be relatively easy to stop buying the comics themselves but it is so much harder to actually give them up; to let go of the things that filled your dreams and made you believe that a man could fly.

A favorite game, in the past and still now, is to ask others what superpower they would most like to have. Some say the ability to soar above the ground, others to read people's minds – for me it is simple: I want to never stop believing in the things that make me happy.

That is one of the reasons why I was so happy that the wonderful Static Movement, the publishers of the book that you hold in your hands, allowed me to put together this anthology. I hope that, in some small way, the following stories bring you back to the days when you had the power to believe in things that, as adults, you may not be able to anymore.

So, never stop looking to the sky because – just maybe – it isn't a bird or a plane that you are seeing. You just have to believe.

About the author: Jay Faulkner resides in Northern Ireland with his wife, Carole, and their two boys, Mackenzie and Nathaniel. He says that while he is a writer, martial artist, sketcher, and dreamer he's mostly just a husband and father.

His work has been published widely, both online and in print anthologies, and was short-listed in the 2010 Penguin Ireland Short Story Competition. He is currently working on his first novel.

Jay founded, and edits, 'With Painted Words' – withpaintedwords.com - a creative writing site with inspiration from monthly image prompts.

For more information visit – jayfaulkner.com

Foreword - Gods and/or Monsters

Cy Dethan

In its purest, most time-honoured form, the hero is the monster who fights on your side.

The hero takes up the practice of evil in the service of good – or, at least, in the service of our best or most immediate interests. His tools are deception, cunning and violence. He wields terror and awe as weapons against his enemies and, if he's "our" monster rather than "theirs", he's rewarded with adoration and celebrated in stories. When our conflicts are resolved, he becomes an embarrassing anachronism at best, an intolerable threat at worst. The greatest crime the hero can commit is to live too long.

This is not a book about heroes. It's a book about the qualities that define them.

Underpinning the hero's lethal glamour is the understanding that his capabilities exceed those of lesser stature, at least in some specific arena. In many cases, no more is required than a superhuman capacity for violence – but the bar is not always set so low. For better or worse, *power* is what separates the heroic from the merely brave. We applaud the efforts of fire-fighters and soldiers, but their sagas are never filtered into our cultural heritage. We remember those who have fallen in battle or in service, but rarely by name and whatever individual stories may survive tend more toward the anecdotal than the epic.

While the great heroes of classical tradition are inseparable from their defining adventures (and there are many about whom only one story is ever told), their modern descendants - the *super*heroes - require more diverse handling.

Modern superheroes exist primarily to oppose modern supervillains - whose sole purpose, in turn, is to provide that opposition in plentiful supply. It's an endless - and endlessly compelling - dance, and a world without these antagonistic reflections is almost by definition a world without heroes in the classical sense. For such heroism to exist, force must be met with opposing force. A hero without a villain of comparable stature is a bully at best and more likely a tyrant.

So it becomes a question of power, with all the fatal flaws and grave responsibilities that entails. Whether manifested as simple, brute force (with the perverse accompanying assumption that mere strength somehow lends weight to one's moral decisions) or in the more whimsical forms of shape-shifting Martians and invisible girls, we expect power of our heroes and their enemies. We *require* it of them, whether they have earned it, stolen it or had it forced upon them. As long as they possess it, we will consider them candidates for heroic stature, and call them monsters when they harm, betray or disappoint us. These definitions are ours to impose. The Great Responsibility has always weighed upon our own frail, human shoulders...

... and we *will* believe a man can fly.

About the author: Cy Dethan is a British comics writer. He has scripted *Starship Troopers* series for *Mongoose Publishing* and *Markosia Enterprises*, and his creator-owned credits include *Cancertown: An Inconvenient Tooth, Slaughterman's Creed, The Ragged Man, The Indifference Engine: A Holographic Novel* and more. Website: cydethan.com Blog: raggedman.com

Crappy Birthday

Gary McKenzie

Carl stood at the edge of the ledge. High winds whipped around him as he looked over the scenic view of Chicago. How could a city, which he loved so much, fall apart within a few years? A rise in crime had turned his once quiet neighborhood into a concrete and metal version of the old west. Corruption among the city leaders had caused taxes to skyrocket.

The currently unemployed stock trader walked back to the center of the 30 story apartment complex's roof. Taking in a deep breath, he sprinted toward the ledge; there was no backing down now. With a powerful leap, he jumped off of the roof and into his destiny.

Two Days Ago...

"... Happy Birthday to you!" sang Carl's family while the candles melted into pastel pools on top of the dark chocolate cake.

Carl looked around at his smiling family. For 30 years they gathered to celebrate his birth.

"What a waste," he thought. *"Why even bother with birthdays anymore? Once you reach 21 there's nothing more to look forward to but retirement age. I don't get any cool toys anymore. All I get is more socks, more underwear, more bills and less hair."* He could never tell his family his true feelings, so he put on a phony smile and took it like a man.

"Make a wish and blow out the candles, Uncle Carl," shouted Brandon. The little boy innocently looked up. Shadows from the candles flickered across his face.

"You know what?" Carl asked as he bent down to his nephew. "Why don't you blow them out for me?" He then finished the rest of that sentence in his mind. *"It's not like it's gonna come true, anyway."*

The little boy's eyes widened. "OK!" he shouted.

"Now Brandon," called his mother, Iris, from the other side of the table, "be sure to make a wish before you blow out the candles."

Cynical Carl held back a laugh. Why should he ruin a little boy's fun?

After taking a second to formulate his wish, Brandon took in as much air as his little lungs could hold, and blew out with all his might, sending little specks of spit to land all over the top of the cake. But his mission had been accomplished; he managed to blow out all the candles with one breath. He couldn't wait for his wish to come true.

"I did it!" he triumphantly called.

"Good job," Carl said as he patted his nephew on his back. "So what did you wish for?"

Just as Brandon was about to answer, his mother called out, in her nasally voice, "Don't tell him, Brandon. If you tell your wish, it won't come true."

"Sorry, Uncle Carl," Brandon said with a shrug of his shoulders, "Mom says I can't tell you."

"That's all right," the birthday boy said as he cut the cake. "Mommy's always right," he added with a touch of sarcasm.

Yesterday...

"Damn it!" Carl yelled as he jumped out of bed. Sunlight shone in his bedroom and his alarm clock flashed 12:00 over and over. He ran into the kitchen before he realized that the clock on the microwave would display the same flashing time.

It never failed. Every time there was a storm, his electricity would cut off just long enough to wipe out the digital clock's memories. Grabbing the remote control off of his couch, he turned on the morning news. The correct time, 7:45, was displayed on the lower left part of the screen. If he hurried, he could still make it to work on time.

He decided the hell with personal hygiene. Skipping his shower, he elected to run his fingers through his thinning, greasy hair in attempt to look somewhat presentable. Picking up yesterday's clothes from off of the floor, he quickly put them on, wrinkles and all, slipped on his shoes, and ran out the door. He didn't even care that he didn't brush his teeth or gargle. *"I talk on the phone all day,"* he thought. *"Who'd even care?"*

Half a block away from the corner, Carl saw the bus pull up to his stop, but the light quickly changed, and it pulled away.

"No!" Carl yelled and sprinted after the overpriced public transportation vehicle. "I can't be late again! My boss will kill me!"

Houses blurred past his vision as his legs pumped faster than they ever had before. He couldn't believe how fast he was running. He was going to catch the bus! Unfortunately, he didn't see the dog until it was too late.

Momentarily sailing through the air, Carl crashed back to terra firma and skidded across the sidewalk, chin first. The bus, which he had been so close to catching, kept its speed and left Carl lying in its dust. He could almost hear the bus driver chuckle as he drove away.

Walking into his office, 20 minutes late, Carl snuck past his boss's office and crept directly to his desk only to find his boss, sitting in his chair, waiting for him.

"A little late today, aren't we Carl?" Mr. Hurley asked as he twirled a pen in his hand.

"Yes, sir," Carl shrugged. There was no use in lying. He was busted. "The storm last night..."

"It doesn't matter," Mr. Hurley interrupted. He reached over and grabbed a sheet of paper off of Carl's desk. With a fluid motion, he presented it to his tardy employee. "Sign it."

Looking at the paper, Carl realized that he had been written up. Unfortunately, it was the third time this quarter which now placed him on probation.

"But Mr. Hurley, I tried..."

"Stop wasting time with excuses," the tubby supervisor with the bad comb-over said as he waddled out of Carl's cube. "You're already late. Let's not waste any more time. Trying to convince me of anything will only put you further behind. Now, sign the paper and get to work."

Carl grudgingly signed the write up notice, handed it to his supervisor, then flopped into his chair. It was still warm from Mr. Hurley's wide ass, which sent chills down Carl's spine.

He noticed that the red light on his telephone was flashing. He picked up the receiver and pressed the button to retrieve his message.

As soon as he heard the voice on the message, his nuts shot up into his stomach. It was one of his most important, and demanding, clients.

"What the hell happened, Carl!" the angry voice bellowed from the receiver. "I wanted one thousand shares of Demoguard Security, not one hundred! The stocks skyrocketed and I'm nine hundred shares short! Do you know how much money I should have now? Do you?! I will be calling your boss today and notifying him that I am closing my account with your company, immediately!"

Dumbfounded, Carl gently replaced the telephone receiver. Everything around him seemed to fade away. It was as if the world had stopped. Once the shock wore off, the adrenaline started to flow.

"Today is not a good day," he thought. *"In fact, today really sucks!"*

"Damn it!" he shouted and slammed his fists on to his desk. Normally, when he did this, there was only a thundering sound, which caused a few of his surrounding co-workers to look up from their cubes. But today it was a bit different. He managed to break his desk in two.

A half hour later, he found himself walking the streets of downtown Chicago, unemployed. He was still in a daze. Had he weakened his desk from previous poundings? Did Mr. Hurley want him gone so badly that he tampered with his desk? Not knowing what to do or where to go, he decided to do like all the other losers he knew and go home and drown his sorrows in beer.

Walking into his sparsely furnished apartment, which somehow always seemed to look in disarray, he took his key out of the lock and angrily slammed the door behind him. The thundering noise caused Carl to jump.

"This can't be good," he thought as he turned around. "Aww, what the hell?" he whined out loud as he surveyed the damage.

The door was cracked down the center and one of the hinges had come loose from the trim, causing the door to lurch to its left.

"Cheap piece of crap," he mumbled. Shaking his head in a helpless *'what the hell am I gonna do now'* type of way, Carl huffed and shuffled into the kitchen.

Slowly, he opened the refrigerator door, since everything he touched today seemed to break. He reached in a grabbed the six-pack of beer off of the shelf. As he removed the nectar, the cardboard handle broke, sending all six bottles toppling to the tile floor. Before they hit, Carl had managed to snag all six bottles out of the air; saving him from another mess to clean up.

Shocked and amazed by his skill, he actually managed to smile.

"Finally," he said to himself, "something has gone right today."

He placed one bottle on the counter and put the other five back into the refrigerator. Still pleased with himself at his amazing feat, he grabbed the remote control, switched on the television and plopped down into his recliner. As he opened the bottle, to begin his pity-party, the beer fizzed up out of the bottle and all over Carl and his suede recliner.

"Shit!" he yelled. His good luck appeared to be gone.

Early This Morning...

"You're such an idiot!" Iris yelled into the telephone. "What the hell are you going to do now? That's the third job you've lost this year. Did you tell Mom yet?"

"NO!" Carl quickly answered. "Don't tell Mom! You know how obsessed she becomes whenever she thinks that one of our lives isn't perfect." He could hear his sister hiding her laughter on the other end of the line.

"All right, Jobless Wonder, what do you have planned for today?"

Carl looked at the clock. It was 7:45am.

"I don't know," he mumbled. "I guess I'll start looking for another job. Can I use your computer?"

"What's the matter with yours?"

"I had to cancel my Internet service, you know, to save money."

"But I bet you didn't cancel your cable, did you?" Iris said in her *'I know how you are'* voice.

"No," Carl rolled his eyes and answered in his *'yes, I'm stupid - thank you for pointing it out'* voice. "I didn't cancel my cable."

"Fine," Iris said smugly. She loved being right. "You can come over and use my computer but you have to watch Brandon. I have stuff I need to do and he would only slow me down. Besides, he loves having you around."

15 Minutes ago...

"Uncle Carl!" Brandon yelled from the elegant living room of his parent's luxury, fortieth floor apartment. "Can I have some cookies?"

Carl turned away from the computer screen and glanced at the digital clock.

"No!" he called back, "it's almost lunch time. You can have some then." He then went back to his online job search.

"Uncle Carl! Can I have some pop?"

Carl slammed his head into the desk. *"Like that kid needs any more sugar,"* he mumbled. "If I give you some pop, will you be quiet for a while?"

"Yes!"

Pushing back the chair, Carl got up and walked into the kitchen, grabbed a can of pop and poured half of it into a green plastic cup. "I'll keep the rest for myself," he said and took a sip out of the can.

Walking into the front room to deliver the cup of caffeine to the child, he noticed Brandon sitting inches away from the television. The little boy was hypnotized by the magic box.

The intro music for The Mighty Bullet Power Hour, Brandon's favorite cartoon, had started. The boy's entire bedroom was a tribute to the colorful superhero; from bed sheets to action figures, from posters to comic books. You couldn't go anywhere in there without being under the watchful eye of the make-believe champion.

The sound of a gunshot echoed and a streak of blue and silver flashed across the screen. Standing in front of an approaching tank, the hero bent down and easily lifted the assault vehicle over his head. Bending his muscular legs, the Mighty Bullet leapt into the air and flew off into the cartoon sunset. Giant letters filled the screen. The Mighty Bullet Power Hour had begun.

Brandon turned around with a huge grin and reached out for his pop. Carl noticed that his nephew was already wearing his Mighty Bullet T-shirt.

"So, that's the Mighty Bullet, huh?" Carl asked. "What makes him so special? I mean, why do you like him so much?" He wasn't really expecting an answer, figuring that the child didn't want to be bothered during his television show.

"He's the best, Uncle Carl!" the boy said, full of excitement. "He's really strong. He's super-fast and he can fly, too. Can other superheroes do that?"

Carl, being no stranger to comic books in his youth replied, "There's a few." But there was no need to knock this hero off of his nephew's pedestal.

"Yeah," Brandon said indifferently, "but none of them are as cool as The Mighty Bullet."

A few seconds later, Brandon's eyes got a bit larger. He looked around with a bit of guilt on his face. He slowly inched his face closer to Carl.

"That's what I wished for, Uncle Carl," he loudly whispered.

"What?" Carl cluelessly asked. "What wish? When?"

"For your Birthday," Brandon answered in a 'how-dare-you-forget' type of way, "when you told me to make a wish before I blew out your candles, I wished that you were The Mighty Bullet." A huge, innocent grin spread across the child's face.

All of a sudden, it hit him. Carl now realized why strange things had been happening to him.

The flash of blue and silver - He caught up to the speeding bus and saved his beer from breaking on the floor.

Lifting a tank over his head - He broke his desk in half.

Leaping into the air and flying off into the sunset.

"Wait a minute," Carl said to himself. "Brandon, can the Mighty Bullet fly?" he asked just to be sure.

"He sure can!" the little boy answered and went on to tell, in vivid details, about one of the hero's adventures, but Carl had already blocked out the sound of his nephew's voice.

I can fly! he thought. Snapping out of his daydream, Carl reached out and grabbed his nephew by the shoulder. "Brandon, I've got a big surprise to show you."

Now...

As they made their way to the rooftop, Carl told Brandon about his newfound powers.

Brandon was so proud of himself; he had turned his uncle into a real-life superhero.

Kneeling down to look Brandon directly in his eyes, Carl spoke in a serious tone.

"Now don't do what I'm going to do. I have superpowers, now. Remember, YOU... CAN'T... FLY."

"I know, Uncle Carl. My wish was for YOU to be a superhero."

"Good," Carl said as he exhaled in relief. "Now stay right here and watch as I fly just like Super Bullet."

"Mighty Bullet," Brandon corrected.

"Right."

Carl walked over to the edge of the skyscraper; his heart beat a mile a minute. "Don't look down," he said to himself as he eventually looked down. The ground seemed to fade even further away while he looked at it.

Shaking his head to clear his mind from its hypnotic state, he walked back to the center of the roof before he chickened out. Taking in a deep breath, he sprinted toward the ledge; there was no backing down now. With a powerful leap, he jumped off of the roof and into his destiny.

Carl stuck out his arms and willed himself to fly, but nothing happened. It was as he plummeted down, past the fifteenth floor, when he remembered his sister saying, "If you tell your wish, it won't come true."

About the author: Gary McKenzie is the author of the children / young adult Gingerbread Kingdom books (conveniently available at Amazon.com) and has also entered the horror market with short stories found on HouseofHorror.org/uk (Issues 9 & 13). He has been a comic book fan since the age of 4 when he picked up his first Spider-Man comic.

8

The Tripwire Trio

T. L. Barrett

1.

I have always harbored a secret love of all thing super-heroic. I was just eight years old when the New York tragedy occurred, but I can remember crying when I heard that my heroes had died at the hands of Dr. Devious. I remember my dad hugging me when the remnants of Team 7 took the madman down. I knew that I must have a meta-power somewhere inside of me, and I dreamed of one day joining that erstwhile band of teen heroes. When Team 7 disbanded, I guess I put those dreams away. Recognizing that I would never exhibit the powers of my heroes, like the rest of America, I picked up the pieces of my life and moved on.

When the editorial office gave me this assignment, those dreams, soaked in the primary colors of youth assailed me. Thusly, I found myself driving up a winding hillside on a bright Hollywood day to meet one of the originals, a real honest-to-God Golden Age meta-hero.

I had stopped my editor mid-sentence when he went on to tell this wet-behind-the-ears reporter just who Tommy Winfield, Soup Boy, was. That Christmas of 93', American Meta-Toys had reissued a commemorative line of Minute-men action figures. I had begged my folks for a Captain Dynamo. Of course, the last leader of the MM had sold out of every store. My parents winced as I opened up my consolation prize, a combination pack of the complete and original Golden age Minute Men: Minute Man, Lady Liberty, Clarion, Red Dog, Mr. Dark, and Soup Boy. Soup Boy, in his GI helmet with his cherubic and grinning face was my favorite for three reasons. 1. He came with a little container of sticky blob goo. 2. None of my friends knew who he was. 3. My parents told me he was still alive.

Almost seventeen years later, I parked in front of a classy art deco house with a magnificent view of the valley with wet hands and a lump in my throat. A housekeeper came out, guided me onto a tiled veranda overlooking la-la land and into a chair with an iced-tea at my elbow. She also left an ash tray for me. Feeling like I had stepped into a different era and a little vindicated in avoiding relinquishing my vice, I lit up.

Frankly, the embarrassment I feel for my lack of observational skills overwhelms me. The ornately molded tub sat only six feet or so from my feet, just in the shade. I should have noticed that the glistening contents of the tub were not in fact water. When said contents rose up and formed the rudimental shape of the top half of a man, I admit to yelping, spilling my iced-tea, and burning my lap with my cigarette.

As I recovered myself and apologized, a surprisingly human voice chuckled good-heartedly at my lack of composure.

SB- My apologies Mr. Raymond, I never can resist the temptation. I guess what they say is true; those things really are bad for your health.

50 Stars- I guess you're right. Thanks for taking the time to talk to 50 Stars.

SB- Heck, kid all I have is time, these days. But, I really can't complain. You'll forgive me if I don't get up. I have a lot of trouble these days maintaining my original shape. The government docs always said that something like this might happen. But, I thought: heck, what do they know? What did any of us know, for that matter? I'm just getting old in my own way, I suppose. My memory is still intact, I'm thankful for that at least.

50 Stars- You'll celebrate your eighty-eighth birthday this October. Looking back, does anything surprise you, or stand out after all these years.

SB- It all stands out, I suppose. I still can't believe New York is gone. I suppose that's at the heart of all these groups crying out against metas. I can understand their fear, but I think it's sad that folks forget how many good people lost their lives protecting us.

50 Stars- You're granddaughter, Tia Okada, the Oddity, was Time Magazine's most influential meta-human. Do you ever worry for her in this climate considering the growing hate group trends?

SB- Sure I worry, but I try to remind her to still live a life: get married, have kids. Time goes by so quickly, and in the end there'll always be one more problem to fix. She's a good girl, but I worry she takes too much on her shoulders.

50 Stars- Of the original Minute Men, you and Joseph Redfeather are the only known survivors. He lives under protection of the Navajo Nation. Do you ever speak with him?

SB- Red calls me every year on my birthday. Mostly to rub it in my face that he's still older and wiser than I am. I can't imagine he'll let himself go before me. He's too stubborn to die. I guess, you can't teach old dogs new tricks.

50 Stars- What about the rumors that the FBI still believes that Rhett Faraday is still alive and behind the meta-terrorist group, The Third Shift?

SB- No comment. Don't believe everything you read, kid.

50 Stars- Some people say that the book Mr. Faraday wrote in '73, *The Third Shift*, might have inspired metas like Dr. Devious. Do you have an opinion on the subject that you would like to share?

SB- Is it J.D. Salinger's fault that Lennon died? Give me a break. I guess there's one thing I can say I've learned from eighty-eight years of living: there's always enough fools to believe the damnedest things.

50 Stars- Back in the seventies you became active-

SB- Hold it right there. I was so hoping you wouldn't bring up the seventies. Yes, I made quite a bit of cash as a regular on variety shows. I let the studio execs drop me all over nubile models and actresses. I probably know Goldie Hawn's body better than Kurt Russell does. I still cringe whenever I hear someone call "soup's on!" I did it. I'm not proud of it, but in the end it's what paid for this tub and the view, so it is what it is. I was hoping we would talk about the stuff that mattered.

50 Stars- Actually, Mr. Winfield, I was about to ask you if it was true that you actually poured yourself all over Richard Nixon while he was golfing.

SB- (laughing) Yes, that is true. I got that weasel good. It wasn't my idea, actually. Tommy Smothers put me up to it.

50 Stars- You said you hoped we would talk about the stuff that mattered. What does matter to you? What would you like to talk about?

SB- Well, the documentaries I've seen always talk about the love between Lady Liberty and Minute Man, and how Clarion went nuts in the fifties and everything. Rhett, Red and I are always just side notes, but we aren't. We were our own team: the Tripwire Trio. We might not have had as flashy powers as the rest of them, but we fought bad guys. Once, we very nearly saved the planet, as far as I can figure. Not very many people know about that.

50 Stars- Sir, 50 Stars, would be honored to help you inform America about these events if you feel like you're ready to tell them.

SB- You bet I am. As you know, we three were the only real successful subjects from the first meta-human experiment after the Boston Initiative. The government already had the Minute Men fighting on the front lines and in the front pages. They wanted to create a covert operation unit of metas to get behind enemy lines. It was called Project: Tripwire. Many of the brass were worried that the Axis had begun their own meta experiments. I believe that was going to be our first task, to find these operations and shut them down. Things didn't really end up happening that way, but nobody did too much complaining. It was back in December of '43. We had been held up in a base in Nevada for months. We were young and we were stir-crazy. We were also nervous that any day they were going to drop us into enemy territory with a parachute and a prayer...

2.

Private Thomas Winfield lay in the bed and wished he had lied. He had lied before. He had told Mrs. Carmichael down the street that he wasn't virgin on that sweet hot day before he shipped off to base. He had figured that she figured that out halfway through the too quick experience they had anyway. He wished he had lied on the damn questionnaire they had given him when General Gaines had come onto the base. The enlisted men weren't allowed to talk about the 'tests', but Tommy could tell most of them thought the General and the exams were a loud of horse manure. Tommy could also tell that the pretty young assistant holding up the cards was impressed with Tommy's performance. That just encouraged him. He hadn't seen any ghosts, he didn't know the future, and he sure as heck didn't read minds, but he was lucky; and he said so on the questionnaire. The Winfields had always been a lucky people. Everybody back in Harrisburg knew it. Tommy had come on to the varsity baseball team half way through the season in his Junior year and the team had suddenly gotten all kinds of wins and took the regional championship. People lined up at the county fair to watch him at the game tents. Heck, he had fulfilled his all-time adolescent fantasy with Mrs. Carmichael, talk about luck.

Tommy had been selected along with 32 others for Project: Tripwire. They were going to be superheroes, just like the Minute Men. In a bus with covered windows they were driven at night to new location. Tommy didn't like remembering the days after they had emerged from the underground chamber with the awful Tuning Forks resonated him so that he felt like he would break apart. The General had put him in isolation for a while, when his body parts started to liquefy. Finally, when it didn't appear like the stuff that Tommy was becoming was toxic, Tommy had been placed in with the two of the other survivors, Joseph Redfeather, a Navajo with an infectious laugh and the smooth talking Rhett Faraday. Rhett talked Tommy through the worst of it. He convinced him that he could control his body, solidify it when he needed. When Rhett talked him through it, the lights would dim. That got the General's attention in a big way. Both Tommy and Rhett had stayed by Red's side when the big Indian had begun his first painful transformation in to what looked like a huge hell hound.

Now, they suffered through long hours of physical and mental drilling. It soon became apparent that 'The Tripwire Trio', as they had begun calling themselves, was not being groomed for front page appearances. Red had surmised that eventually the three of them would be dropped behind enemy lines.

"Let's face it," Rhett agreed, "we're a guy who casts shadows, a red skinwalker, and a guy that turns into a mucousy blob. We're not the shaking-hands-with-the-mayor types."

Tommy didn't know if he had it in him to drop behind enemy lines into god-knows-what kind of Nazi hell. He knew he probably would see combat when he got the draft notice, and being a superhero had sounded great. It wasn't looking so glamorous now. The people in the project had started calling him 'Soup Boy' for crying out loud.

"I can't sleep."

"I know," Red said from the darkness of the next bunk.

"How do you know?"

"You aren't snoring, are you?" Red said. Hearing the Navajo's voice in the dark had weird effect on Tommy. He had only had younger sisters growing up. Now he had two very strange older brothers. "But you haven't been thinking too much about Mrs. Carnegie, at least."

"That's Mrs. Carmichael, Red," Rhett corrected him from Tommy's other side.

"Whatever," Red sighed.

"How do you know if I'm thinking about her?" Tommy asked. Red shook his own bed in a rhythmic creak of the springs.

"Oh..." Tommy said, feeling the heat of his own reddened face in the dark.

"Leave the poor boy alone, Red," Rhett said. "What's got your crank in a yank, Tommy?"

"I wish I lied," Tommy said. He felt guilt for saying it. All three of them were in this together.

"Lied about what?" Rhett asked.

"Lied when I took that stupid test that got me sent here. I'm not cut out for this kind of thing. I mean, I can't keep myself together, some days, literally." Red laughed. It was what Tommy loved most about the big Injun. He always laughed.

"I never took a test," Red said. "Did you take a test, Hollywood?"

"Uh, no. I didn't."

"Yeah, you guys must have," Tommy said, rolling onto one elbow. "You know, the test to see if you were all weird and everything?"

"No. Didn't take a test," Red said, suddenly pensive. "I didn't have to. My grandfather is a medicine man."

"How 'bout you, Rhett? What's weird about you?"

"Other than my extra-long lady pleaser? Not a hell of a lot, kiddo," Rhett said.

"You see spirits," Red stated.

"Cut that spooky Indian shit out!" Rhett snapped. "Fine, my grandmother used to con the famous and rich out of tons of dough back around the turn of the century doing séances and that spiritualist stuff. What did they find so weird about you, Tommy?"

"I guess I'm lucky."

"Lucky Tommy," Red said, and reached out and affectionately patted Tommy's arm.

"What about the others?" Tommy asked. "There were thirty of them. Did they all die?"

"No. Some did. I think the General hid the others away," Red answered.

"You mean they were worse than us? Worse than turning into soup?"

"No. Maybe they were better. Maybe the General is afraid of what they can do. Maybe we were the rejects." Tommy lay on his bed and thought long on what that could mean. He started to drowse.

"Fellas," Rhett hissed. Tommy jumped and snorted. Rhett was standing over him. "Get suited up. Be quiet. We have to leave."

"What?" Tommy asked.

"Just do what Hollywood says," Red said. Tommy got up and started pulling on his uniform. None of them had any other clothes. They were property of the United States Government. No, scratch that, Tommy thought. They were the personal property of General William S. Gaines, and he wasn't going to be happy about this.

"Rhett, what is going on?" Tommy said, struggling into his boots.

"Do you trust me, fellas?" Rhett asked.

"Sure, Rhett, we trust you," Tommy said.

"Then each of you take my hands and don't let go no matter what; and keep up with me. We are going to have to run."

"There are at least three guards out in the hallway!" Tommy hissed.

"We won't be going into the hallway," Rhett answered. "Red, you sure we're in Southern Nevada?"

"Pretty sure."

"Pretty sure will have to do. Grab hold, fellas." Rhett grabbed Tommy's hand. Red took Rhett's other hand. Rhett turned them to the far wall and took a deep breath. He lurched forward, running them full tilt at the wall.

"What the heck!" Tommy gasped. Then blackness engulfed them.

Tommy ducked his chin and winced, closing his eyes. He expected to feel the impact of the concrete wall against his skull. Instead, they ran unimpeded through the darkness.

Strange sounds came to them as they ran pell-mell through a dark universe. The sounds owned a consistency, a solidity all their own. They implied shapes that flashed by as the Tripwire Trio tore through the oblivion. Tommy's mind tried to make sense of the shapes around him, but his mind raced faster than his feet.

As they ran for what seemed forever, and Tommy's lungs ached with fire, he heard, but did not see, the shape of great looming architecture on the horizon. Strange shapes screamed their flight above them. Tommy focused on the sound of his friends' breath, the feel of Rhett's hand, and hoped that his legs would not give out.

And then the world returned to them. They were out in the winter desert night. They let go of each other's hands and bent over panting. Tommy looked up and saw a strangely familiar sight.

They stood just fifty yards from the warm light that issued from Big Abe's All Night Diner and Truck Stop.

"We're in Arizona?" Tommy panted. "How the heck did you get us in Arizona, Rhett?"

"I'll... explain... inside, Tommy. I need some grub and I need it now. Jesus, that took a lot out of me." Tommy caught the scent of grilled beef on the air. His stomach growled.

"Big Abe's!" Red shouted. "Wahoo!" He laughed and started to jog toward the familiar spectacle.

3.

As Frank Sinatra crooned about stardust from the juke box, the Tripwire Trio took a booth as far away from over-hearing ears as they could. Tommy ordered everybody the hamburger plate as Red sat across from Rhett and studied his friend impassively. Tommy had seen plenty of soldiers shirk from the Indian's stare before, but Rhett just stared back with an uncharacteristically somber look. Tommy looked from the handsome stony face of Red, to the dashing face of Rhett, who despite his obvious fatigue and pallor, still managed to look sophisticated with his pencil thin bit of moustache.

"All right, already!" Tommy hissed. "Will somebody tell me what the hell is going on?" Rhett's eyes broke in their stare and he rubbed his eyes.

"I don't cast shadows," he said.

"Well, you can do a whole lot more, I'll tell you that! I mean, we went what... hundreds of miles in a few minutes?"

"That wasn't me, Tommy."

"Then who is it?" Red asked.

"During the experiment, I thought I was going to die," Rhett began.

"Join the club," Tommy said.

"I called out for help, and my grandmother answered."

"She's dead, isn't she, Rhett?" Tommy asked his eyes wide. Rhett nodded.

"She told me that I had the gift, but I always knew I did anyway." Here he looked up at

Red for a second and looked down again. "She told me that she had someone I needed to meet. That's when I met my little shadow."

"You mean when you do that... what you do... It isn't..?" Tommy swallowed.

"It isn't me, kiddo, not entirely. My 'friend' is in me, he joined with me somehow."

"Jesus, Rhett," Tommy uncharacteristically swore.

"It isn't evil," Red stated.

"No, it isn't, and it's here for a reason, a pretty important one."

"Wait. How do we know this shadow thing isn't evil?" Tommy asked. The two other men gave Tommy a look. "Fine," he said and held up his hands.

"It's okay Tommy, it is weird. They don't really come from anywhere. It is hard to describe. You know that we have free will? Well, every time we make a decision we bring more potential worlds into existence. Well, no, sometimes we can do really bad things, like killing or enslaving... look it's too complicated. The point is that they come from the place where all that potential exists. Each time we think and make a decision we carve reality out of that darkness. They call it the void."

"They," Red stated. Rhett nodded.

"Yeah, there's a lot of them, probably countless."

"Wait, that weird place...that was it. We ran through the void?" Tommy asked.

"Keep your voice down, kiddo." Rhett said, but nodded. "Look, you remember I told you that the brass are worried that the Axis is working on developing a project like ours, people with powers?" Red and Tommy nodded. Rhett had used his shadow casting abilities to slip out during the night. One night he had overheard the General and some officers discussing it. He had also brought back a bottle of hooch once.

"Well, it turns out they are, but not like us. The Nazis have this weird group, the Thule society. They aren't nice people, black magic, sacrifices, end of the world, that kind of stuff. Anyways, they found a way to reach into the void with magic and scoop out shadows and force them to bind with their soldiers. These shadow-Nazis have been ripping apart our forces over in Europe. The shadows are enslaved, against their will. They have never seen such hate, or pain before. The shadows are all connected. They are disgusted by what they have seen."

"Join the club," Tommy quipped. "Rhett, why didn't you just tell the general?"

"They can't know," Red said. Rhett nodded.

"As it is, the shadows of the void are ready to swallow this whole reality because of what the Nazis have done, as it is. They sent the shadow to me in a last ditch effort to free their comrades. If the allies found out about it, they would be forced to find some way to do the same thing."

"So what are you... we supposed to do?" Tommy asked.

"The Nazi shadow-warriors are on the move-" The waitress arrived at Red's side bearing three huge hamburger platters with fries and coleslaw.

"There you are soldier boys. Eat up!" The tired waitress smacked her gum and winked at Rhett. Rhett managed a tired smile. The men fell to devouring the best meal they had eaten in months.

"The shadow Nazis have been coming stateside for the past few weeks, meeting with Nazi sympathizers on the east coast. The sympathizers are going to dress up like superheroes and raid a munitions factory as a decoy. This will keep the Minute Men busy and distracted," Rhett muttered around a mouthful of hamburger.

"Well, we have to warn them somehow!" Tommy said, and winced at the volume of his voice. "The Minute Men will be able to kick these shadow-Nazis back to Berlin."

"There isn't time. The Nazis are sending the shadow-warriors to the white house tonight, while everyone is distracted. They're going to assassinate Roosevelt."

"We have to stop them," Red stated. Tommy swallowed. He felt the burger lodged in his esophagus. He took a long drink of water and looked around.

"Hey, guys, some girl is staring this way," Tommy said.

"I get it all the time," Rhett said. "They always think I'm a movie star or something."

"Sorry, Rhett, I don't think she's staring at you. She's staring at Red, and she's coming this way." A pretty brunette in a striped work shirt approached.

"Joey Redfeather? Is it really you? How's uncle Sam been treating you?" Red looked up at her and a sly smile crept across his face.

"Nancy Fellows. No complaints, really. What keeps a farm girl like you out so late?"

"Just got off shift about an hour ago. Doing my bit for the cause, you know? You sure are a sight for sore eyes, Joey." Red grinned.

"Are you a riveter, Nancy?" Red asked.

"Just call me, Rosie, sweet man. Look at me, now." Nancy rolled up a sleeve and curled her arm so that her bicep bunched into a hard knot. "Feel that steel, will ya?" Red laughed and reached up and squeezed her pale arm with his long dark fingers.

"Hitler better hope they don't send you over there," Red said. Nancy blushed.

"Get your damned fingers off her, you dirty injun!" someone said from across the diner. A big man in his thirties had risen up from his seat and walked forward. He still had dirt on his forearms from a long day of work. "Just cause you wear that uniform doesn't give you the right to fondle our women, boy."

"Carl Webb, you just go sit yourself down and have another beer," Nancy said.

"Your poor father might not have minded you playing in the dirt with the reds when you were a kid, Nancy Fellows, but I'll be damned if I'm going to sit back and watch while you embarrass yourself like a damned floozy."

"Uh... Red," Tommy said. Red stood up. Across the diner three other big working men stood, as well.

"We really don't have time for this," Rhett said wearily.

Red stepped in front of Nancy. Webb strode across the diner, knocking over a chair as he came. Webb's cronies came on, as well.

No one noticed Tommy lean over as he were diving toward the floor. His body changed as he fell, a great rush of peachy protoplasm landing on the floor and sliding under some tables. Webb came within swinging distance of Red. Red stood his ground, giving the bigot his impassive stare.

Webb hawked and spat in Red's face.

Red's fist flashed out and caught Webb in the jaw. The man flew back and broke a table with his fall. Someone screamed. Webb's cronies came rushing forward.

Suddenly, their feet slid across the greasy protoplasm and flew out from under them. They fell in a pile, rapping their heads on tables and each other.

Tommy sluiced back into his discarded uniform and stood back up. Webb struggled to rise.

"Ah, Tommy-" Rhett said and pointed to his friend's midsection. Tommy looked down to see that he had reoccupied his pants backwards and one arm had solidified inside his shirt.

"Darn it!" Tommy said. "I thought I had that down."

Webb lifted the chair with which he had used to rise. Rhett rose, grabbed Tommy's free hand and took Red by the shoulder.

Darkness flooded the diner. Many people screamed.

"Come on, scrapper," Tommy heard Rhett say. With a great commotion and clamor they made their way out of the diner and into the cold night wind.

"Let me go, Hollywood!" Red said. "He deserves it."

"And you gave him a broken jaw, I think. We have other matters to attend to, if you can think past the pretty riveter for a second. It's happening now." The darkness receded. Tommy and Red looked at their friend in shock.

"Right now? You're sure?" Tommy asked. Rhett nodded.

"You guys don't have to come. But, I hope you do. There are three of the shadow-bastards."

"Let's go, Hollywood," Red said and put his hand out. Rhett took it.

"Tommy?" Rhett asked.

"'All for one, and one for all', right?" Tommy said, and forced his right hand out of the arm hole in his shirt. He put the shaking hand into his friend's.

"Get ready to run again," Rhett said.

Red let out an eerie howl that filled the desert night. The Tripwire Trio ran into the void.

4.

The tripwire trio stumbled exhausted from the void and tumbled down onto the floor of the state dining room of the White House.

"I'm going to throw up," Tommy wheezed from where he lay on the carpet.

"Get up," Red said and looked about the darkened hall. Tommy looked at the room where some of the most important people had broken bread together. He was really in the white house. That meant that there were really Nazi shadow-warriors and they were really going to kill the president. Tommy swallowed and stood on shaky legs.

"I've been here, when I was eight. My grandmother brought me here. She insisted that I come. Mrs. Coolidge had invited her to a dinner," Rhett whispered. Red went to the door and looked out at the Cross Hall. A body lay on the floor. Red crept up to it. He turned and slid a finger across his neck. Tommy and Rhett scurried to his side and looked down at the dead security agent. Red led the way toward the center of the hall, where pillared columns stood on the left. He stopped. Tommy almost bumped into him. Rhett's face wore an awed expression. Rhett stepped forward and acted as if he was listening. Then he nodded and saluted.

"What is happening?" Tommy hissed.

"Was that-?" Red asked. Rhett nodded.

"We go upstairs to the second floor," Rhett said.

"How do you know that?" Tommy asked.

"Honest Abe doesn't lie," Rhett whispered and led the way through the columns to the left. They mounted the stairs.

At the top of the stairs they entered a smaller hallway with halls leading to the left and right. Another slain agent lay just inside the landing area. A shadow moved on the left. Further down the hallway a shadow moved on the right.

"Find the president, Tommy. Protect him," Rhett said. He turned and said something in a strange hissing language to the closer shadow on the left. The shadow coalesced into the shape of a man, and then faded. A huge Aryan soldier stood there. The shadow wrapped about him, forming a dark suit of armor. The Nazi raised his hand and a blade of shadow grew from it.

Tommy heard the sound of cloth ripping and saw his other friend transforming into his huge red canine alter ego. He growled and his eyes glowed infernally in the dim hall light. The shadow to the right stopped and ran down through a doorway. Red dashed down the hallway after it.

Protect the president. Jumped up Jesus on a pogo stick, Tommy's grandfather would have said. He jogged after Red, moving instinctively. He scanned and saw doorways leading off to both the right and left. He stopped and tried to clear his mind.

Left, that inner voice that he had learned to trust told him. He went left into a huge oval room decorated in yellow décor. He suddenly wished he had spent more time listening to his history teacher rather than staring at the Susie Allen's glorious rack. He turned to the right and came to a closed door. It was locked. He looked down. Could he squeeze under the crack at the bottom?

He'd have to try.

He flowed out of his clothes and pressed himself as thin as he could, flowing back halfway across the yellow room. He pressed himself against the door jam and felt a great painful pressure throughout his amorphous body. He slid underneath and slowly, ever so slowly, began to expand back on the other side. Finally he was through. With relief he solidified in the private sitting room as naked as a jay bird. He crept across the sitting room to a door opposite of the one he had just passed. He tried the door knob. It was not locked.

Something began to growl as he opened the door.

***

Rhett watched the shadow knight bear down on him. The Nazi gave him a grin of triumph as he prepared to strike. Rhett let his own shadow fly around him. Rhett's hand tightened on a shadow sword as thin as the rapiers he had used in boarding school fencing club. His shadow flowed from his neck like a musketeer's cape.

Rhett feinted to the side just as the Nazi bore down on him. He twisted on his feet and spun his shadow out. The edge of the Nazi shadow blade just sliced him on the upper arm as he did so. His shadow cape slipped around the Nazi's legs. The Nazi staggered to his knees cursing in German. Rhett felt himself falling with the spin and let himself fall lengthways across the German's back. He brought an elbow down and knocked the Nazi flat on the floor. The Nazi rolled and brought the spiked edge of a shadow gauntlet against the side of Rhett's arm. Rhett fell heavily against the wall.

He looked at the blood coming down his torn uniform sleeve. He looked up and saw that the Nazi was grinning now, raising his shadow sword high over his head. Rhett held his tiny blade out in front of him as he lay against the wall where he had fallen.

The shadow rapier extended with great speed until it entered the space just above the Nazi's armor and just below the Nazi's jaw. The shadow blade kept going until it slid out the back of the Nazi's impressive skull. The Nazi's sword and armor disappeared. The Nazi stood like that for some seconds before falling forward at Rhett's feet.

"That's the problem with you jack boot types," Rhett said and winced while he struggled to regain his feet, "your total and utter lack of imagination."

***

Red Dog bounded after the shadow-warrior into the private dining hall. The shadow warrior slid over the large dining table and Red Dog slid under it, snapping with his vicious jaws as he came out on the other side. The shadow-Nazi dove into the kitchen on the other side of the split door. Red Dog pounded through after, only to find himself in darkness. A terribly cold pain pierced Red Dog's flank and he gave out a load yip of pain. He darted forward and spun around knocking down all manners of cutlery and glass cake stands. His iridescent eyes fixed on the heat signature of the Nazi like a shadow within a shadow. He recoiled and then sprang forward. The Nazi tried to swing his shadow blade out at the beast.

If Red Dog had truly been the savage hell hound he appeared to be, leaping in wrath at the source of his pain, the Nazi's blade would have found purchase in his throat. Red Dog was not a savage, he was a member of the Navajo people, with much experience defending himself from angry older boys off and on the reservation. He twisted his great neck as he flew and snapped his mighty jaws. The Nazi's hand came off at the wrist.

Red Dog's clawed front paws came down on the Nazi's shoulder and flung him against the edge of the kitchen counters with a nasty crack. The Nazi made one shuddering groan as his bowels released and he fell to the floor. He shook, staring at the stump of his arm as Red Dog lowered his head and covered the Nazi assassin's head with his jaws.

***

The dim lamplight from the sitting room cast a shadow of Tommy's naked form as he stood in the threshold of the bedroom of the 32nd president of the United States.

The Scottie dog sitting on a little bed at the foot of the president's growled viciously.

"Easy boy," Tommy said.

"What?" FDR snorted. "Fala? What's wrong?" He fumbled with his glasses and managed to find them. He put them on and pulled a cord for his bed-side light.

"What in the hell is going on here?" the president demanded, his eyes fixing on the young naked man before him.

"Mr. President, sir... you are in danger," Tommy managed lamely, trying to cover his side.

"Are you some kind of pervert?" the president asked, his face going pale in the lamplight.

"No sir, I am not a pervert. I promise," Tommy said.

"Who the hell are you?"

"Private Thomas Winfield, sir," he saluted.

"Did the republicans put you up to this? FDR asked. "Here, Fala! Have they black mailed you, young man?"

"No sir. Sir, you are in serious danger. The security guards...they've been killed. The Nazis have sent shadow warriors to assassinate you-"

"What the hell?" FDR said. Tommy heard noticed movement on the far side of the room in the shadows. Tommy ran forward and leaped up onto the edge of the bed and ran over the president's legs. Fala leapt and snapped in rage at this outrageous invasion.

"Good Christ!" FDR screamed.

The shadow Nazi launched himself forward at the same moment. The Nazi's dark hand caught Tommy by the throat and slammed him down upon the bed against the president's side. The Nazi gritted his teeth and a shadow snaked from his side and flew down toward FDR's chest. When it touched the president, FDR convulsed as if from a great shock. Tommy watched his president pale with horror as the icy touch of the shadow crept up on his heart.

Tommy wondered distantly how things had come to this, as his face turned from red to purple as the shadow Nazi squeezed his thorax. It was so hard to breathe.

He looked at the black clad Nazi and got an idea. Tommy dissolved and slipped out of the Nazi's grip. Then he shot up the grasping arm and poured himself into the fascist warrior's nostrils and mouth. As the mucous-like substance filled the Nazi's air ways, the Nazi's shadow retreated from its hold upon the president. Tommy blindly forced himself deeper into the soldier. The soldier gurgled and wheezed, clutching at his own throat.

For what seemed like eons, Tommy burrowed deep, filling the cramping lungs of the assassin. Then finally, the blood burst from the Nazi's mouth and nose. He collapsed on the ground, a lifeless SS officer.

Tommy slid from the ruptured insides of the officer and took form again. His head and shoulders were covered in mucous and blood.

"Mr. President, are you okay?" The president sucked in a great wheezing breath.

"Yes, young man. I'm all right. How in God's name did an SS soldier get in my bedroom?"

"He was a shadow warrior; he walked through the void to get here."

"Who are you, again?"

"I guess you can call me Soup Boy," Tommy said. He looked over at the dead man on the floor. "Oh my God." He said and fell on his naked rump on the floor. He put his face in his hands and sobbed.

FDR struggled to pull himself across the bed and reached a hand down to Tommy's shoulder.

"You've never killed a man before, have you son?" Tommy shook his head.

"Well, I've never killed a man, but I've broken hearts before. What you have done here is a far more noble deed, young man. I thank you for it. Your country thanks you for it." The little black Scottish terrier licked FDR's ear excitedly. "Fala thanks you for it, too."

"Tommy!" Rhett shouted from the doorway from which the shadow-Nazi had entered. He ran in and looked at the mess.

"This young man is all right, I think. He saved me," FDR announced. Rhett bent over Tommy.

"Tommy, are you okay?" Tommy looked up and wiped his face and nodded. Red came running in. Tommy saw that he had tied a cook's apron over his front for makeshift loin cloth. For decency's sake they were going to have to work on the whole clothing issue. Tommy noticed the wound on Red's side, leaking a trickle of blood down on the white apron.

"Are they all-" Tommy managed.

"Dead. Yes," Red said.

"We're not out of the woods yet, gentlemen," Rhett stated. "Mr. President, the men who attacked tonight had enslaved a group of shadow beings. Those shadow beings have returned to their home. Their people are not happy, and since they have all returned, are about to extinguish our entire reality for the crimes that they have been forced to commit."

"This is all very dumbfounding, I assure you, gentlemen," FDR stated.

"I appreciate that, Mr. President, I do, but we are going to have to act now or everything we know or could know will pay the ultimate price for what the Nazis have done."

"I understand. What needs to be done?" Tommy could hear the security agent reinforcements moving down the hallway outside.

"We need to take you to the void, Mr. President. We need to have you speak to the Queen of Shades, herself."

5.

Tommy decided that he would never get used to these visits to the void. At least, this time they weren't dashing pell-mell through it, so he had time to adjust to hearing the shapes of things. A sprawling metropolis of looming structures and whispering shadow-folk teemed around them. Thankfully, the shadow-folk, disgusted by the three intruders, had kept their distance. The tripwire trio rested on the edge of an entrancing shadow fountain and waited.

"I hope old FDR can talk some sense into the shadow queen," Rhett said.

"If anybody can do it, he can," Tommy said.

Three shadows approached them.

Thank you. The freed shadow beings bowed low. They sang a song of thanks then, and many shadows danced and added their grace. Tommy, Red and Rhett sat and listened to it all, tears tinkling from their eyes to counterpoint the melody.

Great shapes were formed by the song, commemorating these heroes forever in the land of shade. The sounds reverberated across the multiverse and somewhere a young boy in another reality heard the song and it stayed with him. Later, when his children were nearly the age that he was when he first heard it, he would sit down and begin to write about Red, and Rhett and Tommy. The thought of it made Red laugh his wonderful laugh.

"Well, Cairo and Teheran had nothing on this. I'll tell you that, men." FDR said as he walked proudly out of the infinite chambers of the Queen of Shadows. The men turned to see how gracefully their crippled president sauntered. "Stalin and Churchill are not nearly as formidable as her ladyship; but then they aren't as pleasing on the senses, either."

"You did it, then, Mr. President?" Rhett asked.

"Yes, I believe so. Our reality has been given a reprieve. But there are things that must be done. But first if you will..." In the land of shadow, Franklin D. Roosevelt danced for all the multiverse to see.

6.

In the oval office, the tripwire trio listened to the president of their country quietly squash the hopes of the man who had dominated their lives for the past few months.

"I understand, General Gaines, I do, sir. I want you to know what a fine job you've been doing... Yes, I appreciate that. No, sir, I assure you, the matter is one of utmost importance. Yes, well you have a good day then. Thank you... I will, Good-bye General Gaines." He hung up the phone and lit his cigarette. He smiled and patted the desk, and winked at the trio.

He pushed a button and said: "Send in the Minute Men, will you?" A moment later, the original three meta-heroes for the Allies, or the world, for that matter, entered the room. Tommy gawked at just how small, yet formidable the minute man looked. He finally got the whole 'mienoot man' quip that everyone enjoyed. Standing at just shy of four and a half feet tall, the miniature yet perfectly-proportioned leader of the world's premiere super team might have picked a different name. He was noble looking, a real hero type, though. It didn't hurt that he wore a three cornered hat, revolutionary style upon his head. The little man shook hands with all of the three. Tommy could feel the power in his gentle grip, however, and in his presence, which seemed to crackle with energy.

Lady Liberty followed. The three men sucked in their breath as they took in her entrancing eyes and long dark hair. There had been rumors that the lady was really a Goddess reborn. Tommy believed it.

Clarion, his head looking like a featureless shining brass bullet, permanently encased as it was in metal, floated into the room. The very air vibrated with a strange muffled sound as he nodded and passed to take his place beside his teammates.

"Minute Men, I'd like to introduce you to your three new teammates. Minute Man, Lady Liberty and Clarion I'd like you to meet, Mr. Dark, Red Dog and Soup Boy." The three heroes looked with bemused curiosity at the three GI's standing before them.

"In a minute, I'll let Mr. Dark fill you in on the background and the details. You need to keep up here. We don't have much time before I'm sending you all back across the pond.

"You see, according to the treaty I hammered out with the good Queen of Shadows, it is our sworn duty to seek out the members of the Thule society, and destroy them utterly."

Soup Boy helped wheel the president to the door.

"I'll be in touch before I actually take off to make sure that everything is going well. I'm afraid after the peace talks I've had to attend that a place called Warm Springs is calling my name. God keep you, my heroes, and Merry Christmas!" FDR said. Just before he rolled out the door he reached up and laid his hand over Tommy's.

"I want to thank you again, son. The world owes you everything." Tommy swallowed, took a deep breath and turned back to face his future.

About the author: T. L. Barrett lives in Vermont's Northeast Kingdom with his beautiful wife and five children, where he also writes weird fiction. His short fiction has been published in many anthologies and magazines. This year, his Fantasy Trilogy, *The Vale of Shade*, will see print at the Library of Fantasy. You can learn more about T. L. Barrett and his work by going to tlbarrett.blogspot.com.

20

The Last Day and Night of Bill Stevens, Superhero

Jude-Marie Green

I owe Bill my life. The debt weighs me down, sobering my every action. To be plain, if he hadn't put himself between me and three guns held by drug-dealing bastards, if he hadn't shouldered his way through them, my shield while the bullets exploded from the gun barrels, I would be mouldering in a grave. For me, there would be no today.

Today, he called me in the inconvenient hour before I absolutely had to be out of bed in time for my morning shift at the bar, a shift I dreaded because only incorrigible drunks and cops looking to ease psychic pain ever came in to Doohan's at 6am.

"Tansy," Bill said. "I need you."

"Sure, what's up?" I blinked, wiped the yellow-crusted sleep from my eyes.

He hesitated. The dead phone air disturbed me. Bill never hesitated, was never vague. He was a man of action. The seconds ticked by in silence and the tension in my neck from straining towards the earphone brought me fully awake.

"Bill?" I said, just as he said my name again. We both uttered sharp barking laughs.

"Tansy, I need help with my birthday party," he said.

"Ah, sure," I said. "I'll be there tonight."

"I need you *now*,"he said.

I called in sick at work, washed up, and drove over to Bill's house. He lived in a quiet fading neighborhood of smallish 1950s houses with deep private yards. I parked across the street from his pink-washed South-western stucco house. Already some caterers' trucks lined his driveway: food and service and entertainment. White plastic tables bloomed in his trimmed back yard, and a white-jump-suited crew had begun to lay a temporary dance floor. I hoped he brought in a band rather than one of those currently fashionable djs with the turntables and spotlights. I preferred the live messy music.

I opened the side door into his bright kitchen. The fresh aroma of percolating coffee counterpointed the sharp tang of an orange that had gone overripe. I stepped deeper into his house, expecting bustle but finding only quiet.

"Bill?" The arched doorway led into his library.

"Tansy."

His expression scared me because I couldn't read it. His usually-smooth face carried an overnight growth of beard and he reeked of old sweat.

"I'm afraid."

His breath washed over me and I flinched.

"I'd be afraid too if I smelled like you," I said. I grabbed his arm. "Off to the bathroom, Bill."

He didn't resist. I shoved him through the door. He turned to me.

"It's my birthday," he said. "My 45th birthday. I was born just before midnight. I'll turn 45 at midnight."

"Yes," I said.

"Tansy," he said.

"Clean up, then we'll talk," I said. I closed the door.

After a moment I heard the water running. I walked back to the kitchen and poured coffee into a thick mug.

We had talked about his 45th birthday before; he was certain he'd die tonight.

I'm not the only one he's saved from certain death. The first time he'd saved someone's life was in May of his sophomore year at Cottonwood High School.

The way he told it, the bright point of any school day for Bill happened at 3pm, when the final bell released him from classes. He anticipated meeting up with Julie, his new girlfriend, over at Volcano Burgers, the student hangout across the street. On that day, he saw her at the crosswalk and ran to catch up with her.

The crossing light turned green. He didn't have quite enough nerve to grab her hand. She waited a moment then grasped his.

"Let's go," she said, pulling him along.

The moment his shoe touched the tarmac he knew something bad was about to happen. He told Julie to run.

"What?"

"Run!" he said, shoving her back.

An exotic car, sparkling blue in the afternoon sunshine, slewed through the intersection, out of control and squealing brakes. Julie sprawled onto the sidewalk. Bill stood smack in the car's path.

When the car hit him, not a glancing blow but dead square with the right bumper, he didn't see his life pass before his eyes. Instead, he remembered what his father had told him so often at bedtime.

"None of us die till we're 44, son," the not-old man rasped in a fake pirate voice. "And none of us live to see 45."

Bill spun across the intersection and knew he wouldn't die. He was only 16.

He lost his shoes in the impact. One stuck in the car's crushed grille. Julie shrieked when she saw that lonely bit of torn canvas; she collapsed beside him on the street and cried.

He patted her shoulder.

"Julie and I are still friends," Bill said to me. "Of course, she didn't want to be my girlfriend any more after that. Too weird. And after that I started my, um, *career* anyway, so I didn't have the extra time anyway."

Time for a relationship, he meant. That was as close as he got to admitting his feelings for me, and explaining why he didn't want to get close to me, all in one short sentence. Since I got clean, after he saved my life, I hadn't had time for other relationships either... or so I told him. Now and again we hung out, got coffee; now and then he let me hostess his parties.

The doorbell chimed.

"I'll get it," I shouted so Bill could hear me.

He dashed out of his bedroom, clean and groomed, tucked in and neat. He stopped me at the door.

"Let me," he said. His hand shook a bit as he twisted the knob.

A scrawny kid wearing a famous brown uniform stood on the doorstop.

"Delivery." He pointed his clipboard at a pinewood-enclosed crate on the driveway. The thing was bigger than a breadbox; as big as a sofa, in fact.

"Can you help me open it?"

"Nossir," the kid said. "I'm only supposed to deliver."

"Fifty bucks in it for you."

The kid held out his hand and Bill slid the money into his palm.

Bill handed out a crowbar and together they yanked the crate apart with the squealing of nails leaving still-green wood. In minutes the packaging fell away to reveal the shining silver of a brushed aluminium coffin.

"Help me carry it in."

The kid held out his hand again and Bill filled it again. They grasped the handles and lifted.

I spoke up.

"Bill, no."

His smile was just an exercise of muscles; the fear in his eyes was more convincing. "Why not? Sandra Bernhardt did the same thing and she only lost a leg."

They carried the coffin into the living room and hoisted it onto the buffet in the center of the room.

I threw my coffee mug at the wall. I didn't mean for it to sail by so close to the delivery kid's head but it did. His eyes widened and he dashed out of the house.

"What the hell do you think you're doing?" I screamed at Bill. I slammed my fist against the silver box. "You're giving up. That's not like you."

He smiled at me, that slantwise curl of lip that used to make my heart race faster than was good for it.

"I'm going to die tonight, I might as well be prepared." He pulled the casket lid open. He must have paid extra for the deep red silk lining.

"The only reason you think that is because your father told you a fable when you were a kid. When you grow up you're supposed to realize that your father's tales were made up," I said.

He began to climb into the casket.

"What are you doing?" My voice cracked on the high pitch.

"Getting ready," he said.

I couldn't stand by and watch him give up. I stumbled out of his house.

I leaned against my car's hood and breathed some fragrant noon air. Jacaranda blossoms drifted to the street beneath the mildest breeze. I opened my cell phone and tapped out a number, never taking my eyes off Bill's house. Shirlee Jones, a reporter with the local rag, answered. Between us we'd cooked up a birthday gift for Bill, a genealogy complete with names and dates and photographs. I hoped the information she'd uncovered would bring Bill to his senses.

"Shirlee, you have to come over now," I said.

She sighed. "Well, I have so much to do, I have to wrap up this photo op, and finish the article, and I have to wait for my date to Bill's party. I'll be there this evening."

"He needs you *now*," I said. "You have to bring that info you dug up for me, the gift? He's going off the deep end here."

"Well," she said, unhappy, "maybe I can get out of a few things."

"Shirlee," I said, and then explained about the coffin.

"Okay. I'll be there in two hours, that's the best I can do." She sounded crisp and determined, not like the fluffy woman I normally dealt with. I hoped she wouldn't let me down. Let Bill down.

I wouldn't be able to help him from out here. I found my courage and returned to Bill's home.

I heard him moving around in the living room.

The coffin still stood on the buffet, the lid closed. Bill wiped a soapy rag on the wall, trying to clean up the coffee stain. He couldn't look at me.

"Lying in that thing gave me the willies," he said. "I guess I'm not ready to give up yet."

I hugged him and got some soapy water dripped on my back.

"Let me help with this," I said.

Superman. Spiderman. All of the X-Men (and X-Women too.) Other strangely-colored and costumed comic book heroes, in bright green and scarlet and yellow spandex suits. Posters, framed in glass and Lucite, some of them signed by either illustrators or writers or perhaps even some actor who'd portrayed that character in television or video or movie, lined Bill's walls, spilling from the hallway into each of the rooms, even into the kitchen, clashing against the more adult décor of his home.

"They all had some weakness," Bill said.

"Yeah?" I was familiar with Bill's musings on the comic book characters. Still, I prodded him, to get him talking about the various aspects of his avatars.

"Yeah. When the Hulk calmed down he returned to normal; Spiderman sometimes ran out of web fluid; Wolverine's a hothead who makes bad decisions. Even Superman couldn't fight against kryptonite.

"But me? No weaknesses. I don't even kill the bad guys and suffer a guilty conscience." He sighed.

We sat at his kitchen table, drinking coffee. He looked into the creamy depths of the cup as if he could read his fortune there.

"I'm a fraud, you know."

"You are no such thing," I started.

He held out his hand to shush me.

"Yes, a fraud. I never risk anything when I *rescue* someone. I know I won't die, I never break a bone or get wounded by bullets or suffer cuts or, hell, I've never even gotten a bruise.

"I just know the date I'm gonna die. That's not such a bad bargain, is it?"

He wasn't asking for my opinion.

"Bill," I said. "How do you *know* when someone needs you?" I'd known him for all these years and I'd never asked before.

He flushed pink. Superhero pink, maybe.

"Ah... I kinda... hallucinate," he said.

I blinked. "'The 60s were good for you'?"

"What? Oh. No. No drugs involved. Just, um, I see a message that tells me where I'm needed."

"A message, huh?"

He blushed even more. "I see a graveyard and the message is written on a tombstone," he said all in a breath.

I laughed. He didn't.

"When you were in trouble," he said, "remember? I was there. 1:54am, in a parking garage, 1 floor down, red Buick? Don't you think it was coincidental that I was right there and ready to help?"

I nodded. I'd always been too grateful to question his help, but that thought had gnawed around the corners of my mind.

"I jerked awake at 1:30 that morning, and instead of my bedroom I saw a graveyard, with some big dark trees, and a tombstone, with glowing letters. Red letters. Like fire.

"So I knew where to go to help you."

I considered for a moment. "If you hadn't shown up I'd be dead," I said. "Have you ever *not* gone?" I wasn't sure I wanted to know the answer.

He didn't blush; this time, the blood left his face white and drawn.

"Yes." He looked like he was going to say more, but he just put his cup on the table and put his hands flat next to it.

"Once."

The doorbell chimed again.

"I'll get it," I said.

For the next hour people arrived, apologizing for being early, dressed for the most part in dark clothes and austere jewelry. They mingled, exchanging smiles and sipping wine.

I kept an eye on Bill, who talked with the people, his friends, the good people he'd rescued from harm over the last three decades. I was familiar with most of the stories, of course; Bill didn't keep his exploits secret from me. Here was the teenager he'd saved from drowning and the businessman he'd saved from being crushed by a bus and the nun he'd saved from a heart attack. I was still fuzzy on details about the nun and I wondered if perhaps Bill hadn't fudged the tale about how he saved her; but she was there, in modern monastic regalia of blue suit and flat shoes, looking quite happy to be alive. She hugged him; I noticed that most everyone had hugged him, put their arms around him, touched his shoulder or patted his head. Touch. We all needed to touch him.

Shirlee Jones was later than she promised; I sighed when I saw her park her van across the street from the house. She stepped down, a short, blonde, and perky girl-reporter, carrying a thick briefcase in serious brown leather. A man stepped out behind her, lanky and dressed in black jeans and a tee-shirt with generic white letters spelling the word 'EVIL.' He carried a handheld camera and aimed it at the house as he approached.

Bill and I met them at the door.

"You sure took your time," I whispered, a bare edge in my voice.

She ignored me and grabbed Bill's hands.

"Oh!" she chirped - she truly sounded like a bird – "I heard my favorite superhero was having a birthday party and I just had to come."

Bill blushed.

"This is my cameraman, Jayse. Say 'Hello,' Jayse." She smiled up at Bill.

Jayse aimed his camera at Bill and pressed the record button.

"I'm recording this party as a birthday tribute for you," he said. "Shirlee's gift to you, big guy." He grabbed Bill's hand and shook, two rapid jerks, then wandered off. Bill watched him go with a bemused frown.

I grabbed Shirlee's arm. "We have to talk *now,*" I said. "Bill, excuse us for a minute, okay?"

I dragged her into the deserted guest bedroom. I'd slept in here before, after particularly fine parties with Bill and his friends. I liked the washed colors of the Southwest decor, but Bill thought it looked like a hotel room. I sat in an overstuffed chair by the window.

"Do you have the photos? Of his family?" I said.

"Yes, but there's a problem," she said. "Everything I found rather supports his belief. I mean, all the men in his family have died at… I mean, it might be true." She frowned.

"He believes that story?" she said. "That he's going to die tonight? I never thought he believed it."

"Of course he does," I said. "It's all he ever talks about any more."

She bit her lip. "Okay. I have to tell you something.

"About ten years ago we began to get reports of someone being a hero. Okay, that might be too grandiose. Actually I just noticed these similar items in police reports: dangerous situation, a lone man interfering and rescuing some helpless victim, the man always escaping harm. I tried to track him down: no luck. So I wrote a few columns about our mysterious superhero, The Blockade. And he came to me."

I remembered those columns. Bill had read them, collected them in memory books, even wrote corrections of the details she'd gotten wrong. He commissioned a set of silver spandex tights and a helmet with wings; she'd dubbed him 'The Blockade' and he'd played along. For a while. He talked about the silver long johns with me one day and decided to barbeque them.

"He came to you?" I said. "You mean, he looked you up at the newspaper and visited you there?" He'd never told me this. *She'd* never told me this. I felt a twinge of jealousy.

"Sure. He wanted me to reassure him that he was doing good, ya know? I guess it's tiring to throw yourself into harm's way every night. Even if it's not actually harm's way, since he can't be harmed."

I shook my head. "Never mind all that. Do you have the photographs?"

She frowned. "Not just photos, but some other information. Genealogical info. I have his birth certificate." She produced a square of white paper, inked and embossed.

I took it. "So?"

"Note his place of birth," she said. "He was born on the East Coast, in West Virginia." She pointed to the 'place of birth' entry on the certificate.

"Yes? So what"

"Tansy. He was born at midnight, but in another time zone. He'll turn 45 in about…" — she checked her watch — "about ten minutes. At 9pm here in California."

We rushed back into the front room, where Bill and the guests were standing in a circle around Jayse. The cameraman's voice was high and excited.

"Has he saved everyone here?" he said, his dark eyes startled wide. "All of you? I don't believe it. Raise your hands if he's saved you somehow."

The party had gone quiet with his question. People around the room raised their hands, slowly at first. Jayse looked at me for confirmation. I raised my hand, too.

He pointed at one man who crossed his arms over his chest.

"What about you? Didn't he save you?"

"Name's Stu. Bill gave me a kidney. Didn't rescue me from the bad guys like some kind of comic-book hero; he saved my life. He's the real deal."

Julie nudged him with her elbow and he sighed. "Oh all right." He stuck his hand in the air.

"These are great photos," he said. He held his finger down on the shutter button and scanned Bill's guests. As he swerved towards me I put my hand over the lens.

"No," I said.

He pulled his camera away. "Why not? Bill gave me carte blanche!"

"Don't you understand?" I said. "This isn't a birthday party. It's a wake. Bill expects to die tonight."

"Yeah, I know," said Jayse. "But until then, he's a superhero, right? Can't be hurt?" Jayse dug into his pocket and brought out a gun. Small and chrome silver, a ladies' .22 caliber snub-nosed weapon. "Hey Bill!"

Bill looked up.

Jayse fired into his chest.

The guests tackled the man. I heard his skull hit the floor, and I think I heard the camera shatter, or perhaps that was his bones breaking, but I was looking at Bill. In slow motion I walked over to him. In slow motion I reached out to him. In slow motion... then I saw the red on his shirt and time sped up again.

"Bill!" I screamed.

He looked down at his chest but didn't seem concerned.

"We have to leave now," he said. "I know what I have to do."

"We have to call 911 and get you to a hospital," I said. "You're bleeding!"

Bill smiled at me distantly. His eyes were clouded over. "I just saw my tombstone, Tansy. We have to go now. We have to get there by midnight."

Nine o'clock at night racing down the highway trying to cover the 150 miles to the cemetery before midnight.

I had the fastest car, my sweet 8 cylinder job, but Bill insisted on driving. "I know where we're going," he said. He switched on the radio; music blasted loud enough to stop conversation. And questions. I'm not sure how Shirlee got into the car with us, but I glared at her a lot. Bill didn't seem to care. The patch of red on his chest expanded but he didn't seem to notice that, either.

We flew down a 100 mile stretch of freeway that turned into an asphalt road shrouded in mist and dust.

"It's eleven o'clock," Shirlee screamed from the back seat, barely audible over the howling wind and thumping music. "We'll never make it."

"Sure we will," he said. "We're almost there." He grinned; or maybe that was terror skinning his lips back from his teeth. My own face when I caught a glimpse in the rear-view mirror looked like a death mask, thin and tight. The cold night air couldn't stop the sweat pouring down my back and dripping off my palms. The speedometer edged over the 100 miles an hour mark. One lane of asphalt in the dark. I trusted him but still held on to the door brace and jammed my legs against the engine bulkhead.

He muttered something and lifted his foot off the accelerator. Shirlee screamed, "What?"

Bill braked hard and made a sharp left turn.

"We're here."

I gulped air as the car slowed. The music bounced hard through someone's drum solo – the car doors bellowsed over the woofers – then Bill reached over and snapped the music off.

"We're here," he said again.

My watch read 11:45 pm when we got out of the car and walked into the headstone garden.

Bill went from stone to stone, running his hands over the tops.

"This is the place," he said, "the cemetery that shows up in my dreams, visions, whatever."

Goosebumps traveled along my arms.

"You're creeping me out," I said.

"Some details are different," he said.

"Like: you don't have a headstone here?" Shirley was clearly rattled: she didn't have her camera out.

The last names were all the same, the same as Bill's.

I did some hurried math and confirmed that they all died at age 44, some on the day before their 45th birthday.

"I'm here, I'm ready," he said. "What do you want from me?"

He stood next to his father's headstone.

The light in a cemetery isn't like other light. It's cold and cruel, throwing the bodies and faces of the living into sharp contrast. The mist and dust that had followed us for 50 miles of back road had stopped short at the cemetery's gates as if afraid to venture into this place. The hot white stars overhead, unsoftened by any phase of the moon, glared down on us.

The night deepened to midnight.

"Bill, are you sure you were born at midnight?" Shirlee's voice fell flat in the dead air.

Bill ignored her.

"Shirlee, hush," I said. "Something's happening. Can't you feel it?" I shivered.

Shirlee shrugged but Bill nodded.

"Yeah, something," he said.

Fog flowed over our feet, thick and white as fresh cream.

"Did you hear that?" I said. They both nodded. A sound like squealing air swelled around us. The fog swirled high around our legs and flowed to the tops of the tombstones. The fog found Bill and engulfed him.

He looked terrified.

"Ghosts," Shirlee whispered.

"No kidding," I yelled. "Bill? Are you okay?"

The mass of fog swirled ever faster around Bill.

A shape formed, separating from Bill's body, oozing from the wound in his chest. This red-tinged ghost — or angel perhaps, with its dark hint of wings and perfect, expressionless face — swirled past Bill's head then dissipated: one moment there, the next moment gone.

We stood in the silent graveyard and looked at each other.

"You're not dead," Shirlee said.

"I'm not dead."

"Of course you're not dead," I said. "They released you."

Bill frowned. "Why?"

"You're going to second-guess ghosts?"

Shirlee said, "Your hair is white." I touched my hair reflexively but of course she meant Bill's hair.

Bill checked his wristwatch. "It's after midnight. I'm 45." He fell in a dead faint and knocked his head against his father's tombstone.

Shirlee screeched and fell on her knees beside Bill. I held my breath; that dark streak on the stone might be blood, or might be condensation.

Bill moaned before he opened his eyes. "Ouch," he said, touching his head gently. "Gosh. I didn't see *that* coming."

We stayed in the cemetery for another hour, sitting between the stones and talking. The light from the stars above seemed kinder somehow.

I drove us back much more slowly than we'd arrived. Shortly before dawn I pulled into a Quiki-Mart. The Pakistani man behind the counter unlocked the liquor cabinets for me when I produced two twenties. I grabbed a bottle of champagne and some plastic cups.

Shirlee snored in the back seat. Bill snugged his jacket over her shoulders then joined me sitting on the car's trunk.

I opened the bottle and poured two glasses.

"Hey," I said.

He smiled. "Hey." He took the champagne. "Pretty sunrise, huh?" He sipped.

I put my arm around him. "Yeah."

A phone call woke me up moments before my alarm would have blared.

"Ummng," I said.

"It's Shirlee. Our superhero friend is at it again."

I bolted upright in bed. "So soon. It's only been a month. Are you sure?"

"Yes, we had photos." She paused. "I'm not going to do a story on him. The photos were, ah, lost."

We agreed to meet for lunch then hung up.

Though he hadn't confided in me, I'd known he'd start up again. What else could he do?

About the author: I have recently sold stories to *Global Warming Aftermaths*, *RetroSpec*, and *Dark Tales Of Terror* (all three anthologies coming out this year.) Also, I am a Clarion West 2010 graduate.

Dreaming of Nick Savage

Simon Forster

Bruce Gray was a low-level accountant by day, working in a drab office. It was a dull job but it paid the bills and allowed Bruce to live his life; although, truth be told, Bruce didn't really have much of a life. He had few friends and no girlfriend.

Bruce had a routine that he normally stuck to: daily he would awake at 6am when his alarm sounded, shower, eat breakfast, brush his teeth, get dressed and head off to work. He always caught the 7.30am tube, reaching work with time to spare before he started at 9am. He would work through the day, take his lunch at noon in the café around the corner (with his usual order of a ham salad baguette and a latte, all washed down with fresh orange juice), finish work at 5.30pm and he would generally catch the 6pm tube and be home for 8pm. Then he'd make his dinner, eat in at the table while reading his paper, watch something on the television or read a book (depending on the day and what was on), then be in bed by 10pm.

At the weekend he did his chores and his shopping, saw his few friends and relaxed. Sometimes he went to the pub with a friend or work-colleagues, but never went to any clubs or late-night cinema showings. No matter what he did, he was always in bed before midnight and awake no later than 9am.

It was a safe, deep-rooted routine that made Bruce feel secure and at peace. Most people thought he was a nice but dull person, uninspiring but easy-going. Bruce was boring, drab and lived up to his family name and he knew this, even liked it.

But when he slept, when he dreamt, it was another matter entirely.

In his dreams he was...

***

...Nick Savage ducked behind the burning car as the robot's weapon fired, pelting the car chassis with hot lead. He checked his own weapon (a pistol of his own design) and found that he had but one bullet remaining. The rest of the ammo was hidden in his car, which was parked a whole block away.

The robot - one of Doc Foster's killer-bots - clunked across the street, its heavy feet tearing chunks out of the tarmac. It kept firing as it approached, shattering the remaining window of the car and ripping the passenger door away.

CLUNK-CLUNK approached the killer-bot.

The firing stopped, followed by a thunking-whir as the 'bot reloaded.

This was the moment Nick Savage was waiting for. Seizing his chance he vaulted over the bonnet of the burning car, ducked under the sweeping arc of the 'bot's arms and brought his pistol up to the weak-spot on the 'bot's head.

BLAM!

BOOM!

The killer-bot's head exploded in a fiery burst. The mechanical killer staggered a little, as if drunk, then collapsed in a heap at the feet of Nick Savage.

There was a moment's silence.

Then a great cheer went up from the crowd that had sprung up to watch, followed by a tremendous round of applause from all the civilians and police that stood watching their hero, the mighty Nick Savage.

As the clapping faded away, the policeman in charge, Lieutenant Davidson, walked up to Nick Savage and shook his hand warmly.

"Thank you, Mr. Savage," he said with deepest sincerity, "don't know what we would've done without you."

"You would've managed," said Nick Savage modestly. "Now, if you'll excuse me, I have a prior appointment I must keep." He headed to his car, a souped-up black Cadillac, leaving the police to go about their business of cleaning up, taking statements and maintaining the peace.

He drove off to his appointment: a dinner engagement with the delightful Miss Cassandra Reynolds, daughter of the great physicist Dr Reynolds.

Cassandra Reynolds, Cassie to her friends, family and especially to Nick Savage, was dressed in a fetching, figure-hugging long dress when Nick Savage pulled up in her driveway. She was standing on the steps, tapping her foot and glancing at her watch impatiently.

"You're late," she said as Nick Savage get out of his Cadillac. Her voice was scolding, but had unmistakable warmth to it.

"Sorry, honey, but there was this 'bot on the rampage downtown and I was needed," he explained. Somewhere along the way he had changed into an immaculate pinstripe suit.

"So I heard. Come on, Nick, let's go. We're already fashionably late."

Nick Savage loved Cassie. Not only was she beautiful, intelligent and fiery, but she wasn't awed by his heroism and reputation. She saw beyond all that, to the man beneath, something no one else had ever managed to.

They drove to the party, a charity event hosted by Cassie's father, chatting about their day and current events, behaving like a normal couple. This illusion was shattered as they arrived at the venue and saw a trio of killer-bots clomping across the neatly mown lawn.

Parking the car around the corner and leaving Cassie in the driver's seat in case they needed a fast get away, Nick Savage grabbed his pistol, loosened his tie and went to confront the killer-bots.

The 'bots had reached the mansion by now and had taken up positions outside of the front entrance. Inside faces were pressed up against the windows, arms gesturing and pointing. The 'bots were leaving them alone: they hadn't come for them; they were here for Nick Savage.

That was the problem with being a super-hero: there was always someone out to get you.

Nick Savage walked out on to the lawn and blew the head off one of the 'bots, just to get their attention.

He winced as the headless 'bot toppled over, scraping down one wall and breaking a couple of windows.

The other two 'bots spied him immediately and started towards him, their laser-armed hands raising and taking aim.

Nick Savage remained still as the first laser bolts flashed around him, then he leapt into action.

Diving into a forward roll, Nick Savage dove between the two giant robots, causing them to twist to keep him in their sights, their laser-fists still flashing deadly rays.

One killer-bot was faster than the other, its rays cutting into the steel casing of its partner. Before it could react to this misfire, the other 'bot's casing melted and its valves and servo's exploded and the 'bot screeched an electronic scream that sent a shiver up Nick Savage's spine.

Nick Savage rose to his feet, intent on dispatching the last 'bot.

But the still screaming robot was falling towards him and he couldn't move out of the way in time.

He braced himself and...

...Bruce woke up, his alarm clock ringing. It was 6am on another drab Monday morning in a winter-wrapped London.

This moment was always the worse, the transition between dream-filled sleep and awakened reality. It always made Bruce quite sad to leave the adventures of Nick Savage behind, but he cheered up when he remembered that he could continue the story that night.

That was something Bruce had never questioned, nor wanted to question: he never dreamt of anything else, just the life and adventures of Nick Savage, hero of the nation, protector of the city, lover of Cassie Reynolds. The dreams continued on from each other, an on-going and linear narrative that Bruce always vividly remembered.

He never told anyone about his dreams, for they were personal, private, precious, and he didn't want to share them with anyone. To Bruce it was the only thing in his life that set him apart from everyone else. So he went to work, following his daily routine, looking forward to going home so he could sleep, dream and continue the story of Nick Savage.

Bruce declined the offer of a drink after work with a colleague and rushed home. The outcome of last night's dream had been on his mind all day, distracting him from his work like never before.

He had a quick dinner, then had a relaxing bath and went to bed early. He fell asleep quickly and was soon dreaming...

Nick Savage blinked and woke; he felt sore, which was to be expected as he lay under the remains of the fallen killer-bot.

It was dawn, the sun slowly peeping over the roof of the mansion. The mansion itself was pockmarked with craters, had gaping windows with shattered glass and the front doors were hanging off their hinges. There was no sign of the party guests.

Cassie! Where was she? thought Nick Savage, recalling that he had left her in his car. With his impressive strength he pulled himself free of the dead robot and hurried to where he had left Cassie in his Cadillac.

He spotted it immediately, further down the driveway, on its side and looking crumpled. He searched it and the surrounding area, but there was no sign of his beloved Cassie. On the chance that she had headed to the mansion for safety Nick Savage ran towards it, pistol drawn. He drew to a halt outside the broken doors, then cautiously entered.

The interior was a mess: toppled tables, broken ornaments, burn marks on the walls where laser-bolts had splashed. There were no bodies, for which Nick Savage was grateful, and a frantic search of the rest of the mansion revealed that there was no one inside.

So where was everyone?

Nick Savage returned to his car, reached in and grabbed his unique car-phone, called the police and informed them what had happened. He was surprised to discover that they already knew about it.

"How do you know about it?" he asked the policeman on the other end of the phone.

"We've just had a call from Doc Foster himself," explained the policeman. "He's just told us his terms for the safe release of his hostages..." There was a pause and Nick Savage knew what was coming. "...and that includes Miss Reynolds."

"Don't do anything until I get there," ordered Nick Savage in a tone that the policeman had no wish to argue with.

Nick Savage righted his car with a mighty shove. It was just about drivable and so he drove as fast as he could to the police station, vowing revenge on Doc Foster if anything happened to Cassie.

Doc Foster's terms were the usual: a large amount of money to be delivered in a short amount of time. For all his evil genius and his deadly inventions, Doc Foster sometimes lacked imagination.

While the police got on with arranging a fake deal and some sort of plan, heroic Nick Savage decided to do things his own way. He knew where the hostages would be held, where Cassie would be imprisoned, the only place where Doc Foster felt safe: his fortress-island out at sea. All Nick Savage had to do was get there.

He drove to the coast in a borrowed police-car. He met his old friend, Captain Wise, at the docks and boarded the old, reliable *Neptune's Wave*. Captain Wise had served with Nick Savage in the war, where they had brought about the demise of several German U-Boats using nothing but the *Neptune's Wave*, crates of junk and their wits.

Nick Savage explained the situation to captain Wise, who shook her mane of red-hair in half-serious dismay.

"It'll be a difficult journey getting to the island safely," she explained once they were under-way.

"I know, but Cassie's there and it looks like we're already on our way."

"Well, how could I refuse to help my former captain," said Captain Wise with a wry grin. "Besides, this was your ship."

"Yours now," said Nick Savage, his eyes on the distant horizon, looking beyond it to where Doc Foster's deadly island lay.

"Get some rest, Nick," said Captain Wise, "you'll need your strength when we reach the island."

Never one to ignore his friend's advice, Nick Savage agreed and headed below to get whatever rest he could. He lay down on the lower bunk of his old cabin and shut his eyes...

...and the alarm went off, waking Bruce.

Tuesday morning, back to the tedium of work and another dull day at the office. There were times when all Bruce wanted to do was sleep and dream. Life was better in his dreams.

There were problems with the tube that morning, as sometimes happened, so Bruce had to get the bus. Today, however, the bus was diverted from its normal route due to some flooded roads, and Bruce found himself taking a new course to work.

On his journey the bus passed by a small, run-down building that advertised itself as a museum. On a large notice-board there was a poster announcing a new exhibit. Bruce stared in amazement as he saw what it was: the recovered remains of the lost *Neptune's Wave*.

How on earth could something out of a dream be advertised in the real world?

But no, that was a stupid thought. Of course a dream couldn't manifest itself in reality, that was ridiculous. It was a coincidence, nothing more. In fact, it was more likely that he had briefly seen that same advert elsewhere and as such it had seeped into his subconscious and entered his dream.

Bruce got to work and amidst the tedium of his job he soon forgot all about the poster and the museum.

That night Bruce dreamed...

...Nick Savage was awakened by Captain Wise shouting his name.

He hurried up to the bridge. "What's up?" he asked as he stared out of the window.

"We've arrived," she said, pointing ahead.

It was dusk, the last rays of sunlight vanishing behind the horizon and painting the clouds red. Ahead, dead-centre and growing larger lay Doc Foster's fortress-island, lit by searchlights and the glowing eyes of patrolling killer-bots. A high wall blocked the sea from the island and there was no way in that could be seen.

Nick Savage knew better, he had been there once before and he had escaped using an underwater outlet pipe that led directly into the fortress. It would be the means of his re-entrance too.

"OK, Captain, slow to a stop and hold us here. I'll break out my equipment."

Dressed in his wet-suit and SCUBA gear, Nick Savage waved goodbye to his old friend and former war colleague and dove into the cold sea.

Under the water all was dark, the lights from the island failing to penetrate very far and the lights of the Neptune's Wave switched off to avoid detection. Nick Savage went deeper until it was so dark that he couldn't see his hand in front of his face. He switched on his powerful spotlight, triggered his underwater-jet and headed in the direction of the island.

The killer-seabot swam across the outlet again, its searchlight sliding back and forth. Its lobster-like claws were as long as Nick Savage was tall; twin torpedo launchers flanked its single-eye sensor; and its legs ended in thick webbing that aided its movement through the water when propelled by the twin water-jets that stuck out of its rear like over-sized exhausts. It looked dangerous and fast.

Nick Savage watched and tracked its movements, his finger taut on the trigger of his personal torpedo-rifle. The 'seabot made another pass and as it turned to retrace its route it momentarily disappeared behind an outcropping of bedrock. As it did so, Nick Savage pulled the trigger and let fly his torpedo.

It whizzed through the sea like a pike after its dinner and as the 'seabot reappeared the torpedo struck it dead on the 'nose' and the explosion tore the machine apart.

Nick Savage waited for the concussive blast to settle, then he swam up the outlet pipe and into the fortress. Emerging on to dry ground in one of the refinery and recycle plants, Nick Savage shed his wet-suit and moved off in search of Cassie and the hostages.

It took a while to find his way out of the internal workings of the island's fortress, but eventually Nick Savage found his way into a lit corridor that he vaguely recognised having spent time here as a prisoner. If the layout hadn't changed then he knew exactly where he was and where the prisoners would be kept.

But first he needed to ensure their escape.

Nick Savage hurried down the corridor, clutching his trusty pistol. Up ahead the corridor opened on to a large room, which turned out to be just what he had been looking for: a hanger.

There was a killer-bot on guard, watching over a sea-plane and a stack of attack-bots, their wings folded underneath them as they 'slept'. The sea-plane looked intact and fuelled, large enough to whisk all the hostages to safety. Now all he had to do was find them, rescue them and defeat Doc Foster's killer-bots along the way.

All in a day's work for Nick Savage. He moved off towards the prison block.

The prison block was a collection of cells guarded by mini-bots, which were simply smaller, man-sized, killer-bots. The hostages were herded together in three of the narrow cells, subdued but otherwise unharmed. Nick Savage watched them from the doorway, wires from the prison's alarm-system dangling in his free hand.

Sizing up the opposition Nick Savage choose his moment and ran in, pistol firing, taking out three of the five 'bots before they had a chance to react. He dove behind the control panel for the cells, ducking lower as the 'bots opened fire. As he had planned their bullets tore holes at the panel, shorting the controls. The cell doors slid open, momentarily distracting the mini-bots as the prisoners surged towards the exits. The 'bots turned to deal with them.

Nick Savage popped up and dispatched one 'bot by blowing off its head, then sprang over the panel and pistol-whipped the last 'bot so hard that its head crumpled. It fell over, twitched, then its head exploded in a colourful array of sparks.

Nick Savage helped the hostages out of their cells. He knew them all, since many were friends and colleagues. He sought Cassie amongst them, but as he guessed she was not there.

"Where's Cassie?" he asked Colonel Thomas, an old colleague from the war, although he knew what the answer would be.

"That evil mastermind took her," said the Colonel, confirming Nick Savage's guess. "He's using her as insurance against you."

"Then he'll regret that action," vowed Nick Savage, his anger quietly bubbling. "Come on, I'll get you all to a place of safety."

Nick Savage lead them to the hanger and the sea-plane. There he quickly defeated the killer-bot on guard, then loaded the released hostages on-board the sea-plane, telling the Colonel that if he wasn't back in two hours then the Colonel was to fly them all to safety. Then Nick Savage headed off in search of his beloved Cassie.

As he made his way along another corridor the sound of distant drilling filled his head. Steadily it grew louder and louder until Nick Savage turned a corner and...

...Bruce awoke to the sound of workmen drilling in the street. He looked at his clock: it was 5am. He knew he couldn't get back to sleep, so he got up earlier than normal and got ready for work.

For a change Bruce decided to travel to work early, with the intention of grabbing a coffee in a café he sometimes visited. In fact, since he was having a change, he decided to get the bus again.

Just like the last time the bus was diverted and once more the bus passed the museum, which Bruce had forgot all about. This time there was also someone outside the museum, unlocking the faded doors.

Bruce took a long look at the woman as the bus drove by and was surprised at what he saw: she looked like an older version of Cassie, even down to the cut of her dress. Had he seen this woman before? She glanced up as the bus moved on and for a moment their eyes met. A look of what Bruce thought might be recognition passed over her face, then she was gone as the bus sped up and left her behind.

That look and her face stuck with Bruce throughout the day. It seemed highly coincidental that both the woman and the museum were so similar to his dreams. He must have seen them at some point in the past, maybe on television or in the paper and they must have influenced his dreams. What other explanation could there be? Maybe he should check the museum out, to see whether or not he recognised anything or remembered being there at some point in his past, maybe from his childhood. He was free at the weekend, so maybe he would visit the museum then.

That night, he thoughts filled with the museum and Cassie, Bruce took a long time to fell asleep, but when he did...

...Nick Savage had found his way to the lair of Doc Foster, deep in the heart of the fortress. He stood outside the huge, thick titanium doors staring into the video-camera that rose above the door and was staring right back at him.

"I'm here," he said. "Let me in."

With a shuddering hiss the doors swung inwards and Nick Savage strode in with a confidence he only half-felt. Although he was generally fearless, the fact that Cassie was in there made him fearful, more for her than himself. He didn't want her harmed in any way.

Doc Foster's lair was a large oval with long, thin windows high on the curving walls. At the opposite end from the doors was a semi-circular dais on which a throne-like contraption sat. In that chair, flanked by killer-bots, with Cassie at his feet, sat the evil genius that was Doc Foster.

Between Nick Savage and Doc Foster was a large pit, from which wisps of steam issued forth.

With a satisfied smile Doc Foster rose from his chair, closing the doors with a flick of a switch. The doors slammed shut with a resounding thud.

"Nick Savage," droned Doc Foster in a nasal tone, 'how glad I am that you could join us."

"Let her go," said Nick Savage.

"All in good time, Savage, all in good time."

"What do you want, Doc?"

"What do I want?! Why, I want what I've always wanted: you!"

With that, the killer-bots advanced.

Nick Savage drew his pistol and fired. The shot ripped through the eye-piece of a killer-bot, shattering its positronic brain. It fell to the floor, as the second 'bot moved to the side and opened fire.

With the agility of a tiger and the strength to match, Nick Savage dove, ducked and fought like a man possessed. The killer-bot never stood a chance.

Nick Savage stepped over the remains and walked up to the edge of the pit. He briefly glanced down, staring into bubbling magma far below. A wave of heat washed over him, bringing sweat to his brow. He looked back up at his nemesis.

"Give it up, Doc, it's over."

"Do you really think so?" said Doc Foster, brandishing a pistol, which he pushed up against Cassie's temple.

"Come on, Doc, don't do this. You know you've lost. You never could defeat me. Just let Cassie go, surrender and go to prison peacefully. You'll live longer that way."

"Never!" Doc Foster screamed , gesturing wildly with his pistol; which was just the reaction that Nick Savage had been waiting for.

With astounding speed Nick Savage aimed and fired.

Doc Foster"s head flipped back with great force, a spray of blood coating the wall behind him. His body crashed to the ground, leaving Cassie safe.

"Is he...?" began Cassie, visibly shaking.

"Yes, he's dead. Are you OK?"

"I am now, Nick, I am now."

The chamber shuddered.

"What was that?" asked Cassie as she ran over to where Nick Savage stood, gazing at the corpse of his former nemesis.

"SELF-DESTRUCT INITIATED" said a computerised voice from hidden speakers.

"Blast, he's booby-trapped the island," cursed Nick Savage.

"You mean the entire island is about to explode," said Cassie incredulously.

"I'm afraid so. Lucky I have a plane full of passengers waiting for us. Let's go."

Together Nick Savage and Cassie Reynolds ran to the hanger, where the Colonel was waiting for them, the sea-plane all ready to fly. Nick Savage and Cassie boarded. Once inside Nick Savage slid into the pilot's chair, the Colonel taking the co-pilot's seat, with Cassie behind them. He started the engine and pressed the button that would open the hanger-doors.

Nothing happened.

"SELF-DESTRUCT IN T-MINUS THREE MINUTES" said the computer.

"What now, Nick?' asked Cassie, brave as always in the face of imminent danger.

"I'll have to get the doors open," he replied. "Colonel, once the doors are open, you know what to do?"

The Colonel met his eye and nodded. He knew what to do.

The exchange wasn't lost on Cassie. "No! You are not leaving us like that," she said.

Nick Savage smiled sadly, kissed her passionately, then knocked her out with a swift punch. He strapped her into a seat, kissed her lightly on the forehead and turned back to the Colonel.

"You won't have time to wait for me once the doors are opened," he explained quickly. "Fly as fast as you can and get everyone to safety."

"What about you, Captain Savage?"

"I'll dive into the sea and swim to the *Neptune's Wave*; it's not far from here. I've done it before," he added with a smile.

"Good luck."

Nick Savage left the Colonel to it, made his way across the hanger to the door-controls and got to work.

In less than a minute he had bypassed the controls and the hanger-doors slid open. With a roar the Colonel flew the sea-plane out of the hanger and away, carrying the passengers and Cassie to safety.

"SELF-DESTRUCT IN T-MINUS 30 SECONDS."

Nick Savage quietly crossed himself, gave a short and silent prayer to whatever gods were listening, then ran for the open doors.

The ten second countdown began as he reached halfway across the bay.

"NINE SECONDS."

Nick Savage leapt over the killer-bot he had dispatched earlier.

"SEVEN SECONDS.'

He vaulted over the railings of a gantry and climbed the steps to the walkway that surrounded the bay.

"FIVE SECONDS."

He ran along the shuddering walkway as distant explosions sounded deep within the fortress.

"TWO SECONDS."

Nick Savage reached the open doors, jumped on their edge, looked over at the sea below and took a deep, deep breath.

"DETONATE."

KABOOM!

The explosion made Bruce sit bolt upright in his bed. His ears rang from it, his mind still full of Nick Savage, Cassie and the exploding island.

Another explosion... but no, it was just someone knocking at his neighbour's door. The voice of his landlord demanding late rent could be heard. Then silence once more. Bruce glanced at his clock: 5.55am. Almost time to get up.

So Bruce got up early and got ready for another day at the office.

He didn't go pass the museum that day, taking the tube to work instead. Last night's dream had left him feeling anxious and unsettled, so he just wanted a normal day to make him feel make him feel safe and secure again.

The day passed swiftly and he returned home, sat in front of the television whilst eating his dinner, then headed to bed to sleep and dream.

But that night he didn't dream, at least not that he could recall. It was possible that he dreamt of cold, of darkness, but when he woke he wasn't sure.

Bruce had dreamt of Nick Savage each and every night for as long as he could remember. Without the dreams his life felt empty, almost meaningless, although he knew that this wasn't really the case.

The rest of the week was the same, no dreaming of Nick Savage. Bruce began to feel restless, uneasy during the day and his work suffered. On Friday morning his boss told him to take the rest of the day off, to go home and relax.

Instead Bruce went to the museum.

The museum was open for business and was still advertising the recently discovered remains of the *Neptune's Wave*. It was free to enter, with only a couple of tourists looking around. To anyone else the museum would seem an oddity; a small, specialist museum that could only be of interest to certain people.

For Bruce it was both astounding and impossible, because this museum was nothing short of a memorial to Nick Savage and his adventures. It was clearly impossible, but nonetheless it was all here to see, to read and to touch.

Every adventure he had dreamt of, each character Nick Savage had encountered, were housed in this small museum. Most were extracts from newspapers, but there were also old photographs, exhibits of parts from killer-bots, sea-bots, ray-guns and even Doc Foster's monocle.

Bruce thought that either he had seen all of this before and simply forgotten about it, or else he was going mad. The latter option seemed more likely when he came face-to-face with a life-sized figure of the legendary Nick Savage himself.

It was like looking in a distorted mirror.

The man before him was younger, more muscular, stood with a better posture and confidence (although it was just a mannequin), but otherwise he was staring at his mirror-image.

"This isn't possible," he murmured to himself.

"Nick?" enquired a soft feminine voice behind him.

He turned around. There stood the woman he had seen a few days earlier, the one who looked like an older version of Cassie from his dreams. Up close he realised that he was wrong: this was no version, this *was* Cassie!

"Nick?" she asked again, one hand half-raised as if she meant to reach out and touch him. Her expression was a mixture of uncertainty, fear and hope.

"No, my name's Bruce?" he heard himself say, although he no longer knew if that was true.

"No, it's you," she said in a quiet voice. "I'd know that face anywhere." She stepped closer, her hand reaching out to rest softly against his cheek. "I've missed you," she said, tears welling in her eyes.

"Cassie?"

"It's me, Nick, it's me."

Then something snapped inside Bruce's mind and he collapsed.

Nick Savage dreamt.

In his dream he was a dull accountant who plodded through life in a sedate manner, living comfortably but without passion, want or ambition. When he slept he dreamt of a better life, where he was a hero loved. In those dreams he was himself again, but they weren't really dreams, he knew, but memories.

He recalled the events leading up to the island's explosion, but beyond that there were only fragments. He remembered a badly damaged ship, the *Neptune's Wave*, rescuing him from the cold sea and Captain Wise taking him ashore to the hospital. He remembered the doctors talking in concerned voices.

Then he heard Cassie's voice, older than he remembered, but just as warm and loving.

"They said you'd lost your memory, but that with time you'd regain them. It's partly why the museum was built," she was saying from some dark place. "Then one day you disappeared. You just walked out of the hospital and we never saw you again." She broke off then, sobbing from both regret and relief. She added: "That was twenty years ago."

But now he did remember, he remembered everything. The museum and dear, sweet Cassie had worked their magic.

Bruce Grey opened his eyes and ceased to exist.

Nick Savage smiled up at his beloved Cassie.

"I'm back, Cassie," said Nick Savage, "I'm back."

About the author: I have been writing since I was a child, although I would only consider myself to have been writing seriously for the past 13 years. In that time I have written over a million words of fiction, encompassing nine (9) novels & novellas, forty-four (44) short stories, and an illustrated children's book as a Christmas present for my niece. I have had several short stories published in small magazines, and have self-published two short-story collections that are available from on-line stores (notably on and through Lulu.com).

The Night Ghost Returns

Christopher McKittrick

Good men stay out of alleys, thought Max McDonnell. He hated that the quickest way home from the parking garage where he worked nights was through alleys, because it forced him to take the long way home most nights. But tonight he promised Eileen that he'd rush home, since she always worried when he worked the late shift – mostly because she worried that he'd find his way into one of those late night bars where the clocks always seem to be stuck at half past one. But he wouldn't do that, because he promised her that he wouldn't. In fact, tonight he was hurrying as fast as his tired old legs would take him.

Max had trouble catching his breath for a moment as he wondered why he still had to work at sixty-one. He had voted for Roosevelt four times, yet he still had to wait four more years for his Social Security checks. He should've been able to retire years ago, but he had never recovered from the thirties – Eileen said it was because he started to drink too much after they lost the house, but Max knew that had nothing to do with it, as most men know there are other explanations for such things. By the time the jobs came back, Max was too old to start over – it wasn't his fault that God kept the world turning and the sun rising but the bankers kept the stocks falling. They had no choice but to move into a cheap place in the city, where the streets were getting worse every year, and put off having kids until they were both too old to have them anyway. These were the thoughts that consumed Max now, almost as if he had a premonition that his life, which was already so full of regret, was about to change again.

Distracted by his thoughts, Max didn't hear the shuffling next to him in the alley until he heard the metallic click of what he thought was a gun. Max had only heard that sound before in movies, yet in this moment it sounded much quieter, but far more chilling. He turned to see a man hunched over in a curious way. If it wasn't for the gun that was now pointed at him, Max would have no reason to feel threatened from the crooked mass before him that only vaguely appeared human.

"Give me your jacket and your wallet, Pops," wheezed the man. "Give them over or I'll kill you where you stand and take 'em anyway."

If it were ten years ago, Max would've gone for a punch. If it were five, he would've ran. But now, he wasn't sure if he could outrun the man's aim, even in the man's poor condition.

"Please... I don't have much," whimpered Max. He held his hands up, shaking as they were.

"Who cares?" shouted the man. It was less a question than a declaration of authority. He stepped forward and shoved the gun into Max's ribs. Because of the proximity, Max could finally see the poor condition the man was in. His bruised face was covered in small bandages, as if he were a badly beaten prize-fighter, and he was bleeding heavily through a hole in his gut that looked to be about four inches wide by the bloodstain. This man, if you could still call him that, had to have been in some fight.

"You need a doctor..." whispered Max. He didn't know why his reaction was to say that.

"I said hand them over!" yelled the man, his voice rising yet again. "You have about three seconds before I make you bleed worse than me!"

Max started taking his jacket off, but then he heard a rustle of cloth that didn't come from his jacket. In fact, it sounded like it came from above them.

"What was that?" Max asked, momentarily forgetting that there was a barrel of a gun in his ribs.

The bleeding man looked up quickly, but nervously. "Shut up, you old windbag! Hurry up!" he harshly whispered in a shaken voice.

Suddenly, the little light in the alley was eclipsed, and a large form dropped from the sky. Max couldn't see the form clearly in the midnight darkness. It appeared to be a man, dressed in a cape and costume, but Max (even with his glasses on) couldn't make out if it even was a man.

"Leave that man alone," said a deep, scary voice from the direction of the dark shape, though to Max it seemed to almost come from the deepest depths of the earth.

The wounded man turned the gun in the direction of the shape. "Why don't you just leave me alone, you freak?" he muttered in a voice full of dread. "I'm dying on the streets cause of you!"

"You have no one to blame but yourself and your dirty deeds, O'Grady," the dark voice.

Suddenly, the man the dark shape called O'Grady fired his machine pistol into the darkness. Though the gun was no longer pointed at him, Max was frozen where he stood. Not even the sudden boom of the rapid gunshots could get him to move.

When the gun clicked empty, O'Grady laughed. "You see that, old man? I did it! I iced the Ghost!" The dark shape at the end of the alley was no longer visible.

Knowing that the gun was empty, Max went to run. However, O'Grady shoved him against the wall with newfound intensity. "You ain't getting away that easy, Pops," said O'Grady in a threatening tone.

Unexpectedly from above the costumed man dropped down on O'Grady. Max was knocked back and his glasses fell off, yet he could still make out that the mysterious stranger was dressed in a dark, double-breasted jacket and a dark green blindfold-like mask that covered his head like an executioner's hood. If it hadn't been for the mask and cape, Max would've sworn he was looking at a Park Avenue doorman or a chauffer. Had Max read the papers, he would've heard rumors of this man.

"I told you to leave that man alone!" growled the costumed man as he wrestled O'Grady to the ground. Bleeding as he was, O'Grady could not put up much of a fight. Though Max knew he could now run, he still could not move from where he stood. Using some sort of wrestling hold that Max had never seen the grapplers at Madison Square Garden use, the stranger subdued O'Grady. He then stood up and turned to Max, who had been standing there watching in awe. The dark green cape wrapped around the stranger's entire being and seemed to almost envelope the entire alley.

"Go. Call the police," the stranger commanded.

Without responding, Max set off to do what he was told. He didn't worry about losing his breath while running for a police callbox, and his only concern was with whether or not Eileen would believe his story.

But after making it halfway down the alley, he turned to catch another glimpse at the mysterious stranger who had saved him. But the man – if it even was a man – had disappeared, and the only evidence of him being there was a bloodied would-be robber and the vague sound of cloth flapping in the wind.

James Jeffers might have been the only man in Manhattan who didn't wear a fedora to his day job, but that suited him just fine. He had just gotten off his early morning Midtown beat and was ready for his almost-daily long afternoon nap. Still, he would stay awake long enough to read the lead story in the *New York Post* that he had just bought off of a paperboy. The headline on the paper read *MYSTERIOUS "NIGHT GHOST" STRIKES AGAIN,* which made him smirk. After walking past a group of laughing teenagers in front of the ice cream parlor storefront that made up the ground floor of his apartment building, he turned around to watch them for a moment and his smirk turned into a smile. The teenagers waved to him, and James felt a small measure of pride over how respectful the neighborhood kids were on his block; not just to police officers like himself, but to everyone. He pulled open the side door to the building and went inside.

James' well-furnished apartment came as a surprise for anyone who knew that he lived on a cop's salary. Furthermore, one would be even more surprised at its cleanliness, since James was a confirmed bachelor. Then again, since he rarely had visitors it was unlikely that anyone ever had or ever would have these thoughts. While some men facetiously claimed that they had no time for a serious relationship, James was one of the few who legitimately did not, though he still had time enough to maintain a tidy apartment.

He threw the newspaper on his coffee table and almost sat down on his couch, but he instead walked over to his radio. He had yet to buy himself a television, though he recognized its usefulness in both of his lines of work.

Upon turning on his radio, James chanced upon the report of the story he had bought the newspaper for. In the typical booming anchor voice, the announcer proclaimed: "...back on the street less than twelve hours after an anonymous tip directed law enforcement to O'Grady, severely wounded, in a Hell's Kitchen alley. His lawyers easily secured his release, with O'Grady being charged with only possession of an illegal firearm. O'Grady, well known in organized crime circles, appears to have been apprehended by the mysterious vigilante that the media has dubbed The Night Ghost though the businessman did not comment on this speculation. It is known that the vigilante was out again last night, two months after his first appearance. The rumored Phantom Protector of Manhattan was credited with stopping seven crimes in the course of four hours along with the capture of O'Grady. But is he really helping? Some say that..."

He shut the radio off. The law that he served both day and night failed the people yet again, thought James. To him, O'Grady was a monster who took advantage of a system that was founded upon the naïve impression that men were too good-hearted to do so. He walked into his bedroom, crouched down next to the bed, and pulled out a large briefcase. James opened the briefcase, revealing his Night Ghost uniform.

"O'Grady isn't getting off that easy tonight," James muttered, as he wished the hands of the clock would move faster.

1964

O'Grady ran across the roof of one of the many buildings in Hell's Kitchen that had once belonged to him. In his whole life he had never run faster than he did now. But buildings, like everything else in life, have to end somewhere, and O'Grady found himself standing on the edge of the old, cracked concrete. The alley below looked much further down than the six stories that it actually was.

The night was cold, much colder than the weather report had forecast. A thick early autumn fog made it difficult to see anything beyond one's immediate surroundings, which didn't help the fleeing man. O'Grady's lungs stung from breathing so heavily on such a cold night. With his entire being disoriented by his wheezing and the deafening sound of sirens approaching ever closer, O'Grady didn't notice the dark shape approaching him until he was close enough to corner him.

"Give yourself in, O'Grady. You have nowhere else to run," the Night Ghost commanded, his breath coming out in plumes of steam that drifted ominously from his silhouette. It had taken the Ghost an entire decade to finally corner O'Grady like this. He had to finish this tonight, for he doubted he would have O'Grady as vulnerable as he was now ever again.

"You stay the hell away from me, you hear?" O'Grady desperately snarled. "You've been hounding me for a decade and two prison sentences, and I wanna know why!"

"Why?" asked the Night Ghost, half in surprise.

"Yeah, I want to know why! Why me?" O'Grady screamed in attempt to sound forceful, though his voice wavered nervously.

The Night Ghost didn't speak for what seemed like an eternity to O'Grady. When he finally did speak, his voice seemed to surround O'Grady from every direction. "You are everything that is wrong with humanity and with this city. You prey on the weak to become stronger, and the law can barely touch you. But I'm not the law." That last part came out of the Night Ghost's mouth awkwardly, because Jeffers, still a police officer in his civilian guise, was, in fact, the law, despite the ten years of APBs to capture his nocturnal alter ego. "But I'll never stop haunting you until you're no longer a threat to all those who you would hurt and you answer to all those you've already have."

The Night Ghost then took three slow steps forward. Each word he said to O'Grady he had said in honesty. Over the last decade O'Grady had run the most corrupt and destructive mob in New York City. Others had been bigger and stronger, but none had been so ruthless, so wicked. Murdered priests, orphans used as drug couriers, arson, small business racketeering – O'Grady and his boys never gave up, even as one by one his associates and thugs were thrown in prison for longer and longer sentences. Yet throughout the years the Night Ghost could never make anything stick for long on O'Grady. That was until tonight, when the Night Ghost cornered O'Grady – alone, desperate, and above all, scared.

O'Grady, who had yet to process the words the Night Ghost had said, backed up toward the edge of the building. "You can't do this! I won't go in again, especially if it means going in from you." Shaking, O'Grady turned toward the edge.

The Night Ghost saw what O'Grady intended to do, and he reached his right hand out. In a weakened voice that was more from Jeffers than the Night Ghost, he shouted, "Step back from the edge!"

"I told you," O'Grady growled, "Don't come any closer."

"Step back!" shouted the Night Ghost. Several police cars swerved into the alley below, their loud sirens and bright lights only confusing the already desperate situation.

"You have to give up, O'Grady," The Night Ghost said in a voice more forceful than before. "You have no other choice now – now you can finally pay for all that you have done."

O'Grady looked down at the police cars below and laughed a nervous laugh. "I've always got choices, Ghost." He turned his body slightly toward the Night Ghost. "Come a little closer, will you? I'm afraid I'm gonna fall." His voice was more unsure than before, and he sounded vulnerable.

The Night Ghost was confused by O'Grady's request, but he hadn't the time to think it over. He slowly approached O'Grady with his right arm still extended. "I'm only trying to help you."

O'Grady chuckled. "Go to hell, Ghost," he snickered, and then spit in the face of his adversary. In a handful of rushed moments, the Night Ghost sprang to grab O'Grady, but the man who evaded paying for his crimes for so long leapt backwards over the edge. The Night Ghost almost tumbled over the edge himself as he reached forward to grab what was now only empty air. He could do nothing but watch as O'Grady fell. Though he could not see for certain, the Night Ghost was convinced that O'Grady was smirking all the way down.

1984

James Jeffers sat in front of his black-and-white television – the same RCA he bought in 1955 and never saw a need to replace with a color model – as he did nearly every night since he retired from the police department. When he saw what was coming on the channel four evening news he wanted to get up and change it, but he could never find the motivation to do anything in his retirement except work out and dream about his past. They were the only aspects of his life that made him feel good about himself in these days.

The lead story featured Matthew O'Grady, a young man who spent most of his days on both the front pages of the city papers and in the headlines of the gossip section. Though James couldn't stand the sight of him, he was at least happy that his black-and-white television wouldn't show the false sparkle of his playboy smile and the colors of his undoubtedly flashy suit. James was prone to thinking that black-and-white always showed things the way that they truly are, and that certainly held true for Matthew O'Grady.

Matthew O'Grady was speaking in front of City Hall, surrounded by several local politicians and the press. Closest to him was a taller, thinner man wearing an equally slick suit and an equally false smile, which was fitting since he was essentially O'Grady's copycat puppet.

"We are here for perhaps the most important announcement of my life," Matthew shouted into the dozens of microphones, "Or perhaps the most important announcement in the history of my family. After all, it is because of my father that I am taking part in this historic moment."

James winched in the way he always did whenever he heard mention of the elder O'Grady. He saw so much of the father in the shadow cast by the "squeaky clean" son. Most of the city probably secretly did too, but as long as Matthew O'Grady kept opening wings of children's hospitals and donating large sums to museums they all seemed to ignore what James had observed for years. It was easy to turn a blind eye when the other eye was seeing so much "charity."

"Though I was not old enough to really get to know my father before he was so ruthlessly murdered by an unprovoked act of illegal vigilante justice," Matthew continued, "He left me with several profound lessons. One of these, of course, was to provide help for others, and I believe that Patrick Robert McKinley has the heart to help the people of New York!"

James heard little else of what Matthew had to say, as the first part of his endorsement address dredged up old memories of the night that the elder O'Grady was "ruthlessly murdered by an unprovoked act of illegal vigilante justice." It had been twenty years since O'Grady had taken a suicide dive off the roof of a Hell's Kitchen office building through the windshield of a parked police car. The fog made it difficult for anyone to see anything clearly, but a few officers – ones who James knew to be of the anti-Night Ghost faction of the department – believed that they saw the Night Ghost push O'Grady. All the newspapers, even the ones which should have known better, ran with it. It was the more interesting story, after all.

An immediate investigation into the Night Ghost's activities was publically called on by the then-mayor, who of course had several advisors who had been on O'Grady's payroll. James tried to carry on as the Night Ghost for the better part of the next month, but it was impossible now that most of his fellow officers could no longer turn their eyes away from his nocturnal mission. By the end of the month, James shoved the suitcase that contained his uniform into the back of his closet and requested the night beat in the hope that he could cover at least a fraction of the Night Ghost's nightly route in a police officer's uniform. He never could stem the growing tide of crime that quickly rose with the Night Ghost's disappearance, and by the time he finally retired from the force crime was far worse than it had ever been in the city, making the Night Ghost's impact totally negligible. It was enough to drive any man to despair.

Suddenly, the newscaster's voice snapped James back to attention. "Strong words from Matthew O'Grady, who has certainly the most responsibly for McKinley's latest high poll numbers. Curiously, tonight also marks the twenty year anniversary of the last confirmed sighting of the Night Ghost, who remains the primary suspect in what many believe to be the murder of Matthew O'Grady's father. The Night Ghost's true identity remains unknown. Criminologists continue to debate if the Night Ghost's eleven year vigilante crusade against crime had a positive or negative impact on the city's crime wave. Indeed, we may never know for sure many things about the Night Ghost – who he was, what drove him to be who he was, and his relative success or failure – yet I believe we all can safely agree on one thing about the Night Ghost – only in New York!"

That last statement was too much for James to take, and even if he had been nailed down to the couch he would still have found a way to get up and shut the television off, as he did now. "Only in New York" – what a stupid thing to say about a man who gave up more than a decade of his life to defend the city that he called home from those who would choose to turn it into a playground of sin. That was the legacy of James' sacrifice? To be a historical oddity, an urban legend akin to alligators in the sewer? How could the city hold up a man like Matthew O'Grady – a man as corrupt as his father, yet all that conveniently ignored because of his good looks and charitable donations with blood money – as a saint and still have doubts about the Night Ghost? How could this city even consider a man supported by a member of the O'Grady crime family – and it was still a crime family, despite what the papers said – as the favorite candidate for next year's mayoral elections? Murders in the street, escalating deaths from crack, crimes among the homeless in public parks, and criminals contorting the election process – had the Night Ghost done anything to help the world? It was enough to drive any many beyond despair, but more so a man who had stood up to stop it all only to be stopped himself.

He heard a scream from the street outside. It was a woman's scream.

The respectful teenagers that had treated him kindly in the fifties were long gone. The ice cream shop that had once been below Jeffers' apartment was now a hole-in-the-wall bar, and at least once a week James heard women screaming outside in the street, no doubt at the hands of men who ought to be treating them better, no matter what kinds of women they were. For years, Jeffers never did anything about it. He didn't care anymore – he wasn't a vigilante; he wasn't a police officer.

Tonight he started to care again, and he decided to finally do something about it.

He got up and stepped over the debris that had accumulated on his apartment floor since the last few years. He had stopped keeping it tidy a dozen years ago when he came to the realization that since he had no friends or family, nobody ever visited him. That was what made him the perfect candidate for the Night Ghost, but the worst possible candidate for early retirement. He took a left into his bedroom. He opened the closet door, the inside of which was covered with newspaper clippings of unsolved crimes that James had collected over the preceding twenty years. He knew all of them had a connection to Matthew O'Grady. He glanced over all of them briefly. They were all the inspiration that he needed.

He reached all the way back in the closet for the suitcase he left there. It was covered in a thick layer of dust. When he opened it, he saw what he had left behind almost twenty years ago.

"Thank God I still work out," he said aloud to himself while standing in front of the mirror and putting his former uniform on, "I'd hate to see what I'd look like in this if I didn't."

The uniform fit as well as it ever did, which James took as a sign that what he was doing wasn't crazy. True, he was fifty-four, but that wasn't a death sentence – didn't Satchel Paige play until he was almost sixty? But most of all, he didn't feel like an old man, like he did when he was sitting on his couch. He was so much more than that, and was meant to be so much more – he wasn't made for retirement; that much was for sure. He tightened his hands into fists and smiled when he heard the leather crease.

Then he remembered that he had heard a woman scream.

The street outside his apartment was always pitch black at night. This was by no fault of the city – he knew because he called them whenever a bulb was out – but was caused by local vandals who knew it was easier to rob in the darkness. The Night Ghost stood atop his building and looked down upon the street level entrance to the bar. Even though it had taken him nearly ten minutes to get into costume, the woman who had been screaming was still in the alleyway next to the bar's entrance, but now was unconscious. The man who must have put her in that state was standing over her, preparing himself to do what the Night Ghost rather would not say. The Night Ghost was lucky – had Jeffers spent even a minute longer changing into his uniform the situation might not be as salvageable.

For the first time in a long time, the Night Ghost leaped off a rooftop. The problem with observing a crime from above is one was never quite sure of the size or the ability of the criminal one was about to pounce on. As the Night Ghost fell, he realized the man in the alley was large indeed. When he landed, he lost his footing – he was out of practice, of course – and tumbled over into a pile of garbage bags.

"What the—" the man grunted in surprise. He turned to see a costumed figure struggle to his feet. The Night Ghost coughed in an attempt to catch the wind that had been knocked out of him, and then rose to his feet.

"What is it, Halloween?" the man shouted, although with a nervous chuckle that betrayed his air of confidence. He was young – he looked barely old enough to be the recently-raised twenty-one drinking age. Nevertheless, he was built like a linebacker, though more like one who had retired from the field and spent more time at the dinner table than the weight room.

"You're going to want to leave that poor woman alone, son," the Night Ghost commanded. Jeffers was somewhat surprised by how easily he was able to speak in the gruff voice that he hadn't used in so long – in fact, he was more surprised that he instinctively called the man "son."

"What are you gonna do about it, buddy?" In contrast to the Ghost's "son," the man couldn't tell how old his "buddy" under the hood was due to the uniform and the darkness.

"Just this," the Night Ghost answered. From under his cape came his hand, which held a lasso of fiberglass rope with a loop tied at the end. The Night Ghost tossed the loop over the man's neck and pulled it tight. Immediately the man started to thrash about, struggling to breathe again, completely forgetting about the woman who he had only minutes ago considered a lucky opportunity. Jeffers was wise enough to admit that despite his conditioning his advanced age probably prevented him from winning any sort of fistfight with the man, so choking him out was his best option.

The man attempted a desperate charge at the Night Ghost, but because he probably hadn't seen the inside of a gym since junior high school he couldn't get very far without oxygen. The Ghost only had to make a half-hearted dodge to get out of the way of the charging man. Soon it was all over, and the Ghost used the rest of the rope to tie up the now-unconscious man. The woman remained out cold, but she was at least breathing. Jeffers thought it was funny that his big comeback featured a damsel who was too drunk to know she was in distress. He made a mental note to ask for an ambulance when he phoned the police for pick-up. Aside from the awkward landing from the rooftop and the fact that his uniform had twenty years of wrinkles in it, he felt confident about his return.

"Okay, so jumping off rooftops is off the list," he said aloud. "But now it's time for Michael."

The Night Ghost started to climb the closest fire escape when he came to the conclusion that he talked to himself way too much in his old age.

Even years ago when the Night Ghost was regularly scaling buildings, nobody spent much money on rooftop or high story security. Nowadays, it was relatively unheard of. Half of the windows of the sixty-fourth floor of the O'Grady Corporation Building – not only the top floor, but the floor of the executive office suites – had even been left open. The Night Ghost had no trouble breaking the jumper prevention bar and climbing into Michael O'Grady's office, which he recognized from a photo spread that had been published in *Forbes* magazine last year. He knew that O'Grady was still up and working. His kind did their real work only at night.

Though the office's lights were on, it was empty, although when he was outside the Night Ghost saw numerous people shuffling in the other rooms on the floor. The décor of the office could only be described as exceptional – though Jeffers had memorized the layout from the *Forbes* article, he still couldn't help but be amazed by the sheer wealth that surrounded him. Michael O'Grady's desk – made out solid mahogany and over a dozen feet long – alone was probably worth tens of thousands of dollars. Jeffers never had an eye for art, so while he couldn't tell the prices of the paintings and sculptures that lined the walls of the office, they certainly had an expensive look. The sheer amount of them cluttered the office, making what could have been a showcase of sophisticated art a gaudy display of wasteful overabundance. Yet it provided Jeffers with one advantage – there were lots of places to hide. The Night Ghost shoved himself into the gap between two sculptures of nude women and waited.

Almost half an hour later, he heard the voice of Michael O'Grady long before anything else of him reached the Night Ghost's senses. He was talking to a handful of others about the election three weeks away.

"Face it folks," he heard Michael say, "The polls are saying we have this one in the bag."

There were a few voices that expressed congratulations, although the Night Ghost was only focused on the one he came to hear.

"I got to make a few calls about that shipment coming tomorrow," Michael said while opening the door to his office. "I'll catch up with you at my club later."

Michael entered the room with a slick smile on his face, the kind people have when they think they know something the rest of the world doesn't. His tie was loosened and hung around his neck like a lasso that hadn't been pulled, and his shirt was halfway unbuttoned. He looked relaxed and confident.

As Michael walked across his office, the Night Ghost leapt out and grabbed him by the shirt. Before Michael could speak, the Night Ghost flipped him on top of the desk and covered Michael's mouth with his hand.

"We've never formerly met, boy," the Night Ghost growled, "But I'd hope you'd do us both a favor and not call for help."

Michael's eyes were filled with a mixture of rage and fear. If you scream, I'll make it so you can't scream ever again. It's as simple as that," the Night Ghost threatened. He obviously didn't mean it, but Michael didn't know what he was or wasn't capable of.

The Night Ghost removed his hand. Michael was breathing heavily, but he did not shout. "It's you," he said between breaths, "You could be anyone under there, but I somehow know that you're the same man who killed my father."

The Night Ghost shook his head as he backed away. "I didn't kill your father. He committed suicide. Whether or not you want to believe that is up to you."

The young businessman looked like he was about to laugh. "Like I'd really believe that. My father was the most powerful man in the city. He'd do no such thing."

"Believe what you want, kid. I'm not here about your father anyway." The Night Ghost began to slowly circle Michael, who remained lying on the desk.

"Then what do you want from me?"

"I'm here to warn you. There's a reason why your father died alone in an alley. His way of life left him with nowhere else to run, and it was the only escape left."

"Nobody – not the police, a judge, or even you – was ever able to pin anything on my father. So I'm not inclined to believe you or anyone else who tries to tell me that my father was a horrible human being. At worst you could say he did a few dishonest things." Michael sat up and turned his back to the Ghost as he said this.

"Seems like you have a pretty broad definition of the word 'worst,' son," the Night Ghost answered, almost with a chuckle.

Matthew stayed frozen with his back toward him for a few moments. After the sting had abated, he turned around. "I could shout out to my bodyguards and have you killed right this minute. Or I'll just have them beat you, I'd rip off that stupid mask, expose your face to the world, and ruin the lives of anyone you've ever loved or anyone who ever loved you. I'd enjoy it, too. You took my father away from me."

"And your father took my dream away from me," the Night Ghost shot back, "But considering I didn't kill your father, I'd say I'm being pretty generous that I'm offering to call it even." He took three slow steps forward. "And now that we're even, I'm asking you for a few favors: withdraw McKinley from the race, turn your tail, and get out of this city."

Matthew laughed. "Seriously? I've got more money and power in this city than half of the pretenders on Wall Street combined. You'd think I'd give that up because of the threats of an old man in a cape?"

The Night Ghost stepped forward also, and only a few feet separated him and Matthew. "You talk big, son," he replied, "But I'd bet you're as big of a coward as your father was."

The punch that Matthew suddenly landed on the Night Ghost's chin wasn't one of the best-thrown ones the Ghost had ever taken, but the shock and surprise stung with a unique kind of intensity. Jeffers hadn't been punched in over twenty years – not even during his night beat. He had forgotten how much a punch, even a bad one, hurt. He didn't let Matthew throw another one. Though he moved slowly at first, the Night Ghost's body accelerated like the gears of an old clock finally rewound after decades of idleness as he took down Matthew with a sweep of his legs and an old stranglehold that he had learned from his high school wrestling coach. He's probably dead now, thought the Night Ghost, though he wasn't sure why that crossed his mind just now.

The hold cut off Matthew's air and prevented him from speaking or shouting out to his bodyguards. As the young man thrashed about, the Night Ghost lectured him much like a father would scold his son, only the worlds were different.

"I will watch everything that you do. You won't see me, you won't hear me, but you'll feel my presence with every step you take. Every time you take something away from the people of New York, I will take something away from you – something that costs a lot of money, because that's the only way to get to you O'Gradys. And eventually the press will catch on, and they'll wonder – why is the Night Ghost back, and why does he seem to only go after Matthew O'Grady? Then they'll start digging, and they'll find what I already know about you."

The Night Ghost released Matthew, and the young man fell to the ground. He almost slipped into unconsciousness, but managed to remain awake for the entire lecture. He tried to cry out for help, but was too busy rasping for the air that he had no connection with for over a minute. By the time he was finally able to call for help, the Night Ghost was gone.

1985

"How many years did you say you were on the force?" the little inquisitive man asked with some skepticism.

"Thirty-two," Jeffers answered. He adjusted his tie for the fourth time in the last twelve minutes. It had been so many years since he had to wear a tie that he needed to buy a new one for the interview. "I retired four years ago."

"Please don't take that question personally; it's just that you're older than our usual hires. But your experience is invaluable, and you've obviously kept yourself in superb shape, as your physical shows."

"That's understandable," Jeffers answered. Working out and watching television were just about the only things Jeffers had done in those four years.

"Well, I guess I can officially say 'welcome' to O'Grady International. You should fit in perfectly with our Executive Security team."

"I was hoping you'd say that. I'm a great team player."

"All that's left is to have you sign your contract and our non-disclosure agreement. I have to emphasize how extremely important privacy is to our executives."

"I'm not surprised," Jeffers replied, although he anticipated breaking that agreement as soon as he had all the information he needed to take Matthew O'Grady down. If he got caught, so be it. He had always been willing to give his life for his cause, and this wasn't any different.

"Come meet the Boss," the little man said. "I'm afraid he has his own bodyguards from his... associates, so you won't be protecting him directly, but you'll certainly see a lot of him in passing."

"I can't wait," James said with a smile, but not for the reasons the interviewer thought.

James followed the little man through a series of the most ornate and overindulgent offices he had ever seen, each greater than the last. He finally entered a familiar office, where Matthew O'Grady stood speaking with Executive Secretary McKinley, who had held that position ever since he had dropped out of the mayoral race due to an undisclosed medical condition.

"Mr. O'Grady," the little man announced, "I'd like you to meet James Jeffers, our new front desk security guard on the Executive Level."

"Ah! I read your background file and such," O'Grady answered, flashing his phony smile. "I look forward to seeing you around the office, although, as I'm sure you know, I am extremely private man – you won't see too much of me, I'm afraid!" Next to him Executive Secretary McKinley chuckled.

James Jeffers gave O'Grady a firm handshake. "It's nice to finally meet you," he responded. "I'll be watching you."

About the author: Christopher McKittrick is an instructor of English at the C.W. Post campus of Long Island University, Suffolk County Community College, and Briarcliffe College. His first published short story, "The Wicked Giant," appeared in *By Mind or Metal: A Fantasy Anthology* from Static Movement Press. His previous creative nonfiction work has appeared in *Newsday* and *Good Times Magazine*. When he is not teaching, he likes to flex his creative writing muscles to find out if they still work.

Seven Years after Midnight

John X. Grey

-Thirty Miles East of Gibraltar – December 29, 1938, 11:32 P.M, Central European Time-

The 40' Coastal Motor Boat had cast off from a smaller dock of Gibraltar's Royal Naval base, this gray-painted craft flying its British Naval Ensign (the red St. George's Cross on a white field and Union Jack in the upper left corner). Three navy-blue uniformed sailors were the crew: one at the wheel, another for moorings and a commanding petty officer. They conveyed two passengers (instead of depth charges, mines or torpedoes) standing beside the aft small mast.

The first figure was a 6' 2" man in his wide-brimmed dark-gray fedora and flowing overcoat, the light-gray suit (no tie) and black boots, completed by that black domino mask above rugged, tanned, square-jawed features. The gentleman removed his hat to allow the Mediterranean Sea's breeze tousling cropped black hair with neat high bangs above that firm nose and sharp blue-gray eyes. Standing at that man's left was one male Chinese teenager in his traditional black kung-fu belted jacket and loose trousers with short slippers. The black-haired youth stood 5' 6" and also sported a black domino mask over hazel eyes. At each side, he flexed hands from fists to knife chop positions, every muscle tensed for action. The man replaced his fedora as they approached a 3-mile diameter rock far out of sight from Gibraltar's horizon itself.

"There 'tis," Petty Officer Second Class Mickey Bath in the red-piping marked blue uniform moved near the American's right, pointing at the fog and smoke-shrouded mass they approached, a Cockney accent betraying his common origins, "Smoke Island or *la isla del humo* to the Spanish. Why did you and the Chinaman wanna be stepping onto that deserted rock, Sir?"

"I already discussed that with your base's commander, John Bull," Professor Midnight soon informed the shorter British sailor, using the clear commanding Midwestern accent, "I've also read two Royal Navy warships were recently lost here. They each sank quickly with no storms, indications of an attacking submarine or forgotten mines being the cause."

"'Twas strange, each sinking," Bath briefly removed his bill cap to scratch balding crew-cut red hair, "the *HMS Justiciar* and *HMS Rampart* goin' to the bottom fast. I knew blokes servin' on them frigates. They were good ships, but not one man survived 'em."

"Well, I'm known, from the news boys in the States, as a 'mystery man,'" Midnight pulled at his overcoat's lapels, thankful the night was cooler on the sea in this semitropical area, dressing as he had, "and those sinking ships sound like the sort of mystery I've investigated the past few years now. Just wait. We'll get to the bottom of it tonight."

"Well," Bath rubbed at his reddish nose, the broken capillaries one sign he took the rum ration like other Royal Navy sailors, "our orders were just to deliver you two fellows right 'ere."

Moving near the wheel man, the NCO ordered his steering five degrees starboard for a black sand beach to the south. Donning black leather gloves, Professor Midnight put a restraining left hand on his partner's right shoulder, as Shade acted as if prepared to evacuate this CMB before reaching their destination.

"I thought you seemed more tense than usual tonight, Wu," this 35-year-old man behind the mask, Dr. Carl S. Krytchek, M.D., had been 16-year-old Wu Jan Ming's legal guardian almost three-and-a-half years during their working partnership, "focus on a calm *ch'i* and pay attention to the here and now. There's nothing much we can do about the future."

"There are times, Professor," the teenager tightened that black belt around his jacket's middle, a symbol of the fighting school this orphan had begun at age eight in Macau, "when you often almost sound more like my old *Wing Chun* master than he did. I think your time in my homeland rubbed off on you somewhat. Is that not so?"

"I've rubbed off on you a bit too, Friend," Professor Midnight now rechecked his overcoat's various inner equipment pockets and the twin .45-calabur Colt (M1911 A1) automatic pistols in the shoulder holsters beneath each armpit, "your Cantonese accent is getting less pronounced the more you've traveled."

Smiling and nodding in accepting the complement (some Asians might have considered it as insulting); Shade crossed both arms, waiting beside the psychiatrist-turned-crime-fighter while the CMB cruised toward their landing beach. The Royal Navy anticipated arrival by a squadron of its warships after recent maneuvers between Crete and Cyprus. The Admiralty was concerned about those vessels also being lost. Civil war-torn Spain had been one minor British concern during the recent Czechoslovak crisis and Munich Pact. Germany and Italy maintained active interests, granting aid to General Franco (whose nationalist forces were finally winning), as former Soviet-sponsored volunteer brigades bolstered flagging republican fortunes.

"Right," Bath informed the duo as his men lowered a rowboat, "from 'ere, you row in. Good luck, Gents. Another patrol should be back this way after 18 hours."

"Luck's something I've often had in life," Professor Midnight almost bragged, climbing into the 6' dingy over that larger boat's port side, awaiting Shade's joining him for their fifty-foot row, "a pleasant voyage for you and your men tonight, Petty Officer."

Shade hesitated for a few seconds under Petty Officer Bath's mistrustful gaze, soon joining Midnight in rowing to reach the volcanic black sand beach minutes later.

"What's wrong, Shade?" Professor Midnight tied the craft to a tall narrow gray rock, using the teen's costumed alias. "We can always use this boat for return to Gibraltar if necessary."

"Yes," this youth admitted, waving at the CMB to signal its sailors they made landfall, before that craft turned about for Gibraltar, "but I never liked boats living in Macau, especially after my parents both died during that typhoon on their sailing junk."

The masked mystery man then reconnoitered this narrow beach seeking any means around or higher up the rugged island's interior, discovering a well-traveled, gradually-inclining pathway that wound northward. The night winds were gentle breezes, not enough to scatter the volcanic vents nearer the plateau summit that gave this island its name.

There were times, the psychiatrist reflected, as he and shade climbed one inclined rock face toward a cavern 20' above them, his sanity was questionable, putting on this costume and mask to thwart evil doers, after some mobster killed the man's parents exactly seven years earlier.

-Chicago, Illinois – December 29, 1931, 9:00 P.M., Central Standard Time-

Dr. Carl Stanislaus Krytchek, M. D. departed Lakeshore Hospital's psychiatric unit, stepping into a cold snowing night after another late shift, numbed at aiding broken minds caused by the Depression gripping this nation more than two years now. Pulling both his black overcoat and fedora tighter, and adjusting the gray wool scarf, tan gloves and black earmuffs, the man heard a clock's chime somewhere off in the Windy City's distance.

"Hey, Carlos," Krytchek spun in the black snow boots at the 2' drift he walked through on the sidewalk, before the vision of loveliness he had met during the internship caught up to him, "did you forget that offer about an escort toward the El station?"

Carmelita Juanita Sanchez, R.N., the only Puerto Rican nurse on staff here, wore a long blue cape with its Red Cross symbol, a matching cloche hat and fur-lined black snow boots, the woman almost sliding to fall on some ice before Krytchek caught her.

"Yeah, it slipped my mind, sorry," Carl smiled for this green-eyed, cinnamon brown-haired lady, the man often attracted to exotic-looking women since he was a teenager, "I'd better keep that promise, or you might break your neck walking through this weather."

"I forgive you," the nurse kissed his right cheek, "this time, *hombre*. I heard you'd finished a tough day and saw some part of your hard night's work to boot on my shift."

They continued toward the nearest elevated train station arm-in-arm, as few other pedestrians around neither noticed nor cared about a 'mixed-race' couple during this freezing evening's late hour. Nurse Sanchez lived at the YWCA hotel, and her boyfriend still rented his bedroom from two almost-elderly parents in their Park Ridge grocery store's upstairs apartment.

"I had to calm one man down from his violent rage, after he'd injured two orderlies. Mr. Roy Fitzgerald Pike lost all he had for two reasons – criminal extortion and financial ruin. The fellow buckled under those pressures."

"I still thank God we both have jobs," Carmelita tried to inject one small ray of sunshine into his thoughts, despite a dour Marxist-oriented upbringing, as Carl brushed fingertips at her hair's tight lower bun, "and each other, every night when praying."

Saying goodbye to each other, before Nurse Sanchez boarded her train (Dr. Krytchek waited for another train, transferring to the Union Pacific Northwest Line headed past Park Ridge), the psychiatrist indulged in more passionate kisses than usual. The Latina responded with eagerness to that advance.

"Carl, *mi madre* and *padre* always ask me when we're moving in together," the woman then mentioned while catching her breath at this sheltered platform, "or even getting married. You know they didn't wed until after having all eight of us kids, three *hermanos* and five *hermanas*. They're both tradition-hating Marxists."

Kyrtchek felt flushed after that inquiry, shaking his head to clear it as the train pulled up to the platform, searching for some answer before she left him that night. "Lita, I love you, but I'm just finishing my internship, planning to be a medical professor, and you're three years out of nursing school. We should know each other better before taking such a big step. The country's going to hell in a hand basket, and any future seems risky."

"*Si*, I understand what you're saying, Carl. I emigrated from San Juan here when everything looked brighter, but don't regret too many of the days I've lived on the mainland. We can't be afraid of tomorrow, not when mankind progressed so far after that awful world war."

As she entered the nearest El car, Krytchek was speechless at her parting words.

"Just think about *our* future together, not the world's, *mi amante*."

The psychiatrist lowered his head, after seeing her kiss the glass between them in affection, waving while the train pulled out again. Krytchek loved Carmelita Sanchez more than any woman he had ever dated during the past decade, uncertain if that was enough.

-Park Ridge (northwest of Chicago), Illinois – 11:55 P.M., CST-

Maybe I can wed Lita after getting tenure as an instructor. Krytchek carried a wrapped ham sandwich in its brown paper bag from Kohl's All Night Diner, walking the final two blocks to his family's modest grocery store, having worked there as a delivery and stock boy up until college. The Krytcheks were struggling to keep their market afloat, having started it in 1902, and often seemed worried, Carl noticed, but not about whether the business might go bankrupt. *Not being raised by Marxists, I never know what to say when my gal talks about shacking up.*

The psychiatrist ceased pondering his love life and again considered the Krytchek Grocery's survival, now turning the corner from Garden Street onto Prairie Avenue in sight of the two-story building he had always called home. Carl glimpsed two (flat cap and coat-clad) figures fleeing from the alley leading to the store's delivery entrance and staying in the shadows, until they got into an idling gray sedan half-a-block away. Suspecting he had witnessed thieves making their getaway, the young doctor quickened his pace toward the store as another distant clock chimed the Midnight hour. Before the man stepped from the icy street onto the snow-shoveled curb at the store's front, that building exploded and knocked him backwards five feet.

Oh – my – God... no. Sprinkled with some broken glass but not seriously hurt, the dazed physician slowly sat up off the frigid pavement and beheld that entire building engulfed in roaring flames, radiating heat so great it partially alleviated the chilled winter air. "NO – MAMA, POP – NOOO!"

Retrieving his dropped, wrapped sandwich almost as an afterthought, and not quite believing the horror before him, Carl Krytchek could not get near the inferno, or reach the rear door leading to the family's second-story living quarters. Every window was filled with flames.

-Smoke Island – December 29, 1938, 11:58 P.M., CET-

Professor Midnight reached his right hand to Shade, assisting the teen onto that ledge beside the cavern they now entered, pulling the Chinese ally upward as both heard a strange crackling electrical noise on the island's summit, followed by an eruption of bubbles from the sea (in the approximate location where the Royal Navy's Coastal Motor Boat might have reached).

"What was that?" Regaining his footing, Shade spun clockwise to the phenomenon.

"I hope our ride didn't meet with disaster," Midnight adjusted his fedora against the shifting winds, "by moonlight there's nothing afloat, and I can't hear the boat's motor now."

"Does it mean," Shade shook his head before leading their way inside the cave, as Midnight handed him the metal headband (containing a newer battery-powered electric mining lamp) and attached another around the fedora's brim, "their naval craft was just lost here also?"

The psychiatrist-turned-adventurer had no answer for that or two missing frigates yet.

Professor Midnight and Shade crept through the rough tunnel, extinguishing their lamps and hugging the walls upon hearing drifting voices through this cave speaking Spanish, soon noticing the warm light glowing ahead. The darker-clad duo glimpsed the gleam and caught the odor of a campfire around the bend to their right. There, two men wore dark-green uniforms, garrison caps and carried Mauser bolt-action rifles slung over shoulders. Midnight signaled Shade to distract the men by one tap at his back. The teenager leaped into that passage and faced the guards, as the mentor brought pistol handles down across their skulls. The youth then made one spinning leap over the campfire, kicking a nearby third soldier there in the head.

"Yep, they're all Franco's soldiers," Midnight examined the unconscious men's uniforms and equipment, "on an island Spain has never legally claimed, even after defeating the Moors."

"This one is an officer," Shade noted the third man's epaulets and pistol sidearm.

Hearing other voices echoing with work sounds from deeper inside this mountain, Professor Midnight and Shade dragged the unconscious soldiers into a side passage and extinguished the campfire before moving onward. Reaching a lighted intersection minutes later, they surprised two more Spanish soldiers, Midnight kneeing his opponent's stomach and following with a right cross, while Shade chopped the other man's jaw and flung him to the ground, employing one short sharp punch for rendering that guard unconscious. The partners dragged these soldiers into the shadows of the preceding passage (not needing the lamps beyond this point).

The cavern walls soon changed, having been cut square by mining operations, and contained modern electric lighting every few feet hanging from spikes and attached to cables. After they had covered more yards, hearing voices in Spanish coming from elsewhere, Professor Midnight glimpsed a metal door labeled with that language as the 'Generator Room' in black paint. The psychiatrist tried the door's turning handle, only to set off a flashing red light mounted upon the ceiling hidden above and the whistling siren blaring around them, before one disguised smooth floor section beneath Shade and he suddenly opened its trapdoor.

Booby trapped – I should've known.

The mystery men crashed across a rocky floor 10' below, before the space filled with gas from several low circular shuttered vents around the walls. Midnight fumbled for his small war surplus gas mask inside the coat, but soon succumbed and passed out alongside Shade.

-Park Ridge, IL – December 30, 1931, 2:12 A.M., CST-

My selfish desires are all gone now, maybe even loving Carmelita.

Carl Krytchek sat on the frozen curb in front of the burnt-out ruined structural shell which had been his family's small grocery store on Prairie Avenue almost three decades. He now cradled a half-empty white coffee mug some neighbor had given him earlier that was already growing colder between both hands, the uneaten ham sandwich from Kohl's Diner on his lap. The local volunteer fire company was finishing around the building, this frigid weather making it difficult to fight any flames here (semi-frozen water hampered their efforts), but they contained that blaze and kept it from spreading to other buildings. The police had taken Krytchek's statement a half-hour ago. Illinois' Fire Marshall would not begin his investigation until after dawn.

"I don't want to slur your parents in a time of loss, Mr. Krytchek," Chief Daniel O'Rourke's clear brogue revealed one damning discovery to this survivor, "or cast any aspersions upon their good name, but the firemen found evidence of stored alcohol in the basement. For the moment, it looks like someone was distributing hooch out of this establishment. Do you know about that, Son? There's no point protecting the dead now."

Krytchek restrained himself from decking that blue-uniformed, white-haired heavyset man. Smashing that round face and wide nose would be assaulting a police officer. Collecting hints and signs of this accusation in recent months, the psychiatrist responded with his well-acted denial.

"That's Doctor Krytchek, Chief, as a licensed psychiatrist ready to start practice next year. No, I don't know about alcohol on the premises. It was just a grocery store and my home."

After the officials departed the scene, and Dr. Krytchek accepted an invitation to bed down at the Relief Mission half-a-block east for tonight, the man was standing and staring toward ruins of his personal life in that blackened building's rubble, as one black touring sedan with a white hard top pulled beside him on the curb.

"Hey, you, get in," the hard-nosed, ice-blue eyed driver in that black suit and gold tie insisted, after the automobile's right rear door swung outward as the one passenger opened it, "the Boss wants to talk wit' ya now, Pal."

Swallowing fear from his grief-numbed body, and abandoning all care this might be the last ride he tool anywhere ever (due to the greater Chicago area's crime epidemic), Dr. Carl Krytchek slowly stepped inside and sat on the comfortable seat beside a large man with shining black hair wearing that tailored ice-cream suit and black tie.

"Drive around the block, Vince," the heavyset gentleman then shifted to face his passenger at the right, "so I can get better acquainted with this unfortunate orphaned soul."

Comfortable from the car's heated interior, Krytchek placed the sandwich in his coat's right pocket, setting the mug between them, realizing: "I've seen you somewhere before."

Alberto Pannucci chuckled and wiped at the clean-shaven jaw with its small horizontal scar, shrugging both broad shoulders. He held a mahogany cane by the left hand against the floor, the white Panama hat on his lap, continuing their conversation.

"I was distressed to learn of your misfortune before New Year's, Dr. Krytchek. Please accept my condolences at the untimely passing of both parents. It is regrettable when anyone has to die because of someone's stubborn refusal about reasonable business proposals."

"Are you insinuating something, Mr. Pannucci? I've seen and read your story in the city's newspaper before, disturbing various alcoholic beverages to the communities all around greater Chicago's suburbs."

"I give the public what it wants," Pannucci stated in a matter-of-face tone, "even when the law says 'no' to their desires. I'm simply a businessman, as your father was."

Tiring of the philosophical debate regarding Prohibition, Krytchek sighed.

"What exactly do you want from me?"

Pannucci gestured with his right hand explaining their meeting's purpose.

"In this competitive enterprise, I have rivals, and your father was working with one of those other businesses – the Finnegan Gang – distributing their product in secret through his basement almost two years now. When that Mick clan was peanuts, I didn't consider them a threat to my annual profits, but things have since changed."

Krytchek clenched his lower jaw tighter, and both fists inside the gloves, considering jumping from the moving sedan to escape this harsh reality he had denied (after hints of the evidence from Mikhail and Sophie Krytchek's ability to keep their small grocery store solvent during these hard economic times).

"My father's a good man, and my mother's a saint," Carl defended their memory, "they didn't deserve to die that way! I believe the police will figure it all out."

"The police," Pannucci rubbed at his upper lip and shook the head 'no,' "I own them in Park Ridge. And the state's Fire Marshall will probably discover the blaze was started by that rotgut Finnegan pushed on your father. It's getting late, Vince – time to drop off our rider.

The sedan stopped in front of the Relief Mission minutes after Krytchek and Pannucci began their conversation. The psychiatrist was barely able to find the passenger door's handle behind him, still absorbing the fact Pannucci had done everything except confess to planting whatever explosive was used in that grocery store's destruction. Stumbling onto the icy curb and grabbing the mug from the seat before Pannucci tried handing it toward him, Krytchek felt powerless to say anything during the mobster's parting words.

"Do yourself a favor, Doctor, stay out of trouble. Taking care of the sick is a fine profession. Consider yourself fortunate you weren't home when the place went up in smoke."

Watching the sedan drive off into the light snowfall that started then, Carl Krytchek felt white heat behind his eyes before strolling toward the mission and knocking to let the older lady running this place, Sister Aimee McGrath, know he had finally arrived.

My life changed at the stroke of Midnight. Somehow, I must make him pay for 'their' sake and that of others.

-Smoke Island – December 30, 1938, 2:15 A.M., CET-

Stirring out of the dream he was having about finding some odd tropical world straight from Burroughs or Doyle, Professor Midnight felt nauseous after being gassed, but thankful it had not been toxic. The Spanish forces apparently wished him alive for now. Seeing Shade face down to his right asleep, the Professor found their hands were bound against the back. He shook the Asian's body until that young man awakened. Shade rolled into a seated posture, before taking a tiny knife from one of his belt's rear hidden pouches.

"Where is this, Professor? We were not killed by the gas."

Feeling his pistols, extra ammo clips, concealed holsters and most other gear had been taken, Krytchek watched Wu Jan move the knife in delicate hands to free bound wrists. His fedora was perched on the head, but the mining lamp and its metal band were gone.

"Cut me loose next, Kid," the man shifted to face away, as Shade worked on his ropes, before considering dim surroundings (lit by its 15-watt bulb), a 15' by 10' metal box enclosure with one door containing only its high-placed 2' square barred window, "I'm cleaned out of tools."

Shade helped his mentor stand and examined the jacket's belt and its hidden small pockets, smiling to inform the American: "I have not been. Our luck holds, Professor."

Peering beyond the door's window, Midnight glimpsed no guards, but this exit was locked from the outside. The corridor beyond had been cut through gray rock and lit as the other earlier hallways they traversed.

"That remains to be seen. Still got your pick among those things, Shade?"

The youth shook his head in reaching for one of the belt's right compartments and pulled out the small nickel finish lock pick tool. Clinging on the bars in order to reach out of their cell, Shade leaned downward and discovered his arms were not long enough to reach the lock. Rubbing both aching temples, Professor Midnight realized another odd detail.

We weren't unmasked by our captors. Why?

"I cannot quite get there."

"I'll try it," Midnight shook cobwebs from the mind to concentrate on this skilled task, taking Shade's place reaching through the door, finding his arm was long enough, but could barely stick the head outside those bars even after removing the fedora, "this is gonna be tricky."

Straining, struggling and grunting while engaged in the difficult work, Professor Midnight worked the pick into the keyhole and managed to shift this door's tumbler after twenty seconds. Shoving the door outward and extricating himself from the window with Shade's assistance, the man replaced his fedora as they checked their exiting had not been overheard.

"Which way should we go next, Professor, left or right?"

The corridor stretched off to the right and left by 30' with rectangular doorways at each end, and five other cell doors holding no prisoners behind them. They then heard multiple sets of footsteps and Shade replaced his lock pick as Midnight handed it back. The psychiatrist and youth flattened themselves to either side of the left doorway, ready for anyone approaching this area. They had to wait mere minutes, before two Spanish soldiers entered with rifles slung over the right shoulders. Midnight grabbed the big man to his left and slammed him head first into one wall. Shade gave his taller opponent a low kick against the abdomen, followed by the sharp chop in the forehead before that man collapsed. Midnight heard gasps from the third person entering this cell area at the doorway, grabbing and pulling the woman inside, shoving his new adversary into the wall to face him. Rearing back for inflicting a wide roundhouse, Krytchek stopped when he beheld that familiar exotic female visage.

"My God, Carmelita, I can't believe it's really you. Of all the places in this world, I never expected we'd meet again on a barren forsaken Mediterranean island." "Carlos," recognizing the voice and face behind that mask and beneath the fedora, Carmelita Sanchez (hair dyed black now) was wearing a green Spanish army jacket, matching knee-length skirt below the light-green blouse and red tie, shod in black jack boots, "is it really you?"

-The Iron Horse Roadhouse outside DeKalb, Illinois – September 12, 1934, 8:02 P.M., CST-

Clad in his black suit, fedora and domino mask, Professor Midnight smashed the spoke-back wooden chair across a tall cropped-haired blonde Bundist's square jaw as the man lunged with the stylized dagger, knocking him into two more brown-haired goons in black shirts, trousers and jack boots becoming involved. Midnight then dove across this honky-tonk bar's main room, shoving and upending a round table at one big bushy black-haired Bundist swinging to miss the mystery man that had broken inside their lair. Pulling both .45-calabur pistols in blocking the front door, Midnight fired two shots at the ceiling warning his two dozen opponents against advancing.

"Okay, Boys, it's been fun, but I won't hold back the lead next time. Drop your weapons and raise those hands high above the heads, just like when saluting that *Fuhrer* you all admire so much, only put them both straight up in the air this time. I mean it."

The masked mystery man had learned about this American-based paramilitary group from another doctor's patient beaten for betraying The Blood Circle by contacting the FBI about its activities (organizing workers in dockyards, factories and trucking firms). Investigating their organization on his own, and even posing as a warehouse worker (heavy lifting experience from years laboring in Krytchek's Grocery) to attend one meeting, Dr. Carl Krytchek found the gang's main headquarters in eastern Illinois. Professor Midnight tipped the Bureau on the location and waited for impending arrival of federal agents from his car, until he saw one silver touring sedan pull into view and a half-dozen well-dressed persons head inside this rough establishment.

"He's just one guy," the blonde man he just hit noted, "and can't kill us all." " I can slow you down, Creep," Midnight straightened to aim for that one foolish Blood Circle member, feeling more confident after twenty-eight months experience at fighting crime as a local vigilante, "and stop enough of your buddies without killing them. It's your choice."

Sixteen thugs in the room backed away from the fight. Eight hard core troublemakers threw some furniture at Professor Midnight before charging with their blades or reached for pistols. The masked man dodged all but the corner of one square table catching his left shoulder, knocking him against the nearest wall as they closed in. Two bullets missed his head and right side, before he fired both automatic pistols, wounding two men through their kneecaps, disarming a third of his Luger 9-mm pistol (hitting the wrist with one trick shot), grazing another man's neck and a fifth's skull, as every other shot missed him.

Being a doctor, I know where to shoot 'em that hurts, not kills.

Professor Midnight dodged a thrown knife and ended across the floor on his back, before firing every last bullet in each clip, hitting one man's right collarbone, damaging another's left shoulder and disarming the last pistol wielder through the palm to the appendix; a bullet grazed this masked intruder's lower right rib cage (causing Krytchek minor irritation).

"Okay, Cretins, the Federal boys will be here soon, thanks to Professor Midnight."

Midnight discharged the spent clips and pulled out new ones before he rolled and stood with his back to one large square-pane window (containing this bar's smaller neon sign), seeing those men that backed off now fleeing toward a door behind the bar counter. Odors of perspiration and blood mingled with pitch and wood (from the roadhouse's manufacture), as the lone man charged across the bar, avoiding wounded Blood Circle men (those man now unwilling to fight).

I'd better find the ringleaders.

"Hey," one man on the floor cradling both bleeding kneecaps demanding of their assailant, "just who are you supposed to be again, Mack?"

"Professor Midnight," Krytchek vaulted over the counter as he introduced himself, "fighting darkness from the shadows, that's my motto, Jackboot."

Kicking the next inside door open, the hero presented pistols at an empty hallway leading to another door 10' ahead, behind which excited voices and hurried noises emanated. Bashing that door open with the right shoulder, Professor Midnight ducked the first man who was swinging one double-bladed axe, his tool embedding in the door's frame, before kicking that attacker's abdomen to shove him crashing through a window at this room's left side. Those other nineteen men and two women inside the room, all dressed in black work attire or more-fashionable evening clothes (the latter wearing steel-gray armbands with a red circle containing three white pointed arrows), either threw furniture, fired pistols at this pursuer, or took the one back exit into a nearby pine barrow. Midnight dodged projectiles, bullets, and the gunpowder cask almost hitting his head. He fired again at many assailants, and wounded five armed ones until the remaining conspirators fled. The crusader shot at those fugitives, wounding two men's legs, grazing one man and woman's heads. An unscathed assailant pausing at that exit threw his cigarette lighter toward spilled gunpowder, its trail formed by the hurled cask's uncorked hole.

"You can rest in pieces, masked man!"

"What the—?"

Professor Midnight fired at him but missed, glimpsing that fast burning fuse headed toward nearby stored ammunition here. He stumbled after the escaped conspirators, but halted when seeing the lady's face he had just wounded.

Oh my God, Carmelita?

The man threw this familiar woman over his right shoulder and jumped through the door as gunpowder exploded, landing in the dirt a few feet away when other explosives inside that room detonated and cooked ammunition went off from the heat and flames. Soon half of the building was on fire, as the doctor's training took over and he wrapped a makeshift bandage around that cinnamon-haired woman's bleeding right temple after having dragged her clear.

"What are you doing here? I know we drifted apart when I started wearing this costume and mask, spending more time avenging my parents against Pannucci, before finding other evil men to thwart in Chicago and surrounding towns."

The man recalled Nurse Sanchez's impassioned words to him during 1933, talking about her idealistic parents immigrating to newly-republican Spain for joining that socialist revolution. The daughter had drifted in an opposite direction, admiring strong men like Benito Mussolini. FDR's election had radicalized her more toward extreme nationalist political views. She had joined this Blood Circle since it shared those beliefs.

I can't turn Lita over to the Bureau. I still love her on some level.

Midnight carried the unconscious lady to a hidden high-speed black roadster (his first cousin Stosh – a backwoods mechanic – built it from wrecked scrap Indianapolis 500 racing cars), parked just off the nearest road. He drove Carmelita away, leaving her for attention at the nearest hospital (the man briefly removing his mask while performing that merciful act).

Professor Midnight continued receiving press for crime fighting efforts, even after relocating to Miami Beach the next year. He never saw Carmelita Sanchez again, but learned she emigrated in 1936 and joined the Spanish nationalists.

-Smoke Island's mountain interior – December 30, 1938, 2:28 A.M., CET-

"You know her, Professor?"

"Carl," Carmelita disbelievingly shook her head, "it is actually you?"

Shade dragged the Spanish soldier he had just subdued into their vacant cell, soon returning for the other man Midnight vanquished. The Professor kept Carmelita cornered against the rock wall in the meantime, noting her small scar from that 1934 bullet.

"Yeah, back in Chicago we worked together at a psychiatric ward." Dr. Krytchek sighed and shook his head in amazement and disappointment, before addressing the nurse. "I knew you drifted toward the Fascist cause after we started dating, Lita, and see you've darkened the hair. It suits you."

"Carl, you shouldn't be here," the woman glimpsed Shade locking that door to trap the guards who escorted her earlier, as Midnight stooped to collect the black medical bag she dropped when he pulled his ex-girlfriend inside this corridor, "it's Spanish sovereign territory."

"I'm here because two British warships were sunk in sight of this island as their last reported positions, after securing the Royal Navy's permission to investigate. The Coastal

Motor Boat we arrived in, I think it sank returning to Gibraltar. Would you know anything about that?"

Carmelita tried to take the bag, but Professor Midnight stepped back and opened it for further examination, while Shade grabbed the woman's right arm and restrained her. The satchel held medical supplies – needle and syringe, an alcohol bottle and cotton balls, and two vials filled with clear liquid (marked Sodium Thiopental – Krytchek knew this was commonly called 'truth serum').

"What were you planning, Lita, getting us to talk without applying a rubber hose?"

"I was only told that two intruders had been found on the island," for one moment, Krytchek was reminded of their brief tender past from her soft innocent expression while confessing a small role here, "and assigned to prepare prisoners for interrogation, our chief medical officer Dr. Munoz being occupied. I never knew it was you, dressed like that."

"The papers call me Professor Midnight."

The psychiatrist sighed relief Carmelita did not remember their prior meeting in 1934, after he began this extra career. On that night, he wished to take his ex-girlfriend away and propose marriage, doubting the woman would renounce Fascism. Tugging the fedora's brim, Krytchek kept the mask on even though she recognized him; his eyes then met hers when continuing.

"Carmelita, I'm not here to debate philosophy, or forgive your spurning me. Something's happening on this island. It might have cost the lives of sailors on two British warships and that smaller motor boat. I need to know what your superiors are doing and why before more people die. A Royal Navy squadron returning from maneuvers must soon pass here headed for Gibraltar. Will you help us?"

The woman reflexively clicked both boot heels together while appearing to think the matter over, as Shade released her at Midnight's behest and they stepped back from that nurse closer to the doorway. Looking at Krytchek, Carmelita Sanchez smiled in wistful affection then nodded with her answer.

"I only worked here for a few weeks with the small medical staff, after serving at hospitals on the mainland behind battle lines, caring for a Nationalist platoon and scientists under Doctor Juan Satana, our island's project leader. There is one volcanic lava tube I heard about that should lead directly inside the main operations cave where the strange experiments happen."

"We should not trust her, Professor," Shade stared at Sanchez with daggers in his eyes behind the mask, arms crossed and alert for suspicious actions, "she works as a Fascist. They are always loyal to the group. We both know this from past cases." "I agree, Shade," Midnight noted, "But I'm willing to trust her part way for now." He then looked to the nurse again. "Will you come with us later and get off this island?"

Carmelita moved closer, caressing Krytchek's shoulders when answering.

"After I show you the tube, I'll return here and pretend to be knocked out in the cell with those guards. No one else need know my involvement guiding your clandestine search."

Professor Midnight nodded, reaching for his revolvers out of habit under the overcoat, only to rediscover he remained disarmed, as Carmelita peered out the cell area's nearest exit to see whether that way ahead was clear.

"Can we also retrieve my weapons and other gadgets by any chance?"

"I'm sorry, Carl," Carmelita wet her lips in facing the duo again, "I don't know where the armory is located down here, but your confiscated equipment would most likely be there."

Shade then handed Midnight a Mauser rifle with two extra clips (from Carmelita's escorts) and took the other while observing: "We will find whatever is needed from our hosts."

Smiling at his partner, Professor Midnight shouldered the new weapon, kept the medical bag in the left hand and urged Carmelita: "Lead our way, if you please." The nurse stayed just ahead of Midnight and Shade taking them through stone corridors, but most passages were largely deserted at this late hour so the group seldom hid. After ten minutes, they reached the 4' diameter lava tube's entrance in its rocky side tunnel.

"I'll recommend the British authorities go easy on you, when they investigate this affair after today," Dr. Krytchek rubbed his former love's small chin from lingering affection, "just as I pulled strings with the Bureau sparing your arrest about that Illinois roadhouse."

"Ah," Carmelita looked at the man's costume closer, recalling the incident, "it explains why I wasn't deported afterwards. *Muchas gracias*, Professor Midnight." Watching the nurse headed back toward the cell area in a casual manner, after returning the medical bag to her, Professor Midnight decided she would not raise any alarm, restraining Shade from following Carmelita for confirming that fact.

"We've still got a job to do."

Nodding agreement, Shade preceded his mentor into the natural lava-formed passage; both men crouched inside the 4' diameter opening to maneuver forward. After two-dozen yards, they reached a metal net grill across the exit, looking down at one metal catwalk bolted onto the rock wall 6' below. Beyond that object, the main (50' high and 100-yard diameter) cavern was filled by large-scale apparatuses and technical-looking support equipment, the crowning item here one huge long cannon-like device topped by its big magnet emitter instead of some barrel's opening. The 'weapon' sat upon a round platform within the cavern's central floor, designed to be raised by hydraulic lifts through a metal-shuttered opening placed overhead along the ceiling.

That thing must be the star attraction in this circus.

"*Med leng yea?*" Shade pressed against the screen for a better view. "It is huge gun, but not exactly, Professor."

Professor Midnight smiled at his young aide's 'colorful' Cantonese, knowing that profane expression himself (words corresponding to decades later familiar English initials 'w t f'). The man had learned various Chinese words and phrases from Ming since 1935.

"That's a super-sized magnet on the end," the psychiatrist pondered their discovery, "clearly some sort of weapon. It must have something to do with those two British—"

The concealed crime fighters then heard voices and movement from behind them inside this tube, soon realizing they had to go forward. The cavern contained some civilians around control panels in green uniforms and others wearing white volcanologist protective gear near a lava pool in the area's center left side. The grill seemed fastened on the rock, but flexible to the touch.

"We'll have to kick it open," Midnight moved to place his boots against the area, while Shade was already positioned, "and hope that machinery's sounds cover our entrance."

"Whatever happens," the Chinese teen added, "I have experienced amazing things traveling in your company, Professor."

The two men then kicked the grill open all along its bottom section after three strikes, sliding over the side for dropping onto the catwalk below. Unfortunately, the noises attracted attention from male civilian scientists, one younger dark-haired and the other snow-white with a beard, as they cried out with different warnings.

"*Alarma*! *ALARMA*!"

"*Guardias, presura*! *Intrusos*!"

Professor Midnight and Shade scrambled along the catwalk, dodging behind some stalactites as soldiers from the lava tube fired Mausers at their heels jumping downward in hot pursuit.

They found a ladder inside one cylindrical metal grated enclosure and alternately climbed or slid down its length to reach the ground floor, while Fascist troops continued firing or chasing after them above. Midnight and Shade took their captured rifles and fired in response from cover, as enemy soldiers closed with greater caution to contain these intruders. Hearing boots running near from behind, Midnight turned toward the approaching men until their commander ordered his forces to stop the firefight, giving these intruders time for reconsidering their situation.

"*Cesar fuego*!"

"That's far enough, gentlemen," Midnight declared as he and Shade crouched, back-to-back there now, the teen watching those men emerging from the catwalk by ladders or some additional routes, while the psychiatrist aimed at the forward guarding row.

"*Yanqui*, you and your accomplice are completely surrounded and have no hope of escape," the brown-haired officer's English was acceptable and formal, "surrender or we will be forced to kill you both."

"From where I'm standing, *Caballero*, we have something known in the States as a 'Mexican standoff,'" exaggerating his position's strength, Midnight ejected one spent cartridge by the bolt, "and it usually ends badly for everybody concerned."

"Except now, *Profesor Medianoche*, the self-assured Spanish baritone voice then interjected, as a balding, round-bespectacled, black-haired man (in his long white lab coat with its double row of brass buttons, crisp black trousers and jack boots) emerged from behind the soldier skirmish line, "*Coronel* Calabreese, have your men stand down."

"But, Doctor, that *Yanqui* and Oriental have discovered our base."

Midnight saw a self-satisfied smirk across this scientist's thin lips; those beady hazel eyes now studied him as if potential prey or another guinea pig. Two newer shadows loomed behind the soldier ranks under lower lighting inside that next cavern section.

"They will surrender without a fight, I believe. Also, I have the power of command over this special project from *nuestro Caudillo* himself, do not forget."

The middle-aged Spanish civilian's words had some effect and Colonel Calabreese signaled his men on either side to lower their rifles and holstered the revolver he carried. The two newer shadows stepped forward, one holding the other by its right arm, into the light. The tall man in a gray uniform had cropped sandy-blonde hair beneath the combination cap, and held his own Luger 9-mm pistol to the head of the familiar woman beside him – Carmelita Sanchez.

"You will lay down your arms, *Mein Herren*," the German-accented gentleman insisted as his cold blue eyes looked toward that captive, "or this woman dies in five seconds."

Glimpsing Carmelita's body trembling, the pitiful expression and tear-streaked eyes pleading him to comply; the psychiatrist sighed once and looked at the floor a moment.

It's probably all an act, but I can't take the chance.

"They got us, Wu." Midnight declared as he dropped the Mauser and stood with upraised hands in acknowledgment. "We surrender."

Shade shook his head once in disgust when disarming, as soldiers moved around them to herd these captives toward the scientist and two officers for closer examination.

"So," the Professor came face-to-face with the German officer, "you're a Nazi. Aren't Hitler and his chum Mussolini doing enough to their poor country already?" "I am Major Landau, German military attaché to this project," the man released Carmelita's right arm and pistol-whipped the American once across the mouth, "we provide technical expertise for Doctor Satana's groundbreaking work here."

"I'm sorry, Carl," Carmelita kissed Krytchek's slightly-bleeding lips despite his wincing at that act right after the whipping, before she embraced and kissed Dr. Satana, "my loyalty toward the state must take priority over our past relationship."

Seeing one 'I told you so' gaze by Shade to his right, Professor Midnight licked some residual blood off that cut lower lip.

"You haven't changed, Lita. I won't ignore your loyalties again. Next time, you'll suffer the full consequences for siding with these people."

"They should both be shot immediately," Landau injected, aiming his pistol.

"There won't be a next time," Dr. Juan Jorge Satana decided, "or the quick death provided by a firing squad. Execute these spies in the lava *caverna's ahorcamiento jaula*."

Dragged away with Shade, Professor Midnight understood the last two Spanish words as 'hanging cage.'

-British Hong Kong Island, Edinburgh Plaza – July 4, 1935, 9:45 P.M., Hong Kong Time-

After crossing from the Kowloon Peninsula by ferry to Victoria, the gray-suit clad Professor Midnight tailed his quarry near the pier into that evening's bustle within Edinburgh Plaza by a hired rickshaw, the half-Japanese/Peruvian lady he sought was in another rickshaw ten feet ahead on this crowded street. Madam Inez Yohoshita took her longer route to the Imperial Japanese consulate northwest of the ferry's pier, carrying a special jade box Midnight sought for his own reasons.

The scenes to either side of his own rickshaw seemed more primitive than a major American city's sidewalk crowded with busy pedestrians, but Midnight had only traveled to the Orient on two other occasions (engaged in this globetrotting 'side career' from the lucrative Miami Beach psychiatric practice of Dr. Carl Krytchek, M.D.). The lady's rickshaw took its right angle turn, headed northwest instead of southeast onto one of the city's main roads, as the sun was almost set. Professor Midnight knew that Madam Yohoshita carried an odd artifact recently uncovered from one Amazon jungle ruin, the clear crystal wrist bracelet with strange symbol writing alien to this world. The Imperial Japanese government had similar goals as the German Third Reich about collecting unusual mythical objects reputed to contain power, arranging inspection of that item provided by this loyal South American *Nisei* agent inside their Hong Kong consulate rather than Tokyo itself.

Where'd she go?

There were only parked rickshaws ranged along that street's north side, none containing one dark-haired passenger in the green silk dress and black pumps with a large black handbag. Scanning the walkway, Midnight then spotted her bobbed haircut and its small round light-green hat moving among the similar hair colors of Asian pedestrians. Telling his driver '*mai jhau*' ('stop' – Krytchek had picked up Cantonese words during this trip), the masked American soon handed that man a five-Pound note, hurried through other walkers, and shoved irate locals aside until he saw Madame Yohoshita turn into an alley at her right. Professor Midnight reached the alley's exit and found his quarry had vanished. Watching each doorway at either side adjusting his gray fedora, the foreigner glimpsed local brutality in a connecting perpendicular alley he could not ignore.

Five Chinese men in dark-green and black fighting tunics, trousers and slippers surrounded one smaller youth, taunting him in Cantonese with occasional shoves or swings. Seeing no sign of the half-Japanese lady before or behind him, Professor Midnight then reached into his gray suit jacket's special openings with gloved hands beneath each arm for holstered automatic pistols he carried, brandishing them before directly challenging this encircling quintet.

"Hey, five versus one in any fight seems 'quite unsporting,' as the Brits might say."

The two men nearest Midnight spun in mirror images to each other, hurling small throwing knives at his pistols, knocking those weapons from both hands before he could dodge the attack. Two other Chinese then leaped through the air above their missile-wielding allies to land at the Professor's sides, the American shifting backwards barely in time to avoid blows aimed for his cranium. Knowing little of the Asian martial arts they utilized, Midnight employed street fighting tactics against his adversaries, while the other trio again concentrated on the smaller boy in the tan belted tunic, matching pants and black slippers. The hero dodged behind one roof's wooden support to avoid the next attacker's flying kick, before grabbing it to swing around and employ his own kick against the second man, missing and causing a brief scuffle. He barely heard the other ongoing 'uneven' battle.

Damn, I'm in deeper than that boy I just wanted to help, never mind losing the woman.

Midnight could not reach his pistols on the cobblestone pavement several feet away, grappling with one opponent while employing a tight headlock, until the second Chinese kicked him across the alley toward an opposite brick wall. Dazed, Midnight saw something unexpected to his left.

*That kid, he's cleaning house over there on those guys. He didn't need **my** help.*

The small boy had downed one fighter with a spinning kick, and bashed the others aside using short punches or chops, making yells with each strike and never showed fear as he awaited their next assaults. Midnight then ducked one chop meant for the throat and tackled the nearest Chinese man to collide with the second thug in mid-alley (they fell into that entangled huddle), before the American rolled right and scrambled toward his nearest pistol. The men then pulled melee weapons and sprang from the ground to get between Midnight and his lost firearms. The left warrior brandished a foot-long barbed knife, as the other whirled one of two sticks attached by their linking chain (Krytchek once heard that weapon called *nunchukkas*).

Those rods will bash my brains in, and I'd get a close deadly shave from that blade.

Crouched and prepared for their next attacks, Professor Midnight was stunned when the knife wielder's eyes widened before he was struck by one flying comrade from deeper inside that alley, dropping the weapon as the other man paused while swinging those *nunchukkas* ('nunchucks' to Westerners). During that confused pause, the American dove for the nearer pistol, fired once into the air, and half-circled the last fighter briefly after chambering another round.

"I've got a longer reach with my weapon than you using those things," Midnight added some condescending words he overheard a British gentleman employ earlier here, "understand in the King's English, my Good Fellow?"

The hero then saw his opponent react to something near the man's right side, swinging one *nunchaku* in that direction as a fast-moving tan figure, before the rod weapon was caught and then slammed against his jaw, knocking the disoriented man to the left unconscious.

"Easy there, Kid," Midnight held his fire, seeing the boy now in possession of the knife and *nunchukkas*, wielding both as if a master fighter, "I'm on your side here, just trying to help."

Realizing someone had to make the first trusting gesture; Krytchek holstered that pistol, with an eye toward the other gun a few feet off to his left. The crop-haired boy relaxed, sticking that divided-staff weapon in his tunic's own silk tan belt.

"Please tell me you speak English, Kid."

"I learn some, my Good Fellow, from our British rulers."

"Okay, but I'm American, so don't hold it against me that I share their language." The man then stepped forward with an outstretched right gloved hand. "My name is Professor Midnight, looking for a half-Japanese woman carrying one special item—"

Realizing his quarry was getting closer to the Japanese consulate every second he delayed here with the child (who now seemed older than his size first suggested), Midnight paused from shock when the boy crouched into a fighting stance and flung that blade toward the left.

Why'd he do that? Wait, I wasn't even the intended target.

Diving for his other pistol with a right-side shoulder roll, Midnight landed in the crouch, one gun ready to fire at the boy, until he heard another gunshot from behind and saw it ricochet off the cobblestones between where the American had been standing and the Chinese youth's position. Spinning, Midnight viewed Madame Yohoshita, coughing blood and swaying on her feet at the intersection (where he first spied the boy's earlier fight).

She'd doubled back, saw me and planned to end our chase with a bullet from behind.

Professor Midnight holstered the second firearm and moved forward, as the half-Japanese lady fell onto her back in the silk dress, that knife clearly through its victim's heart.

He knelt at this adversary's side, kicking her dropped 9-mm pistol out of reach across the pavement, seeing in those almond eyes that the spirit would soon depart its body.

I almost feel sorry for her.

"So, *Senorita* Inez, you just couldn't resist sneak attacking an enemy? Distracted by that fight, I might've missed your skulking away into these shadows." Coughing another blood trickle and grasping at the knife's handle, Madame Yohoshita almost seemed an innocent maiden. She stared; confused this moment was her career's end.

"I have failed my father's people, the Emperor and our honorable ancestors. You take nothing else from me here tonight, American Devil."

Using final strength, the Spanish-accented Yohoshita plunged the blade deeper through her pierced heart, making one half-scream, followed by convulsions and the death sigh. Midnight searched her black handbag for that jade box she had allegedly possessed, but found nothing.

Damn, the package isn't on her. She took its hiding place to the grave.

Professor Midnight then stood to see the boy now vanished from view, but he knew his own attention had been on Madame Yohoshita and could have missed any exit. Looking around him in each direction, Krytchek removed the gray fedora and wiped perspiration from the short black hair using a blue handkerchief out of one inner jacket pocket, frustrated by this failure.

"Hey, Mister American," the familiar high-pitched voice called as he started toward the main street again, "this thing she had you wanted, how much it worth?" The boy held up a small parcel wrapped in brown paper tied by one white ribbon.

Laughing at this good fortune, Midnight saw the boy's confusion about his reaction and held up both hands while forestalling any further misunderstanding.

"Well, it's worth a good hot meal for the finder, and a generous reward to someone's family as an added bonus. Where do they live here, Kid?"

"No family left, I all alone," the child pouted and stared at the package with disappointment until adding. "My master was killed tonight by these men. I fled, but they hunt me down."

"Gee, that's a tough break," Midnight engaged him in stepping closer with both hands down at each side to foster trust, "what's your name and how old are you, Son?"

"Wu Jan Ming is name, and was 12 on last birthday."

"Well, Wu, if you've got no particular place to go, I'd appreciate your guidance to the closest restaurant that doesn't serve British or Japanese fare. I'd promised you a meal."

Thinking over this unexpected offer, the hazel-eyed 4' 10" boy finally shook his head as the Professor urged the surrender of that package. The American then tousled Wu's dark hair and allowed his taking the lead, leaving one dead and five unconscious bodies behind. Reaching the street, Midnight untied the ribbon and unfolded the wrapping paper, finding a jade jewelry box (the lock's key later discovered hidden within its bottom compartment).

"Hey, just why that so important to you anyway, Mister?"

"I'm Professor Midnight, at least in US newspapers," Krytchek carried the re-wrapped parcel beneath his left arm as he followed in Wu's wake, "and it's supposed to contain a crystal jewelry item with strange powers the Japanese wanted. I first found out about it two weeks ago from an archeology contact in Peru."

He would use this artifact in two years, failing at rescuing Howard Philips Lovecraft from an eldritch dimension (aided by Shade and a New England sorceress called the White Arcana). Later at his Kowloon Peninsula hotel room, Krytchek opened the box to confirm its contents, uncertain if Madame Yohoshita's death had been worthwhile.

I could improve this kid's future tonight.

"You serve as my new shadow in life, Wu Jan," Krytchek confessed as they both gazed on the crystal object, "and after everything you've told me about your situation, I've decided to adopt you when we go back to the States, if that's okay."

"Yeah, okay," Wu was grateful for the full belly, even though he would have to sleep on the room's couch tonight, "with Master Han dead, and my parents gone when junk sank in storm four years ago, you need someone watching your *mou gwai tyun* as shadow."

Midnight would learn those Chinese words' meaning sometime later (roughly 'stupid foreign ass'), but realized Wu meant the description in growing, grudging affection.

-Smoke Island's Main Magma Cavern – December 30, 1938, 3:05 A.M., CET-

Professor Midnight and Shade had been disarmed and the psychiatrist stripped of his overcoat once they entered this hotter cavern and the bubbling lava pool dominating its center. They were placed inside the 6'x4'x4' stone cage attached to the thick conveyor chain passing through a wheel built into the rock face near the exit and one securing ring atop this cavern. The wheel was driven by an electric-powered motor, but also included handles for manual effort to raise the cage above that lava and another lever to lower it into the molten magma. Both dotted by perspiration after minutes here, Midnight and Shade saw few possible escape options available.

"Once raised above the pit's center, *mi enemigo*," Satana flexed black rubber-gloved hands folded together and smiled at their predicament as one guard secured the door's lock, "then you are lowered to slowly burn, prolonging that agony until death is final."

Major Landau and Carmelita were also there with Colonel Calabreese and six soldiers, four to guard the prisoners until inside the cage, and two for operating the room's controls as an execution squad. Landau seemed to bask in the heat, unable to resist bragging further.

"This project will achieve the super weapon for our Reich and the Spanish state, negating Britain's considerable naval advantages from every ocean, and in due time even that of your own decadent country. Die slowly, *Amerikaner schweinhund*." "Carmelita," crouched inside the cage, Krytchek leaned against the bars, holding on during the rough ride caused by that rising pulley chain, "I've had a weakness for exotic ladies. But what in Heaven's name did I ever do to deserve falling for some Fascist whore?"

"I'm sorry we couldn't make beautiful music together, Carlos," she almost sounded convincing, wiping perspiration from her quivering upper lip, "we're too different."

The cage shuddered to its halt at the top of the ring. The support cable took over and started lowering the object with a slower pace. Midnight saw the tortured purpose from prolonging their wait for death until that lava oozed past the cage's floor lattice, instead of giving them two quick rifle bullets. They grew uncomfortable in the increasingly warm stone structure.

"*Adios, Yanqui*, enjoy our salubrious climate," Satana led everyone out of the cavern, except two guards at the control panel right of the cable's wheel, "I must use my weapon again tonight on that British flotilla you mentioned to Carmelita, after sinking those three other boats."

"At least they left us your belt sash," Midnight whispered, before Shade checked it.

Professor Midnight stood at the locked door, smiling for the two Spanish soldiers below, as one man worked the lever to lower the cage, while the other kept his rifle pointed toward these doomed prisoners. Appearing to suffer from the heat, Shade removed his belt and then the tunic, feeling for the secret compartment holding any suitable tool to that stone lock.

"Once open, Professor, they'll start shooting at us like sitting ducks," the teenager pointed out the main flaw in this plan, "and I've not become immune to bullets since we met."

"When the door is open, you use that belt to slide down the chain and subdue those guards," Midnight rubbed perspiration off his face, judging the distance Shade would need to jump and then get clear before being shot, "and I'll follow soon as I can. If we stay, without trying to save our bacon somehow, this mission's over just the same."

"Got the one we need here," palming the curved pick, Shade dropped that tunic to the cage's floor, wrapped the belt around both hands, knelt on the cloth against heated bars and reached for the warmed granite lock, setting to work at it, "wait until I'm finished."

"Midnight unbuttoned his tie-less shirt, rolling up both sleeves, and removed the fedora as a makeshift fan. One guard offered the other a cigarette and lit both off the same match, both oblivious to Shade's efforts in assuming their captives would die.

"It's done," Shade smiled at Midnight, removing his left hand from the belt and dropping the hot tool as they both shoved the door loose with combined effort, "we go now."

"I'm getting uncomfortable in this oven," Professor Midnight saw one guard notice this small change and shifted the lever to lower their cage faster, taking the container's chain at an increased speed toward the lava, "let's leave before we're deep-fried."

Shade leaped from the cage after Midnight kicked the door outward, catching the chain and wrapping his belt over it for sliding down at an angle along metal links. Replacing his fedora, Carl Krytchek had to make a standing leap (there was no room for any running start) almost five yards for reaching the chain, as the lava's surface was getting closer.

Either I make this crossing, or I'm toasted ashes.

Midnight leaped as bullets careened off the cage and chain, missing himself and Shade as the shirtless teen caught that nearer guard while swinging off the diagonal route, kicking the man into his comrade using both feet. The Professor caught the chain with his left hand at about halfway down its length, the hero's body swinging precariously at first until he wrapped both legs around the metal, beginning an arduous quick-sliding hand-under-hand climb. Shade then executed the clockwise spinning kick at the second guard, moving the man's rifle aside and shoving him to the floor. The youth was grazed by the other guard's next shot across the left side ribs. He sprang the separating distance, just when the soldier ejected one cartridge and prepared to fire again, subduing the brown-haired Spanish man with two chops against the neck. Midnight glimpsed the dazed black-haired soldier raising his rifle toward Wu Jan from behind.

I can't let the Kid down now.

Eight feet from the ground, Krytchek forced his legs off that chain and began swinging as the Fascist guard was regaining footing, releasing the grip to fly into the target when taking aim on Shade. They collapsed together, as the rifle discharged and hit that cage's control panel, before Midnight gave his disoriented opponent one head butt and right cross. The panel shorted as the heroes saw that cage submerged into lava, relieved they had escaped.

"Are you okay, Shade? I see blood, but the wound looks superficial."

"It is, Professor," the Chinese teen winced in tying his belt against the 2" flesh wound, "but I will survive. We have more important matters now."

"Yeah," Midnight nodded as he and Shade were armed with Spanish rifles once again, "we're the only ones that can stop their terrible super weapon for world peace."

Looking into each other's eyes, realizing the act might require complete sacrifice, Professor Midnight and Shade retraced the route they were brought here from that central cavern.

-Smoke Island's Super Weapon Cavern – 3:20 A.M., CET-

Dr. Juan Jorge Satana rubbed hands together in the black rubber gloves, before straightening the long white laboratory coat and adjusting the round spectacles, peering at the master control panel to the amazing giant electromagnetic-based projector on his right, now atop this control platform with Major Landau and Colonel Calabreese flanking him. The two dozen other scientific personnel tended to various cable connections and geothermal generation equipment below this point, as twelve guards covered cavern exits. Carmelita Sanchez stood among other base personnel for observing Satana's impending triumph. At that moment, another Spanish officer hurried past two guards in one tunnel, exchanging Fascist salutes before the black-haired man ascended the scaffold stairway to reach Calabreese's side.

"*Coronel*, that British flotilla is approaching from the east, and almost within the weapon's optimum range. As *Senorita* Sanchez learned earlier, they are destroyers and frigates.

"*Gracias, Lugarteniente* Diaz," Calabreese returned the salute, "take all precautions."

"The British are in range soon." Landau looked to his left at that exchange, as Calabreese's aide Diaz departed with those orders. "Is your super weapon now prepared for its greatest test, *Herr Doktor*? I will at last witness it sinking an adversary's squadron."

"I say," Satana handed goggles to the officers and placed a pair over his glasses,"there is no time like the present. That flotilla might uncover our activities, land marines or bombard us."

The scientist signaled every other witness present to put on protective goggles they wore as he activated the super weapon's brilliant electrical charge phase. Satana started the kinescope monitor on its latticed metal stand left of the main panel, adjusting control knobs.

"Witness tomorrow's miracle," Satana smiled at the device's grainy black-&-white image coming into focus, after stepping back from it, "a picture beamed by the special iconoscope 'eye' atop the mountain at our camouflaged weather station."

This American technological ingenuity was also available in Britain and Germany, but had not yet been put to practical usage. Satana and the others could see the distant dark silhouettes on the cloudy Mediterranean water's horizon and the smoke stack plumes trailing behind them. The British were rumored to develop their own long-distance tracking system involving radio waves bounced off solid objects. This cutting edge innovation proved just as useful.

"They could become curious about this island," Landau sounded more insistent as the power buildup's brilliance subsided, "commence your test with all speed, Satana."

"Wait until it's charged," Satana seemed cool and collected, as others wiped perspiration or shifted positions removing goggles, "then watch as they all become heavier than the sea."

-Smoke Island's interior – 3:28 A.M., CET-

Professor Midnight and Shade had subdued additional soldiers, soon acquiring long-handled grenades, one rifle and an automatic pistol each. They took officer caps and jackets (Midnight storing his folded fedora inside a pocket) for tricking other guards until close enough for attack, and eventually found one tunnel leading to that big weapon's cavern.

"You still with me, Kid? And are you sure that doesn't need medical attention?"

"No, Professor, the bleeding has stopped. I am not hindered by it and can fight."

"The Royal Navy's squadron should be passing this island soon," Midnight stared at the black leather band windup wristwatch he had taken from one recent victim, "if things their Rear Admiral Roberts mentioned about his fleet's operational timetables were accurate."

"So, our main plan is still to destroy that super weapon?"

Midnight nodded and patted Shade's mid-back, peering around them to see none now noticed their presence, before telling his partner: "It's been a pleasure fighting the good fight with you, Wu Jan, and if we don't survive, I just wanted to say it once"

"The feeling is mutual, Carl," Shade addressed him as a friend, "we must begin now." The two men surged forward into the tunnel, creeping inside the shadows until they saw two guards with slung rifles facing each other at that exit. Shade ran, executing the high leaping kick that struck the right man's head, and Midnight heard the neck's snap distracting the other guard long enough to close the distance. The American pistol-whipped that next soldier, followed by a left to the stomach and kneeing his groin, before they were both spotted.

"*ALARMA – INTRUSOS*!"

Midnight and Shade then opened fire on the nearest guards, wounding two men and forcing the others to seek cover. The scientific personnel and all other bystanders sought shelter from that ensuing battle, Krytchek spotting Carmelita pulled along a catwalk with the panicked group there, before she was shoved by two additional people (one man and another woman) straight over the railing, barely hanging on as those colleagues fell screaming to the rocky ground below.

"Kill the meddlers!" Landau's eyes blazed with bloodlust when he pulled out his sidearm, Colonel Calabreese following that lead before moving to organize the remaining guards present as a scratch defense force.

"Watch, as I show how my scientific genius," Satana activated the cavern's metal roof cover and raised the weapon at the main panel, boasting, "ends Britannia's rule over the waves."

Midnight and Shade threw their first two grenades toward a lava pool nearest the weapon, splashing three charging guards with molten rock, as they fell burning in agony. The other guards reciprocated their grenades, but those heroes had already charged and crept forward toward one of the weapon's support pillars. They could hear more guards storming into the cavern behind them, and used pistols to hit two more soldiers at their front. One wounded Spaniard dropped his live long-handled grenade blowing self and two more men apart. Calabreese's right leg was injured from that blast.

"Come on," Midnight urged his ally as gunfire ricocheted on rocks behind them, "the weapon will soon be deployed outside this mountain!"

Discarding an empty rifle, Shade pistol-whipped Calabreese and then disarmed him.

"All right, Colonel," Midnight kicked the injured officer onto his back, as he and Shade took cover near a square power regulation console, before Shade shot one more Spanish soldier in the head as that man took aim at them, "I'm not letting your mad scientist do whatever he plans against Britain's ships with that thing."

Before Calabreese could reject the American's interpretation, Landau moved from behind another console ten feet away, firing his automatic pistol in rapid order. The bullets tore through Colonel Calabreese first as others hit Shade's torso, abdomen and legs. Midnight suffered a graze to the right temple since the Chinese teen shoved his mentor aside. The German's hammer clicked on an empty chamber before pulling the empty magazine to reload. Midnight returned fire, riddling that preoccupied crouched officer's upper body seconds later.

"Sorry, Midnight," Shade smiled through pain, "I did not move fast enough that time."

Professor Midnight could see from bleeding bullet placements that Wu Jan Ming might never walk again. Taking Calabreese's pistol off the floor, he gave the Chinese teen a nearby dropped rifle (five shots in its clip) before Shade returned him two long-handled grenades (of four they had left) and then his belt's last small concealed knife.

"I'm sorry this had to happen too, Kid. Perhaps you'd have been better off in Hong Kong, even as a Tong-hunted orphan."

"I regret our adventures together not one moment, Krytchek," Wu Jan flinched when bullets whizzed through the air above them, "but must hold off others now. Stop the madman from doing whatever he intends. Please go, Professor, before it's too late."

"I won't forget this, Shade," replacing his fedora, Midnight hurried to the control scaffold.

Never looking back while dodging more shots in reaching the metal staircase, Midnight soon heard explosions from Shade's grenades that hindered their attackers several seconds. Reaching Dr. Satana on the platform, the American realized this super weapon's noises were building as that device turned eastward toward the approaching British warship column.

"This ends now, Madman! Step away from that console!"

"Foolish Meddler, your nation has the seeds of greatness within it, hampered by a lack of will to dominate weaker people, and from inviting the world's mongrel refuse settling there."

"I won't say it again – move!"

"Midnight was then struck across the skull from behind and fell dazed across the metal-grilled floor. Dropping a wooden baton, Carmelita stepped over him toward Satana, where they kissed and embraced. She then reached for the disoriented Krytchek's dropped pistol.

"I loved you once, Carl, but have since desired men of greater destiny. Juan Jorge is making a better and brighter future here."

"Damn you," Midnight snatched his weapon away first, firing at Satana as Carmelita accidentally got in the way. She fell from the first shot into Satana and they collapsed against the floor, other bullets damaging the console. This caused a sudden targeting malfunction as the weapon slowly turned back into the cavern, releasing energy toward its supporting platform and the magma pool.

"You're too late, American," Satana held bleeding Carmelita, oblivious to his weapon's new misdirection, "those destroyers and frigates will join other warships I sank."

Abandoning the dying lady and her lover, dropping that empty pistol, Midnight scaled the weapon's grillwork (clear of its pulsing interior) to utilize his grenades.

I can't deactivate this contraption. Will these do enough damage?

Hearing the bullets ricochet off metal near him, minutes after seeing grenade explosions at his wounded partner's last known position, Professor Midnight was halfway up the long barrel as he spotted the cavern's top metal opening starting to close again. The weapon still discharged its effect toward the floor, frying the geothermal generation equipment and causing the platform base to sink from increasing mass. As soldiers and civilians fled exploding machinery, Midnight flung his grenades into magma near this super weapon and resumed climbing.

"If I die, at least I've saved the world from this machine."

An artificial eruption from detonating grenades sprayed equipment, generating feedback through power cables and triggering the master console's explosion. Midnight could see Carmelita crawling away from that area, but lost sight of Satana before the blast caught her. The weapon platform fell down into magma, as the American leaped onto a hanging chain, getting clear of that collapse and destruction. Reaching the stopped roof shutter, others evading the new eruptions, Professor Midnight could see little below through lava smoke. He climbed along the shutter's scaffold to grip the exit's edge with both gloved hands, rising onto the summit and a smooth false plateau. New explosions shook the island's foundations, and Midnight struggled to maintain his footing off the buckling shutter onto solid ground under this overcast night. From the rearward volcanic illumination, he spotted a square metal building two dozen yards ahead, with its mounted antennae and a strange round sphere (camera) facing east, all beneath camouflage nets. Racing there, he ignored rising lava plumes melting those shutters.

I'd say Smoke Island is blowing itself sky high.

Midnight realized he needed a way off this island. Reaching the corrugated-steel building on its raised hill, the American burst inside and subdued two Spanish scientists panicking at eruption tremors. Midnight found their wireless transmitter and signaled a Morse warning to those approaching British ships. Within minutes, the land shook as naval bombardment added to the eruption's shaking. The man fled this station with shells exploding nearer the summit. Lava now blocking nearby mountainside paths, he spotted shadowed objects tethered against the station's east wall.

Of course, they're using balloons for atmospheric readings. But could one of these carry me aloft to safety?

Returning there, Professor Midnight prepared the nearest camouflaged tethered balloon, lashed himself to its line and severed the object from a mooring railing with Shade's knife. The magma plumes doused that building after those warships ceased attacking (firepower never equaling natural destructive force). The American was carried higher into the dark sky by volcanic heat, before one sudden wind caught and moved his balloon toward the Royal Navy's battle line. Scaling the rope, Midnight utilized Shade's small sharp blade to puncture enough holes to reduce the balloon's altitude, landing across the destroyer *HMS Sovereign's* foredeck minutes later.

"Blimey, did you escape that volcano?" An armed khaki-clad British marine, among the dozen men surrounding this new arrival from the darkness, asked in genuine amazement.

Standing slowly, Midnight dropped the knife and raised both hands. Smoke Island's summit exploded, lighting up the overcast night's sky as that flotilla began rescue operations.

"Yup," he admitted before asking. "Permission to come aboard?"

-Office of Gibraltar's Naval Base Commander – 3:35 P.M., CET-

"So this Spanish weapon was destroyed," Rear Admiral Cecil Roberts sat at his desk, clad in a dress blue uniform, the graying blonde-haired man with large gray eyes sipping tea, and offered the American guest some included with 'biscuits' (cookies) on a sliver tray, "and we took every Spanish survivor into temporary custody for interrogation after the eruptions subsided."

"Except Dr. Satana, Admiral, that's assuming he could have survived." Seated cradling his fedora and clad in the soot stained attire from last night, Professor Midnight sipped Earl Gray tea and nibbled one shortbread cookie (puzzled by the British 'biscuit' label). "The crazy Spaniard tried executing me and Shade by lava inside a stone cage. It was lucky for us, since bullets would've been quicker."

Carmelita and Wu Jan will never leave Smoke Island.

"Quite, Professor," Roberts agreed, before they were interrupted by a knocking on the cabin's door, "enter."

"Excuse me, Sir," the sandy-blonde yeoman in blue fatigues peered inside, "that envoy from the States has arrived across the Spanish border."

"Send him in, Briggs, straight away."

I wonder who this could be.

Roberts stood to greet the sober-faced firm-jawed American visitor in a sharp gray suit as the man removed his matching fedora. Professor Midnight stood to shake hands, unacquainted with this gentleman.

"I don't believe we've had the pleasure. Are you with the US government?"

"In a matter of speaking, Professor, or I should say Doctor," this guest took the other armchair to Krytchek's left, as the mystery man wondered if he should remove his mask (the visitor seemed to know him); "I'm William Donovan, former US Army Colonel. Being the war veteran, former politician and attorney, I offer President Roosevelt counsel regarding foreign affairs."

The psychiatrist sized up this middle-aged graying-haired man with the East Coast manner, suspecting Donovan might be some sort of spy from those guarded admissions. The visitor then got down to business after politely accepting the Admiral's offered tea.

"Ah, thank you, Sir. Professor Midnight, I recall that label from newspapers, we have been aware of your colorful adventures for some time now."

"Yes, newsmen print an occasional reminder about my exploits to the world."

Donovan nodded agreement and continued.

"Especially after the business last year around Arkham and Providence, when you and your sidekick, Shade I believe is his name, got involved regarding the disappearance of that obscure horror writer Lovecraft."

Shade, White Arcana and I failed to rescue him from that hellish dimension.

"Yes, the authorities cleared me and my now late partner of culpability in the case."

“M-hmm, and the white-haired lady linguistics professor you worked with then, supposedly a dabbler in magic powers, had something to do with the outcome. I’m sorry your young Chinese ally didn’t survive last night, Midnight, but life goes on.”

Krytchek set his tea and half-finished cookie aside on the tray, discerning: “Should I assume, Colonel Donovan, you’re here today for reasons other than socializing?”

Clearing his throat, the bright-eyed American officer nodded, gesturing toward this mystery man in confirming Midnight’s supposition.

“I’m on a tour of Europe, having just met General Franco days ago, and heard some strange things happening near Gibraltar I wanted to confirm. Would you consider working for Uncle Sam, strictly off the record, of course?”

“I’m not a spy,” Midnight protested with gloved hands upraised in protest.

“No, you’re just a Miami Beach psychiatrist, moonlighting as the globetrotting adventurer who fights various evils and experiences more excitement and perils than most people. Your peculiar expertise could prove useful to Washington, especially if another general European war, one Mr. Roosevelt and I fear is inevitable, materializes in the future.”

This fellow is used to being in control, and thinks he holds all the cards here. Maybe I’ll play along for now.

“After today, I’m returning to my practice,” Midnight shrugged in response, “and mourning Wu Jan’s death. But I might help in special circumstances when needed, rather than be conscripted someday. There are limits regarding what I’ll do, however.”

“I’d say we’ve the start of an understanding, Sir,” William Donovan and Professor Midnight shook hands again, as Krytchek entertained one negative thought.

Holy cow, did I just make a Devil’s bargain about my future here?

About the author: John X. Grey is the more memorable pen name of Edwin R. Haney, still dwelling hermitlike in the same Southern Ohio hometown he often thinks of as ‘parts unknown’ or ‘terra incognita.’ Writing fiction since August 1999, Grey has completed nine novels (from rough to revised draft form) and fifty-two short stories or novellas, a few of those published by Aurora Wolf Press, Lame Goat Press, Leucrota Press and Static Movement in various anthologies since November 2009. Currently unemployed between day jobs, the writer still clings to his unrealized dream of professional success as an author, but believes he is coming closer to it with each accepted story for publication.

Family Secrets

Rob Rosen

Lester walked into the wall and kept right on going. Strange as that may sound, it wasn't all that unusual. For Lester, at any rate. See, Lester could walk through anything really: walls, doors, trees, sand dunes, hotdog stands, people. You name it, Lester could walk through it. It had something to do with his innate physical make-up. Seems that the atoms that comprised his body were spaced farther apart than your average person's, so that when he encountered another object, his atoms allowed their atoms to pass between. Well, it went something along those lines; Lester was never entirely sure how it all worked. He just knew that nothing ever got in his way if he didn't want it to. Literarily.

Luckily for Lester, his atoms were just barely spaced farther apart than normal. Had there been additional space between them, even a tiny fraction, any-and-all objects would have passed right through him. Clothes would go on and then fall right to the ground. Food would go in, down, and out. Chairs, beds, and couches would be unsittable and unlayable. Theoretically, Lester could have been born, passed right through the doctor's hands, then the floor, the ground, the earth, etc, etc. The thought of it gave Lester the creeps, and rightly so.

But Lester just barely had extra space between his atoms, so that he needed to push himself through other objects. He had to will it, in other words. It was an active versus passive sort of ability. Thankfully, Lester could, indeed, lie on beds, knock on doors, shake hands, pet dogs. Well, you get the drift. Thankfully, as well, Lester could also *not* go through objects, if he so desired. You see, usually he liked to keep his little talent hidden from the world. Early on, he found that it sort of made other people freak out.

It should also be noted that Lester's clothes didn't go along with him when he passed through things, and that public nudity, as he was to discover, is frowned upon almost as much as incredible feats of unexplainable trickery, such as walking through walls. Ghosts walk through walls, people do not. And they certainly don't walk around naked, at least out in public. Usually.

Still, as a child, he had his moments of fun with his abilities; though he was quick to learn the drawbacks: his mother screamed when he'd poke his head, and then the rest of his body, through the crib slats; his teacher screamed when she walked in and found half of Lester's arm buried inside the chalkboard; the lady on the corner screamed, and then promptly fainted, when Lester ran into the ice cream store while the front door was still closed, and then ran out naked as the day he was born. The list goes on and on. Suffice it to say, Lester's abilities caused a lot of screaming. In other words, the *fun* wore off right quick.

Fortunately for Lester, most people couldn't or wouldn't believe their own eyes at those moments he was having his fun. And for those who did, Lester's mother knew how to convince them otherwise. She explained that her son was practicing to be a magician. It was all done with mirrors, she would say, and then quickly walk away with Lester firmly in tow.

So you see, Lester rarely utilized his natural-born talent, once he reached a certain age. Rarely, but not never, that is. On occasion, he needed to walk through walls, especially on the one occasion near the very start of this story.

That day started off like all the rest usually did. Lester woke up, got dressed, ate some breakfast, and left for work. He never made it, though. Not even close. "Take the next right," came a voice from behind the driver's seat, which was quickly followed by a *click*, and then the feeling of something cold and steely hard against the back of Lester's neck. It didn't take a rocket scientist to figure out what was pointed Lester's way.

"Wh...who are you?" Lester stuttered, as his heart began to race hummingbird-fast, a trickle of sweat suddenly cascading down his cheek.

"You don't need to know. But we know who you are and what you can do. Oh, and your mother's waiting for us with a gun pointed at her head," informed the man, his voice gravelly.

Clearly, he meant what he said. "All you have to do is follow our instructions and nobody gets hurt. Okay?"

Lester gulped and squeaked out an okay. He'd always been afraid that his abilities would get him into trouble, though he never imagined his mother would be involved. Or that their very lives would be at risk. So, with no options, he took the next right and awaited the bad guy's directives. Minutes later, they arrived at their apparent destination.

"Out of the car," the voice commanded, and Lester obeyed. Both men got out, and Lester was pushed forward and into a rear door, which slammed quickly and loudly behind them. Once inside, he was promptly blindfolded. He never saw the man who kidnapped him, nor did he see the other two men who were waiting for him. He did, however, hear his mother's sobs, and every muscle in his body tensed at the sound, anger rising from the pit of his belly, fear a short step behind.

"Um, just so you know," Lester said, as he stood there in total darkness with his knees knocking together, "I can't steal anything for you guys. Only I can go through things. Anything in my hands will be left behind when I return."

"Yeah, buddy, we figured that out already. You're a merely okay hero, nothin' *super* about you," said another voice off to Lester's side, followed by a sinister laugh. "Anyway, you don't need to take something; you just need to memorize something. Simple as that."

"Oh," Lester said, and then sighed. His mind was going a mile a minute. What could these guys possible want with him? And did they know the other family secret? He prayed not. It might be their only hope. "Okay, just let my mom go free, and I'll do whatever you want."

"Yeah, we know that, too. So just shut up and listen," the guy to his side spat out, then gave the instructions. "You're gonna walk through the wall directly in front of you. You'll be in a room with several filing cabinets. The room is locked from the outside, not that that matters to you, but you'll obviously have no clothes on, so trying anything funny will be a definite no-no. Now, all you have to do is search the cabinets for a folder marked *Codes*. On the page inside there will be no names, just numbers listed. Look for number 103. Memorize the code associated with that number, tell it to us, and you and your mom go free. If not, or if the code isn't legit, you're both dead meat. The office opens at nine, so you have half an hour to find the file. If I was you, I'd hurry."

And that is just what Lester did. He walked right into the wall they pushed him to, with his clothes and blindfold dropping to the floor as soon as he went through, and, naked as the day he was born, he emerged on the opposite side. The room, as forewarned, contained nothing but filing cabinets. Lester started opening each drawer until, fifteen minutes or so later, he found the folder marked *Codes*, just as he'd been told.

In the folder was a single sheet of paper with a list of seventy-five numbers and codes associated with them. The numbers started at 100 and went to 174. 103 had a six-digit code next to it, which Lester promptly memorized. With fifteen minutes to spare, he decided to have a quick look around. The door was locked, but of course that was no barrier for the likes of Lester. Still, there might have been someone in the office already, and a naked man walking around would have caused a fair bit of alarm. He couldn't risk it. His mother was still in grave danger. There was, however, something else in the room that caught his eye.

He walked across the floor to a phone hanging on the wall. Marked across the paper beneath the plastic cover imbedded in the phone was the number 106. Clearly it was an extension. Lester picked up the phone. There was a dial tone, and so he punched in the code associated with 106. Within a second, Lester knew what the kidnappers' plans were. So, next, he dialed 103. Someone picked up. Lester quickly told the man on the other end what he needed to do. Then he hung up and walked back to the wall.

"Well," he whispered to himself, "Let's hope this works." Then he walked back through the wall and reemerged on the other side. The room was dark. He was quickly blindfolded again, and then the kidnappers flicked the lights back on.

"Did you find the folder?" asked the voice.

"Yep," Lester responded, already knowing what would happen next.

"And you memorized the numbers?" it was asked, anxiously.

"Yep," Lester said again, and then reeled them off. "Now let me and my mother go, like you promised."

"Wait," said the voice. "I need to test it." Lester could hear the man flicking open his cell phone and punching the numbers in. Less than a minute later, the voice said, "Okay, those are the numbers. You did good, boy."

"So now let us go," Lester pled.

The gravelly voice returned. The same one with the gun. "Can't do that. You both know too much."

"But we don't know what you look like," Lester tried to reason. Though, again, he knew it would get him nowhere.

"Doesn't matter," came the reply. "You can still go to the police and tell them what you know. Eventually, they'll figure out what happened, and that's no good. Sorry, but you both gotta die." In an instant, Lester heard the gun fire. But an instant was all Lester needed. The bullet sped across the room and went right through him, hitting the wall on the other side.

"Sorry," Lester said, but that's no good either. "What's plan B?"

"Plan B?" the voice asked, with a devious chuckle. "Plan B is we shoot your mother and then figure out a way to kill you later. Say goodbye to your momma, boy."

And again Lester heard a shot ring out in the small room they were in. But at that same moment, a door was violently kicked in and Lester heard the voices of several officers yelling, "Freeze! Drop your weapons! Hands behind your backs!"

Lester ripped the blindfold off and watched as the three kidnappers were surrounded and handcuffed. He quickly got dressed and then ran to his mother, who was seated in a chair. She too was blindfolded. The second bullet fired didn't go straight on through its target like the first one did.

"Mom, mom! Are you alright?" Lester shouted at his mother, and then tore her blindfold off.

Lester's mother opened her eyes and smiled. "Come on, son, you knew that bullet couldn't hurt the likes of me."

Lester returned his mother's smile, wiped the sweat off his brow, and then looked around the ground at her feet. The bullet had rolled beneath the chair. Lester did indeed know that the bullet couldn't squeeze its way between his mother's too-tight atoms. They were just fortunate that the men now in custody weren't aware of this. Luckily, his mother's innate abilities weren't as readily apparent as his own.

"Are you ready to go home now, mom?" he asked, his heartbeat, at last, returning to normal.

"Sure, son," she replied, with a heavy sigh. "I think I've had enough excitement for one day." Which was a gross understatement, if ever he'd heard one.

Lester helped his mom up, and then the two of them walked out of the room and into the warm, morning sun. They were greeted by a man in an expensive looking suit, looking at them in utter confusion.

"Are you the guy that called me and told me to call the police to come rescue you?" the man asked.

Lester smiled. "That would be me, sir, yes."

"And can you tell me why the President of the company that's in direct competition with my company has just been arrested for kidnapping and attempted murder?"

Lester looked to his mother, and the two of them let out a little giggle. "Go ahead, son, tell the man," his mother said, patting his back.

"They wanted the password to your voicemail. Guess they could have learned a lot from that, and you'd never be the wiser," Lester explained.

"Makes sense," the man said. "But how'd you call to warn me if you were in the same room with them?"

Again Lester looked to his mom, who promptly answered for him. "Lester walked through the wall and called you." Then she smiled at the man and nodded to her son. The truth, as she well knew, could be a heck of a lot stranger than fiction.

The man looked to Lester and then to his mother, and then said, "Okay, so don't tell me. Anyway, I'm just glad you're both okay and that jerk's on his way to jail. He used to work for me. Guess that's how he knew about the codes. Oh, and if you're ever looking for work yourself, I've got a position for you if you want it. It's the least I can do after what you've done for me. What is it you do for a living, by the way? Or are you just a full-time hero?"

Lester laughed and looked at his watch. "Actually, I'm a magician, sir. And I'm late as heck for a child's birthday party right now. But thanks for the offer, just the same."

The two men shook hands, and Lester kissed his mother before he ran back to his car. Lester's mother waved to her son and shot him a sly wink before he sped off.

"I bet he's a great magician," the man said to Lester's mother, scratching his head, a wry grin spreading across his face.

"The best," she replied, proudly. "Super, in fact. He's been practicing ever since he was a little kid. You should see his fist through the board trick. It's a real scream." She chuckled, knowingly, and shook the man's hand before she excused herself. She then walked around the corner and out of his sight.

"Strange pair," the man said, when he was once again alone. "And that mother, boy, that's some strong grip she's got."

If he only knew. Then again, he'd probably never believe it. Some family secrets are just too unbelievable to be true. Especially Lester's.

About the author: Rob Rosen, author of the novels *Sparkle* and *Divas Las Vegas*, has had short stories featured in more than 100 anthologies. Please visit him at therobrosen.com

Secret Origin of the Sack Man

Martin Zeigler

Gerald Finney took a deep breath, pulled open the bathroom door, and made a less than grand entrance into his parents' bedroom. With all the enthusiasm of a kid forced to wear his Sunday best when he'd rather be outside playing, Gerald uttered a tepid, "Ta-da."

His mother, perched on the edge of the bed, her hands folded expectantly in her lap, positively glowed. "Why, you look dashing. That fits you very well, don't you think?"

"Ma," Gerald said, giving himself the onceover, "I look like a circus act. I told you I didn't want a costume."

Seeing the downcast look pass over his mother like a thundercloud, Gerald immediately regretted his abruptness. He felt he should add something to soften the blow of his remark, but couldn't figure out what, and was relieved to see his mother's customary cheerfulness return to her face—that is, until she remarked, "Why, of course you want a costume. You're a superhero now, and superheroes need costumes."

Gerald instantly hit upon a clever response, but before he could figure out a more charitable way to phrase it, his mother canted her head slightly, touched an analytical finger to her lips, and observed, "Hmm. Now that I look at it, I do see where I need to take it in a bit. And it seems to be bunching a little at the shoulders."

Gerald considered his right arm, and then his left. "It's not the wrinkles. It's the patches. Ma, I'd just as soon be caught dead than go out there wearing these lightning bolts."

His mother smiled wanly, trying to hide the hurt. Gerald recognized the look. It was the same look she'd given him years ago, when he'd passed on her homemade ketchup, refusing even a taste. She had cooked it up for him, knowing his love for ketchup, and he had turned it down. But why had he been so adamant? It wasn't as if he'd been asked to pour the watery effluence onto his hot dogs.

And now as he thought about it further, Gerald was beginning to recall, in succession, the many other ways he had engendered this one specific look in his mother, and he felt ashamed, at least for the moment.

He sat beside her on the bed and gently placed a hand on her shoulder. She wrinkled her nose slightly and shifted away from him, and Gerald shifted along with her. "Ma, I appreciate what you've done. I really do. It looks like you went through a lot of hard work. These lightning bolts must have taken days."

"I made a pattern first," she explained stoically. "It wasn't so difficult."

"But I did tell you, didn't I? Even before you started sewing and making patterns? I mean uniforms or costumes or whatever they're called work great in comic books. But in real life, they don't look the same. In real life, you end up seeing all the...." He hesitated, searching for a delicate way to put it. "You see all the... well... bumps and stuff."

She smiled and gave his leg a pat. "Honey, you're in pretty good shape, despite what you eat. You have no...." She paused in a moment of realization. "Oh."

Gerald nodded, pleased that he had got through without having to elaborate. In fact, he was almost on the verge of believing that the bumps and stuff had put an end to this whole costume business, when his mother, with another look of hers—the hope-in-the-midst-of-a-crisis look—bubbled, "Leather!"

"Huh?"

"Maybe a sturdier material would do the job. You know, down...you know, where... anyway, leather might just be the answer."

"Leather? You mean, like, lederhosen? You want people around here to think I flew in from the freaking German town of Eisen-Schmeissen?"

"Eisen—what?"

Gerald sighed. “I made it up, Ma. What do I know about Germany, except they wear lederhosen and yodel.”

“Eisen... Eis....” His mother, still fumbling with the name, suddenly hit an epiphany. “Eyes!”

She leapt off the bed and swung around to face him. “Your mask! That’s what’s missing! I knew there was something! Where’s the mask I made for you? You didn’t put your mask on. Go... go put your mask on, honey. It’s probably there in the bathroom. You need to wear your mask.”

“What for? To hide my shame and humiliation?”

Right then and there, even before looking up at her—for he hadn’t faced her when he’d said this—he knew he had done it again.

“That’s unfair,” she pouted, sinking into the chair by her dresser. “It’s to protect yourself. Aren’t superheroes supposed to have secret identities?”

“Ma, listen. Please. It’ a mask, for God’s sake. It covers my eyes, that’s it. Friends can still tell this is my hair hanging down like this. That it’s my mole here on my cheek. And guys who made fun of my nose back in high school, once they see me on the news after I’ve thwarted some villain, will be sure to call me up in the middle of the night and say, ‘Hey, saw you on the TV there, *Ger-aaald*. Great job, Bugle Beak. But why the mask? And what’s with the lightning bolts?’”

Gerald regretted that last part, but he couldn’t help it. Those words had been gathering a momentum of their own. If his mother noticed, though, she didn’t let on. Her maternal instincts, evidently, were attuned to a more urgent matter as she looked her son in the eye and insisted, “Gerald, there is nothing wrong with your nose.”

He looked at her right back. “Not according to Dad.”

“Your father criticized your nose?”

“Indirectly.”

“What do you mean, indirectly?”

“The other day I was watching TV,” Gerald explained. “Dad put down the paper, and he said to me, ‘Gerald, I hope you’re not using your nose as an excuse to avoid job interviews.’”

“Your father means well.”

“That’s what you always say when he doesn’t.”

“Honey, don’t talk like that about your father. He wants what’s best for you. He just feels you shouldn’t be so self-conscious about talking to people because of your bulbous—because of your crooked—oh, honey, you know what I mean.”

“Yeah, I know. Because now, with the uniform, I have a better reason to be self-conscious.”

His mother slapped her hands on the arms of her chair. “All, right. You win. Let’s forget the uniform. Let’s forget how many hours I spent designing it and putting it together. All the time I drove to and from the fabric store trying out different materials, matching colors, picturing my flesh and blood soaring proudly through the clouds. And spending my own time—Gerald, I have interests, too, you know, things I’d rather be doing. It’s not all about you. I—”

“Ma, please...”

“Honestly, Gerald, what else would you wear? Have you even considered that?”

“Yes, I have, actually. You wait right here, and I’ll show you what I have in mind.”

Gerald raced out the door and down the hall into his own bedroom. In the time it takes to tear off something ludicrous and don something truly heroic, Gerald was back in his parents’ room. He’d brought his mother’s uniform with him and now shoved it in an out-of-sight, out-of-mind fashion into his mother’s half-open armoire. His mother, in the meantime, was pacing the carpet, evincing little of the joyous expectation as before.

“Ta-da!” Gerald declared with open arms, feeling much more enthusiastic than he had at his first unveiling.

She looked at him with an expression he couldn’t quite discern, something between total apathy and a complete nervous breakdown.

"That's it?" she said blankly. "Slacks? A tee shirt? Sneakers?"

"It's the simple look. For the superhero of today."

"Slacks? Whenever we go out as a family and I plead with you to dress in a civilized manner instead of in your torn-up jeans, you always find some excuse. Last time, it was the air-conditioning in the movie theater. It was too cold, you said. With loose slacks, the air would get inside your pants and freeze your legs, ruining your movie-going experience. Honestly, the things you come up with to avoid looking presentable. And now...now all of a sudden you want to wear decent clothes?"

"That's why it's so perfect," Gerald said. "No one will guess it's me wearing them."

"You actually went to the store and bought slacks."

Detecting a troublesome shift in tone in his mother's questions, Gerald said, "Ma, there's no reason to get bitter just because I don't want to wear some skintight Halloween costume. Yeah, I bought slacks. Out in Mayville."

"You went all the way to Mayville? We live three blocks from the mall. And how'd you get there? You don't drive."

"Bus."

"Did anyone help you?"

"I know how to ride a bus, you know."

"No, with selecting the pants. You've never bought any clothes in your life. Did you have a salesperson assist you?"

"Why should I?" Gerald huffed.

"Okay, then, what size do you wear?"

"What difference does that make?"

As his mother shook her head in hopeless frustration, Gerald figured, with her acting so irrationally, that now would not be the time to bring up the fact that because he had no idea what size he wore, and because he was afraid to admit it, he had purchased every last pair of pants off the store's rack and taken them all home, where he was able, in the comfort of his room, to try them on one at a time.

Money had been no object, because Gerald, believe it or not, had followed his father's advice and saved. The fact that, over the years, the money had come from his mother in the form a duty-free allowance without his father's knowledge was neither here nor there.

"And what about your mask?" his mother asked. She seemed to have put behind her the issue of the pants size.

"Simple," Gerald asserted, now back in familiar territory. "I've decided to, well, put a bag over my head. A grocery bag."

Somehow, now that he said it aloud, the idea didn't carry the same elegant genius as it had when he had formulated it in his mind. But he continued nonetheless, in the hopes that the additional information would prove how carefully he had thought this through. "I plan to cut out holes for the eyes and mouth."

His mother nodded in a way that suggested she was not in agreement. "I see," she said. "Not the mask I made you. No, sir. And no lightning bolts. Heaven forbid you wear something with a little pizzazz. Because now you're sporting the perfect thing to strike fear into evildoers and to get people's hearts a-stirring—a pair of wrinkled Dockers and a plain brown paper Shop-'n'-Gobble bag—with holes, no less."

Gerald smiled. "The super hero of today."

"And what if it rains, Mister Super Hero Of Today? One downpour and you'll be one drenched little Gerald Finney for all the world to see."

That was something he hadn't considered. But a solution presented itself immediately, surprising even him. "Simple," he declared. "Double bag."

"Double bag."

"That's when you put one bag inside another. What you do with heavy groceries."

"I know what double bagging means, Gerald, honey. I do it whenever I go out to the Shop 'n' Gobble to buy you your family-sized bags of barbecued potato chips and your cans of baked beans and your endless bottles of...." She closed her eyes as if recollecting a grim misfortune from the distant past. "Ketchup."

She let the word hang, giving it significance that Gerald found disconcerting. It seemed to suggest that, decades from now, long after he'd made his name as a crime fighter, she would still be reminding him, on a daily basis, of a certain skintight outfit into whose genesis she had sacrificed every fiber of her being.

"And what do you plan on calling yourself?" Her mother then asked. "Bagman?"

"Hey, that's close, Ma. In fact, that was one of my original ideas. Which shows we're on the same wavelength. But I've chosen to go by the name: Sack Man. You see, a bagman is a guy who does dirty work for the mob. Plus, if I ever get a—well—partner, I wouldn't want her to be called Bag Lady. That wouldn't be very flattering."

His mother softened, suddenly. Her discouragement seemed to vanish. He was her son, after all. "Partner? Female partner?"

"Of course. Why not?"

"Is it Cheryl by any chance?"

"Cheryl?"

"Our neighbors? The Colliers? They live a few feet from us? They have a daughter? The one I see you talking to whenever I come home from work?"

"Oh, *that* Cheryl. Gee, I don't know. Could be."

"Well, personally," Gerald's mother said, nodding approvingly, "I think she would make a lovely bag lady. Or what would it be—Sack Lady?"

"Sack Gal."

"Heaven help me."

"Don't worry, Ma. That's down the road a ways. First of all, she'd have to be willing to spend a night—"

His mother's hands flew to her ears. "I don't want to hear it! Please!"

"Not with *me*, Ma," Gerald corrected. "But, I mean, if she ever feels that being my sidekick is something that sounds kind of appealing, she'll have to be willing to do like I did and spend a night at the power plant, by the 750,000-volt transformers."

"And what would *she* wear?"

"At the power station?"

"No, honey, when she goes off gallivanting with you."

"Oh, probably a very, very, very, very short skirt."

"Oh, honey, that's awful. The Colliers are lovely people. How could you possibly—"

"I'm joking, Ma. I don't know yet. That's a few years down the road. I've got to prove I can go it alone first."

"Any maybe by that time you'll change your mind about the uniform." Gerald's mother didn't ask this as a question, but nevertheless raised an eyebrow at him for some hint of confirmation.

Gerald sighed. "Yeah, maybe, Ma. Maybe."

He felt good saying this, because of the way it brought to his mother's face that other look he recognized, the look of being needed and worthwhile. Never mind that if he had his way, he would never wear that uniform again even if some super foe threatened to suck out his eyeballs with an eye-suck ray.

His mother beamed. With renewed, purposeful vigor, she slapped her hands together and got down to business. "Well, until that day, let's make sure you look nice. That when you make your debut as a superhero, people will look up to you and see that you're clean and well-groomed." She took a seat once again on the edge of the bed. "Now come here. Turn around. Let's see how they fit in back."

Elated that he had won the day, Gerald went over to his mother and turned his backside to her. She tugged at his belt a few times to adjust the fit of his slacks, and then suddenly let go. He heard her muttering something. It wasn't a word, but more of a cough, and not really a cough, but a kind of gagging sound.

"Ma, you all right?"

Gerald turned slightly and watched with a puzzled fascination as his mother worked her way frenziedly along the comforter toward the far edge of the double bed, all the while gaping at him in horror, as if he were cursed.

"Ma, what is it?"

"Honey," she stammered, "when—when was the last time you—?"

"When I, what?"

"Changed your underwear? Oh, my goodness."

"Huh? A couple days, I guess. Why?"

His mother escaped from the corner of the bed and bounded toward the window, the back of her hand to her mouth. "Oh, goodness. Oh, my goodness. Goodness gracious. Two days, you said?"

"Okay, a week. What's the big deal? I was busy."

"Busy?" She reached out toward the window, threw the latch, and shoved the sash upward with a desperate muscularity. "Busy doing what, for goodness sake?"

"Organizing my comic books," Gerald said, trying to restore a sense of reason and calm to the proceedings. "I've been putting together a database, so I can access them by different search criteria."

His mother braced herself on the sill and inhaled the night air with ravenous gulps, as if having been deprived of oxygen for countless eons. "Oh, goodness me."

"Ma, you said that already."

Desiring more of that delicious air, she leaned in closer to the open window. "Goodness, goodness, goodness. And oh, my goodness. There's your father pulling into the driveway."

The panic that seized Gerald Finney rendered the state of his underpants moot. "That can't be," he stammered. "I thought he wasn't due back till tomorrow."

His mother stepped away from the window, the color having returned to her cheeks. "You know your father, how he hates business trips. He probably finished up sooner than he thought and took an early flight back."

"I know him all right," Gerald said, trembling. "And he's going to kill me."

"Oh, honey, don't be silly."

"You don't know Dad. He told me just before he left, he didn't care what job I had, just so long as I had one by the time he returned."

"He means well, honey. After all, you're twenty-three years old. He just feels you should be working by now."

Gerald shuddered at the sound of the front door slamming and his father announcing, "I'm home, everyone!"

"Ma, you haven't told Dad about my super powers, have you?"

"No, I haven't told him a thing," Gerald's mother said. And then, making a megaphone of her hand, she shouted out, "Be right down, Sweetie!"

"Because if he ever finds out, he's going to whap me a good one, and super powers or not, that'll smart like hell."

"Gerald, your father has never laid a hand on you in his life."

"Yeah, well, just wait and see what happens when I tell him there's no way I can put in eight hours and also be expected to fly over the rooftops keeping tabs on this big city."

"Darling?" Came a call from downstairs. "Gerald? Gerald, you get that job I asked you to? Oh, Gerald?"

"We better go down," mother suggested.

"Not me." Gerald went to the window, climbed up on the sill, and crouched into the open space. Facing the black, starless night and imagining that everyone in this vast city could hear him except for his father, Gerald proclaimed, but not too loudly, “Dear citizens, the time has come for you to know the name, to heed the deeds, to witness the wattage of the mighty Sack Man.’

From behind him he heard his mother say, “Mighty Sack Man, you’re not planning to go out like that, are you?”

Gripping the window frame, Gerald leaned back into the bedroom. “I’m wearing nice pants, just like you’ve always wanted me to. What’s the problem?”

“No, I mean—“ She pointed to his face. “Your mask.”

“Oh, yeah. Good point. Well, when you go downstairs can you grab a sack and bring it back up?”

“Darling!” his father called from what sounded like the foot of the stairs. “I’m coming up! I hope you’re indecent!”

The color in her cheeks even more prominent, Gerald’s mother shouted back, “No, no, you wait there, Sweetie! I’ll be right down! I’ll make you a sandwich. You must be hungry after that long flight!” And then to Gerald she whispered, somewhat frantically, “What reason could I possibly give for bringing a shopping bag up to the bedroom?”

“Tell him you have stuff for the Goodwill.”

“That’s a thought,” his mother said. She looked over at the streak of lightning peeking out from her armoire. “Some poor, destitute little boy without a penny to his name would be proud to wear a nice little suit. I bet you wouldn’t hear him complaining to his mother. And if I threw in the mask, he’d be absolutely delighted and wouldn’ grouse about it like one ungrateful son I know.”

“That’s a terrific idea,” Gerald said, thinking what a break this turned out to be and hoping the poverty-stricken waif would cherish the thing forever.

“Anyway,” his mother said, “I better go down and see to your father.”

She was closing the bedroom door on her way out, when Gerald noticed something and whispered a shout to her. “Ma! Wait!”

“Don’t worry,” she said, poking her head back into the room. “I won’t forget your Shop-‘n’-Gobble sack.”

“Better make it two,’ Gerald said, holding up a couple of fingers. “Feels like rain.”

About the author: Martin Zeigler enjoys writing fiction, dabbling in music, and taking long walks, sometimes off of short piers. His fiction has been published in various small print anthologies. He lives in Portland, Oregon with his sweetheart.

Dinner Guest

Frank Byrns

I knew who it was as soon as I heard the doorbell. I opened the door anyway.

My best friend Kenny stood on the porch, right where I knew he would be. For the first time all summer, he had brushed his hair. He even had on a clean shirt. "Is he here yet?" he asked.

I wanted to kill him. "Is who here yet?" I said, playing dumb.

"Don't play dumb with me."

I shrugged. "I don't even know what you're talking about."

Kenny frowned, the same look he had whenever he was about to punch me. I flinched in anticipation; luckily, my mom came down the stairs just then, saving me from a rabbit punch to the kidney.

"Hello, Kenny," she said, coming over to put her arm around me, embarrassing me. "I'm afraid Patrick can't play right now – we have company for dinner."

"Oh, I'm sorry," Kenny lied. "Patrick didn't tell me that."

I squirmed free of my mother's arm, glaring at my friend. "I was about to," I said through clenched teeth.

"Have you eaten yet, Kenny?" my mother asked, incredibly. "I could put out another plate, if it's all right with your mother."

"Oh, no, she's out of town at a conference," Kenny said. "I promised my dad I'd be home in a bit – we're going to heat up a can of soup together. Just us menfolk tonight."

I knew for a fact that this was nonsense – Kenny had called his mom that very afternoon for a ride home from the pool.

"That's nonsense," my mom said, eating right out of Kenny's hand. "A growing boy like you? You need a full balanced meal. Use the phone in the den and call your dad, tell him you'll be eating with us tonight."

Kenny looked down at his shoes, feigning embarrassment. He was good at this. "Oh, I don't want to be – "

"I won't hear of it," my mom said, cutting him off with the tone she usually reserved for me when I didn't want to take a bath before church, or give my grandmother a kiss on her leathery cheek. "Patrick, help Kenny make his call, then you boys go ahead and wash up. The meat should be done in a few more minutes."

As soon as my mom left the room, Kenny turned to me and grinned, nodding his head, his tongue visible between his teeth. "How'd you like <u>that</u>?" he asked.

"I hate you."

"So," Kenny said, ignoring me, rubbing his hands together. "What's for dinner?"

***

Kenny had been waiting for this moment all summer long, ever since I let it slip that Brian Nakamura was my dad's college roommate.

"No shit," he had said, dropping his ham sandwich into the tall grass beneath him, where we sat on a small hill looking down into the high school football stadium, watching the drill team work on their routine in preparation for the fall. A few of the girls were wearing bikini tops. It was a nice view.

Kenny picked his sandwich up, brushed off a couple of quick-reacting ants. He gave it a once-over, then took a bite, satisfied. "That must be weird," he said, his mouth full of Wonder Bread.

"Weird how?" I said, my own mouth full of tuna on wheat. My mom had been on a health food kick lately, and it sucked. There hadn't been a cookie or a soda in our house all summer.

"Weird how, like your dad's friend being famous and shit." Kenny had also decided to practice his swearing as much as possible before we started middle school in the fall, a would-be sailor perfecting his craft.

"I don't know," I said, chewing it over. "It's weird to me when I see him on TV, not when he comes to our house."

"Holy shit! He comes to your *house*?"

I didn't get why the idea of the weekend weatherman for Fox-5 having dinner at my house with my parents got Kenny so excited. "Dude, he's just a weatherman. He's not even the regular guy."

Kenny launched a bite of his sandwich out of his mouth, eyes bulging in an exaggerated double-take. Last summer's well-practiced skill – I have to say I preferred the potty mouth. "Just a weatherman?" he said. *"Just a weatherman?"*

I've known Kenny since kindergarten, but that doesn't mean that I always understand him. "What are you talking about?"

"You don't know?"

"Don't know *what*?"

"Oh, I see. You *do* know. You're just in on the secret. That's cool."

I was beginning to lose my patience with him. "Don't. Know. *What*."

"Come on, dude, don't give me that shit."

"*Kenny.*"

"That Brian Nakamura is really Whirlwind." He watched for my response, his eyes wide open. "You *had* to know."

"You're an idiot."

Kenny shrugged – *maybe I am*. "Your dad has to know, at least – I mean, c'mon. Asian guy, does the weather on TV? Asian superhero, controls the weather? It's so *obvious*."

I stared at him like he'd lost his mind.

"OK, maybe not obvious to *you*," he said. "Look – it's not the first time your parents have lied to you." He leaned in closer to me and lowered his voice. "And it won't be the last."

My thoughts bore repeating. "You're an idiot."

Kenny shrugged again. "*Everybody* knows."

"Yeah? Who's this *everybody?*"

Kenny shook his head – *simplest thing in the world, man*. "Everybody. The same way that everybody knows that Jamie Lee Curtis is a hermaphrodite. The same way that everybody knows that Mr. Rogers was a stone killer in Vietnam."

"*Mr. Rogers*?"

"Yep. A Marine sniper – over a hundred and fifty kills to his name. That's why he wore the sweaters. To cover up all his service tats."

"*Servicetats*?"

Kenny shook his head again – *so disappointing*. "Dude, it's like you don't even have the internet."

"The *internet*?"

"What's that saying? Two people can keep a secret, as long as neither one of them has a wi-fi connection?"

"I don't think that's how that saying goes."

"Well, whatever. All I know is, people talk."

***

That was in June. Kenny didn't bring the subject up again until a few weeks later, over the Fourth of July weekend. We were sitting on the sidewalk outside the pool, drying out in the mid-afternoon sun, our bikes on their sides in the grass. We were waiting for Gemma Matthews' older sister Marley to finish her lifeguard shift, hoping to catch one more look at her cherry red bikini top before the pool's one day closure for the holiday.

We'd been out there the better part of an hour with no luck. I was about to give up and head home when a city Metro bus rolled past, a large billboard for the Fox-5 Storm Tracker team on its side. Brian Nakamura was among them, a stupid grin plastered across his three-foot-tall face.

Kenny's eyes followed the bus down the street, then turned to me. "Let me ask you something," he said.

"Jesus, this again?"

"Now, now, no need to take the Good Lord's name in vain, I just wanted to ask you a simple question."

I sat there, staring at my friend, waiting. "So ask it already," I said finally.

"Have you ever seen Brian Nakamura and Whirlwind in the same place at the same time?"

"Are you kidding – "

"Well? Have you?"

I scratched at my forehead, staring at the grass. "No," I said. "No, I haven't."

Kenny nodded sagely. "*Exactly.*"

"Actually, I've never seen Whirlwind *at all.*" I shrugged – then another thought occurred. "By that logic, I've never see *you* in the same place as Whirlwind, either. Maybe *you're* Whirlwind."

Kenny dismissed me with a quick, violent shake of his head. "That's ridiculous."

"For that matter, I've never seen you in the same place as Kobe Bryant, either," I said, rolling now. "Maybe you're *him*, too."

"That's stupid – "

"I've never seen you in the same room as my grandfather." I tilted my head sideways. "That you, Grandpa?"

"Shut up."

"Darth Vader."

"He's not even real – "

"Jay-Z."

"Stop it – "

"Jerry Seinfeld."

"You made your point, asshole."

"I'm just saying – "

"Forget it," Kenny said, standing up. "I'm going home."

Kenny got on his back and pedaled down the street, never looking back. I felt bad. But only a little.

***

We didn't talk about Whirlwind again for a while. Then, on Monday: "You know, I read on the internet last night that white people are genetically incapable of telling Asians apart. They really *do* all look the same. To us, anyway."

We were sitting on Kenny's roof, baking in the midday sun, waiting for Greg Malthus' mom to come outside for her daily hour of backyard sunbathing next door. Kenny said that she sometimes did it topless. "Evens out the tanlines," he said.

I looked at Kenny and shook my head. Only a quick glance, though, since I didn't want to miss Mrs. Malthus stepping out onto her deck. "You're insane," I said. But it got me thinking, though, my dad and Brian on the back porch, drinking beers, saying the same thing. I always assumed that they were joking, but maybe. . . *No.*

"Insane," I said again.

Kenny shrugged. "I don't why you're always so quick to dismiss proven scientific facts, but whatever."

"And now, thanks to you, that's all I'll be able to think about Thursday night."

Kenny turned his full attention to me now, Mrs. Malthus' possible toplessness no longer a priority. "Thursday? What's happening Thursday?"

Shit. Kenny's profanity was starting to wear off on me. "Nothing," I lied.

Kenny tilted his head. "You're seeing Nakamura on Thursday?"

I looked up, squinting into the bright summer sky. "Man, is it that late already?" I said, as if I could tell time by the sun. "I gotta be getting – "

"What, you're going over to his *house*?"

"No," I said quickly. Too quickly, in fact, as I was overly eager to say *anything* truthful in this conversation.

I looked away from the sun and back at Kenny, who swam in and out of my now-spotted vision, a knowing smile on his face. "Whirlwind is coming to *your* house."

Never a quick thinker, I held out one of my rapidly-pinkening forearms to Kenny. "Look at this – I told you we should have used some suntan lotion – Hey, how much lotion do you think Mrs. Malthus is going to be using – Can't wait for that, huh – it's gonna be awesome."

"So, Patrick," Kenny said, ignoring my idiotic rambling. "What time are we eating on Thursday?"

***

"This brisket is delicious, Mrs. Baskett."

Kenny dabbed the corner of his mouth with his napkin, the perfect gentleman.

"Thank you, Kenny – I wish it were that easy to get a compliment out of Patrick sometimes."

I kicked Kenny in the shin under the table – *hard.* He choked down a scream.

"We're only having meat because there's company here," my dad said. "Ordinarily, we'd be eating a big bowl of grass and leaves." He looked around the table for confirmation, and, getting none, stumbled on. "Once school starts back, we'll be lucky to get Hamburger Helper, or a frozen pizza – and I for one can't wait."

I couldn't agree more – my mom taught third grade, and spent every summer vacation trying to turn back the clock into some sort of Susie Homemaker lifestyle. This summer was healthy, home-cooked, hormone-free meals – next year she might be vacuuming in pearls and pumps.

"You could try cooking something yourself sometime," mom said thinly.

"Oh, I don't think any of us want that."

I couldn't agree more with that one, either. Mom's annual June trip to Houston for an Educator's Conference was the worst week of the year. My dad could have just played it smart and ordered a pizza, but <u>no</u>; he had to be a 'modern' man and cook dinner for the two of us. Which he promptly ruined, every time, leaving us to order a pizza anyway. Every time.

"Oh, God forbid," my mom said, her eyes rolling towards the ceiling as she poured herself another glass of wine.

"So, Kenny," Uncle Brian said from across the table, in his impossibly smooth, deep television voice. "You boys are starting middle school in a couple of weeks?"

"Yessir," Kenny said, his teeth still clenched.

"Boy, how the time flies. I remember when this one –" Brian pointed at me and winked – "I remember the day he was born. I was there, you know, out in the waiting room."

"I did *not* know that," Kenny said.

Brian looked at Kenny, then at my dad. My dad just shrugged.

"If you don't mind, sir, I'd just like to take this chance to tell you that I love your work," Kenny said.

"Thanks, Kenny, always nice to meet a fan." Brian said this without looking at Kenny, narrowing his eyes instead at my father.

"In fact, I find it inspiring. I hope to one day follow in your footsteps."

"That's nice of you to say – you know, the station has an internship program for interested students. If you're still interested when you're a little older, I'm sure that I could put in a good word – "

"Oh no, this is embarrassing," Kenny said, somehow *willing* his cheeks to redden. *How does he do that*? "I was *actually* talking about your other job."

I sighed heavily, and banged my forehead against the edge of the table.

"Patrick!" my mother said.

"Oh, I'm sorry," Brian said, raising an eyebrow at my father. "When you said you were a big fan, I just assumed you were talking about the meteorology. I've never met anyone who considered themselves a fan of my other work."

Kenny nodded – *a perfectly understandable misunderstanding*. "Sure. But like I said – *inspiring*."

"Uhm, Kenny, you *do* know that I edit science textbooks during the week, right?" Brian's eyes were pleading with my dad for help. My dad took another pull on his beer, clearly enjoying the show.

Kenny nodded again. "Sure. Among other things."

I banged my head again.

"Patrick! What in the *world* is the matter with you?"

My dad finally decided to add something to the conversation: "Do that again and I'll break my foot off in your ass."

I sat up immediately – Henry Baskett was not a man of idle threats.

Now my mom was unhappy with everyone (except maybe Kenny): "Really, Henry, is that sort of language necessary at the table?"

"Sorry, dear," my dad mumbled, pulling at his beer again.

"Boy, *this* is exciting," Kenny said.

I kicked Kenny under the table again, as hard as I could this time, a little higher, right in the kneecap. A muffled scream leaked out of his mouth, like helium from a pinhole in a balloon.

"Everything OK, Kenny?" my mom asked.

"Mmm-hmm," he said, his mouth clamped shut in apparent fear of what could escape.

"Well," Brian said, standing up, his palms placed flat against the table. "Joanie, it was delicious, as always, but I really have to get going."

"Long night ahead," Kenny whispered, nodding.

Polite table manners went out the window at this point. "What's with your friend?" Brian said, looking directly at me.

I banged my head.

"Patrick!" My mom and dad, in unison, together again.

"OK. Well, like I said, I *really* have to get going. Henry, I'll let you know about the ballgame next week?"

Kenny stood and limped over to Brian, offering his hand. "So nice to meet you, Mr. Nakamura."

Brian took Kenny's hand and pumped it twice, bewildered. "Pleasure's all mine, Kenny."

Brian made as if to pull his hand back – but Kenny wasn't ready to let go quite yet. "So I'll call you at the station about the sidekick thing?"

Brian snatched his hand away from Kenny, like a man caught in a bear trap. "The internship program?"

Kenny winked. He actually, honest-to-God, *winked*. "We can call it that if you want."

Brian ran both hands through his hair. "Uhm, good night, everybody."

He had his hand on the doorknob, pulling it open, before Kenny spoke again. "Mr. Nakamura?"

Brian's shoulders sagged deeply. "Yes, Kenny?" Brian seemed afraid to turn around, but did so, anyway.

"I just wanted you to know. Your secret's safe with me."

Brian looked up at my dad, who turned his palms over, shrugged, and shook his head – *You got me, buddy*. "Hey, man, thanks for coming," my dad said. "Next time bring a date."

"What, and subject her to *this*?" I added.

"Patrick!" my mom said again, just as my dad smacked me in the back of the head so hard I saw stars.

Without another word, Brian slipped out the front door, and just like that, he was gone.

"Man, he's fast," Kenny said. "Like the *wind*."

"I think it's time for you to go, Kenny," my mom said. Rather graciously, I thought, all things considered. She opened the door and ushered him out, a firm hand steering the small of his back.

"I just want you guys to know how touched I am that you trust me enough to have me over tonight like this," he called over his shoulder. "I don't want you to worry about the tabloids showing up. Or Fox-5, or anybody like that. 'Course, they probably already know. They'd have to, wouldn't they?"

"Good night, Kenny," my mom said, shutting the front door in his face. She turned and stared and me.

My dad smacked me in the head again.

"What'd I do?"

About the author: Frank Byrns lives and writes in suburban Maryland. His third collection of superhero short fiction, *Things to Come*, was published in 2009, joining *Requiem* and *My Father's Son*. He is also the editor of *A Thousand Faces, the Quarterly Journal of Superhuman Fiction*. Visit him online at frankbyrns.com.

Space Scouts

David Perlmutter

In this universe, disorder and chaos abound. The enforcement of justice, therefore, must be handled with care by people who are well-versed in the art of mediation and law enforcement. Alas, those kinds of people do not exist on Earth, so it is up to us to do it. My name is Portia, and I am a Space Scout.

You should be familiar with the basic concept of our organization, for your planet has many paramilitary groups of minors similar to ours. The difference is that we, rather than confining ourselves to badge-earning or selling cookies, enforce from our interplanetary base of operations the name and word of the law as we, and only we, define it. Because we are Scouts, we think and act correctly- *always*. Anyone who does not agree with us, particularly those smelly boys and men who cause the majority of our problems, gets swiftly annihilated.

I am a Space Scout, 1st class, and command a unit of three who operate in the area which comprises what you Earthlings refer to as the Milky Way. My uniform is similar to what many of your scouts wear: a blue blouse, skirt and beret with white shoes, having the appropriate hash marks on the side to designate my rank. When I get my blond-haired, black-eyed self into it and get to work, I am in complete and total Zen.

I am assisted at all times by my associates, Corporal Dulcinea and Petty Officer Hortense. Dulcy, as we usually call her, possesses ashen red hair and dark eyes like mine. She is unique among the Scouts in that she can bench press ten times her own weight. Most of us can barely do two, and my own ability to do five is somewhat rare. This is one of the few things I envy her for; usually she envies my superior intellect, since her own is... inferior to mine, and she is also unable to sustain objectivity the way I do. I rarely, if ever, show my emotions on duty, like a good Scout. The third member of our group, Hortense, is our resident strategist and interpreter, since she can read and interpret any language known to man and alien, a handy trait that most of us are expected to have to some degree. Hortense is also capable of understanding the true emotions of people on sight, regardless of the level of subterfuge employed by an opponent, another valuable trait. She is an albino; the only color related to her is her uniform. She is very shy and does not tend to associate with the other Scouts much, myself and Dulcy excepted. She is also unique in being unable to lift her weight in anything, but she makes up for it by being the most intelligent- and overly conscientious- of the three of us, which can be both a positive and a negative trait at different times.

Together, we comprise a unit that is fearless and efficient in enacting our duties, as our enemies well know. The following is one of our exploits, to give you just a hint of what we do and what we are capable of doing:

On November 8, 2007, the squadron leader called me into her office to brief me on a new assignment.

"What's up, Ophelia?" I asked.

"Trouble on Tiberius."

Tiberius has always been the place where we have been forced to intervene most. In the past year, we were sent there more than to anywhere else combined. The immense size of the planet's population, coupled with the passionate militarism and stupidity of its residents, are key reasons why we have to keep bringing our brand of "enlightenment" to it. They still haven't got it. They don't own this galaxy. We do.

"Yeah." Ophelia replied.

"Who's responsible?" I queried.

"The Tiberian Broadcasting Corporation."

"What's wrong? I thought they were clean."

"Not anymore, they're not."

"What happened?"

"The old ones are easing out. And the younger ones are sticking their fingers in the sockets. No good."

Ophelia sighed. I knew what was going on, so she didn't need to explain it to me. But you need to know about it.

You see, the residents of our galaxy, bordering yours, are unique in that we, with some freakishly abnormal exceptions, do not age physically past the age of thirteen. However, our brains, which can be dislodged and placed into new bodies when and if necessary, reflect our natural and more advanced ages. This allows us to continue our duties in new bodies should our old ones get destroyed in battle, a rather convenient way of confusing our enemies.

Because we don't advance past thirteen in terms of our physical appearance, we consider it the premium age of intelligence and sophistication. Therefore, every person past that age physically, by our standards, is an idiot. Because most of the people on Tiberius are well beyond this age physically, you can just imagine how we feel about *them*.

But to continue. We had much to fear from this new generation of fiends from Tiberius. Not only did they fail to respect the traditions, morals and ethics of their elders, but they also had no sense of the world beyond their own faces. For this reason, we had become diligent in confronting the grave menace they posed to everyone in the universe. When I knew of their infiltration of the most venerable public broadcaster in the galaxy, the one most likely to disseminate the proper messages of empowerment we want our associates to express, I got worried. Rare for me, so that's a sign of how bad it was.

"We have to stop them!" I said instinctively "There's no telling what those demons could do if they get control of the whole network!"

"Why do you think I called you in?" said Ophelia.

"My unit and I will take care of it." I replied firmly. "There's no way that those uneducated mental inferiors will keep broadcasting on media they don't know how to use properly so long as the Space Scouts are around!"

"You know they won't give up without a fight," my commander warned me as I exited the room.

"That's what I expect." I returned, with as little emphasis as I could muster during the situation. "In fact, I'm counting on it!"

I gathered up Dulcinea and Hortense, and we flew to Tiberius promptly. And I don't mean in an airplane.

The TBC building soon stood before us. Getting admitted was no problem for us. Apparently, they get a lot of visitors and, though we resented their patronizing attitude, we were used to such treatment on account of our appearance. Until they learn to treat people of our appearance with more civility and respect, Tiberius will never evolve to their proper and useful mental potential.

Our first target was the offices of what had once been one of the best comedy shows on television anywhere but one which had fallen on hard times since they had been forced by network fiat to bring young people into the cast. We were to track down and arrest Crack Lousy, one of this newer breed, for the crimes against good taste he committed while in the envelope of this institution. Lousy was particularly dangerous to us because he was a sketch comedy expert and able to assume any guise he wished. We could only hope that we could stop him before he could assume a disguise that would allow him to best us in some way.

When we encountered him, he was practicing his teeth-grinding impersonation of the planet's Prime Minister. Evidently, he was plotting to capture said individual and install himself in his place. In reality, he was a lonely and bitter young alien who was using the manipulation of an audience to succeed at the expense of enlightening them.

When we called his name, he turned around, looked us over, and insisted he hadn't ordered any cookies.

Dulcy wanted to kill him for that slight, but I tried reasoning with him, and I signaled

Hortense to hold her back, if she could.

"Lousy, you're on thin ice with that attitude!" I snapped at him.

"Why should I be afraid of *you*?" he returned, arrogantly. "You're not cops!"

"We're SPACE SCOUTS!" I rejoined. "And our job is to handle malfeasants like you, regardless of who, what and where they are!"

"What's a *malfeasant?*" he shouted, revealing his ignorance.

"Have you an *education*?" I requested.

He was nonplussed.

"No!" he answered "So stop *riding* me!"

"We'll ride you ALL WE WANT!" I replied "Our authority is greater and more all-encompassing than any "law-enforcement" group on this planet or any other! Our decisions about you are not simply charges you can bargain out of with your accredited agents of the law. When we tag you a criminal you are marked for immediate destruction, with absolutely no chance of your escaping. If you're willing to change your ways, then we'll let you go, but if you aren't, we have full authorization to kill you on sight!"

"What have I done to get you on my back like this?" he said, trying to be reasonable. "I'm just a comedian!"

"You're not *just* a comedian, sir!" I retorted. "You are an ANARCHIST! You use the label of "comedian" to get people to pay attention to you, to laugh with condescension at exactly the same things you would laugh at, or you would have them laugh at *for* you. Keep on burning your bridges like that and soon *nobody* will laugh with you- only *at* you."

"You're asking for it, you little brat!" he responded, with an uncivil tongue.

"Nice talk-from an unfunny comedian!" I returned.

"WHAT DID YOU JUST SAY?" he screamed.

Now, I know from experience that the last thing a comedian wants to hear is that he is not funny. Generally, a variety of results can be expected, but anger and rage are perhaps the most obvious. Lousy looked like he was going to burst a blood vessel after I uncorked that one. He jumped at me with the intent of ripping me and my colleagues apart, but I had already motioned to Dulcinea to do her thing. She dropped him quickly, ripping his arm and then his head off in quick succession. The removed body parts were deposited into our gunny sack to be exhibited in our Space Scout headquarters as a warning to any would-be malfeasants.

"Impressive." I said. "No quick blood flow this time."

"I get it done quick-like always." said Dulcy.

We still had some other miscreants to deal with, though, and soon we were on the way down the hall to the radio studios. The reason for our trek there was simple and precise. What had occurred was that the network, in its efforts to continue getting its customary large sums of cash from the planetary government, had begun mirroring the government's "police action" in the wilds of Athabaska by hiring a bunch of stiffs and hacks to stand in a studio and pretend to be soldiers. This is something we Scouts neither accept nor condone, since we have all faced to a certain degree exactly the kind of warfare which these cretins were faking on a twice-weekly basis. War is a life experience to us. I have the campaign ribbons and war wounds to prove it, as do my colleagues and friends, from many an interplanetary war and political campaign against injustice and tyranny. No level of technical expertise in a radio studio can possibly replace the experience and dedication of the real soldier in action. Even to attempt a simulation of this dedication by outsiders who know absolutely nothing about it is an expression of the greatest arrogance imaginable.

For this reason, our march down the hallway was particularly brisk and passionate. We ignored the battery of signs warning us that their precious program was being recorded and entered the studio. I commanded their attention, only to be hushed by a rather snotty-voiced engineer. Noticing that the big red "RECORDING" sign had been turned on, I motioned to Dulcy to take it out. She promptly advanced on it and, to the shock and astonishment of everyone save me and Hortense, smashed the glass, pulled the red light bulb from its socket, and threw it at the producer and writer in their comfy chairs at the control panel.

"We're talking to you, jerks!" she snorted.

The producer, an arrogant-looking female, got up and shook with the fury common to her type of Tiberian.

"What do you kids think you're doing?" she snapped.

"Madam, we are not 'kids'!" I replied. "We are duly commissioned Space Scouts, designated to disarm and shut down any individual and group deemed by us to be in violation of the laws of morality. By this authorization, we have come to shut down this flagrant misrepresentation of the arts of war!"

The writer, a small, emaciated looking fellow, was quickly on his feet.

"Athabaskanaadabananastan" is *not* a flagrant misrepresentation!" he spat out at me, in such a manner that a fair amount of his saliva ending up landing on my nose. "We have an *actual soldier* as a technical consultant!"

"Besides..." added the producer "...the TBC does not accept this kind of direct input from the public. If you're willing to perhaps send an e-mail, we might be able to..."

"Both of you will SIT DOWN and SHUT UP IMMEDIATELY!" I screamed.

They did so.

"Now understand this." I continued, with a greater level of calm in my voice. "We are professional soldiers, and we understand that you media people take great pride in the level with which you can create 'accuracy' in your productions. And, to a degree, you are able to succeed in spite of your limited resources. However, the creation of scenarios based on actual events, which are so clearly designed to enflame the most ignorant and prejudiced people who live within your boundaries to persecute creatures unjustly painted as "the enemy", is a situation we will not abide. Your generation of human beings is unable to create realistic narratives of war because you are totally unacquainted with the realities of war. War, madam, may be something as abstract and unimportant as a cheap potboiler for public consumption for you, but for people who have actually experienced it, IT IS NO JOKE!"

My tirade left the producer and writer speechless. The actors, enclosed in the recording booth around the microphone, had also heard it, and were making their way towards us.

"The petty internal conflicts you're trying to deal with here don't matter to us," I reminded them. "You must cease and desist immediately. We demand that you shut this infernal production down or you will face the consequences."

"The day we take advice on programming decisions like that from you *civilians* is the day hell freezes over!" replied the producer, arrogantly. "This show is going to be on the air for a long time, whether you like it or not!"

By this time, Dulcy had clenched her teeth and was patting a fist against her left hand. I knew what that meant.

"Can we kill them now, Porty?" she asked.

"Yes," I said, through clenched teeth. "This is the *perfect* time!"

And before they knew it, that bunch of fools was in a hell worse than any they could possibly fake on the air.

Next up on the list of people we had to eliminate was a little green protoplasmic form named J. N. Gitcheegoomee, who had apparently gained a twice-daily radio timeslot. On his "show", he could mumble nonchalantly about topics he and only he was interested in, related to what little existed of the "arts" scene on Tiberius. A more egotistical windbag could not be found elsewhere on the radio transcriptions of Tiberius.

Before we commenced the operation, however, Hortense filed an objection with me about the gore we had inflicted on our previous rounds. She suggested, with tactful respect for the superior rank of her colleagues, that we try to find a more subtle way of eliminating our next target.

"Doesn't it seem a bit excessive to you two that we kill these people on sight?" she asked "We could easily transport them back to base for a fair trial, couldn't we? It would save us a lot of paperwork- and bloodshed!"

"You forget who is the sergeant here!" I reminded her in gentle but firm tones "When you have your own unit, you can proceed as you wish, but under my command you will proceed as ordered."

"But do we really have to *kill* them?" she persisted "Couldn't we try talking with them?"

"That's what they *want* us to do!" Dulcy seconded me. "But we don't want to do what they want us to do, or else they'll force us to do what they want us to do and we can't force them to do what we want them to do. Got it?"

"Most of it." said Hortense. "But I still think..."

"Enough out of you!" I snapped. "We were instructed to *terminate* these people, and that's exactly what we're going to do!"

And we proceeded to do that, entering Mr. Gitcheegoomee's studio while he was in the midst of broadcasting his one-and-a-half-hour ego trip, "Coup". We had been warned about two things related to him: first of all, that he talked faster than most stenographers can type, making him difficult to understand at even the best of times. Second, that he surrounded himself with a phalanx of sycophantic producers whose very jobs and lives depended upon him, and who would give those very lives in the name of protecting him. We were to observe both in short order.

As soon as we began to approach his inner citadel, that previously named phalanx of producers quickly surrounded us. The idiots seriously thought they had a chance of destroying us but, like all Tiberians, their vainglorious bark served to reinforce the ineptitude that inhibited what little bite they had. After a moment of this folderol, they had severely tried my patience and I silently instructed Dulcy to discharge the contents of the nearby fire extinguisher upon them. This was done, and the fools scattered away in panic like the sheep they were.

We soon entered the inner fortress of Mr. Gitcheegoomee and heard him in the midst of speaking with typical inane nonchalance as we approached his booth.

"Hi, there. I'm J.N. Gitcheegoomee and this is 'Coup'." he seemed to be uttering. "You know, I'm so glad to be a Tiberian because we rock harder than any other planet in the galaxy. We kick anybody's ass when it comes to music, film, television and everything else. I think it's high time the galaxy got down on its knees and begged us to spare them from the onslaught of cool which only we on Tiberius can deliver..."

At this point, the door was kicked open by Dulcy and we entered.

"It'll be a cold day in hell before the Space Scouts allow you to continue this reign of jingoistic nationalism, you self-absorbed little fool!" I shouted at him.

"Don't talk to me like that!" he spat out with an awe-inspiring rapidity. "I'm better than you 'cause I know the arts scene better than..."

"Shut up!" I commanded. "What you are is an intolerant nationalist who assumes everything on your planet is the greatest thing ever produced, when more likely the opposite is the case. Have you no knowledge of or interest in the work of other countries? Other planets? Other galaxies? You should, because their work will always matter *considerably more* than the trivial tripe which you seem to think everyone is interested in. It is simply you and you alone who are interested in it, and you who force-feeds it to the rest of your countrymen by means of your so-called charm!"

Gitcheegoomee sprang from his chair towards me, intending to do me grievous bodily harm. His ropy tentacles sprung at me in all directions, but I deftly used my speed and agility to avoid them. Quickly exhausted, he returned to his seat and continued verbally attacking us.

"Look, you guys," he said very quickly "I'm not giving up my career simply because you think I'm biased, okay? I have a contract with the TBC, and they want me to promote Tiberian culture 'cause it's better than anything else. Besides, you little kids wouldn't understand my complicated thought process anyway..."

Dulcinea grabbed him and smashed his head into the control panel.

"Don't call us kids, you self-centered little ELITIST!" she commanded.

He recovered almost immediately, due to the surprising thickness of his head, and continued his arrogant tirade against us further.

"Okay, that does it!" he slurred "Get out of my studio! I can't believe mothers like yours would let their kids run around in broad daylight and bully people like that in order to get..."

Dulcy grabbed him by the throat and choked him while pulling him down to my eye level, where I shot back at him.

"First of all, *sir*..." I said. "we have no 'mothers'. On our planet, we are fully formed, mature adults, with an ethical and moral sense superior to anything you Tiberians could possibly obtain. Second, we are *not* bullies. We are enforcers of our own brand of law, a law that excludes no one, especially not arrogant fools like yourself who falsely believe broadcasting elevates them to a status akin to deification!"

"Did you swallow a dictionary or something?" Gitcheegoomee replied "'Cause you couldn't possibly be this smart at the age you're at!"

"Oh." I said "and my "age" is some kind of barrier to you, is it? What kind of society is your Tiberius? One where people are not allowed to succeed based solely on some abnormal, freakishly defined barriers that place you within a totally obtuse social structure? In my territory, sir, it is actual wit, intelligence and thoughtfulness that matters in the world, not the immature, fast-talking posturing you seem to assume is of value in promoting the half-witted "culture" of your native land. You are a disgusting, exploitative, filthy creature who should be exhibited in a cage like the freak of nature you are! WHAT DO YOU THINK OF THAT?"

"I'm supposed to be asking the questions around here, you..."

"Shut it!" Dulcy answered, cuffing him around the neck With a potent squeeze she twisted his head sideways on his neck. He quickly used his protoplasmic form to wiggle out of her arms, but we were prepared. Drawing our Swiss Army knives, we dislodged the sharpest blade and quickly stabbed him at his pressure points. There was a slow, virtually inaudible moaning sound as Mr. Gitcheegoomee faced a death as rapid as his typical pattern of speech. He uttered nothing, save the slowly descending tones I have come to expect to hear from a dying alien. When we had finished our attack, the cold corpse fell to the ground.

There was one bit of business that needed to be fixed. I motioned to Hortense, and she promptly approached the microphone and uttered the phrase we had rehearsed for this event:

"One moment please."

***

We had to hurry onward in order to destroy our final target, since its taping was to begin fairly soon. This was a surprisingly popular comedy program called "The Rebaters", in which untalented alien "stand-up comedians" thoroughly debased the noble act of debating. They followed the formal procedures of debate all Space Scouts are fully instructed in, but used said structure as a forum for inflicting their cheap and racist "humor" on an unsuspecting public. That they performed these tawdry routines in various states of inebriation and hallucination only made things worse.

We did not reveal ourselves immediately, but simply presented ourselves as ticket-paying members the audience, one full of idiots and hicks. Clearly, these stupid fools were to be entertained only by a base level of poppycock; anything more sophisticated would obviously be far above their heads.

This was made most obviously apparent when the show began. A gap-toothed, stupidly-grinning creature introduced the show by [barely] playing the guitar, at which time another such nitwit took the microphone to introduce the program.

"HEY, EVERYBODY!" he shouted into the microphone. "I'M A STUPID IDIOT WHO DOESN'T KNOW WHEN TO SHUT HIS FAT MOUTH! ON MOST PLANETS, I'D BE CONFINED TO AN INSANE ASYLUM, BUT ON TIBERIUS, I'M PERFECTLY QUALIFIED TO ANNOUNCE RADIO PROGRAMS - LIKE THIS ONE, "THE REEEE-BAAAATTEEERS!"

The audience, except for we three, exploded in laughter and applause.

"AND NOW..." continued the jerk "HERE'S THE RINGMASTER OF THIS CONVULUTED CIRCUS, SPEEEED PABLUMSON!"

This was the host, a shambling, green-skinned illiterate who entered holding an open liquor bottle. That gives you an idea of the oh-so elevated tone the proceedings were to take.

As if things couldn't get any worse, they did. The "debate" portion of the program commenced. Topic: "Do We Really Need Law Enforcement?" (We Scouts naturally were enraged by the fact that anyone would *dare* consider this idea, but we kept our cool for the moment.) The two "debaters" entered soon afterward. The pro side was supposedly taken by Mr. Pablumson's green-skinned countryman, Booger Face Johnson, a backwoods rube with an entirely inarticulate speech pattern, and the anti-side by Alberta Brown, an arrogant purple-skinned woman in an oversized cowboy hat. Like the host, they were not sober whatsoever.

The "debate" continued for a little while, both combatants "talking" for a few minutes under the haze of alcohol. They could barely be understood by us but somehow the audience got it, being the morons they were.

Finally, I'd had enough, not only of the program but of the whole horrible network. I leaned in to Dulcinea and Hortense and commanded them to unpack our secret weapon: the portal. I could see my colleagues shudder for they, like I, clearly knew the power of the portal.

The portal is by far our most powerful weapon, for it is one of the most potent connections between our world and yours. Just off our planet is a well-guarded, impenetrable facility on an island moon to which we deliver the most unredeemable criminals who have ever set foot in this or any galaxy. Nobody is able to escape this enclave once they enter, and the portal is the only way to enter the place for those who are not members of the Space Scouts. The portal and the prison are the bedrock of our authority, and it was high time that these fools knew we meant business.

I rose from my seat, followed by the others, and stalked to the front of the stage, whipping the microphone out of Pablumson's hand. He protested drunkenly, and he, Johnson and Brown attempted to attack us, but we quickly subdued them. Then I addressed the audience.

"Ladies and gentlemen..." I said solemnly "we of the Space Scouts have determined, through our moral authority over this galaxy, that this "entertainment" program is to cease here and now, FOREVER! Comedy certainly has its good points, but it cannot, it will not, and it should not be used as a forum for serious social discussion. When exactly did you determine that comedians had an authority greater than the duly elected leaders of your countries and the professors of your universities to decide what the vital issues of the day really are? These *vipers* are no more qualified to discuss these affairs than infants! And so I say to you, return to your homes immediately, before you risk invoking our wrath!"

The crowd did not choose to heed my warning; rather, they rose as one and moved towards us, seemingly with the intent of lynching us. That was all I needed to act.

"Turn on the portal!" I ordered my colleagues.

They did. The strobe light was turned on, and quickly began to emit the gale force winds and ectoplasmic energy so common to these dimensions between worlds. As we temporarily fled the room, the prone bodies of Pablumson, Johnson and Brown and the captive, sub-human audience were transported completely and directly to our prison moon. Our mission completed, we packed up and left.

"See" I said to Hortense as we left the building. "We didn't kill *everybody!*"

"Thank you!" she said, respectfully but with a detectable hint of sarcasm. I'll have to be more careful around her in the future.

As we flew home, I contacted Ophelia via satellite image phone watch and informed her of our success in achieving our objective.

"Hopefully, they won't give us any more trouble." I said.

"It would be good if they got the message." she concurred "but you don't know with these Tiberians. It takes them *forever* to get ethics and proper manners through their simian skulls."

"We can only hope that this little episode will get the TBC on our side, at least." I said.

"Amen to that, I hope." she replied.

"And if they don't, we'll have to come back!" interjected Dulcy.

And we laughed.

That's all for now. Don't make us come to deal with you - or you'll regret it!

About the author: David Perlmutter is a freelance writer and university graduate student living in Winnipeg, Manitoba, Canada, where he has lived his whole life. His passions are American television animation, literature (especially science fiction and fantasy) and music (rhythm& blues, soul, funk and jazz.) This explains why much of his writing is as unconventional and defiant as it is. He is challenged with Asperger's Syndrome, but considers it an asset more than a disability.

Super Cleaners

Michelle Ruckoldt

Wyatt Epstein met Lydia Day while he worked. He pulled the cleaning van up at a house with a neat, colorful garden and a caved in roof. As he parked at the curb, he tsked.

Yeah, a Super Hero has been here, he thought, and prepared to call his contractor.

The woman who answered the door was startlingly beautiful. Her hair was short, black, and fashionably messy. Her eyes were wide and blue. Her figure was ample in all the right places and spare where it wasn't ample. There were tears on her face. Wyatt had seen many women cry after they'd had their roofs torn off by Super Villains.

"Good morning," Wyatt said, smiling in his most trustworthy fashion. "My name is Wyatt Epstein. I own Super Cleaners."

The woman sniffed and said, "Please, come in. Captain Amazing has trashed my house again."

Wyatt blinked at the "again." "Okay," he said. "I'm glad you called. I'll have this cleaned up in a jiffy. Where would you like me to start?"

The house, as Wyatt stepped inside, was a mess. One of Captain Amazing's Super Powers was the ability to make a storm with himself as the eye, and it looked like he'd done just that right there in the living room. Furniture was scattered as if by a huge, unruly child. One couch was on its back. A lamp was broken and ceramic pieces glittered in the beige carpet.

Wyatt tsked again. "Wow, he really did a number on you. Who was he fighting?"

The woman chuckled grimly. "That would be me."

Wyatt blinked at her, growing suspicious. Maybe she was some new Super Villain he hadn't yet heard about. Wyatt's hand started to drift toward his cell phone. He was sworn to report any evil activity to the Super Hero Bureau.

The woman noticed what he was doing and put a prettily manicured hand on his arm. "Not like that," she said. "I'm Lydia Day. I'm Captain Amazing's girlfriend. She appeared to reconsider her statement as she looked around the destroyed room and said, "Well, I'm his ex-girlfriend."

A flash of memory sprang into Wyatt's brain. He had seen this woman in the news a million times. She seemed to be a magnet for Super Villain activity. She was always being kidnapped by Herr Doctor or being hog tied and thrown onto train tracks by Willy the Kid.

"Hey, wow!" Wyatt exclaimed. "It's an honor to meet you, Miss Day! I'm a huge fan!"

Lydia smiled at him, a smile like a pearly sunbeam, and it was then he fell in love.

As Wyatt cleaned the living room and called the contractor in to fix the roof, Lydia sat down on the newly upturned couch. At first she only watched Wyatt clean, but soon she seemed to want to talk. "So, how did you get into cleaning up after Super Heroes?" Lydia wondered.

Wyatt smiled at the memory and began, "Well, when I was a kid I was in a bank while it was being robbed by the Terrible Twins."

Lydia whistled. "I haven't heard that name in a while."

Wyatt nodded. "Yeah, they're doing a five year stint for armed robbery. Anyway, it was a rainy day and when they came into the bank they tracked mud everywhere. Three seconds later, who should vault through the window But Domino Louie?"

Lydia laughed. "I know that old relic is retired."

"Yeah, to Acapulco. He's living like a king on that Super Hero pension. By the time Domino Louie had rounded up the evil twosome my mother, God rest her soul, was muttering, 'I would hate to have to clean up this mess.' And that's when it hit me."

"Super Cleaners," Lydia mused. "That's ingenious."

Wyatt shrugged modestly. "I see a need and I fill it."

By the time Wyatt was shampooing the carpet he felt confident enough to ask, "So, what's with you and Captain Amazing?"

Lydia shrugged and sighed. "Well, you know Super Heroes. They think they can do whatever they want. I saw him on TV schmoozing with Terrific Tina. I confronted him about it, and he blew up and took the roof off my house. So much for Captain Amazing."

Wyatt tsked. "That's awful. Have you ever seen the schnoz on Terrific Tina? She's not half as pretty as you."

Lydia smiled her gorgeous smile, placing a hand against his shoulder. "Do you really think so, Wyatt? I figured since she can lift a car— "

Wyatt cut her off with a wave of his hand, feeling himself swell up with hope at Lydia's touch. "She's too butch. Myself, I prefer a lady. Obviously Captain Amazing is not so bright if he left you for Terrific Tina."

Lydia beamed. "And to think of all the times his nemeses attacked me to get at him. Can you imagine! I still stayed."

"He never deserved you," Wyatt told her sincerely and turned on the vacuum cleaner.

They started with dinner, and nine months later Wyatt bought Lydia a ring. They moved in together and bought a yellow cat named Tilly. True, Lydia wasn't Jewish, but Wyatt's mother was dead, so who was to care? They had a peaceful relationship, which was primarily characterized by the two of them sitting snuggled up on the couch, eating popcorn and watching television. They liked the same shows, the same music, and the same food. If they ever saw Captain Amazing or Terrific Tina on the news, one of them immediately changed the channel.

Wyatt's business grew with every Super Hero that moved to Metro City. Lydia sold insurance out of her house, so between them they made a fair amount of money. They had saved up enough that the wedding would be a nice one even though they were both orphans.

Such were Wyatt's thoughts one Saturday evening as he drove the white van into the driveway he now shared with Lydia. As soon as he stepped down from the van, Wyatt noticed that one of the windows facing the lawn was broken.

Wyatt tsked. How strange. Lydia normally would have called him if a window had been broken. He took his cell phone out of his pocket and checked his messages even as he made his way across the lawn. There was nothing from Lydia.

Wyatt touched the doorknob, and it swung open. It hadn't been shut properly. A chill moved across Wyatt's skin like a cool breath. He readied his cell phone to dial for help and pushed the door open. He noticed at the threshold that the coffee table had been knocked over. His heart thrummed with fright as he stepped inside.

Tilly, frightened as well, bolted past his ankle and into the street.

"Lydia," Wyatt called, still alarmed. "Are you home?"

There was no answer. Slowly, Wyatt made his way into the depths of the house. There were multiple signs of destruction but there was no sign of Lydia. When Wyatt reached the kitchen he saw a piece of white paper taped to the refrigerator. It read:

Captain Amazing,
If you thought you could put us in the slammer and escape unscathed, you were sadly mistaken. Now we have your girlfriend! If you hope to see her alive again, come to dock nineteen and do battle!

It was signed:
The Terrible Twins.

"Oh, no," Wyatt breathed. The Terrible Twins had been in jail for the last five years, apparently captured by Captain Amazing. They would have no way of knowing that Captain Amazing and Lydia Day had broken it off. Wyatt gasped and dialed the police.

When a nasal sounding woman answered, "Metro City Police Department," Wyatt could barely contain his fear.

"I need you to put me in touch with Captain Amazing," Wyatt demanded. "My fiancée has been kidnapped!"

Irritated, the woman said, "You can't talk to Captain Amazing. He's got his own girlfriend to save."

"Then you have to send the police to help me!" Wyatt begged. "My fiancée is Lydia Day, and she's been kidnapped by the Terrible Twins because they don't know that she broke up with Captain Amazing. They want him to do battle at seven o'clock tonight!"

The woman sighed. "Look, buddy. I don't know what you think this is, but this is the Metro City Police Department. We have two men on duty. I don't know how you think we can help you. If you want someone to save your girlfriend, call a Super Hero." And she hung up.

Wyatt swore violently for the second time in his life and then threw the ransom note neatly in the garbage. What was he going to do? He had no idea how to get Captain Amazing's attention, short of committing a crime. He had never met the famed Super Hero and didn't know where he lived. Lydia had kept his secret identity as if it were her own. That was one of the ways Wyatt knew he could trust her.

The clock on the stove said 6:30. He had half an hour until the Terrible Twins would be expecting Captain Amazing. Wyatt realized he was pacing back and forth across the kitchen linoleum. Somehow, he had to let the Terrible Twins know that Captain Amazing wouldn't be coming.

Wyatt stopped short. He could tell them. He certainly couldn't "do battle" with them, but he could explain the situation.

Wyatt darted for the van. He paused to lock the door carefully behind himself, but barring that he was off like a shot. He arrived at dock nineteen four minutes before seven and got out of the van to wait for the infamous pair.

The dock was a mess, he noticed immediately. There were piles of wooden planks stacked haphazardly, and someone had left the contents of a tool box scattered around for anyone to trip on. Nervously, Wyatt bent and put a crow bar, a hammer, and a pair of screwdrivers into their proper place. Then he glanced at his watch. The Terrible Twins were a minute late.

Those are Super Villains for you, Wyatt thought cynically.

The kidnappers arrived in a convertible with the top rolled down. They screeched up behind his van at high speed. Wyatt flinched; the driver missed hitting it by an inch or less. Then they jumped spryly out of the car without opening the doors and pulled Lydia out after them.

She noticed Wyatt right away and called, "Wyatt!"

"Lydia!" Wyatt cried, and took a step toward her without thinking.

The Terrible Twins were dressed identically in black, and they each wore a face mask. They had grown pot bellies since that day they had robbed Wyatt's bank, and they were both balding and sunburned where they'd once had hair.

One twin regarded Wyatt menacingly and said, "Who's this? Amazing's mild mannered alter ego?"

His brother snorted and said, "Not unless he's lost seventy pounds and become Jewish in the last five years."

Lydia groaned and threw her hands up in the air. "I told you two! Captain Amazing and I broke up! That's my fiancé, Wyatt Epstein."

"It's true," Wyatt agreed, as the Twins exchanged a look.

"I don't believe it," the first Twin said. "It's got to be one of Captain Amazing's ploys."

Suddenly, a deep, masculine voice boomed, "Did someone call for Captain Amazing?"

All four of them looked toward the voice. Hovering three feet above them, cape billowing heroically in the breeze, was Captain Amazing. Wyatt's mouth gaped of its own accord. Captain Amazing was a gigantic, golden gentile of a man with biceps the size of Wyatt's waist. His mask emphasized the squareness of his chin and the red leotard definitely added to the illusion of being a Defender of the American Way. Wyatt instantly hated him.

Scathingly, he said, "Why don't you get down here and do battle with your own enemies so the future Mrs. Epstein and I can go home?"

Captain Amazing squinted near-sightedly at the group and said, "Lydia? Is that you?"

"Hey, Amazing," Lydia called warily and waved with her fingertips.

Captain Amazing looked around again. A smirk was growing on his dimpled features.

"Wow," he said. "Mrs. Epstein, huh? I bet right now you're wishing you still had a real man around to rescue you."

Wyatt's mouth dropped open. "Why, you flying schmuck," he growled. "Why don't you come on down here and say that to my face instead of floating there like a sissy?"

Captain Amazing narrowed his eyes at Wyatt and dropped gracefully in front of him. Wyatt immediately saw that he'd made a mistake. Captain Amazing stood nearly seven feet tall to Wyatt's 5' 9" and had at least seventy pounds on him. Wyatt deflated a little, but Lydia was watching. He had to back up his mouth.

"You think I'm a sissy, Epstein?" Captain Amazing growled. Wyatt puffed up his chest and hoped he looked tougher than he felt.

"Maybe you just fly like that because you're light in the loafers," Wyatt said. "You want to make something of it?"

Captain Amazing popped his massive knuckles, and Wyatt prepared to feel Super Strength first hand. Then, suddenly, he heard a car turn over.

They both looked up. Crumpled on the ground were the Terrible Twins. The crow bar Wyatt had put away lay between them. In the driver's seat of their sport's car was Lydia, gunning the engine. Both of the combatants' mouths fell open.

"Wyatt, get in the car," Lydia said coolly. "Amazing, feel free to take credit for my hard work just like old times."

Wyatt and Captain Amazing exchanged looks. Slowly, Wyatt walked over to the car and got into the passenger seat.

"You hit them with the crow bar," Wyatt observed, amazed.

"Of course I did," Lydia said breezily. "You can't really expect me to sit around and wait for some Super Hero to save me, can you?"

She put the car in gear and drove away.

About the author: Michelle Ruckoldt, 26, is the mother of three and works in the escalation department for Sprint customer service. She has been writing since kindergarten. Born in Brownsville, TX she relocated to Pueblo, CO at the age of eight. She attended New Mexico State University for English with an emphasis in creative writing. She has published a number of poems, including one in the independent magazine 'Iconoclast' and one in the New Mexico State University newsletter. She is a member of the Prose Three writers group.

Spandex

Alexander Bentley

The first time Hector met Marigold, she was hiding from her own fourth birthday.

Hector suspected there'd been some kind of mix-up - whenever his parents had parties, they were friends with every guests. Hector had no idea whose party this was, and therefore must not have been invited, but he didn't want to say anything and embarrass himself. So he just slipped out of the main room when no one was looking, and decided to explore. Never in his short life had he seen a house so big, and so empty. His home was tiny and packed to the brim with stuff; horrible, easily broken stuff. A distant clang and crash broke Hector from his reverie. Confused and intrigued by what could be making such a racket, Hector set out to investigate.

Peeking his head from around a corner, Hector laid eyes on the cleanest, whitest kitchen he'd ever seen. Everything was spotless. Even the slowly growing pile of pots and pans were silver and shiny. A measuring cup came flying from a half-open cupboard and landed with a clang on the mound. Suspecting kitchen gremlins (or at least some sort of appliance-goblin), Hector threw open the cupboard doors. He was met by the brightest pair of lightning-blue eyes he'd ever seen. The little girl they belonged to had obviously been dressed up against her will. The red bows in her midnight black hair had been done up with one hand, the other hand needed to restrain her. Her dress had a tiny drip of ice cream on it, a remnant of the bribe necessary to get her to finally stand still.

"Hey!" The small girl yelped, "How'd you find me?"

Hector moved aside, revealing the stuff piled on the floor which, with a mighty crash, promptly collapsed under its own weight.

The kids shared a moment of silence for the lost mountain of silver.

"I'm Marigold. Wanna build a kitchen-man?"

"What's a kitchen-man?"

"It's like a snow man, but made of kitchen bits."

It took three hours before anyone noticed two kids were missing, and by that time, Marigold and Hector had made the world's most awesome kitchen-man, agreed to be friends for life, and had eaten all the candy they could find in the drawers.

***

As Hector stood in the middle of the deserted country road surrounded by wreckage, a piece of the truck's bumper sticking out of his hair, it occurred to him he may not be normal. He noticed Marigold grabbing his fingers, counting them, then patting down his arms, then checking his torso and face. Making sure everything was still there, he supposed. She had the biggest splash of mud on her from where he'd shoved her into the ditch. It had been a very rude thing to do, so he apologized.

Marigold stopped prodding him, and just stared. Then she laughed. She laughed so hard she had to hold on to him for support. Slowly it all came back to Hector.

The two of them had been shipped off to summer camp. The place had been a nightmare - for two kids that made fake crop circles in their spare time, the constant adult supervision was suffocating. The only logical course of action was escape. That's how they'd found themselves in the middle of nowhere, walking down a dirt road in the dead of night. It had been a stupidly dangerous thing to do, now that he thought of it.

Marigold gasped for air, face red. "You okay, dude?"

Hector nodded.

Marigold turned away from Hector, towards the ruined remains of the truck. She cupped her hands over her mouth. "YOU OKAY TOO?" A hand poked out from a broken window and gave a thumbs up. Satisfied, Marigold turned back to Hector.

"What do say, keep going?"

Hector smiled. "You know it."

***

Being invulnerable was, for the most part, totally awesome. Hector and Marigold kept it between themselves - superpowers were still too underground to be cool. Although, it would have been difficult for them to be any less cool than they already were.

Middle school, as it turns out, isn't a great place to be unique. Hector was, for the most part, left alone (the irony of that didn't escape him) but Marigold most certainly was not. Her abstract way of thinking, mixed with a distinct lack of social filters and verbal grace, made her the perfect target for everyone looking to put someone down. Marigold didn't care for the most part. In fact, she hadn't cared at all until earlier that day.

Hector usually liked Marigold's weird tirades, but sometimes on those long and painful days there were just irritating. Today, she'd pushed his patience to the breaking point with her "Macbeth was a time-traveler" argument. He'd snapped, asking her to, for once in her life, stop it with the crazy. Marigold had stopped, stood up, and walked out of the classroom without saying a word. Hector felt like the biggest jerk alive, so when he'd received a rather urgent text message from Marigold to get to her place ASAP, he'd wasted no time.

As Hector walked up the hardwood stairs to Marigold's room, he went over all the apologies he'd prepared. With a deep breath, he opened the door to her room.

"Marigold, I'm sor-" Hector couldn't finish the sentence.

A metal sphere with spider legs and giant mandibles snapped and stabbed at dome of off-green energy huddled in the corner of the room.

"Took your sweet time!" Marigold shouted from inside her protective sphere.

The spider-robot turned to Hector. Recognizing easier prey, it leapt at him. Its jaws snapping shut around Hector's head with enough force to slice steel.

It was an awkward moment, the spider just hanging off of Hector's indestructible head. Hector didn't move, his brain working furiously to process exactly what was going on.

"What?" It was all Hector could manage, pointing to the thing now completely stuck on his noggin.

"Sorry."

"*What?*" Hector repeated.

"I,"Marigold rubbed her neck sheepishly, "I was mad, and the thing just sort of came out evil. But I didn't mean to, honest!"

Hector felt he wasn't articulating his point properly.

"*WHAT?*"

"I thought you hated me, okay! There! Are you happy?" Marigold huffed, "You really know how to kick a girl when she's down."

"WHAT IS THIS THING CHEWING ON MY HEAD?"

"Oh. Spiderbot." Marigold said, like it was the most obvious thing in the world. "And there's no need to shout."

"WHERE THE DID IT COME FROM?"

"I just sort of... *built* it. Out of a lawnmower. Don't know how, really. And seriously dude, you're blowing out my eardrums."

"WHAT?" Hector pointed to the green globe around Marigold.

"Force-field. Built it too."

At once, all the gears aligned in hector's brain. "You're a mechanist!"

"Yeah, looks that way," Marigold said, her voice not giving off even a hint that her newfound mechanical might surprise her at all. "How about after you smash the spider on your face, we build a scale replica of the Hindenburg, but with rocket engines? You know, if, uh," Marigold looked away, "If we're still good."

Hector's response was a smile and the sound of crunching metal.

***

Hector was a bit of a late bloomer, but when the blooming happened, it happened all at once. One day girls (not Marigold) had been icky cootie-monsters. The next, girls (not Marigold) had transformed into the most awesome thing ever. He'd never understood what the big deal was about having a girlfriend until then, but for the last three months it was all he could think about.

"Hey!"

Hector jumped a foot in the air. Before he could fully recover, Marigold moved out from behind him and shoved something into his chest. Hector took one look at it, and quickly hid it in his pocket. His eyes darted left and right, making sure no one had seen anything.

"What are you doing?" Hector hissed, "What if someone saw this?"

Marigold raised an eyebrow. "Dude, no one cares about what we're doing" With a wave of her arm, she proved her point. Everyone in the hall was far too busy with their own problems to pay attention to anyone else. Hector still wasn't comfortable with it. He rubbed his fingers over the black domino mask he'd hidden in his pocket.

"So is it..?"

"Of course!" Marigold snapped, "I fixed the perception field *and* bumped the power; you should be safe against anything short of world-class psychics!"

Hector gestured for Marigold to keep it down. The mask was a work of beauty, there was no denying it. He didn't really understand the mechanics, all he knew is that the tiny piece of fabric could completely conceal his identity from even the smartest of investigators. And now psychics too, apparently. Hector supposed it's always good to be prepared.

"I still can't believe you became a superhero just to meet girls," Marigold huffed, "I don't get it at all."

Hector put an arm around his short friend, "One day, when you're older, you'll understand."

"Ugh, just shoot me now." Marigold brushed Hector's arm off her. "How'd you break the mask in the first place?"

Hector crossed his arms over his chest, a smug look creeping onto his face "I might have been fighting Soktar."

"Wait, *the* Soktar? As in 'Soktar, Destroyer of Civilizations?'"

"Yeah."

"Crusher of the Weak?' 'Killer of a Thousand Capes?'"

"Yeah."

"Okay, that's pretty wicked," Marigold sighed, "But don't do it again. I hate working on the same thing twice."

Hector saluted, face a mask of joking faux-seriousness. "Yes, Ma'am!"

***

There was something sublimely therapeutic about punching a bank robber. It didn't make a lot of sense, but breaking up bank robberies always made Hector feel warm and fuzzy. Fighting non-super bad guys was a good thing too, especially tonight - there was a B-movie marathon in an hour, and Marigold was in charge of candy. By some dark magic, she always managed to get huge quantities of the most teeth-rottingly awesome snacks conceivable. Hector's thoughts drifted as he swung one robber into another, knocking them both out and sending them crashing to the floor. He wished he had something more romantic to do on a

Friday night, but watching some dude in a cardboard robot costume destroy all the humans with a platonic friend wasn't so bad.

The roar of an engine snapped Hector out of his train of thought. He cursed himself. Of *course* bank robbers would have a getaway car. He sprang into action, grabbing a chunk of the bank's wall as he dashed outside. The criminals' car was already halfway down the street. With a mighty heave, Hector hurled the hunk of cement. The improvised projectile embedded itself into the car's trunk, crushing metal and breaking glass, but not slowing the vehicle down.

Indeed, it would have been clean escape for the driver, if a blinding bolt of white fire hadn't cut through the car's hood and melted the engine.

Hector was aware there were a couple other superheroes out there, but had never actually seen any in person. There weren't enough of them to form any kind of league, and it's not like you can post personal ads. "Hero seeking other heroes for hanging out and saving the world" wasn't something to put in the classifieds.

Hector considered himself to be moderately attractive. He was no movie star, but wasn't hard on the eyes either. The woman floating slowly towards him made Hector feel painfully plain. She was clothed in the minimum legal amount of white spandex, leaving next to none of her perfect figure to the imagination. Her hair was ablaze with soft white flame, and her eyes glowed like twin stars. She was the White Witch. Hector had seen her on the news, but never thought she was the type to dirty her hands with something as trivial as a simple bank robbery.

"Fluh." Hector stated as the she touched down in front of him. The White Witch just smiled. She got that kind of reaction a lot.

A tingle raced up Hector's spine. It was a primal feeling, something from deep in the past when sabre-toothed tigers hid around every corner. It was the feeling of being watched. In an instant his hero instincts overrode his more primal ones. With one smooth motion, he swept the White Witch behind him, shielding her from the loaded weapon in the getaway driver's hand.

Marigold had designed Hector's costume. Despite his natural resistance to being killed, they'd agreed to armour plates, mostly because it looked wicked awesome. The only downside was that it was a pain to dig bullets out of the thing. Hector didn't even feel the shots burying into his suit as the driver emptied his pistol in the heroes' general direction. Hector waited patiently for the tell-tale click of an empty gun before walking over and clocking the guy in the jaw.

"Not bad." The White Witch said, impressed, "I like a big, strong guy. But you have a little..." she gestured to her cheek.

With an embarrassed smile, Hector reached up and flicked a squashed circle of lead from his face. Before he could react, the White Witch wrapped her arm around his.

"I'm going to go bust Doctor Deviant - I was on my way there when I saw you. Interested?"

Hector couldn't disagree. Partially because his brain had turned into goo, and partially because they were already half a mile in the air, rocketing towards their destination.

***

Hector was on cloud nine. The fight with Doc Deviant so simple the Witch didn't even have to lift a finger, and the rest of the night had been spent just hanging out with the White Witch. It was amazing, she laughed at his jokes, and showed genuine interest; all the other girls he'd hit on hadn't given him the time of day. But alas, all good things had to come to an end, and the White Witch offered Hector a flight home. They were soaring through the night air, the Witch's arms wrapped around Hector's chest and her head beside his. If Hector had died then and there, he would have died a happy man.

"You know," the White Witch whispered in Hector's ear, just loud enough to be heard over the wind, "I think you'd look good in spandex."

It took all of Hector's might to form complete sentences. "I'm not really-."

"Aw, come on. I think you'd look hot in something skin-tight."

"I don't-"

"Do it for me?" The squeeze accompanying her request was more than Hector could endure.

"Okay," he squeaked.

***

Absentmindedly, Hector thumbed the tiny card for Vlad's Custom Costumes the White Witch had slipped in his pocket. He was waiting for Marigold outside her house, like he always did, but she was being slower than usual today. A soft groan caught his attention. Marigold shuffled, hunched over, out the front door. Hector put an arm around her and guided her to a big rock in the garden they could sit on.

"Dude," Marigold muttered, "You didn't show."

It all came back to him. Hector had completely forgotten about B-movie night, and he left her alone with all that candy. Naturally she'd eaten it all; self-control wasn't exactly a staple of Marigold's personality. All Hector could do now was keep her mind off what must have been the mother of all stomach aches.

"So, I met the White Witch last night," was all Hector could think of to say.

"She's the one who wears the transparent eight-inch stilettos, right?"

"No! ... Maybe. I wasn't really looking at her feet."

Marigold let out a sound somewhere between a grunt and a laugh. Hector smiled.

"Don't get cocky, I still haven't forgiven you." Marigold poked him in the chest. "Tonight, you're helping me with this new idea, and you're gonna like it Okay?"

Hector grimaced. Helping Marigold wasn't a problem; in fact, it was a lot of fun. The only problem was:

"I sort of have a date tonight."

Marigold half-smiled, "Sorry, I didn't quite catch that over the agony in my intestines."

Hector frowned. That wasn't funny.

"Dude," Marigold's face fell, "You totally blew me off. The Witch can wait." Silence. "I'm your best friend! C'mon!" Marigold glowered in anger, "You meet one girl willing to suck on your face, and you completely forget about everyone else! I bet she's even got you wearing-"

The look on Hector's face finished her sentence. Marigold's anger turned to horror.

"She's got you wearing spandex," Her horror turned right back into anger, "You idiot! Do you- " She was shaking with fury, "Blind- Useless- RAGH! " Marigold left from her seat, and ran inside her house, slamming the door behind her.

Hector just sat there. In all the years he'd know Marigold, she'd never freaked out so thoroughly. His stunned mind could only come up with one explanation: she didn't like it that he had someone other than her in his life. That must have been reason. Hector stood up. Well, if she wanted to be a possessive brat, then she could do it alone.

And besides, what was Marigold's deal with spandex? The White Witch thought it was awesome.

***

It had been a full week, and Marigold hadn't spoken to him.

Hector shut his eyes. He'd been spending every night with the White Witch, and he was starting to get burnt out. The Witch told him he was having a wonderful time, and his hormonal teenaged brain was inclined to agree with her. She'd introduced him to so many things she said he'd like too, including the spandex. It had been a whirlwind, and Hector was completely swept off his feet.

"Are you even listening to me?"

It took him a moment for Hector to remember where he was, but the cold night air blowing across the roof where the two heroes were sitting helped snap him out of his thoughts. The White Witch glared accusingly at her boyfriend.

"Of course. It's just that this spandex is kind of chaffing."

Silence, then the White Witch huffed.

"It's been a week, suck it up."

The one-sided conversation returned to normal. Week of wearing it or not, his green and yellow spandex suit (colours picked to best match with W.W.) was still really, really uncomfortable. When he'd gone to pick it up, Vlad the Salesman had given him a few tips on wearing skin-tight clothes. Underwear is strictly *verboten*, as it would bunch up and look terrible. "All the support is built in," he'd said. Hector was no prude, but he thoroughly missed the security of his boxers.

His mind drifted as the White Witch endlessly spoke.

***

Marigold had moved her lab out of her house when she'd accidentally de-materialized half the roof. Now, she mostly worked out of an old abandoned warehouse in the middle of the city. Inside the reinforced safety of her mechanical studio, Marigold's fingers flew over the keyboard, writing line after line of complex artificial intelligence. She knew she shouldn't do science when she was angry, but she didn't care.

She missed Hector. He was her best friend - hell, he was her *only* friend. She cursed herself for the four-thousandth and twenty-fifth time. Being Marigold was fantastic, but every once in a while it was the worst person to be. She was furious at Hector, but she just could articulate it. It was all electrical impulses in her head, thoughts that couldn't be translated into language. This sucked even worse than the time she'd fused herself into a wall.

Marigold stood up and stretched. The programming was pretty much done, and she hoped testing would do a better job at distracting her. Giant robots weren't her forte, she was more of a gadget girl, but every now and again Marigold just had to build a ten-story effigy of destruction. This model wasn't fully armed - half the laser cannons were missing, and the other ones didn't actually work. She never intended to use the thing, of course- building it had just been a way to let off some steam.

Program fully loaded, the automaton's eyes flared red, then turned green with painful slowness. The stupid first-time start up for giant robots always took forever. With a deep, booming, metallic voice the robot spoke:

"DESTROY ALL HUMANS! DESTROY ALL HUMANS!"

Marigold smacked her forehead. *This* was why she didn't do science when angry. With the groan of hydraulic pistons, the thing stood up, exploding from the warehouse and sending bits of roof scattering everywhere. It stepped through what remained of the lab and marched down the street, informing everyone within earshot of its intent to destroy all the humans.

Marigold watched it go. She toyed with the idea of going out to stop it, but ultimately decided against it. Cracking her knuckles, Marigold donned her third favourite pair of welding goggles and got to work; she had a lab to re-build, and that whole robot thing would work itself out. Probably.

***

"DESTROY ALL HUMANS!"

Hector's eyes flew open. A brief glance passed him and the White Witch. They sprang into action, the Witch hoisting Hector up and flying towards the noise.

Soaring over the city, Hector saw the problem: giant robot. He smiled, it'd been forever since he'd got to fight a giant robot. As they got closer, the smile fell off his face.

Shiny silver steel covered the monstrosity, overlapping plates protecting all the joints. The thing's head rested directly upon its rectangular torso, eyes staring out of an otherwise empty face. The thing had a half-built cannon resting on each shoulder, with another hooked into its right arm. The arms themselves were long and trashed like tentacles, while its legs were stubby and thick as to support its massive weight. It was a classic B-movie robot.

Hector recognized Marigold's workmanship. She'd probably been building angry again. The robot craned its head upwards, catching sight of the fast approaching heroes. It brought its arm up, and levelled the attached cannon at Hector and the White Witch.

"THREAT DETECTED!" It proclaimed, "NEUTRALIZING!"

The cannon glowed deep red, and Hector really hoped Marigold had been too furious to finish the weapon properly. With a deafening blast, the cannon exploded on the metal giants arm, severing the limb halfway.

"SYSTEM MALFUNCTION! RESUMING MAIN PARAMETER: SMASH!"

Hector and the White Witch were almost on top of the robot. Hector poked the arms holding him - the signal to be dropped. The White Witch released him immediately.

Freefalling in spandex is, without a doubt, one of the least pleasant sensations possible. Wind whipped where it shouldn't be whipping, and drafts drafted where there should be no draft. Thankfully, the experience was over quickly. Hector landed on the robot's right shoulder cannon - an excellent spot. Wasting no time, he leapt over the beast's back, catching a loose plate midway down. Marigold always put the main power-doodad in her inventions' center of gravity. Something about efficiency or effectiveness - Hector wasn't paying attention when she had talked about it. What he did understand was that, with the proper application of force, anything could be disabled by reaching into the right place and smashing whatever was there. This was exactly what Hector did, and the robot hit the ground with earth-shattering force.

The White Witch swooped down to him.

"There's a swath of destruction pointing right to the source of that thing, if we go right now we can catch the mastermind before they get away!"

Before Hector could do anything, the White Witch picked him up and rocketed through the dark sky.

***

Marigold never considered herself to be a villain, so it came as a surprise when a pair of people in spandex showed up at her destroyed lab, interrupting her cleaning, and accused her of being such.

She was even more surprised when she recognized one of them to be Hector. The poor guy looked absolutely awful, like a carnival strongman from Candyland. The other one looked even worse; she could have passed as a dominatrix with a reversed colour scheme. Marigold would have collapsed with laughter if it wasn't so sad.

***

Hector touched down in the devastated building. Marigold watched as they landed, safety pins in her lab coat jingling softly in the night wind, welding goggles reflecting the city lights. He was glad the robot didn't hurt her. Seemed she still wasn't talking to him, though.

"We caught you, villain!" The White Witch proclaimed in her grandiose hero voice. "Give up!"

Marigold didn't move. She stared at him. Hector couldn't see her eyes from under the goggles, but he could feel her looking at him.

"Resisting arrest, eh? So be it!" The White Witch shot an irritated look at Hector.

"What are you waiting for? Go get her!"

The White Witch slapped Hector on the shoulder to get him moving. He advanced on Marigold until they were almost face to face. Still, Marigold said nothing. She just stared.

"What are you doing?" The White Witch huffed, "Stop being a freak and fight!"

Marigold didn't duck. Or flinch. Or run away. She just raised a solitary eyebrow.

Perspective hit Hector like a cruise missile to the head.

His whole teenaged life he'd wanted to have a girlfriend so badly he'd been willing to ignore the simple truth: the White Witch was an awful person. Hector *hated* spandex. He'd stated that clearly the first time he'd read a comic book. He'd made a deal with Marigold the day he decided to be a hero, a promise that no matter what, he'd never be caught dead in anything skin-tight. Marigold had known that there was no way Hector would wear spandex unless some external force had put the thought into his head. No way he'd wear it unless he'd followed someone else's tune. That's why she'd been so upset - the girl had been terrified that her best friend was becoming a mindless drone.

"I never got good grades," Hector said softly to the black haired girl in front of him, "and I never really think things through," he smiled, sad and embarrassed, "but this is the first time I've ever felt stupid."

The smile that crept onto Marigold's face was almost more than he could take.

The squeaking of impatiently shifting spandex brought them back to reality. They both knew what had to be done. Hector nodded, giving Marigold permission. With one fluid motion, she pulled a safety pin from her coat's collar and brought it across Hector's chest, slicing the polymer fabric.

The effect was immediate. The tensile strength of the spandex pulled the cut wider and wider, exploding the entire garment clean off his body. The stretchy thing flew through the air, hitting the ground with a soft plop.

"I just don't think it would work between us."

With a deep breath Hector turned and struck his most heroic pose.

"Our relationship was just too..." Hector smirked, "Drafty." Marigold groaned.

The sudden shock was more than the White Witch could take. She stood rooted to the spot, stunned.

"Maybe if you wiggle around a bit she'll get the hint?" Marigold offered, helpfully.

That snapped the Witch out of her stupor, thankfully before any wiggling was necessary. With a grunt of disgust, she turned and flew away.

Hector wasn't sure if he should be happy or mortified. Either way, what's done was done, and he covered himself before turning around and asking Marigold for some pants.

"Pfft, it's nothing I haven't seen before," Marigold said, dismissing his modesty, "Remember when I went through that clockwork phase, and you were wearing baggy pants?"

Hector sat, cold and naked, on a ruined piece of steel girder waiting patiently for Marigold to find the extra pair of pants she kept around for just such an occasion. He'd just flashed his very first girlfriend, and it probably wouldn't be a good idea to show his masked face in public for a while.

But try as he might, as Hector sat there listening to Marigold tell a surprisingly inaccurate version of their Dancing Zombie adventure, he couldn't stop himself from grinning like an idiot.

About the author: Alexander Bentley is a graduate of Algonquin College's Scriptwriting program, now delving into the deep dark world of short stories and novels. Currently, he's studying Web Development as a means not to starve to death while pursuing his literary passion.

Maxed

Bradley Descartes

Damn, I love this car.

Fifteen years old and it's still cruising like it did back when I first got behind the wheel. For years, people kept telling me to get something new, to buy one of those flashy new sports cars that look like they came here through a time warp from the far future. But I don't care about that. I love this car, my car. My ruby red convertible.

I remember as a kid, every time I saw one of those cars, my mouth would hang open. I was enthralled by them; I wanted to own one so badly. Driving with the top down, wind blowing my hair, in one of those babies was my dream. But I was a stupid kid whose family couldn't even afford rat droppings. The people in those types of cars looked so rich and classy, nothing at all like me. That dream seemed destined to always be a dream. Something that could only attain reality once my eyes were closed.

Yet, look at me now.

Driving on the highway, the top down, wind blowing my hair, doing around eighty. I love swerving between lanes, cutting off those stupid other people driving on my asphalt. I still get a thrill every time they yell and curse me out angrily. The ignorant fools. Getting so worked up by me, yet I don't give a crap about them. But that's people for you.

I crack a smile whenever I think about this car. I'm doing it even now. The dream that insignificant kid had that could never exist, did. It sure was a wild ride getting there, too.

I must have been, what, sixteen, seventeen? I'm pretty sure I was sixteen when it all went down. I guess I should start from the beginning.

Ah, my mother, the woman I love the most...to hate. I know I sound like a victim saying this but that whore messed up my whole life. I never had a father; I didn't even know the guy. I don't think he ever knew he has a son. My mother always told me that my father was a worthless bum who took advantage of her and turned his back on her the moment he learnt that she was pregnant. I believed her, she was my mother, after all, and I was a little kid. At that age, you're supposed to believe in your parents. I mean, sure she would always be out late at night—every night—and would not be back till the next morning, or the one after that, but she was my mother, there was no way she could be up to no good.

Yeah, right. It always takes a stupid adult to ruin a kid's life.

As I got older, I started to hear things. Disgusting things. I'd always run into these lowlifes who kept asking me about my mother, telling me all sorts of stuff I could not understand at that time. Hell, even some of the teachers at my school, both male and female, started telling me things I really did not want to know.

I confronted her one day and that's when she took me to see her late night 'workplace,' the street corner where she meets her clients. Yep, she confirmed it, she was a prostitute. A street walking, body selling, morally deprived whore. She had no idea which one of her clients knocked her up, if she did, she would still be hitting him up for cash before my first diaper was ever soiled.

In fact, that's the only reason I'm even alive. She was sure my father was this powerful senator who'd often acquired her services. Paternity tests proved otherwise. Left without her big payday, she did not know what to do with me. As she put it, eventually I grew on her, like a pet. That's my mother for you, she has a real way with words.

Of course, just because I found out about it, she was not going to stop. Why would she. Who'd care what a pet thinks, anyway.

For a whore, she must have been a cheap one, like the ones who would do it for only five dollars cause we didn't have a damn thing to our names. That's no surprise to me, that woman could do nothing right, except ruin my life, that is.

So that was my life for the next couple years. I watched my mother leave the house every night to do her thing while I stayed home, alone. I got used to it, my dreams were enough to keep me company.

To think, as horrible as my life was, my good old mother was going to make it worse. She hooked up with this hot shot businessman from uptown. The guy was head over heels in love with her. He must have been mentally challenged because I can't see what the hell he saw in her. He wanted her to move in with him and she, of course, accepted. It looked like things were looking up, at least for her. You see, the guy didn't want any kids and he definitely would not want the son of some potential deadbeat hanging around his house. My mother had no problem with that, she was all too happy with that arrangement. She was able to get rid of me and get the life she always wanted in one swoop.

That was what she wrote on the note she left on the door when I came home from school. She never even told me face to face.

So there I was, sixteen, homeless and penniless. I'd been screwed over far worse than anything my whore of a mother could do. I was left with only one real alternative, a life of crime. I mean, what else could I do? Die? That certainly was not an option.

I started off just like all small time criminals. I mugged people and took off running, broke into houses, stole gas out of cars by drilling the tank, anything to help me get by. Getting by was all I could do, there's a reason why people like me were called small time. To really make it big, I had to get involved in the heavy stuff, the kind of things that get you serious jail time. But I could not do any of that on my own, I had to be in a powerful group and no one was hiring. Damn the economy.

But my luck would change. Fate put me in the right place at the right time.

I was sleeping under the stars on my favorite spot in the alley when it happened. A guy in an off-white suit, carrying a briefcase, was on the run. Two guys were on his tail. I got a rude awakening that night from the thunderous gunfire that was exchanged between them. I was a cowardly punk then, I ran and hid behind some old drum barrel.

The men ran down my alley, continuing to shoot at each other. I was lucky that they did not see me. The guy in off-white took one of them out; the other one never stopped chasing him. They went past me, I should have just run off but I didn't. I'm not sure why but I was intrigued. I picked up the dead guy's gun and followed them.

I knew that alley well; it was my unofficial home, after all. There was a dead end, a fitting way to end the duel those men were embroiled in. The guy in the off-white soon found himself trapped, with nowhere to go. The only exit was blocked off by his assailant. To make it worse, he ran out of ammo. That guy in the off-white was finished.

Well, he would have been, had I not shot his would be killer in the back. It was the first time I ever killed anyone, I felt really weird afterwards. I killed this guy I didn't know for another guy I never met. It was crazy, but I felt that it was something I had to do. I don't know what it was, but I had this voice in my head telling me that I should save the guy in the off-white suit.

That guy approached and thanked me for the assist. That was the first time I got a good look at him. He was clean shaven; had neat, straight hair; looked like the ritzy type. A guy like him just did not belong in that situation.

We didn't have the time to talk; the cops were being fashionably late, as always. He ran and I followed him, he did not seem to mind. We kept running till we reached the abandoned fireworks factory. That's where he introduced himself.

Snarky Snider, he said that was what his friends called him. I was elevated to that status for saving his life. He was the son of a big time lawyer but was a delinquent youth. He defied the law and spent a lot of time in juvenile detention centers. Once he was eighteen, he cut ties with his father and joined the Italian mafia. Uncle Adolfo Albertini, now that was one fat bastard. He was the big boss of the mafia. He took Snarky Snider in; I guess he saw something he liked in the guy. He trusted him enough to allow him to pay off the politicians who did favors for him. That was a big mistake; Snarky ripped him off at the first chance. The briefcase he was carrying had over one hundred and twenty thousand dollars in it, more money than I had ever seen.

I still had the gun, I could have jacked him then and there, but I didn't. I wanted to know more about that guy. I felt he was up to something big and I was right.

He told me about his grand plan. He did not want to work for the same old, tired crime bosses that littered the city. He was going to become his own boss and was going to use Uncle Adolfo's 'generous donation' as a start.

He liked what he saw of me that night and offered me a spot in his group. It didn't take me a second to agree, why wouldn't I. My sleeping spot in the alley wasn't exactly luxurious. Besides, Snarky had one hundred and twenty thousand dollars with him. I'd follow him into a septic tank if he wanted me to.

Snarky got me some new attire, a suit similar to his, except mine was dark gray. He said he wanted me to be his enforcer. If only he knew I never fired a gun before we met that night. I doubt I'd be here driving this car right now.

He took me to meet the rest of the group. Lefty McMichaels, Switch and Don Donaldson, three men who were experienced criminals, specializing in anything from lock picking to explosives to computer hacking. They were highly skilled and were all allured by Snarky's promises of grandeur. I was small next to them, but from the way Snarky spoke, he made me sound like a professional hitman. Those guys never learnt the truth, doesn't really matter now, anyway.

Too Jive Crew, that's what we called ourselves. Our goal was to make money and we didn't care whose toes we had to step on, no matter which side of the law they were on. And we sure did step on a lot of toes, the only ones making as much money as us were the podiatrists.

We robbed banks, jewelry stores, other stupid criminals, as long as someone had money, they were a target. It didn't matter what your gender or race was, no one was safe.

We were growing fast, the original five turned into a dominant fifty five a year and a half into it. We were on a roll, no one could stop us. Even Uncle Adolfo was too scared to challenge us, and with good reason, too. The Irish mobsters took us lightly; they thought we were nothing more than an ensemble of punks who had no respect. We soon changed their attitudes towards us. A few bombs in their cars and a couple bullets in their heads were more than enough to do that. I killed at least thirteen of them. I had gotten used to shooting people by then.

I bought this beautiful, beautiful car after that. I'm sure I heard it speaking to me when I went to that dealership. I had to have it and I did just that. My beautiful convertible. I'd kiss it now if I wasn't driving.

It looked like Snarky had pulled through; we became just as big as he said we would be. I went from a kid who didn't know where his next meal would come from to a guy living in a condo, wearing designer suits and driving around town in style. I never thought I would have. I was finally living the life I always wanted, what I thought I could not have.

Nothing could stop us.

At least, that was what I thought.

We were collecting some packages from the docks that were smuggled into the country. Routine stuff. I was there, training the newbies, showing them the ropes. Then I heard a scream and this guy wearing a ski mask came out of nowhere. He took out most of the guys in less than a minute, doing some crazy martial arts moves. He was incredibly strong and fast, above human, even. I tried to take him out but he kicked the gun out of my hand before I could pull the trigger. That last thing I remember before feeling those handcuffs on my wrists was seeing his fist approaching my face.

I went to jail that night. It was the first time I had ever been there. Thanks to our good friends in high places, I did not spend more than a night there. The other members of the original five were pissed, they could not understand how I could mess up like that, especially to only one guy. I could offer no explanation; I took the blame for what happened.

The other guys, however, quickly found out what dealing with that guy was all about.

He started interfering in all our operations. Lefty McMichaels ran into him while robbing the biggest bank in the city. I guess it's more precise to say he ran into his boot. He went to jail.

Switch planted bombs to blow up the bridge to our sister city. One of the biggest contractors in the city was in financial trouble and needed a big job to survive. A deal was struck between them and our politician friends. The bridge is destroyed, they'd cover it up by declaring it was caused by structural weakness, and the contractors would get their big payday. That was how it was supposed to go down, but when Switch flipped the switch, nothing happened. By the time he turned around to tell his boys to check on the bombs, they were all unconscious. That guy with the ski mask was there, he dropped a bag with the bombs in them on the ground, all deactivated. The next one to drop was Switch. He went to jail.

Don Donaldson was making his usual rounds, collecting our protection fee. He was in the middle of physically convincing some old lady to acquire our services when that guy in the ski mask showed up again. Don's teeth ended up on the curb right after that. He went to jail.

After our politician friends got them out of jail, we had a meeting with Snarky. He was royally pissed and had good reason to be. That mystery guy in the ski mask was messing up all our operations and what's more, was costing us money. The media loved this guy, they called him the city's savior, the man who was singlehandedly cleaning up the city streets from vermin like us. That pissed off Snarky even more, because we were losing both money and respect. It would only be a matter of time before other crime bosses tried to move in our turf. We had to make a statement, and a big one. Snarky decided to set up a trap. We'd deliberately leak plans of a kidnapping for ransom, the target being the police chief's daughter. As soon as the goody-goody showed up to save the day, we'd pounce on him for a change and take him out for good. Snarky even wanted to hang his head from that big tree in the middle of the park, a warning to others who wanted to mess with the Too Jive Crew. We had to keep that part of the plan to ourselves, there was no telling how that guy kept knowing what we were up to.

That Friday, we set our plan into motion. We nabbed the police chief's kid when she left school, that part was easy. I had the pleasure of calling him to break the bad news, the cry-baby pleaded for her safety, like I would care. The ransom demands were made, the city was in frenzy, and the media coverage was unending. Where, oh where could the chief's precious daughter be? For two days, the city was at a standstill. We refused negotiations or any further contact. We were just waiting...for him.

He would not disappoint.

He found our secret hideout on the outskirts of the city. He disabled our guys, one by one, making his way inside. I took five guys with me to stop him, I wanted the glory of his death for myself. We found him, rather, he found us. He took out my guys before a shot could be fired. I was the last one left. I tried to shoot him but he knocked my gun out of my hand... again. I had a feeling of déjà vu. We had to settle it, hand to hand. I knew he was very fast so I decided to stay close to him, I did not want to give him time to use that incredible speed of his. I swung at him a bunch of times and missed, he swung at me and had me reeling. His hands were like freaking concrete. I managed to hit him in the face at one point, he flinched, and then I connected with two more strikes. I thought I had turned the tide of the fight but that was far from the truth. He spun around and nailed me in the back of my neck. That hit ended my fight.

The rest I didn't witness for obvious reasons, Lefty told me what went down. He made his way to the middle of the building, where we were holding the girl. The lighting was dim, all that could be seen was the girl and the chair she was strapped to. As he got closer, that's when all the lights went on. Several of our boys surrounded him, there wasn't a place he could turn without a gun being pointed at him. We had the bastard.

Snarky broke through the crowd with his gun drawn, walking pompously. He cursed out the mystery man in the ski mask real good. I wish I could have heard it. Snarky then aimed his gun at his chest and fired. The girl screamed as loud as the gunshot, she even started crying too. Snarky was crying tears of joy. He enjoyed that murder as good as his first. The thorn in our side was dead.

Yeah, if only that was the case.

When some of the boys came up close to take pictures of the body to distribute to our competitors, that guy leapt up and nailed each one of them. All of the boys were in shock, it was like seeing the dead climb out of their graves. That hesitation was used to his advantage, he moved like a hurricane through the crowd, taking them all down with his bare hands. It didn't take long before Snarky, Lefty, Switch and Don were all by themselves. They fired at him but he did not stop. Lefty, Switch and Don were down and Snarky was forced to face him alone. As I heard it, Snarky gave up without incident, he was the only one to leave unscathed. I wish I could have said the same.

We were all apprehended that night, our organization was in dire straits. That crime was not like the others, it was too publicized, not just in the city but across the country. Our friends in high places would not help us. With the Too Jive Crew behind bars, other groups invaded the territory we worked so hard to keep.

After his heroics, that guy in the ski masks fame and notoriety also spread across the country. The people loved him, the media loved him, the entire damn country wanted more of him. With his popularity growing, he needed a name. Guy in ski mask wasn't cutting it. After stopping a hijacking, he left his calling card with his name on it—Mighty Maxed. When I first heard it, my first thought was that it was the dumbest name I'd ever heard. I wasn't the only one. As he explained it in a rare interview, he said the name meant that he was mightiness to the max. I still thought it was stupid. Eventually, he dropped the mighty part and just referred to himself as Maxed.

Whatever his name, no matter how corny it was, he was, without question, ridiculously powerful. There was no stopping him. Other groups, like the one under Uncle Adolfo, met a fate similar to ours. The era of the big crime syndicates was effectively killed. With Maxed around, no group could get enough traction to get big in the first place. Prisons were being packed with criminals like us, they even had to construct a new one to house all of us.

As time passed and I continued to wallow in my anger, forced to sit in that damn prison cell for twenty three hours every day, the outside world was changing. People were actually able to walk the streets at any time of the day or night without fear of harassment. Our old turf, where people feared to even think of going, had mothers with baby strollers and animal lovers taking their dogs for walks. That's what our turf was degraded to. I think I would have punched out one of those hippies if I saw that.

Maxed had also changed. He became a lot stronger and faster. He lifted a ship stuck in the muddy banks of the river with his bare hands, and when he moved, all that could be seen was a blur. He even learnt how to fly, the man could freaking fly. There was one more thing. Snarky, Switch, Don and Lefty all shot at Maxed that night we were arrested and he wasn't fazed at all. It did not make any sense. Another attempt was made on his life by another group. They set up an accident and when Maxed came to the rescue, a dozen guys, all armed with assault rifles, fired at him. People with camera phones caught it all. He should have been torn to shreds but the guy didn't even bleed. Those guys got the surprise and the beating of their lives after that.

That solved the mystery, he was bullet proof, too. Just our luck.

Maxed even got a girlfriend, a police officer by the name of Emma Ramon. She was a dragon of a woman, had a bad attitude, was rude, loud, arrogant and bossy—a typical cop. She was not hiding her relationship, either. She made sure everyone knew she was with the city's greatest hero. No one could see what the guy saw in her but he was in love with her, regardless.

I spent three years in jail for my role in the kidnapping. Snarky was able to convince one of the few friends he had left up top to get us an early release. Don, Lefty, Switch and I re-joined Snarky to start up the old operation.

However, the crime scene had changed substantially.

With the arrival of the superhero came the birth of the super villain. A slew of weirdos and headcases flooded the city. There were guys like Albatross, Chronic, Mister Mephistophelean, Mime Master and Professor Brain Drain. Calling them weirdos didn't do them justice, they were beyond that. However, they were also powerful and dangerous. Albatross looked ridiculous in that bird suit of his but he could fly and had razor sharp wings, sharp enough to even cause Maxed to draw blood. Mister Mephistophelean drew on the power of darkness that he obtained from the contract he made with the devil. That guy was scary; he really looked like a demon. Then there was Professor Brain Drain, I guess he got the title of the arch-nemesis. He and Maxed were always at each other's throats. The Professor constantly let loose his vile creations, whether they were giant robots or mutated grizzly bears.

Yeah, life in the city was becoming that ridiculous and even more dangerous. However, with their hero in the city to protect them, the people were happy.

As for the Too Jive Crew, we became insignificant. We had no powers or gimmick, just a bunch of thugs with guns that became as useless as used toothpicks. The ordinary criminal could not survive without a super villain. Guys who I knew were top level people in their criminal organizations became nothing more than low level lackeys who tried to get the coffee orders right. Too Jive Crew would never stoop to that level, that's what Snarky used to say.

We tried to get things going again but failed at every turn. Maxed was not going to allow us to do that, he screwed us over, time and time again. It was like he could read minds and knew what we were planning. I, personally, think he was psychic, but if he was, he wasn't telling.

Too Jive Crew became a joke. We were no better than the insignificant, nameless, unimportant thugs on Saturday morning cartoon shows the superheroes never wasted a second punch on. With our dilemma and the lack of support or respect from the guys up top, we were forced to split up. Each guy went his own way.

Snarky went crying back to his rich daddy, he took him back without question. Lefty joined a construction company. Switch went into demolition, which really suited him. Don hooked up with his high school sweetheart and moved to the suburbs. Unlike us, he had quite of a bit of cash stashed away, just in case. I wish I took the time to look ahead like he did.

I was forced to give up my condo, my big screen TV, fancy clothes, everything. Well, not exactly everything. I kept my convertible; I'd never give that up. They'd have to pry it away from my cold, dead fingers.

With my record, I could not get a job. I was forced to live in a crummy little apartment, just like the one I lived in as a child. It was funny, real funny. I could not help laughing. I thought I had left that part of myself behind, I had grown above what I used to be. Yet, there I was, lying on the floor of some ratty apartment. I had not grown up, I had only moved in a circle, returning to what I truly was—a pathetic failure.

Eventually, I did find a job as a security guard in a minimart. Yet another irony, I went from defying the law to helping enforce it. Just another chapter in my life. At times, I thought I would chew my leg off in frustration but I found something to keep me occupied. The girl behind the cash register thought I was cute and I thought the same of her. She gave me her number and things picked up from there. Melissa Franklin, the girl of my dreams. After spending my life around slutty women, I never thought I would meet someone like her. So pure and innocent. I didn't think I deserved her in my life, I still don't.

We moved in together—in her place, not mine. It did not take long before we got married and she gave me my first son. He looked more like his mother, thankfully. I don't want him to take anything after me. Two years later, my daughter was born. David and Carroll, I love my kids to death. I wish I could express how much but... well...

The years rolled on and on, I got to see my kids grow up and raised the way my mother never did for me, the right way. I wanted them to be nothing like I was, I wanted them to be upstanding, honest and good-natured people. I wanted that to be the legacy of a man who committed heinous crimes for his own benefit.

If I could only see them grow into adults, I'd give anything for that.

You see, the thing is that life in the city took a dramatic turn for the worse.

Maxed and Emma got married and she quit her job. She used her fame to become a talk show host. She was even reported to soon have her own reality show. I can't imagine how crappy that would have been. She had a lot of power over Maxed, enough to get him to remove his mask and reveal his identity during an episode of her show. He didn't look as grotesque as I'd imagined him being, nor was he the supermodel heartthrob the women wished he was. He looked like an ordinary guy. He even had an ordinary name, Bill Tucker. I guess it's true that greatness can come from anywhere.

He had endorsement deals, did commercials, prime time interviews, the guy was everywhere. He looked uncomfortable doing it to me but since his wife wanted it, he went along. I can't blame him for that, I'd do whatever Melissa wanted me to do as well.

Well, as the saying goes, nothing lasts forever, and this applies even to superheroes. One night, when Emma left the studio she worked at, she was kidnapped by Professor Brain Drain's assistant. I can't remember his name, he wasn't anyone important anyway. As the people who were there reported it, she went with him without struggle. Professor Brain Drain was not the first guy to kidnap the wife of the city's hero; it happened a bunch of times, actually. She followed the usual routine, playing the role of the helpless victim, waiting to be saved by her dashing husband. I'm sure she wanted that sort of thing to happen just so she could get a boost in ratings for her show upon her rescue. Besides, she was Maxed's wife; no one would dare harm her.

That time would be far different from the others.

By the time Maxed smashed through the ceiling of Professor Brain Drain's hideout, he saw what he never thought he would. His wife was lying on the floor, coughing uncontrollably, her eyes could not blink. She almost looked dead. Professor Brain Drain was on a bed hooked up to a ventilator in the same room. Maxed approached him angrily and the Professor revealed what he had done.

Professor Brain Drain, furious after years of failing to kill his nemesis, went to his trump card. He attempted to create a super virus, one powerful enough to kill even Maxed. His attempt backfired and he unintentionally became infected by his own virus. He tried to develop a cure but failed to do so, he created it to be that way. He knew he was going to die, and slowly. He did not want to die without attaining the ultimate victory that was denied him for so many years, so he came up with his end game strategy. He had Emma abducted and administered the virus to her. She, like him, was destined to die. He would have his victory after all. I heard he laughed maniacally before that final cough and wheeze before dying.

Maxed no longer cared about him, he was focused on getting help for his wife. He took her to the best doctors but each one, despite their efforts, failed to cure her. Just as Professor Brain Drain intended, Emma slowly started losing her bodily functions, even her sanity. She could not recognize her own husband. Maxed took it hard and a couple weeks later, took the death of his wife even harder. I know if Melissa died, I'd be the same way. He was a destroyed man, who no longer cared to stop crime in the city. He disappeared entirely after her funeral.

The criminals in the city weren't going to pass up on that opportunity. They ran amok in the city, committing every crime in the book. The shackles were removed.

One morning, I heard a knock at my door and Snarky Snider was on the other side. He wanted to reform Too Jive Crew once more, he was certain that this time we would regain our former glory. I was skeptical; I had a relatively good life with my family, which I did not have to consider before. However, money was tight and expenses were rising. I wanted my family to have a good life, deprived of nothing that they needed or desired.

That's why I accepted his offer.

Too Jive Crew was moving up the ranks in the criminal world once more. We were quickly making almost as much money as we did before. There wasn't a bank manager we could not make pee in his pants. Life was becoming great once more and I had more than enough cash to care for my family. We moved to a bigger house in a better neighborhood, my kids were able to attend private school. My wife went back to college to get her degree. I was even able to give my convertible a much needed face lift. Melissa did not like what I was doing, she asked me to stop, but I could not comply with that request. There is a part of me that loves this stuff, a part I could never fully bury. It's who I am. I guess there wasn't anything that I would not do for my wife.

Yeah, that was one great year. If only it could have stayed that way.

Albatross was up to his usual tricks, robbing high-rise apartment buildings, when Maxed unexpectedly showed up and easily beat him into submission. It looked like the great hero had returned to see that the criminals who plagued his city come to justice. However, he was different, as everyone soon found out.

He did not wait for the cops to arrest Albatross, he grabbed him by the throat and snapped his neck. Just like that, Albatross was dead. He tossed his body aside like it was garbage.

The entire city was in shock. Maxed had never killed anyone in his life, not even when he was a lot weaker in his early days. He obviously was not the man he was before, his heart and soul was covered in darkness like no other. Having to see the woman he loved slowly die before him must have been enough to do that. I can't say I blame him.

It would not stop there. The next week, he repeated his actions, that time laying Chronic to waste. People were becoming frightened; their once revered hero was turning into a ruthless killer. Week after week, another super villain would die. It did not matter if they were in the city or not, Maxed would find them and took them out, permanently. Each murder was done like clockwork, all occurring on a Wednesday at three fifteen. His wife died on a Wednesday at that time. He made the killings symbolic. If his wife would die at that time, then so would everyone else.

Snarky was not worried, though. He was certain that Maxed was only going after the super villains and would leave guys like us, who were insignificant, alone. He was confident enough to continue operations as if nothing was happening. I should have backed out, taken the money I had, and moved away—far, far away—with my family. I chose to listen to Snarky, to follow his leadership.

I guess I never learn.

After the Zen Master, the last super villain left, was killed, we thought that would be the end to the killing spree. We were dead wrong. Uncle Alfredo Albertini, the head of the Italian mafia, was killed. That's when we realized that everyone was a target, not just super villains.

He changed his pattern, killing ordinary criminals every day instead of once a week. There were a lot more of us than the supers.

I noticed that he was not just killing them randomly; he was doing it in alphabetical order. I guess even when it came to murder; he wanted to do it the right way. It's just like him to do that.

It didn't take long for Don to be knocked off; Switch was killed not too long after him. There was a great emigration of thugs and criminals from the city, no one wanted anything to do with the place. Lefty McMichaels took off for Greenland, of all places. He thought he was safe but was dead wrong. Maxed found him and crushed his throat, just like everyone else. Snarky took off for Thailand but it's pointless, really. It doesn't matter where you go, he'll find you. There's no doubt about that.

No one would be spared, that was obvious. All of us would receive the punishment that Maxed believed we deserved. Well, we probably did deserve it. Each of us did a lot of bad stuff in our lives and never truly paid for any of it. The self-proclaimed judge, jury and executioner would ensure that our dues were paid.

Looks like I'm pulling into the driveway. This was a great house, lots of good memories here. It's too bad Melissa and the kids can't live here anymore. It's my fault, really. You see,

Darwin Rubio was killed yesterday and I believe that today will be my turn. I can't think of anyone else who would be before me. That's why I had Melissa and the kids get as far away from here as possible. I don't want them to see what will become of me. Knowing Melissa, she'll come back to bury my worthless self. I don't deserve her, and never did.

It's three thirteen, so I'd better make this quick.

Melissa, my love, you impacted my life in more ways than one. You took a worthless thug and made him a man. I don't know why you took a chance on me, why you decided to waste your time with the likes of me, but I thank you for it regardless, from the bottom of my heart.

David and Carroll, my precious kids. My legacy. I can't express how much I love you; there are no words that can say that. If there is one thing that a worthless guy like me will ask of you, is that you do not become like me. Aim for the stars, become decent people with decent goals and ambitions. Make a living for yourselves with your minds instead of a gun. You two are much better than I am, than I ever could be.

Melissa... Carroll... David... I love you all. If only I could spend five more minutes with you. I'd give anything for that... anything...

Did you hear that? It's a sound I could never mistake, that of feet touching the ground. I don't need to turn around to know that he's here. According to my watch, he's only giving himself twenty five seconds to kill me. I guess I should be honored.

Hey, cops, when you see this, please make sure that you pass this tape to my family. I know you guys will take it in as evidence, but I really want them to have it. It's my final message to them; I really want them to hear this.

It looks like he's starting to approach me. I'd better get out of the car to face him, I wouldn't want my blood to mess it up, not after I detailed it.

I'm going to die now, so this is goodbye. I know I've been a real bastard throughout my life but I really am sorry for all that I've done and I'm not just saying that.

However...there is just one final thing I have to do before signing off. You see, it's the part of me that I cannot bury, it won't allow me to be killed like some cow in a slaughterhouse. No, not me. You see, beneath the driver's seat of my beloved car is a very close friend of mine. We've travelled everywhere together. Fifteen years ago, I killed a man with this gun and that murder shaped the course for the rest of my life.

And with this gun I will face him! I don't care how strong he is, how fast he is, how impervious he is...there is one thing that is absolutely certain! Samuel Roderick is no chump and I won't go down like one, either! You hear me Maxed, you hear me!

About the author: I am a twenty seven year old native of Saint Lucia, in the Caribbean. I graduated from Sir Arthur Lewis Community College in 2002 and am now employed as a Night Wallet Cashier at G4S Security Services.

Fanaticism

Gary Buettner

The Fanatic was not the supervillain that Tommy expected him to be. His long red trench coat accentuated his tall, thin frame. He wore a red domino mask and his black hair was swept back from a severe widow's peak. A red F logo in a gold shield was embroidered over his breast pocket. He was spoken of on the streets in hushed, fearful tones, but he was not as threatening as Tommy had pictured him to be. Without superpowers, how dangerous could this man be? It was his eyes, though, his dark, watchful eyes that made Tommy squirm, made him think that the Fanatic was on to him, as he led him into a hidden elevator and pressed the down arrow.

They began to descend. The elevator was a clear cylinder and Tommy could see the layers of earth and stone pass by the glass. They were going deep.

"So, you're Firecracker's grandson?"

"Yeah." Tommy, on the other hand, actually did look the part of a superhero, with his chiselled body and square jaw. He walked with a slouch, though and hadn't showered or shaved in weeks.

"He kicked serious Nazi ass at like two-hundred miles per hour. He was a real hero."

Tommy couldn't help but grin. He had expected a lot of things, but nerdgasmic hero worship was not one of them.

"Surprised that I respect him so much?"

"A little, yeah."

"Don't be. I *love* superheroes. Love them. The costumes. The powers. But most especially the gadgets. I love it all. Which brings us to the reason for this little visit. Do you have it?"

"Right here," Tommy said, reaching into his backpack.

"Whoa there cowboy," the Fanatic said, pressing a nine-millimetre pistol against Tommy's forehead. "No matter how fast you can move with that belt, I can pull the trigger faster."

"Hey, chill man, I don't even know how to work this thing, okay?" Tommy stood up, holding his empty hands up.

The Fanatic reached into the bag and produced the Speed Belt, a silver belt with a large winged globe belt buckle and two silver wings on either hip. It shined in the elevator's light. "Wow," he said, "you can almost feel the buzz off this thing."

"Yeah," Tommy said, "but that doesn't pay my rent, does it?"

"I can think of several ways that an enterprising young man with the ability to move faster that the speed of sound could make a lot of money."

"No offense," Tommy said, "but, I'm not a crook."

"None taken." The Fanatic looked Tommy over. "Not a hero, though."

"No," Tommy said looking at his shoes.

The Fanatic pointed the gun at him again. "Why not?"

Tommy backed against the wall of the elevator, which, he noticed, was still descending. "My grandfather broke every single bone in his body. Every single one. An adult human body has two-hundred and six bones in it. He broke everyone. On top of that, he died of cancer from a lifetime fighting Dr. Skull."

"Dr. Skull," the Fanatic said. "The Poisonous man." The Fanatic returned his gun to his coat. "I met him a couple of times, total douche bag. I'm sorry to hear about your grandfather. Is that when your father took over the fight?"

"The Silver Age Firecracker? No he was the son of one of Granddad's Army buddies. My dad was less the two-fisted hero and more the two-fisted accountant."

"And you're willing to just give this up?" The Fanatic cradled the belt in his hands.

"For the right price, yeah."

"How do you know I just won't kill you and take it?" The Fanatic handed the belt back to him.

Tommy shrugged. "Word on the street is that you're a straight shooter, for a villain."

"That's the word on the street, huh?"

"Yeah. I mean, they say you've... killed people."

"Really? I've done better than that. I've killed... superheroes. Strictly for acquisitions, never anything personal."

"Anybody that I'd have heard of?"

The Fanatic grinned. "Oh, I'm sure you've heard of a couple of them."

"Like who?"

"Like *whom*?"

"Okay, like whom?"

"I killed the Crimson Eagle. He was a treasure trove, all those gadgets. A lot of people didn't know this, but he used to wear a sort-of backpack under his cape. The way he was always grabbing back there, he looked like he was pulling all those gadgets out of his ass." The Fanatic laughed.

"Anybody else?"

"I killed *America's Man of Action*!"

"Pentagon? You killed him?"

"I got his bullet-proof battle helmet downstairs. Not to bright, Pentagon, ran into everything head-first."

"Who else?"

"Golden Age Skeleton Key. He doesn't really count, I just pushed him down the stairs in his wheel chair. You should have seen the look on his face. I hung his cape on the back of the chair and away he went." The Fanatic had to take a second to compose himself.

"Anybody else?"

The Fanatic's eyes zeroed in on Tommy. "Kid Atomic."

Tommy flinched when he heard the name. If the Fanatic noticed, he didn't let on.

"I shot him in the face, point blank. That was a closed casket funeral for sure."

"I read about that in the paper. I didn't realize that was you. Nobody could believe that you, I mean, ya'know, anybody could get past his force field."

A grinned opened across the Fanatic's face. "I asked for his autograph."

"He lowered his shield to sign an autograph."

"Yup."

"And you shot him in the face and took his Radiation Ring."

"Funny story about that ring. Without Kid Atomic's ability to absorb and control that radiation, I have to lock it up in this big lead vault. More trouble than it is worth, really. That Kid Atomic died for nothing."

Tommy clenched his fists.

The elevator made a soft tone.

"We've arrived," the Fanatic said, as the elevator doors slid open.

"Unbelievable," Tommy said, stepping out of the elevator. The Fanatic's collection rivalled that of any museum or secret headquarters trophy room that Tommy had ever seen. The collection was displayed in an enormous hall. The walls were polished steel and gigantic lights hovered in the air like UFO's. The floors were made from huge slaps of marble.

One wall was dedicated entirely to capes. They lined the wall from end to end like multi-colored silk curtains. The Crimson Eagle. Scaredy Cat. Stargazer. The Green Moth. The Blue Nebula. The Indighost. The Purple Legend. A rainbow of crime fighters. Masks hung above that. Hoods. Cowls. Headbands.

The Fanatic said nothing, but let Tommy soak it all in.

The opposite wall was dominated by an enormous glass case, lighted from below. It contained more weapons and equipment that Tommy had ever seen before. Swords. Secret communicators. Grappling guns. Eagle-shaped boomerangs. Skeleton key-shaped throwing stars.

"Funny story about those keys," the Fanatic said. "They belonged to the Silver Age Skeleton Key. I spent a whole weekend trying to figure out how to throw those things. Couldn't do it. He must have been really chucking them because the first one I ever got was lodged in this burglar's skull. Unbelievable, really."

Unbelievable was definitely the word for it, Tommy thought. He wondered how many of these brave men and women had died at the Fanatic's hands over some trinket or another. It took his breath away.

"Do you wanna see the good stuff?"

The Fanatic led Tommy down a ramp to a massive steel door. The hallway was lit from the floor and gave the whole space a spooky quality. He used a secret decoder ring to open it. He glanced back at Tommy, "I actually got this in a box of cereal. It was a really, old box of the Secret Shield's Secret Flakes. Gag."

The door slid open.

Tommy could not process what he saw fast enough. The small chamber was lined with glass display cases. The display cases varied in size and shape, but the most impressive thing about them was what they contained.

Thunder God's shining gold Belt of Strength.

The Tank's blocky battle armor. Still battle-damaged from his last fight with the Armageddonist.

Retro Rocket's jet pack and ray gun. "Retro Rocket," the Fanatic said, in a deep, Saturday morning cartoon announcer's voice, "the man from the future that never was!"

An enormous vault sat in one corner marked only with the circular, yellow radioactive symbol.

The Fanatic dismissed the lead-lined vault with a flick of his hand. "More trouble than it was worth."

Tommy held the Speed Belt in his hand.

"Can I give you a piece of advice, Tommy? You aren't going to live long enough to actually take this advice, but I wanted you to know how I know that you're a hero, at least a wannabe."

It was Tommy's turn to smile. He didn't see any reason now to continue the charade. "I'd love to take superhero tips from a supervillain."

"You said you didn't know how the belt worked, but the rubber on the bottom of your sneakers is melted. You've been running at high speeds without the proper footwear."

Tommy nodded. "Nice."

"You have a slight sunburn on your face. The pattern suggests that you were wearing a mask."

"I used sunscreen."

"I'm sure you did, but the speeds that you travel at probably wash some of it away. A shame. Secret Identity 101, really."

"You should write a book." Tommy spun around like a tornado for half a second and when he stopped, he'd donned the Speed Belt and his costume, black and red, with the classic exploding firecracker emblem on the chest.

"Ouch, you changed the colors. No more red, white and blue? Granddad must have spun in his grave. At super speed, of course."

"You're under arrest, Fanatic," the new Firecracker said. "For the murder of Kid Atomic."

"Was he like you little buddy?"

"He was my best friend and you murdered him."

"You have some kind of evidence?"

"You confessed and with what is in that vault..."

The Fanatic swung the vault open. It was empty.

Firecracker's mouth hung open. "The ring..."

The Fanatic shrugged. "Which ring?"

"The Radiation Ring."

The Fanatic made a grand gesture out of looking in the empty vault. He clicked his tongue. "Nothing in there."

Firecracker searched the chamber at super speed, checking the entire place in the space of two heartbeats.

"I was just talking smack. You know, *padding my resume*."

"I'm taking you in," Firecracker said. "There's got to be something here that ties you to a murder." He took a small pair of handcuffs from his belt and moved to put them on the Fanatic's wrists.

The villain held out his hands, crossing his wrists.

A ring on his finger caught Firecracker's eye. It glowed. "Oh, shit..."

An explosion rocked the room.

Firecracker picked himself up in time to see the Fanatic levitate off the floor in the force field bubble of radiation that his friend always employed. His fist was a crackling ball of energy.

"You said..."

"I'm a villain, *Tommy*, I lied to you. Ya'know, you really shouldn't believe everything you are told."

"Why didn't you just kill me in the elevator?"

The Fanatic shrugged. "I really wanted to show you my collection."

"Well, thanks." Firecracker raced towards him faster than the Fanatic's eyes could follow and punched the bubble so hard that it sent him flying, force field and all.

The Fanatic cut loose with a volley of radiation blasts, but Firecracker managed to dodge all of them.

Firecracker darted back into the main collection chamber. He figured that the Fanatic wouldn't cut loose in that room and put all of his collection at risk. He would have to launch a blitz attack against the Fanatic, take him by surprise.

Luckily hard and fast was his specialty.

Firecracker launched himself at the Fanatic when he stepped out of the secure smaller chamber.

The Fanatic was wearing the Belt of Strength. He smashed Firecracker in the face with one gloved hand.

"You play with your toys? Doesn't that decrease the value?"

The Fanatic laughed. "I bet you didn't know this, but your little buddy, Kid Atomic didn't die right away. He cried and begged. I had to shoot him *three* times in the face to kill him. Thick skull.

Firecracker raced from one spot of cover to another.

Halfway to safety, he was hit with an energy blast. He looked up to see the Fanatic carrying Retro Rocket's laser pistol. "Designed to shoot down rockets and men in jetpacks. Targeting system works faster than the human eye."

"Thanks for the info," Firecracker said, seizing the pistol from him at super-speed. He smashed it against the wall and it exploded knocking them both off their feet and smashing the glass of a few display cases.

"The reason I pushed the meeting up," Firecracker said, "is because I wanted to make sure that you didn't have time to set a trap for me."

"Clever, I guess, but I had a whole year to set a trap for you," the Fanatic said.

Firecracker stopped running. "How?"

The Fanatic held up the Radiation Ring. "I spent a year researching Kid Atomic, figuring out how his ring worked, what he could do with it if he just didn't give a shit about hurting anyone." The ring began to glow, getting hotter, first red than white. Firecracker could feel the heat off of it.

"The radiation will kill us both if you overload it!"

The Fanatic grinned and stepped back into the lead vault. He dropped the ring on the floor as he pulled the door shut.

Firecracker ran.

After a few minutes, the Fanatic released himself from the vault, picked up the ring and absorbed all the excess radiation in the room.

He walked over to where the remains of Firecracker lay. They boy was covered with radiation burns. The Fanatic wondered if his costume would be salvageable. He'd wanted the belt because of the Golden Age Firecracker's service in World War two, not for some snot-nosed kid's pathetic attempts now. It didn't really matter, and yet...

"You have possibly the shortest career of any crime fighter that I've ever heard of."

The Fanatic unbuckled the Speed Belt and took it over to the display case. There was a smudge of something on it. He took the sleeve of his jacket and wiped it clean. He stepped back to admire the new piece.

"Priceless," he said.

About the author: Gary Buettner lives in Indiana with his family. His fiction will appear in *Rotting Tales* and *Gone With The Dirt: Undead Dixie* both from Pill Hill Press.

The Dragoon

Lane Kareska

She tried to guess the chauffer's race.

His copper face and grassy black hair said some Chinese maybe. A shade of gypsy-gray glinted in his eyes. Mongol silence.

Grace nodded at the driver. He to her.

"Ms. Hunter, I'm to drive you to the manor," he said.

"Thank you."

He guided the young woman into the black limousine. He slid into the driver's seat.

Soon, she rapped on the dark glass divider and he lowered it. The silver bay and the new island-prison Alcatraz blurred by in the windows.

"How long have you worked for him?" she asked.

"Ten years."

"That's a long time."

He didn't say anything for a while but she waited there in the space.

"How long have you worked for the newspaper?" he finally asked.

"Ten years."

The limousine threaded speedily out of the city and into the headlands. After some miles it turned down into a woody, fog-knotted glen. Lonely roads of wet dust.

"What is your name?" she asked.

"Mark Drager."

"Drager. Like The Dragoon."

"Who?"

"Don't read the papers?" she asked.

"No."

The headlights cleaved the rolling wet fog and the car slowed, turning onto a cobbled drive.

"First time here?" Drager asked.

"No."

The manor was elegant, redbrick and ancient. It had an abandoned, mournful look. Grace remembered her previous times here, previous life. She turned the ring on her thin white finger and thought of Adam.

Drager watched her in the rear-view mirror.

He parked and opened her door. Rooks called from the oaks.

In the sitting room, the old man sat parked in his wheelchair. Divided in the still and slatted light, he looked like an old wooden carving of himself. His wispy hair hung like cobwebs about his face.

The tall blue murals on the walls depicted severe-seeming men at hunt with dogs. The center portrait showed a father and a son, both smiling with mischief and pride.

Grace's vision lingered there and she turned to the old man.

"Grace." He smiled.

"Hello, Mr. Barnes."

He struggled to his feet. Drager helped him.

"Call me Laurence."

"I prefer Mr. Barnes."

"Give me a hug," he said.

She held out her hand and after a moment he took it and kissed it with his old, papery lips.

"Please sit," he said.

She sat on the sofa and Drager stood against the wall.

Mr. Barnes returned to his wheelchair and faced the woman.

"Grace, tell me please, are you here as a newswoman or as family?"

"I've never been your family," she said.

"Well, I would say otherwise."

"Your son and I were never married."

"But you would have," Barnes said.

"Yes, we would have."

"So, you're here as a journalist then? It's been ages since I've been interviewed. I would have thought I fell out of relevance years ago."

"Your circus still operates."

"*Sans moi*. I'm involved in name only and it's been that way for long years."

"You founded it," she said.

"I did."

"I don't think anyone else could have. Such a worldly exhibit. Only someone as well travelled, as exotically educated as Laurence Barnes, could have built that show."

"Thank you, yes. I did always love the thrills of travel," Barnes said.

"As did your son."

"Adam, yes. You know he did. You met him on the road—where, in Africa, yes?"

"Capetown."

"Capetown." He looked up at the man Drager. "Mr. Drager, please, get Grace something to drink. Hers is scotch I believe."

"Water," she said.

"Water then, yes."

Drager nodded and left the room, silent as snow.

"Handy that you have him," she said.

"He helps me."

"Where did you acquire him?"

"Acquire? I don't know where one *acquires* people. I met him somewhere along the way. Somewhere in the world," Barnes said.

"Bangkok?"

Barnes didn't answer.

Drager returned with a glass of ice and water and gave it to her.

"Where were we?" she asked.

"Bangkok," Barnes said.

"Yes, Bangkok. The very city where Adam and I were to be married, those many years ago."

"The very city."

She turned to the chauffeur. "Have you ever been, Mr. Drager? No? You must visit. Beautiful city. I'll never return however, too many painful memories. My late fiancée was killed there, you see. Shot twice." She tapped her index finger once against each of her cheekbones. "It was a bandit. Some coward. The police suggested a Tong affiliate. Never solved."

"This is a sad subject for discussion. It will always be. No matter how much time passes," Barnes said.

"Apologies. I don't mean to be melancholy. I'm here to ask about The Dragoon."

"Who?" Barnes asked.

"He's some character running around the city now. At night, mostly. He's been credited with stopping a few crimes, even a murder. Generally, the police want to bring him in themselves. Can't have vigilantes swinging about," Grace said.

"Swinging?"

"He's an acrobat. Dresses in red and black. A masked man, if you can believe it. Straight from the funny pages."

"In our city," Barnes said.

"In our city."

"I'm afraid I'm a poor source for you then," Mr. Barnes said. "I know nothing."

"The police think this man, this gymnast, must've come from some training. They've begun to question the local carnival-men and circus operators."

"If he's from mine, I'm the wrong man to ask about it, Grace."

"He hasn't come from yours. All your performers are regularly accounted for. Rock-solid alibis. So, there isn't any worry there. I'm more interested, though, in motive."

"Motive," Barnes said.

"What would make a man go to such lengths? He must be a psychotic, wouldn't you think? To risk his life nightly. The police think it must be some chronic risk-compulsion. Some outrageous sense of vigilantism."

"What do you think Grace?"

"I think the police are overlooking the greatest of all motivators."

The old man forced one of his woolly eyebrows to rise and curve like the rind of a question mark.

"Guilt," she said. "Guilt can make us behave in unthinkable ways."

"I suppose that's true," Barnes said.

"Certainly. Imagine, for a moment, that you, the great Laurence Barnes were not the wealthy and worldly innovator that you are, but instead, a lowly street thief. A common-criminal. Let's say you were a murderer, the vilest type. A killer of great men. Men with futures."

"Grace—"

"Indulge me. Let us say that you were a bandit in Bangkok. And during a robbery, you murdered the son of a great man. Don't you think that your victim's father would spend his every penny to make sure that you were found? I think a man like Laurence Barnes would never rest until his son's killer was seized," she said.

"And then?"

"*Precisely*. And then? And then, what? Would the killer be killed in turn? Tortured grotesquely? What is fitting?"

"Nothing is fitting," Barnes said.

"Nothing is fitting."

The room was silent for a long moment.

"You know, Mr. Barnes, I have been a journalist for many years. I have witnessed many things, things that stay with me. I frequently dream about them. But the strangest thing I have ever seen was an old woman in Denver. A drunk driver killed her son. Horrible incident. The driver was found and imprisoned. He served his time. But while in jail, the woman visited him every day. She spoke with him, counselled him. And when he was released, the killer rented a room in her house. He worked for her. For free. He became her caretaker. He was atoning, don't you think? All he had to offer was his service and his time, but that's what he did. That was how his own guilt motivated him."

"Guilt."

"I think, Mr. Barnes, that if you ever did find Adam's killer... you would not have him savaged. I know you very well, and I know you're a good man. I think you'd do everything you could to make that murderer want to atone. I think you'd give him the opportunity to redeem himself; to correct the path of his own life. To work off his many crimes. You'd council him, equip him, you'd train him to do it. Even if it took years. I think you would retire from your professional life. I think it would become your life's mission to force the *killer* to see the light."
The room was silent and Grace looked at Drager, then at Mr. Barnes.
She said: "So in that way, I suppose, Adam is the real hero."

Drager drove Grace back to the train station in the city. The day was foggy and the hour impossible to tell.

He opened her car door and stood rigid as iron.

He could not meet her eyes. He was not powerful enough.

After a long time, she hugged him.

That was all.

In this city, at this time, the cable cars ran above the streets. They hung and glided shoulder-level with the towers. They coasted, packed with commuters, like motorized cages on lines.

Grace stood at the rail of a cable car. She slid her wrist through the leather hand strap and looked down at the streets countless floors below. Her car grinded down the line from one stop to another. The end of her work day.

The towers were black and steel and glass. In the liquid shimmer of one, she saw a swoop of savage color. A bold red.

Something landed on her car's roof. None of the other commuters seemed to notice. The car swayed so slightly with the new weight. She craned and tried to see but she could not.

She thought of her late fiancée. The man with a future.

The car swayed again as The Dragoon leapt away. Grace watched him dive out into the void, his body acrobat-taut, holding a crucifix pose as he fell through the cold, singing air.

Grace watched the blur of man descend. She saw him throw out a line that caught somewhere among the towers. She watched him swing away, deep into that city.

About the author: Lane Kareska was born in Texas and now lives in Chicago. He first visited a comic book store as a fourth grader and hasn't been able to stop since.

The Stuntman

Matt Adams

"We're golden, Stan! We're GOLDEN!"

Stan Kirkpatrick wanted to believe his agent.

But he had a feeling, as usual, that Artie wasn't telling him everything.

"So I got the part?" Stan asked, his massive hand engulfing the phone he held to his ear.

His agent cleared his throat on the other end of the line, *"Got the part? No, Stan baby, no! What we've got is an audition. Just you and the bigwigs at the studio. I pulled some strings, called in a few favors, and they're gonna let you audition. You go in there and you kill 'em. Now, not literally. Easy with the superpowers, okay? You're my boy, Stan! You're my boy!"*

Stan shut his phone off before Artie had the chance to douse him with more fake, effusive praise.

It's all up to me.

***

"Unhand him, you villain!" Stan yelled, remembering all the tips he'd learned about voice projection and feeling. He held the pages in front of him and emoted, just like his middle school theater teacher told him.

"I am justice! I am the dawn of a new era! I am the Amazing Marvel! You will release your hostages or I shall be forced to take action! This is your final warning!"

Stan held his hand up in triumph, imagining the movie executives spellbound by his virtuoso performance. But no one clapped or cheered, and Stan snuck a peek to find one executive yawning and another running a file across her fingernails. He ad-libbed, sending a jolt of yellow energy from his hands.

"If this is how you treat others, this is your reward!" he yelled loud enough to shake the room.

The energy blast obliterated the back wall, exposing the cramped space to sunlight.

Satisfied, Stan turned and placed his hands on his hips—his trademark stance—and looked at the horrified movie bosses.

"That, that was great, Stan," one of the men stuttered as he tried to stir a colleague who had fainted.

"Some spectacular work there, Amazing Marvel. We'll get back to you real soon," a female executive promised. Her folded hands shook.

Stan puffed out his chest and saluted the others in the room, doing his best to hide his disappointment.

He couldn't shake the voice in his head telling him the audition hadn't gone well.

***

Stan basked in the bright California sunshine, thankful for another beautiful day on the West Coast. He'd come a long way since his days as an Iowa farmboy.

As the Amazing Marvel, he'd captured the nation's attention. He'd beaten back an alien invasion, captured his arch-nemesis Bloodsport multiple times, and helped solve the crisis in the Middle East. On top of that, he'd built more than a thousand homes for Habitat for Humanity, an accomplishment he ranked as one of his proudest. He knew wars and disagreements were inevitable, but believed he'd helped shape a better world.

Not bad for a 40-year-old man.

Of course, Stan Kirkpatrick didn't look 40 years old. Thanks to a genetic anomaly, he aged at a much slower rate than normal people. Though he'd been on earth for some 40 years, he looked to be in his early 30s, his face retaining perpetual boyish good looks.

He didn't intend to become a celebrity; it just kind of happened overnight. As his popularity grew, he hired an agent and decided to sell his life story. The book, *Confessions of an Amazing Marvel,* sold millions of copies and movie companies found themselves locked in a long battle for the film rights.

Stan's agent Artie worked a special provision into the deal: Stan would get the chance to audition for the starring role in the movie based on his own book.

He figured no one could play the Amazing Marvel better than the Amazing Marvel.

When he picked up a copy of *Variety*, he realized Hollywood didn't agree.

***

"Artie! Artie! Are you seeing this? They're getting the kid from *Transformers* to play me!" Stan screamed. "You and I know the kid messed up the *Indiana Jones* movie!"

Artie chewed gum furiously on the other end, *"Yeah, I tried to talk the studio out of that. But the kid makes money at the box office. That's what they're interested in, sport."*

Stan almost crushed the phone; he hated it when Artie called him "sport."

"But it's not all bad, man. They wanna use you as a consultant on the film. And they wanna rework the script a little bit. I set up a meeting tomorrow with the screenwriter. He says he wants to get some real insight from you, baby. You're the best! You're gold, baby! You're gold!"

Stan pressed the touchscreen to hang up on his agent, leaving a small crack on the surface. It didn't matter what he said to Artie. Hollywood didn't think the Amazing Marvel capable of starring in a movie based on his own life.

Instead, the studio picked some snot-nosed actor parading around like an A-list star. Stan massaged his temples; he'd seen the kid's work; utterly forgettable. He didn't have the stature to play a superhero; certainly not one with Stan's impressive physical presence.

Surely, this was just a bump in the road.

How could Hollywood screw up a superhero movie, anyway?

***

"All right, Amazing Marvel, I have some questions for you," the screenwriter said. "I'm having trouble figuring out your origin story. I mean, the script is good. It's based on your book. But the source material kind of leaves out how you got your powers."

"I was born this way. I did mention that in the book," Stan replied.

They sat together at a table much too small for so large a room. Stan's elbows took up most of the tabletop, and the screenwriter leaned back in his chair holding a legal pad.

The screenwriter sighed, "Well, you see with these superhero movies, especially when we're doing a franchise, we like to do what we call an 'origin story.' Gives the audience something to relate to. Lets them know how you discovered your powers, introduces them to your world. So let's test out a few scenarios, okay?"

"Sure," Stan said, giving the other man two thumbs up before setting his massive elbows back on the table, which bowed at the weight.

"All right, were you bitten by a radioactive animal? Like a spider or something?"

"No."

"Sure, that's been done to death, right? Did you get a huge dose of gamma rays? You know like at a military base?"

Stan shook his head, "No."

"Of course not. What about cosmic rays that changed you and your science team forever?"

"Science team? What science team?" Stan said, crossing his arms.

The screenwriter scratched his head, "Forget I said anything. What about your motivation? Parents gunned down in front of you, forcing you to swear revenge on the criminal element that took them away from you?"

"Dear God, no. That's horrible."

The screenwriter scratched something off his legal pad and looked up, "Right, right. Did you build your own armor? Were you sent here as the last survivor of a dying planet? Are you the son of a god? Are you a man out of time?"

"No, no, no, and no."

"You're not making this easy, Amazing Marvel."

"You can call me Stan."

"Sure. So, Amazing Marvel, how did you discover your powers?"

"Well, I was out in a cornfield when a combine started coming toward me. I was ten years old. And I tried to wave to my dad, who was driving, but he couldn't see or hear me. Somehow, I made the combine stop."

The screenwriter leaned forward and took notes, "That's good, that's good. That wasn't in your book."

"Yes it was. Chapter Two."

"Must've missed it. So you used your superpowers for the first time to stop the combine? Did you tip it over, blow it up, use telekinetic powers to crush it?"

Stan let out a nervous laugh, "No, nothing like that. I just stopped it."

"You mean you didn't inadvertently kill someone with newly-discovered powers you didn't know you had? You didn't throw the combine driver from the vehicle in anger? You didn't obliterate the entire cornfield, destroying the crop and bringing extreme financial hardship on your family?"

"No. I stopped it and then my dad saw me. It's pretty simple."

The screenwriter chewed on his pen, "Okay, okay. So you don't have the snappiest origin story in the history of heroes. No problem. We can work around that. What about your relationship with your arch-nemesis, Bloodsport?"

"We don't like each other very much," Stan said, leaning back and nearly tipping the table with his knees. "He thinks this is all some game. His big goal in life is to defeat me in hand-to-hand combat."

"So, where does his hatred come from? Were you best friends as kids?"

"No."

"Were you archrivals at your high school? You know, you were the popular guy and he was the over-the-top jock?"

Stan shook his head again, "I'm afraid not."

"Did he kill your entire family, forcing you to take a vow of justice to stop him once and for all?"

"Really, again with that?" Stan sighed. "No. That's not what happened, not at all."

***

The meeting left Stan feeling even more skeptical about the film, especially when the screenwriter muttered something about going for "best original screenplay" instead of "best adapted screenplay."

Whatever that meant.

Now the studio wanted him to stop by the wardrobe department to see what they'd cooked up for the movie version of his super-suit.

Once he saw it, he weighed the wisdom of letting Artie sell the film rights to his life story. They got the coloring right, but the costume designer added all kinds of strange swirls to the super-suit and large, metal gauntlets (which he didn't need). He found the flowing, shimmering cape even more distasteful.

He never wore a cape.

In fact, he'd alluded to that in the title of chapter seven of his book.

He also hated the large "A" and "M" logo emblazoned on the chest; his real super-suit didn't have a logo at all.

He walked past several different versions of the super-suit intended for different environments, including an arctic super-suit, a lava-retardant super-suit, an underwater super-suit, and a night-time super-suit.

Stan shook his head; he used one suit no matter where he went.

It didn't have a cape.

Or a logo.

And most certainly not an "arctic diving" mode.

"Oh, very good!"

The accented voice startled Stan, who turned to see a waifish woman who'd stepped straight out of the "Choreography" number from *White Christmas*.

"There you are, Amazing Marvel!"

Stan smiled.

The woman knew who he was!

"Hmmm, let's see," the woman said, using a tape measure to check Stan's measurements. "Yes, underestimated on the chest. We'll have to compensate for that."

Stan stood straight up as the woman struggled to wrap her arms around his thick waist.

"Hmmm. Waist measurement very close. Have to go tighter with the crotch, though. Going to be too saggy if we go as is."

The woman's tape measure snapped as she tried to wrap it around his biceps. She produced another seemingly out of nowhere.

Stan cleared his throat, "Better make sure you get the measurements right for the star of the show."

"Oh, I'm making certain of that," the woman said with a polite smile. "But he's not coming in until later. Right now, I take care of the stuntman."

***

"C'mon, Stan baby! You're the Amazing Marvel! Who better to do the stunts? They're gonna pay ya!"

Stan held the phone an arm's length away and screamed, "I don't care about the money!"

"That's not what you said when we made the deal. You wanted gold! Gold for my money man! Stan the Money Man!"

Stan bit his lower lip before he spoke, "Look, Artie, don't you think it's kind of debasing what's going on here? I mean, this story is based on *my life!* And instead of putting me in it, they've cast some Hollywood hotshot. Throwing me into stuntwork is an insult."

"You said you wanted to be in the movie. And I got ya into the movie," Artie said, letting out a wheezing sigh. "Maybe it'll be your big break. Maybe they'll put you in the sequel."

"The sequel? You're telling me I should look forward to being the stunt guy in the sequel!?"

"Hey, hey, hey. Not everybody starts big, Stan baby. Harrison Ford was a carpenter. Harrison Freaking Ford was a freaking carpenter!"

***

Stan tried not to let it get to him, but couldn't stop seething. Even if Harrison Ford ascended from carpenter to Most Popular Actor Ever, Stan didn't appreciate being marginalized in his own movie.

He was the Amazing Freaking Marvel, defender of earth. He'd stopped numerous threats to global security, but it wasn't until he encountered Bloodsport that people truly paid attention.

Before meeting the villain, most of Stan's foes were common thugs or mobsters. He'd even busted a few white collar criminals.

Bloodsport was a different sort of menace.

He only wanted to defeat the Amazing Marvel in hand-to-hand combat, and he didn't care who he had to hurt to force that battle.

Stan hadn't seen anything like it before. Bloodsport would destroy buildings, set city blocks on fire, and kidnap politicians and prominent public citizens to get his attention. He set off bombs in Bangkok and toppled the Eiffel Tower to draw the Amazing Marvel out.

Of course, Stan would beat him roundly and soundly in an unfair fight every single time, hauling Bloodsport down to another maximum-security prison where he would stay for a week and then bust out and hatch another dangerous plot to force another losing battle.

Stan tired of the game quickly, even if the media ate it up. Everyone knew Bloodsport was no match for him, but the bad guy refused to accept it. He always taunted the Amazing Marvel with some pathetic excuse. "This time, you won't catch me off-guard"; "this time my visor won't malfunction"; "my armor limits my range of motion." Each time, Stan vanquished his foe in just minutes.

Investigators traced the villain's identity back to one of those multiple martial arts leagues. Apparently, Bloodsport—aka Jimmy Kane—had won multiple titles. But the spoils of victory left him hollow, and he needed a bigger challenge. So he came up with the name Bloodsport, invested money in state-of-the-art body armor, and declared his intention to defeat the Amazing Marvel.

Stan defeated Bloodsport time and time again, and his reputation soared. He won high-profile jobs and overwhelming public support. In short, the Amazing Marvel went from defeating small-time hoods to tackling larger crises.

Harrison Ford started out as a carpenter and became an international movie superstar.

Stan Kirkpatrick started out as an Iowa farmboy and became an international superhero.

Surely, the Amazing Marvel could start out as a stunt man and become a global silver-screen legend.

Eventually.

***

Stan's first day on the set came as the crew filmed an early scene in picturesque Iowa cornfields, with their flowing rows of corn.

That's what the producers told him the viewers would see, at least.

All Stan saw was a row of fake corn in the middle of a huge set surrounded by giant green screens. Apparently, for a big-budget Hollywood film, it was cheaper to make a combine and cornfield with computer graphics than it was to go on location somewhere.

The idea blew his mind.

Some handlers brought out a kid, a stereotypical farmboy-type who had more than a passing resemblance to Stan in his youth. The boy ran into the fake cornfield and then fell to his knees, putting his arms over his head before yelling something and then pushing an imaginary object away.

And then the director made the kid do it again.

And again.

And again.

After five or six takes, the director clapped his hands together and motioned everyone over to a small monitor.

"This is going to be brilliant," he said.

Stan thought the director looked old enough to pass for a teenager with his moppy hair and sloppy clothes.

"Hey Amazing, come over here!" the director said, motioning Stan toward the monitor.

"So, you see here, all that green? It's gonna be a cornfield in the final cut. We did a little bit of lighting there on the set. You can see it looks like there's something coming at the boy. And then the kid freaks out, and we're going to have these yellow beams come out of his hands and he's going to blow the *hell* out of that combine."

"He's going to blow the combine up?" Stan asked.

"That's right, Amazing. That's what happened in the book," the director said, throwing him a copy of *Confessions of an Amazing Marvel.*

This was a new edition, one with artwork from the movie poster and an emblem declaring "soon to be a major motion picture."

He noticed the screenwriter's name on the cover alongside his own.

"Those aren't out yet, but it's the source material we're working with," the director explained.

"But I didn't blow up the combine," Stan said. "That's not in the book!"

"It's a movie, Amazing! Sometimes you gotta embellish a little bit."

"So what happened to the person driving the combine?"

"KA-BLOOEY!" the director said, mimicking an explosion with his hands. "The driver's tragic death serves as the emotional lynchpin of the whole film. It makes you determined to learn to control your powers for the betterment of mankind. Heavy stuff, right?"

"But my father was driving the combine. I didn't kill my father," Stan said flatly.

"Ah, well, you know. Rewrites," the director said, turning toward the rest of the crew. "Man, was that kid good or what? I think he's gonna have a future in this town."

***

A week into the shoot, the lead actor hadn't shown up yet. Stan heard he was finishing some pick-up shots on a film that was just winding down. It drove the producers crazy.

By the time the young man arrived on set, he didn't exactly look the part. He was a good six inches shorter than Stan, and had apparently ignored the memo about the "strenuous strength-training routine." The producers ordered the director to shoot around it.

And so he did, telling wardrobe to add more padding to the various Amazing Marvel super-suits.

Stan was starting to resent it.

He'd auditioned for the part, and he would've been perfect. He had the physical presence to pull off the Amazing Marvel. Heck, he *was* the Amazing Marvel. He didn't understand why Hollywood didn't realize how perfect he was for the role.

Instead, they seemed obsessed with inflating the ego of a box office star, just so they'd make a little more money on opening weekend. If they'd concentrated instead on making a great movie, people would come.

Hollywood just didn't get it.

***

"Cut! Cut!" the director yelled, his youthful face red and sweaty.

"C'mon, son! You've gotta give me more than that!"

Stan watched as the director tried to film a scene with the main star. But the kid kept flubbing his lines, and the director's frustrations grew with every take.

The star seemed hyper, nervous, unbalanced.

Stan could sense the crew's frustration.

The director took the actor by the arms, "They've got you wearing a lot of padding. But you're going to need it to step into that super-suit. I need you to get your head right. I don't care about staying on schedule—the studio knows this movie's gonna make money and if we go over, we go over. But I need your performance to be authentic."

The director gestured over at Stan, "Go spend some time with the real hero over there. Talk to him, find out his motivation. Come back here tomorrow and be cash-money, okay?"

The young actor let out a loud "*phhfft!*" and waved off the director, his movements encumbered by the prop suit's ridiculous amount of padding.

Stan didn't like what the director had suggested; he wanted him to mentor the young man who'd taken his part from him. It was like asking a soon-to-be-laid-off employee to train his replacement.

"I'm Stan," he strained through gritted teeth.

He held out his hand and tried to be polite.

"Screw you," the actor said, trying to brush past him.

The kid didn't get very far before Stan grabbed him by the shoulder and lifted him up.

***

In just second, Stan had flown them to a small café not too far from the studio. In Hollywood, no one paid much attention to the superstar who sat down to order coffee, even if he was wearing a ridiculously-padded super-suit.

"This is the worst kind of movie, man," the actor said. "Stupid tacked-on scenes about my family and that clichéd plot about the hometown sweetheart. Who writes this stuff?"

Stan cringed; the hometown sweetheart was actually part of his book.

"I didn't think it was that bad..."

"You're an idiot," the actor said. "People aren't gonna pay ten bucks a pop to see character development and that shit. They want explosions, fighting, hot chicks. Michael Bay shit, man. That's your blockbuster. Not this Iowa cornfield-I have an unrequited love with the prom queen-I solved the Middle East crisis-thing we're doing."

Stan did his best to keep his composure and his thoughts wandered toward all the things the studio and screenwriter had changed.

Stan cleared his throat, "I like explosions. I do. But there still has to be a reason behind them. Who cares about an explosion if there's no story with it?"

The actor snorted, "Dude, did you see *Transformers 2?* Biggest-grossing movie of the year."

"Actually, wouldn't that be *Avatar*? The thing about that movie, is it had heart..."

"I don't know which movie you saw, dude. Contrived *Ferngully* plot. Hair sex. All that money? It was the 3-D man. We're doing 3-D. Did you know that? The studio says it's the future."

"Well, I can see where this is going," Stan conceded. "You obviously don't need my help."

"You wanna help me? Take care of the check."

***

Four days later, Stan finally got a taste of the action.

As the stunt double for the Amazing Marvel, he was supposed to be locked in a bitter battle with Bloodsport. He ignored the fact that the new script had Bloodsport killing his mother and high school love. Instead, Stan steeled himself for one-on-one combat with a very convincing mock-up of his opponent's signature armor.

Bloodsport's armor certainly looked much truer to life than the various yellow and maroon super-suits wardrobe commissioned for the Amazing Marvel.

The Bloodsport doppelganger grunted something—Stan couldn't really hear it, but the producers said they'd loop it in post (whatever that meant). The Bloodsport look-a-like came at him, and Stan dodged, somersaulting over his opponent and landing a punch from behind.

Stan grinned as the fake bad guy went down. He turned toward the camera with his hands on his hips, "Looks like you need eyes in the back of your head, Bloodsport!"

His cheery demeanor vanished when the second unit director started screaming at him.

"Did you even read the script? You don't punch Bloodsport once and then win. And you don't mutter some cheesy one-liner. What do you think this is? A Schwarzenegger film?"

The Bloodsport actor moaned in pain.

"And don't use your super strength on the other stunt guy!" the director pleaded. "All right, Bloodsport, get on your feet. We'll try it again. And remember, stunt guy, you lose this one."

"Lose? I never lost to Bloodsport," Stan said.

"Listen, if you don't want this job, I've got a dozen martial artists ready to step into that suit."

Stan fumed.

He'd fought Bloodsport a dozen times, never coming close to losing, not even once.

But he swallowed his pride and the real Amazing Marvel took a dive at the conclusion of the tightly-choreographed fight scene.

***

"Okay, this is a big emotional scene," the director told the hotshot actor. "But the pyrotechnics are going to be very dangerous. So, we're going to green-screen your interaction later. Stunt guy, I need you up on set right now," the director yelled at Stan.

The scene called for Bloodsport to set off explosions along the entire east coast as the Amazing Marvel tried to stop them. It was loosely based on one of the villain's earlier plots to engage in a personal confrontation with the superhero. Except in this case, the Amazing Marvel had to fight off Bloodsport's army of flying minions as he tried to reach the explosions.

Stan looked over the script, "Flying minions? Bloodsport never had those..."

"Just get up there and do your thing, stunt guy," the director instructed. "Pretend you're swatting away flying bad guys. We'll CG them in later to match your movements."

The director called action and Stan hit his marks, flying from point to point.

He'd expected it all to be computer graphics, so the first explosion actually surprised him. Stan absorbed the blast and continued gliding through the air, moving swiftly as another blast sounded. By the fourth explosion, the surprise wore off and Stan raced through the air, determined to save the east coast—or at least the production crew.

Some 50 explosions later, the crew showed him some respect with a standing ovation.

"That was amazing, Amazing!" the director said, "It's gonna look great when we CG over your face!"

***

"All right, this next scene is a big one, too. We've got a building that's under construction and one of Bloodsport's henchmen is keeping you busy with a wrecking ball. It's huge."

They'd moved outside the safe confines of the soundstage to an exterior location at a rundown Hollywood hotel set for demolition.

Stan remembered the movie version of Bloodsport wanted a henchman do the dirty work.

It wasn't true to life; in reality, Bloodsport's entire motivation was to fight and defeat the Amazing Marvel in hand-to-hand combat.

He sighed, telling himself it was a sacrifice he had to make if he wanted to make it big in Tinseltown.

The director called action and a giant wrecking ball came swooping down on Stan. He knew it was coming, but his reflexes kicked in and he swatted the massive wrecking ball away, sending the rig and its driver several thousand feet into the air.

When he realized what he'd done, Stan took off into the sky and caught the construction rig, bringing it and its terrified driver to a soft, feather-like landing.

"Let's try that again," he said as the director nodded.

The director called action again, and the wrecking ball came swinging in Stan's direction a second time.

Instead of fighting back, he let the wrecking ball slam into him and careened into the crumbling hotel. Stan used his powers to intensify the blow, and the building came crashing down on top of him.

He emerged dramatically from the rubble, choking in the gathering dust and brushing himself clean.

Again, the cast and crew showered him with applause.

"That's great, Amazing. But I need you to climb back under the rubble and stick your hand up through it like you're reaching up for help," the director said. "I need that shot, baby!"

***

"I've talked about pivotal moments throughout this entire filming process," the director said as he coached Stan the Stuntman. "But this is probably *the* biggest moment. It's gonna provide the emotional heft of everything. When this is over and the 'Amazing Marvel' theme starts playing, people are gonna get goosebumps."

Stan looked at the impressive set built for this final moment in the movie. Just midway through filming, the production team was set to film the finale, where the Amazing Marvel met Bloodsport in the middle of a huge industrial complex while machines built cars and sparks flew.

In the Hollywood version, the Amazing Marvel is losing to Bloodsport, and the villain taunts him by deciphering his secret identity and killing his mother and hometown sweetheart.

Again, Stan forced himself to shrug aside the jarring departure from real life.

Stan knew the Amazing Marvel would come close to losing, but ultimately rally and win. He likened it to a professional wrestling match, where the good guy almost gets pinned or succumbs to the sleeper hold, only to react to the cheering crowd and pull off an unlikely victory.

The principal shooting focused on the actors portraying the Amazing Marvel and Bloodsport. They would shoot their scenes together so the director could get several different reaction shots. After that, Stan and the Bloodsport stunt doubles would go through their choreographed fighting routine.

By this point in the script, the villain had managed to clone three different versions of himself, giving the Amazing Marvel the chance to fight his arch-nemesis *and* avenge the deaths of his mother and hometown sweetheart.

Stan shook his head as he thought of the changes Hollywood insisted on making. He always knew those biographical movies were "based on" the life of someone.

By tacking on the words "based on," screenwriters could shift timelines, concoct composite characters, and invent certain "convenient" moments needed for the realization of the character on the screen.

But this film, Stan thought, went too far. His parents were still alive and living in Iowa. He didn't "accidentally" kill his father to stop a "rampaging" combine. Bloodsport didn't deduce Stan's secret identity because Stan never had one... everyone knew he was the Amazing Marvel. Furthermore, Bloodsport didn't kill his mother!

About the only true-to-life connection was the unrequited love he felt for his high school sweetheart. But she'd moved on and married a decent guy.

Bloodsport didn't kill her.

And then there were the parts about losing to the bad guy. The screenwriter changed the entire dynamic of his relationship with Bloodsport. To the Amazing Marvel, Bloodsport was a nuisance; the kind of B-grade baddie who made Stan roll his eyes whenever he resurfaced. Sure, Bloodsport produced plenty of malice and destruction—his quest to defeat the Amazing Marvel went well beyond obsessive—but he wasn't this brilliant, psychologically and intellectually superior supervillain.

And by God, Bloodsport *never* cloned himself; that wouldn't be a fair fight.

Stan let out a sigh as the director called for everyone to take their places. Dressed in the crazy yellow-and-maroon "industrial finale super-suit" (he was sure it would be part of the movie toy line), Stan crossed his arms and watched the "movie magic" unfold.

***

"You killed my mother and my Anna!" the actor shouted.

"And I would've killed your father if you hadn't already taken care of that," Bloodsport taunted.

"You bastard—"

The lights on the set went out for several seconds and then flickered back to life.

"Okay, cut!" the director yelled. Back on your marks. I need that faster, more intense! Faster, more intense!"

"All right, we're doing this again. On your marks! Will someone please show Kyle where he's supposed to stand?"

Stan watched a member of the crew point the Bloodsport actor to the correct spot.

It struck him as odd; the actor didn't miss his mark very often, at least from what Stan had seen from filming.

The director called action, and the scene commenced.

"You killed my mother and my Anna!" the hotshot actor shouted.

Stan liked the conviction in his voice, but thought he could've done just as well.

"It is the way of life, Amazing Marvel. How many times have we fought this battle? How many times are we going to do this?"

Stan tilted his head, realizing how dead-on the Bloodsport actor's voice and body language were.

That wasn't the line, but it sounded like the actor wanted to ad-lib.

"You've brought suffering and death upon those I loved most!" the young actor replied.

Stan admired his willingness to play along.

"I've brought suffering?" the Bloodsport actor responded. "I doubt that. You are the hero. You are the one with the target on his back. And it's people like me who try to hit that target. Collateral damage is often necessary for me to meet my ultimate goal."

"And what is that ultimate goal, you coward? Killing innocent people?"

"I'm not planning on killing anybody, Amazing Marvel. I wish only a fair fight against you."

The hotshot actor turned and looked at Stan.

He also noticed the Bloodsport actor staring at him.

Stan smirked; the guys were playing this scene for him.

"They're going off script," the director whispered. "It isn't working."

Stan froze when he saw the Bloodsport actor produce a large mace from his behind his back.

***

"Back away! Back away!" Stan yelled, cursing his lack of super-speed.

He tried to fly toward the main stage, but the mock factory equipment stood in his way. He powered through it and continued yelling.

The young actor dodged the swing from Bloodsport—apparently he *had* done some training—and Stan made it to the stage, pushing the actor aside to confront his arch-nemesis.

Over his shoulder, he spotted another Bloodsport crumpled in a pile at the bottom of the steps.

The other lead actor.

"You just don't give up, do you?" Stan said, rolling his eyes.

"I will defeat you this time, Amazing Marvel!" the real Bloodsport screamed, charging at the hero with his mace.

Stan sidestepped it, "So, you're using weapons now? That's cute."

He dodged another strike and elbowed Bloodsport in the face.

The villain didn't go down.

Stan massaged his elbow; Bloodsport usually had a glass jaw.

He didn't recover quickly enough from his own shock, and Bloodsport hit him across the chest with his weapon.

Stan staggered backward, feeling a burning sensation around his chest. Trickles of blood began to seep through his costume.

"Learned a few new tricks," he said, coughing.

"You'd be amazed what you learn in a maximum-security prison," Bloodsport replied, taking another swing.

The Amazing Marvel took another step back and then charged, trying to rip the weapon from Bloodsport's hands.

Somehow, his foe managed to hold his ground.

Stan heard the director yell something, and then pyrotechnics began going off and the dormant factory machines roared to life.

The director was trying to give him a distraction.

***

Stan lurched forward as Bloodsport caught him with another hit from the mace. Needles of pain shot through his right shoulder.

Stan hadn't felt pain in a long time, and the sensation threatened to overwhelm even the Amazing Marvel. Bloodsport kept pressing, and Stan couldn't counter.

He leapt off the main floor, and journeyed into the impressive-looking factory machines below.

***

He had to give the special effects crew credit; they'd created a very convincing assembly line full of robot arms, venting steam, and showering sparks.

The sights, the smells, even the sounds seemed pitch-perfect.

Stan figured they'd probably use some Hollywood magic to make it even better. He glanced up to see a series of green screens around the set, knowing the digital artists would use them for something spectacular.

He shook his head and tried to concentrate on giving the crew a great ending.

Bloodsport had returned, and this time the usually pitiable villain meant business.

There was something about that mace; it shouldn't have hurt him. Was it made out of a special material or it had been dipped in some special solution? Stan didn't know; he concentrated on avoiding another blow from it.

A shadow passed to his right, and Stan ducked for cover. Jumping into the darker recesses of the factory wasn't one of his best ideas. The crews hadn't set the lighting rigs yet, so it stayed pitch black, other than intermittent sparks from the machinery.

And his foe wore his trademark black armor suit.

"I can see you, Amazing Marvel. Cowering in the dark! Not as much fun when the odds are even, is it? I can hurt you, and you know it."

It sounded like the voice came from the right side, but with the echoing chamber and the background noise from the machinery, Stan couldn't tell for sure.

"Funny thing for you to say," Stan replied. "You've always been one for hand-to-hand combat. Now you're using a mace? It's beneath you."

"I don't plan on using this much longer," Bloodsport said, clearly enjoying the moment. "But if I can make this into a fair fight, I can finally prove to the world that I'm the greatest fighter of all."

Stan let out a derisive laugh, "Even if you beat me, there will always be someone better."

"Then I'll find them and learn their moves. And then I'll beat them."

A hiss of steam escaped from a nearby machine and Stan leapt over a conveyor belt. He heard the clang of Bloodsport's mace against the concrete floor and breathed a silent sigh of relief.

"This environment is unsuitable for our combat," Bloodsport hissed.

"You're right, Bloodsport. I'm going back up top."

***

Stan rose to the main floor where their confrontation started. He had to give the film crew credit; they were still shooting despite the obvious danger.

Bloodsport made his way to the main stage, gasping for breath as he pulled himself up.

"Sounds like you're out of shape," Stan said.

"Not everyone can fly, Amazing Marvel."

The villain slouched, clearly exhausted, and Stan sped toward him.

Bloodsport responded with a sweeping throw of his mace that caught Stan on his right cheek.

He landed on his back and saw stars, frantically backing away as Bloodsport stood upright.

He sat up, "What's it going to take to end this? A final battle, whoever wins, wins? I beat you, you go away once and for all? You beat me, you stop bothering people?"

"There is only one satisfactory outcome," Bloodsport said, tightening his grip on the mace.

"Killing me? That's not your style," Stan muttered.

"Kill you? Do you think that's my goal? No, I want to beat you in hand-to-hand combat! I would let you live to remind everyone of the true champion who stood above you."

Now back on his feet, Stan dabbed his chin and found traces of crimson on his hand. Whether his opponent meant to or not, that mace could kill him.

"You said you wanted a fair fight, but do you see me with a weapon?"

Bloodsport tilted his head, "Do you see me with superpowers?"

"Look. I'm bleeding from my chin. Blood is seeping through my super-suit..."

"New design? Can't say I care for it. That emblem is tacky. And the cape? Nauseating."

"That's what I told the wardrobe department," Stan said, motioning for Bloodsport to come forward. "Get rid of that mace and show me what you've got."

Bloodsport chucked the weapon aside and cracked his knuckles.

***

The villain came at Stan with a dizzying array of shuffles, feints, and kicks. The Amazing Marvel bobbed and weaved, looking for an advantage.

Bloodsport jabbed and Stan blocked it, launching a vicious counterpunch.

He missed.

Bloodsport responded with a sharp knee to the midsection.

Still weakened by whatever powered the mace, Stan felt every bit of it.

And so their battle continued, with Stan taking blow after blow from Bloodsport. He felt his right eye swelling up. Infant bruises began throbbing as Bloodsport hit the same spots over and over again.

Stan lunged, but Bloodsport caught him and used the momentum to roll Stan over.

He lay on the floor as Bloodsport placed a foot on his chest.

"You have proven yourself a worthy adversary. But with the playing field even, I am the superior fighter."

Bloodsport bowed and then turned.

He didn't take a cheap shot.

He didn't taunt Stan.

He didn't even bother to grab his mace.

"I'll be damned," Stan said, propping himself on his elbows as his enemy walked away. "That really is all he wanted."

***

"What an amazing fight!" the director said as he helped Stan to his feet. "We caught the whole thing on camera. You know what we're going to do? We're going to scrap the original ending, you know the one with the clones? It's a little too obvious with the psychological underpinnings."

"That's fantastic," Stan deadpanned.

"We're going to have to reshoot some of that stuff down in the factory, since we didn't set the lighting grids. Continuity will be a bitch, but we'll make it work in the editing room. I think the audience will really feel the animosity there in the final battle."

"That's great, that's great," Stan said, rubbing his jaw.

"Amazing stuff. Amazing stuff."

"Thanks for setting off the explosives. I appreciate the help."

The director scratched the back of his head, "Um, yeah, yeah. That's why we did that. To help, you know. That guy, uh, you just never know what he was going to do. The only bad thing about it is all the freaking CG work we're going to have to do in that final fight."

Stan looked at the green screens, "Oh, you mean expanding the set?"

The director scratched his head, "Well, more like CGing over your face."

***

"Opening weekend is gonna be huge, baby! HEEEE-UGE!" Artie said, as excitable as ever. *"I'm telling ya, I got a good feeling about this. You're gonna be a star, baby! I've already got calls from three different studios wanting to use you as a stuntman!"*

Stan held the phone to his ear, "I don't know, Artie..."

"The rough cut is getting major buzz, especially with the new ending. Those reshoots

really paid off!"

Stan rubbed his chin, "They liked the ending?"

"The studio was thrilled! They want to bring you and Bloodsport back for the sequel!"

About the author: Matt Adams is a TV news producer who lives and writes in Indianapolis, Indiana. His short stories have been selected for publication in the anthology series *This Mutant Life* and *A Thousand Faces*. He is currently working on a superhero-themed novel.

The Last Laugh

Luke Johnson

The streets of Beacon City were quiet that night. The residents of the neighborhood had long since gone to bed. The only sound to be heard was the faint rustle of leaves; the only movement, the gentle swaying of the branches. Not the kind of place you would expect a battle to the death. But then, this town had a lot of things that weren't quite what they seemed.

The rumbling of an engine pierced the streets' dark serenity, as a large white truck rumbled around the corner onto Hayes Avenue. It was a delivery truck, featuring the logo of Jolly Jack's Bakery. Twenty minutes before midnight would seem like an odd time to make deliveries—not that it mattered, since there was no such place as Jolly Jack's Bakery.

The truck pulled off to the side of the street and slowed to a halt. The driver turned the truck off, opened the door, and walked around to the back. He was a small, slight man; well under six feet tall... but he moved with a surprising grace. He opened the back doors of the truck and climbed inside. The dome light came on, casting its soft glow over the man's face.

He looked better in the dark.

He was just on the wrong side of fifty years old, and looked every minute of it. His hair, which was greying at the temples a few short years ago, now only had a smattering of its original light brown. His wizened face was a lattice of wrinkles, with a couple of scars mixed in. He looked like a man who had seen the world... but if you asked the world, it wouldn't remember him.

The man's name was Dexter Yates, a name known to almost nobody in Beacon City. He did, however, go by another name... one that carried much more attention in the city's history.

That name was Punchline.

Dexter Yates was actually a supervillain—Beacon City's first supervillain, in fact. He had made his debut in the mid-80's, levelling his arsenal of boxing glove guns and bad jokes against the Cowboy, Beacon City's beloved superhero. And what a spectacle it was—Punchline would perform a daring robbery, and the Cowboy would show up to foil it. There would be a fierce battle, complete with clever banter. Sometimes, it would end with the Cowboy landing a knockout blow, and handing the felonious funnyman over to the police. Others, Punchline would make a daring escape—and on occasion, he would even manage to keep the loot that he stole. It provided great entertainment for the civilians, as well as headlines for the newspapers... and best of all, nobody ever really got hurt.

But, as the saying goes, 'time wounds all heels.' Something like that, anyway.

Other costumed villains would pop up over the years, but it wasn't until later that something new appeared on the scene. Superpowered villains.

It was actually not so bad at first—it rejuvenated the city's interest in the Cowboy, and his battles with these new villains provided some great television. Punchline got to know many of them—as it turned out, they were actually decent people, criminal records notwithstanding. They were people with whom he could swap stories and share drinks. Some of the younger ones would even come to him for advice. It was as if they were all members of a fraternity, with Punchline being the founding father—well respected by his lawbreaking brethren, if not by the populace at large.

But as the years went on, things became... darker. New villains popped up, with new attitudes. Suddenly, there were powered beings whose ultimate goal was not to provide exciting spectacle, or even to amass untold riches through dishonorable means. No, they just wanted to destroy. Soon, it wasn't safe for people to hang around and watch the Cowboy's fights. Hell, in some places it wasn't even safe to go out in public. Both the Cowboy and the police had their hands full with these new threats; none of them had time for a glorified clown with a ridiculous gimmick. On top of that, the problems with Denise...

Just a few short months later, the unthinkable happened. A monstrous horror from another dimension attacked the city. Naturally, the Cowboy immediately leapt into battle. It was a legendary fight, and by the end, the beast was dead.

So was the Cowboy.

Beacon City was wracked with grief, and so was Punchline. His old enemy—and in some ways, his best friend—was gone. Dexter Yates delivered a touching eulogy at the funeral, then disappeared from the public eye. The city's beloved hero was gone, but not forgotten... while its first villain suffered a fate exactly the opposite.

Somehow, life went on within the city. New heroes made themselves known, and took it upon themselves to defend the citizens. For a while, things were like they used to be.

It was only a matter of time before someone ruined everything.

That someone had called Dexter Yates earlier that evening, and was the reason why he was skulking around an apartment block in the middle of the night, driving a van loaded with all manner of powerful, if non-lethal, weaponry.

He unzipped a black duffel bag and set it on the floor of the truck. Then, he picked a few weapons from his arsenal and placed them in a row. A shotgun, two .45 semiautomatic pistols, and a snub-nosed .38 revolver. Two canisters that look somewhat like tear gas grenades. His personalized grapple gun with a boxing glove on the end.

Once he was properly armed, he set about loading the weapons. He opened his ammunition locker and pulled out two small boxes, each with a different color of tape around the outside: black and white. These were the real tricks of his trade—he had removed the lead from the bullets, and replaced them with a specially designed device. It was extremely compact when inserted into the shell, but once fired; it would expand and harden, taking the shape of a boxing glove.

The black box held shotgun shells; he removed a handful and loaded them into the shotgun. The white box was full of ammunition for the .45s. He loaded up two clips—one for each—and then two more, just in case. Finally, Dexter dug around further into the ammo locker and found another box, this one marked with red tape. He took six bullets from it and fitted them into the revolver.

Dexter looked at his watch. 11:40 pm. Not much longer now.

He placed the weapons in the bag, except for the grapple gun, which he laid on top. He then stepped to the back of the truck, where another bag was hanging on a hook. A garment bag, to be precise. He unzipped the front and removed the contents. Dark red double-breasted suit, with matching fedora. Black shirt. Yellow shoes, gloves, and bowtie. Domino mask, the same color as the suit. His old villain costume.

"I hope it still fits," he said, to no one in particular. Surprisingly enough, it did. It hadn't taken him long at all to get changed; after all, the quick change is an important skill for a costumed criminal, and some skills you never forget. He hadn't even forgotten how to do the bowtie.

It took him less than ten minutes to get dressed, leaving him plenty of time to prepare himself. He stepped down from the van, grabbed his equipment, and headed toward one of the apartment buildings. Mild-mannered Dexter Yates was gone...and in his place, in the city for the first time in four years, was the notorious Punchline.

He had made his first appearance in Beacon City almost twenty-five years ago. Tonight, he might very well make his last.

***

Dexter Yates got the call two hours before.

"Good evening, Mister Yates. I suppose by now, you've heard about my latest venture. Not quite as successful as I'd like, but there's always a chance she won't pull through after surgery, isn't there?"

"Who is this?!" Dexter shouted. He hadn't needed to ask, of course. He knew exactly who it was. It was the man who had made it his goal to become the most powerful criminal the city had ever seen, and didn't much care what he had to do to accomplish that goal. The man had already filled a few graves in the city. Civilians. Police. Villains.

Dexter wanted very much to find this person and beat his brains in, but he knew that the police and the new heroes were better suited to tackling such a dangerous criminal. Besides, he was retired. He snapped back at the caller, "How many times do I have to tell you; I'm not about to—"

"No? I wonder how your wife would feel about such a decision."

In that moment, the world stopped. "My... what?"

"It wasn't easy, you know. She moved to Illinois, just to get away from you."

Dexter Yates was not prone to fits of anger. Yet he could feel his blood boiling, as he gave his growled response through gritted teeth.

"You bastard. If you hurt her—"

"Tonight, at midnight. Apartment block on the corner of 98th and Hayes. The roof. And if you ever want to see your wife alive again, you'l be there."

Click.

Dexter struggled to fight back the sense of panic that clutched at his throat. He didn't even know where his wife—his ex-wife, actually—had gone. How did that other man find her?

The truth was, he hadn't seen his family in years. Denise had walked out on him, and took their son with her, the day she discovered Dexter's secret. Hell, he hadn' even challenged the divorce. None of that really mattered, though. He still loved her, and the last thing he wanted was to see her hurt.

Eric would be off at college right now, and presumably safe. But then, if that sick son of a bitch found Denise, he could probably find Eric too.

Dexter knew that he didn't have a choice. One way or another, this had to end tonight.

***

A soft breeze blew across the rooftops. With the changing seasons, the night winds in Beacon City became warmer and more pleasant. The birds had not yet returned, so the night was quiet as well. The only sounds to be heard were Pfff, Chnkt, and Whrrrrr.

Pfft! went the Firearm, Punchline's signature grappling gun, as he pulled the trigger. A boxing glove sailed through the air, latching onto the edge of the roof with a heavy Chnkt! Then, the winch in the gun went Whrrrrr as it pulled Punchline up the side of the building. Once at the top, Punchline tossed his bag of weaponry onto the roof, then clambered over as well.

"Wow," he said to himself. "That used to be easier."

After checking his watch—11:55, still plenty of time—he took a look around, in search of a good place to set himself up. His opponent would probably come in out of the east... not because it would give him any sort of advantage, but because it would look cool coming up from the streetlights like that.

The roof access door was closer to the west side of the building, so Punchline went around the other side and set his bag down there. A nice little surprise for later. He placed the revolver in his coat pocket, then pulled out the shotgun. Might as well start with the heavy artillery.

He reloaded the grappling glove into the Firearm and tucked it into his pants pocket—hey, you never knew when something might come in handy. He stepped out into the clear area on the roof, and waited for his tormentor to arrive.

Then, he waited again.

After that, he waited some more.

Punchline groused, "Criminy. Bad enough he's going to try and kill me; the least he could do is be punctual about it."

***

Four days ago. The local news broadcast.

"Good evening, Beacon City. This is Janet Medina, with the KBCN evening news. Tonight's top story: The Crushing Killer has struck again, but both the victim and the authorities have caught a break. This time, the target was Mary MacDonald, better known as the supervillain Hail Mary. Eyewitness accounts say that she stumbled out of a subway terminal, created a blizzard with her weather-controlling power, and buried herself in snow, in an effort to stop the bleeding while waiting for the paramedics."

"She is currently in critical condition, under the watchful eye of the medical staff and several members of the police force, as well as the hero Honor Song, member of the BCDL. According to the doctor's reports, she is suffering from several broken ribs, heavy internal bleeding, and a collapsed lung."

"This was the fourth such attack in the last month, but the first in which the victim survived. Hail Mary was quickly sedated upon her arrival at the hospital... but not before saying a word that, we believe, reveals the identity of the attacker."

"Downfall."

"Police are now on the lookout for..."

***

Punchline checked his watch again. Five minutes after midnight.

"He's doing this on purpose," he muttered. After all, it was said that entering a meeting last gave you a position of power, and made the other person look weak, because he had to wait for you. But it didn't make much damn sense when nobody was around to see it anyway.

Punchline used the time to double-check his equipment, and make sure he had it all where we wanted it. He had retaken his original position, when his opponent finally arrived.

"I hope I haven't kept you waiting. I know how it's past your bedtime." The voice came from below the edge of the rooftop, on the east side of the building. Punchline had called it exactly—he was going for the dramatic entrance, rather than the tactical one.

What an asshole.

Slowly, a silhouette rose into the skyline. It was of an average-sized man, a few inches taller and about forty pounds heavier than Punchline. He had his arms outstretched, as if he were trying to look like Jesus or something. He floated a few feet above the rooftop, before coming down toward his adversary, allowing Punchline to get a better look. The man—and barely that; he must have been half Dexter's age—had a young face, a crooked smile, and perfectly coiffed hair. He wore a sand-colored suit with matching tie, and a white shirt.

Punchline stared at him, and his anger rose again. This was the man who had spent the last month bringing nothing but misery. A man who had used his powers to kill three - nearly four - well known supervillains... for no apparent reason. The self-proclaimed God of Gravity.

Downfall.

"It's been a while, hasn't it?" Downfall asked, the cocky smirk never leaving his face.

"Not long enough," Punchline said.

"Oh, come now. Is that any way to treat a friend?"

"You're no friend of mine."

"That's true. It's not like I have anything in common with your other friends." His smirk grew into a sickening grin. "I'm not dead, for instance."

Anger flashed in Punchline's eyes, but he kept it under control. *Don't rise to him,* he told himself. *Make him rise to you.*

The two men stared at each other for a moment, neither man wanting to make the first move. It was Punchline who broke the silence.

"You know... we had a really good thing going in this town. I guess it was just a matter of time before some ignorant jerk came along and screwed it all up. Thinking that there aren't any rules, just because there's none written down."

Downfall's mouth twisted into an expression of mild displeasure. "You could stand to be a little more courteous, old timer. Not that it will help—I mean, you're going to die tonight. But if you ask nicely, maybe I'll do it quick."

"Yeah, I heard that one already. Try writing your own threats next time."

"Just making my point clear. I want to make sure you understand the... gravity... of the situation."

"You suck at banter, kid. Puns are for hacks."

Downfall paused in his response, obviously trying to come up with one that didn't include a gravity-based pun. Strange that he'd be bothered by that—he had no compunction about theft, assault, kidnapping, or murder... but evidently, he didn't like people thinking he wasn't clever.

"Why are you even doing this?" Punchline asked. "Why not just rob some banks, like any other self-respecting criminal?"

Downfall scoffed. "Money? What good is money, when it can't buy what you really want."

"And what do you really want?"

"Power, of course. I want to do what none of you could—to control the city. I want hatred from the heroes, respect from the villains, and abject fear from everyone else."

"It's not going to happen. Stabbing your own in the back to gain power doesn't work around here—that only flies in Hollywood."

"It's worked well so far." There was that grin again. Punchline couldn't wait to fill it with a boxing glove.

"So... why me, then? Why come after a retired villain who nobody really took seriously anyway?"

"Because—and I'll never understand why—your voice carries weight within the villain community."

"Really."

"I know! I don' understand it either. But for some weird reason, they do respect you. So I figure, if I get rid of you, that gets my name out there. I will have single-handedly destroyed the old guard. The heroes will be next... and whoever lives will have no choice but to think of me as the top dog in Beacon City."

"That's the stupidest thing I've ever heard in my life... and I lived through the Reagan years."

"Yes, well. Too bad you'll never know how it turns out. And now, I am going to bring about your... downfall."

Again with the puns. "Leave the comedy to the bears."

Downfall snarled. "Keep it up, funny man. We'll see how much you laugh when I break every bone in your body. One at a time."

Punchline kept a straight face, but inwardly he was smiling. *Go ahead and get angry,* he thought. *Angry people don't think.*

"I think I've had enough of your smart mouth," Downfall said. "It's time we got down to business."

"You know, one of us isn't coming back from this."

"That's the idea, old man."

***

Ten days ago. The local news broadcast.

"This just in... police have found a clue that might explain the mysterious explosion that occurred a few days ago."

"An abnormally high amount of radiation was detected at an abandoned construction site in the industrial section of the city. The source of the radiation turned out to be a severed hand, encased—and almost completely flattened—inside a lump of twisted metal. Authorities believe that it was a specially-built glove, designed to absorb and store radiation... and that the hand once belonged to Isaac Rothschild, alias Critical Mass, a local super villain whose body had been infused with atomic energy. They speculate that Rothschild was unable to contain his internal power, and used his last remaining moments to as far away from the city as he could before exploding. He is presumed dead."

"Police officials would not comment on whether or not this had anything to do with the so-called Crusher Killer, who had already claimed two high-profile victims..."

***

The two villains stared at each other, like Wild West gunfighters.

Wait a minute, Punchline thought. *I'm the only one with guns. Why aren't I using them?* He leveled the shotgun at Downfall's chest and pulled the trigger.

FOOM!

In a flash, a red blob flew out of the end of the shotgun. As it traveled through the air, it expanded and took the form of a bright red boxing glove. It flew straight at Downfall, traveled at incredible speed...

"Heh."

... and came skidding to a halt, about a yard from the target's feet.

"Hmm," said Punchline. "I envisioned that being more successful."

"Of course you did. You forgot about the powers. How did you ever make it as a supervillain?"

"Charm," Punchline replied, and aimed again. This time Downfall was ready, and motioned toward the gun. With a flick of his wrist, the gun went flying into the air—and if Punchline had not let go of it a split second before, he would have gone with it.

Punchline watched it rise, thereby missing the new gesture that Downfall had made. "I suppose it's too much to ask for you to play fair. After all—yipe!"

Punchline rolled out of the way as the shotgun fell from the sky, its velocity no doubt affected by Downfall's powers. It crashed to the roof, embedding itself into the tar. The weapon fired again upon impact, sending another pugilistic projectile over the edge and down to the street, where it bounced harmlessly.

"Well, that was fun," Downfall said. "Now, I believe it is my turn."

Downfall leveled his gaze at Punchline, who suddenly felt very light. Almost weightless, in fact. He looked down at the ground, and discovered that it was about three feet farther away than he expected, and gaining distance with each passing second. Once he was about ten feet up, his ascent halted... but then, he started to move to the side. Toward the edge of the building.

Downfall gloated, "I realize it's not very sporting, but the longer this takes, the less impressive it will be. You understand."

Punchline, however, was quick on his feet, even though his feet weren't on anything. He pulled the Firearm from his trouser pocket and fired to toward the access door. The glove affixed itself to the door handle, and Punchline reeled himself back toward the ground. His sideways momentum carried him around the brick entrance, and out of Downfall's sight. Once he was obscured, he could feel the return of normal gravity, not to mention the roof.

He's toying with me, Punchline thought. That was good, because it meant Downfall wasn't taking him seriously. That was also bad, because the kid-gloves treatment wasn't likely to last.

"You're not hiding from me, are you? Come out, come out!"

He reached into the duffel bag that he'd hid back here earlier—preparation pays off! —and pulled out one of the canisters. He pulled the pin, and tossed it toward Downfall's voice. It rolled to a stop about a foot away from Downfall, when yellow smoke poured out of it. Punchline peeked around the corner to see if it had the desired effect. Unfortunately, Downfall had only taken the tiniest of whiffs of it. It was enough to make his eyes feel a little heavy, but not much else. He used his control of gravity to lift the canister up into the air, and then sent it tumbling over the side.

"Knockout gas? Seriously? And you were complaining about my puns."

Punchline reached back into his bag and took out another canister, as well as one of his pistols. He pulled the pin and tossed again, only this time he immediately rolled out from his cover and started firing.

FUMP FUMP FUMP FUMP!

The first one was a little-off target, and Downfall had enough time to push it up so that it flew over the top of his head. None of the other three got close. Strangely, the smoke from the knockout gas grenade wasn't rising like it normally did. Downfall's handiwork, no doubt. Downfall smiled at the now exposed Punchline... and instead of disposing with this device as he had the other, he kicked it over toward his adversary. Punchline had just enough time to fire off a shot—FUMP! —that deflected the gas canister away.

"Nice try, Punchline," Downfall shouted, as Punchline scrambled back behind his cover. "It's been fun... but I'm getting a little bored."

Punchline grabbed the other semiautomatic pistol and an extra clip, and waited. He expected Downfall to simply come around the side and get him.

He felt something on his shoulder. Mortar dust. He turned around to see the brick structure which housed the roof access door crumble apart. Bricks were ripped away, and the wall began to tip over—the same wall against which Punchline was leaning. He made a mad dive out of the way, just as the bricks collapsed. A half-second later, he would have been trapped underneath.

Of course, now he was equally screwed. His arsenal had proven ineffective so far, and there was no cover between him and the "God of Gravity."

"Now then," crowed Downfall. "I think it's time I showed you what I can do."

***

Three weeks ago. The local newscast.

"Thanks, Janet. Mitch Wilcox here, outside the residence of Dr. Randolph Uwibambe. You might not recognize that name, because he went by another—the Witch Doctor, a retired villain with an extensive knowledge of both Western medicine and mystical tribal magics. Last night, the Witch Doctor was found dead in his home; coroners are reporting that a crushed trachea was the cause. Foul play has not been ruled out, as there are telltale signs of struggle in the living room."

"No word yet on whether or not this murder is connected to the one from last week, where another of the city's villains—Simon Foster, a.k.a Simon Says, was found crushed to death in his home. Back to you, Janet."

"Thanks, Mitch. At the time of the Simon Says Slaying, our reporter spoke with Monolith, local superhero and head of the Beacon City Defense League. He said, quote, 'The purpose of the BCDL is strictly to protect the people of the city, and to help the police department uphold the law. We do not commit, nor do we condone, vigilante behavior such as this. It is not our place to serve as judge, jury, or executioner, and the members of the Defense League will do everything we can to ensure that the guilty parties are brought to justice.'"

"Unfortunately, our brave heroes have been unsuccessful thus far... and it may have cost another of Beacon City's villains his life. We'll be back with more on this..."

***

Punchline raised one of his guns and tried to fire it, but Downfall bore down on it with his power—more power than he had shown previously, in fact. The sudden increase in the gun's weight nearly jerked Punchline's arm out of the socket. Instead, it pulled him down, trapping his right hand underneath. He groaned in pain as the sheer pressure cracked two of the bones in his hand.

Downfall's mocking laughter filled the air. "Oh, no! You've fallen, and you can't get up!"

Punchline tried to raise his other gun, but it was yanked out of his hand before he could even aim it.

"Come on, Mrs. Fletcher. Don't tell me you're out of the fight yet! I'm just getting started!"

Pressure began to build on Punchline's chest, and it grew rapidly. Within seconds, he was having trouble breathing. One of his ribs broke, with an audible snap.

Downfall framed Punchline's agonized face in between his thumb and forefinger. "You should love this, Punchy! It's like that Kids in the Hall sketch! I am crushing your head! I am crushing your head!" he shouted, and pressed his digits together repeatedly.

"AAAAAAAAAAAAAAARRRRRGHH!" Punchline screamed, as a tremendous weight came to bear against his temples.

"I know what you're thinking. You're thinking that your head feels like it's going to go straight through the roof. Well, you don't have to worry about that. Your skull will implode first."

Somehow, Punchline did not find that comforting.

He tried to fight against the force of Downfall's gravity manipulation, but to no avail. He couldn't lift his right arm more than a few inches off the ground... couldn't lift his left arm at all, as his hand was still pinned underneath his own gun. All he could manage were howls of suffering, and even those became increasingly difficult.

He couldn't believe it. After spending half of his life flouting the law and thwarting danger, he was going to be crushed to death on a rooftop... by someone who would just not shut up.

"And as soon as I put you out of your misery, I'm going back to where I've got your lovely ex-wife stashed, and do the same to her. Or maybe I won't. Maybe I'll have a little fun first."

By this point, Punchline had stopped listening to his rival. Instead, he heard his own voice... but not from inside his head. It was as if it came from outside of him.

Jesus, Punchline, he told himself. *Get up off your ass. This bastard is going to destroy everything you've ever cared about. All your friends. This city. Your wife. Your son. He's going to crush it all, unless you stop him. Right. damn. NOW.*

Summoning his last scraps of strength, he dragged his right arm back toward his body. Somehow, even with all the weight that Downfall had put upon him, he managed to reach that hand into his coat pocket. After a further brief struggle, he slowly pulled out the revolver. He had hoped that Downfall would be too busy gloating to notice, but this would not be the case.

"You're kidding, right?"

Punchline tried to lift the gun, but his strength faltered. Downfall let out a heavy gut-laugh, having finally broken and beaten the elder statesman of Beacon City's villain community.

"Hey, you know what? I can't believe I didn't notice before—you haven't told a single joke this whole time, have you? You haven't! What's the matter, Punchline? Am I not worth breaking out the A-List material?"

Downfall poured on the pressure again, and this time Punchline couldn't even scream. He tasted blood in his mouth, and felt two more ribs go. One of them might have punctured something important.

I'm sorry, baby. I tried. he thought.

And his own thought came back, *Quit trying, and fucking get it done.*

"Come on, motherfucker! Say something funny!"

Punchline tried to choke out a word, but the pressure on his lungs was too great, and he only managed a bloody cough.

An amused smile spread over Downfall's lips, and he let up slightly. Might as well let the old man have his last chance. Besides, letting Punchline's hope bloom would make it all that much sweeter when he crushed it, once and for all.

"What did you say?"

He watched Punchline point the gun at him, ready to swat away another of those ridiculous boxing gloves.

"Newspaper."

BLAM!

***

Now would be a good time to explain the red box.

He'd had it since the beginning of his criminal career, but not once had he ever fired the ammunition inside—not at civilians, not at the police, not at other villains... not even at the Cowboy himself. Hell, he'd never even loaded it.

You see, the red box contained very special ammunition. They were the only bullets he owned that didn't turn into boxing gloves.

Just small pieces of lead traveling very, very fast.

***

Downfall had laughed when Punchline leveled the revolver at him. After all, he hadn't had any trouble deflecting Punchline's other shots; he didn't expect to have any trouble dealing with this one either.

BLAM!

"AARRRGH!"

He also didn't expect that.

In one moment, Downfall was gloating over Punchline, while crushing the older villain with his control over gravity. In the next, a bullet had ripped through Downfall's arm.

"You shot me!" Downfall cried out, in equal parts pain and surprise. "With a bullet! You prick!" He clutched at his arm, doing his best to stop the bleeding. Unfortunately, this left him unable to focus his power.

Punchline saw the opening he'd been hoping for. In an instant, he was up on his feet, anger and adrenaline drowning out the pain.

"What the fuck do you think you're doing?" Downfall screamed. "You don't use real bullets!"

To which Punchline merely replied, "Sunburned zebra."

BLAM!

Punchline had aimed the gun toward Downfall's belly, but this time his enemy knew what was coming, and still had just enough presence of mind to push the bullet away from his vital organs... but not enough to keep it from hitting him in the thigh.

"DAMMIT!"

"Embarrassed penguin."

BLAM!

That one was aimed at the head. Downfall's strength seeped out of his body along with the blood, but he still managed to push the bullet off to the side. It only grazed his ear.

"FUCK!"

Downfall stumbled backwards, no longer able to keep upright. He attempted to scoot away from the enraged Punchline, as if he thought it would help.

It didn't.

"Strawberry-flavored referee."

BLAM!

The round went through Downfall's right hand, taking three fingers with it.

Both of his limbs hung uselessly at his sides, so Downfall tried distancing himself using his one good leg. Tears streamed down his face. He wanted to tell Punchline to stop shooting.

Even if he had, Punchline wouldn't have heard him.

"Two nuns in a chainsaw fight."

The other leg.

Downfall now rested against the precipice. Nowhere left to run. "Please," he begged. "No more. I'm sorry. No more."

This is what Punchline thought:

Now? NOW you want mercy? Where was your mercy when you killed three of my friends? When you put Mary in a coma? When you kidnapped my wife and threatened to RAPE AND KILL HER!!! Now you want mercy, you worthless fuck?!

This is what Punchline said:

"The crosswalk."

BLAM!

Gut shot.

Downfall doubled over in agony, sitting in a pool of his own blood and filth. The very picture of wretched misery. Punchline threw the revolver at him, hitting Downfall in the face. Two broken teeth, one busted lip, and a fresh round of tears.

Punchline spat in disgust; more blood than saliva. He lurched over to where Downfall sat, while tuning out his whimpers. He bent down, ignoring the screaming agony from his chest. Then, he grabbed Downfall around the midsection and hefted him up, just enough to move him back about a foot, then set him back down. Now, instead of leaning against the edge, he was sitting right on it.

He staggered back toward one of his pistols, and picked it up. Pain flared in his arm as he pointed the weapon straight at Downfall.

"Now," he said in a labored, raspy voice. "Now you're going to tell me what you've done with Denise. If she's not hurt, you might live to see tomorrow."

"Please... I don't wanna die..."

"Then you'd better start talking."

"Don't... don't..." Downfall wheezed.

"Don't worry, I won't shoot you, if you tell me where she is." *Maybe,* he added silently.

"Don't... have her..."

"What?"

"Bluff... get you... to fight..."

"..."

"Would have taken too... too long... to get her. Lied to you."

Punchline's head swam, and he lowered his weapon. Denise was never in any danger... and he just went through hell, because some punk kid with fancy genetics or a deal with the devil or whatever, some kid lied big enough that he would believe it? All this had been for nothing?

No, he thought. *Not for nothing. For my friends.*

And he raised his pistol again.

"Hey... hey, what... what are... you doing? I didn't hurt... her."

"No. But you did kill Simon... and Isaac... and Randy. And you tried to kill Mary, and me. All because you had some dumbfuck idea that it would put you on top. Are you really telling me you won't try it again? Or maybe next time, you really will go to the trouble of kidnapping some poor woman who wants nothing to do with either of us. I can't—no, I won't let that happen."

"This... this isn't funny."

For once in his life, Punchline wasn't joking. After this, nothing seemed funny anymore.

FUMP!

The boxing glove-round caught Downfall square between the eyes, knocking him out... and down. Punchline didn't watch him fall, but he did hear the bone-crunching stop.

"It's over. It's all over."

His arms felt heavy, and this time it had nothing to do with someone else's superpower. His pistol slipped from his grasp and clattered on the roof. His torso flared up with every breath he took, but along with the pain came relief. He couldn't save all the people he cared about... but he did save two of them. Maybe not good enough to be a hero, but for a villain, it wasn't too bad.

He took off his fedora—amazingly, it had stayed on through the entire battle. Then, he removed his mask, and looked up at the night sky.

"I know you can't hear this, baby," he whispered. "But... I'm sorry. I'm sorry for everything... and I'm glad you're safe."

Dexter heard the approaching sirens. He started the long walk down the stairs.

***

Dexter Yates offered his arms to the first police officer he came across on the street, and they were fitted with a pair of handcuffs. The cop had been leading the villain toward the cruiser, until he saw the blood coming from his mouth. He waved over a couple of paramedics, who had just arrived on the scene. They rushed over, each one wheeling a gurney to take care of the wounded. One of them was beyond their help, though.

"This guy can go to the hospital," the police sergeant barked. "Leave the other one for the coroner."

"You got it," they replied in unison, and loaded Dexter onto one of the gurneys. As they wheeled past Downfall's body, one of the EMTs looked down and got a weird smile on his face. "Hey, Charlie!" he said.

"Yeah?" replied the other.

The first EMT nodded toward the street, where the blood of the fallen supervillain oozed over the painted lines on the asphalt.

"What's black and white and red all over?"

Dexter Yates laughed all the way to prison.

About the author: Luke Johnson is a common participant in writing competitions on the internet. This should tell you everything you need to know about him. He lives in Vermillion, South Dakota, and does not own a cat.

CPSIA information can be obtained at www.ICGtesting.com
Printed in the USA
245221LV00003B/18/P

9 781617 060717